The
Printed
Elvis

The
Printed
Elvis

The Complete Guide to
Books about the King

STEVEN OPDYKE

Music Reference Collection, Number 75

GREENWOOD PRESS
Westport, Connecticut • London

Library of Congress Cataloging-in-Publication Data

Opdyke, Steven, 1945–
    The printed Elvis : the complete guide to books about the king /
    Steven Opdyke.
       p. cm.—(Music reference collection, ISSN 0736–7740 ; no.
  75)
    ISBN 0–313–30815–2 (alk. paper)
    1. Presley, Elvis, 1935–1977—Bibliography.   I. Title.
  II. Series.
  ML134.5.P73063   1999
  016.78242166′092—dc21   99–11132

British Library Cataloguing in Publication Data is available.

Library of Congress Catalog Card Number: 99–11132
ISBN: 0–313–30815–2
ISSN: 0736–7740

First published in 1999

Greenwood Press, 88 Post Road West, Westport, CT 06881
An imprint of Greenwood Publishing Group, Inc.
www.greenwood.com

Printed in the United States of America

The paper used in this book complies with the
Permanent Paper Standard issued by the National
Information Standards Organization (Z39.48–1984).

10 9 8 7 6 5 4 3 2 1

To Pamela, my best friend, wife, partner, editor, and soulmate.

To Trevor, Jason, and Sara, our family.

To Theresa and Jack.

To a great writer, Bill DeYoung.

Thanks for your support, review, and recommendations.

To Elvis and all those who love him.

There have been more stories written about Elvis Presley than any other entertainer in the world.

—Vester Presley,
A Presley Speaks

Elvis could have pulled "an Eddie Fisher" in the Army Special Services. He could have spent most of his two years in comfort, traveling around the world to entertain the troops by "rockin' and rollin' "–but he didn't.

—William J. Taylor, Jr.,
Elvis in the Army

Certainly Presley was an incredible performer, but he was one whose persona was carefully created and nurtured until he developed an appeal unique in its cross-age, cross-class nature.

—Ray Pratt,
*Rhythm and Resistance: Explorations
in the Political Uses of Popular Music*

Despite his many putrid recordings, Presley's power as a symbol of white Negroism thrived.

—Nelson George,
The Death of Rhythm & Blues

Contents

THE ELVIS COMMENTARIES

A photo essay follows The Elvis Commentaries.

Suspicious Minds:
AN INTRODUCTION TO THE ELVIS BOOKS

Elvis, by contrast, not only had the musical goods, he
strenuously cultivated his public persona, beginning
from the time he was in high school.

–Mablen Jones
Getting It On: The Clothing of Rock 'n' Roll

Even as Elvis became one of the most loved and idolized stars, the
distance between him and his adoring public was vast. During much
of his lifetime, the "quickie" movies he made comprised the only
views most fans had of him. When he did perform regularly in Las
Vegas or on the road, the wall blocking him from paying customers
remained virtually unbreachable.

That was Colonel Parker's plan, to isolate Elvis and leave the
fans wanting more. To fill the vacuum caused by that lack of personal
availability, the Elvis souvenir industry (and ultimately the Elvis
memorabilia and collectibles market) was born. The creation of an
Elvis "Special Projects" venture (the Colonel's brainchild, of course)
enabled fans who "wanted to possess a piece" of Elvis to buy pictures,
bracelets, lunchboxes, and even postcards.

The demand for all things Elvis grew beyond trinkets of all kinds
to encompass not only his commercially released recordings, but
bootlegs as well. People from all walks of life also wanted movie
items, autographs, and so much more, up to and including books
ranging from fan souvenir guides to serious studies. Anyone could
watch Elvis, listen to him, read about him, and gaze at some replica
of his likeness and name.

Today almost every Elvis item has become highly coveted, as a
piece of an icon who "lives" through the various products the average
American has been allowed to own. With Elvis' name on it, anything
could be sold (and increase in value). *Rolling Stone* magazine's
special Elvis memorial edition has remained, even to this day, its

all-time best-selling issue. In fact, "official" souvenir sales have become the primary source of revenue for Elvis Presley Enterprises.

Unfortunately, the Elvis "Special Projects" people rarely gave out any information of import about their star. Elvis himself rarely talked to anyone in a public sense and did not grant any lengthy interviews. He did not allow or participate in any biographical or autobiographical (even ghostwritten) endeavors. Perhaps that was why he was so adored. He was not only unattainable in person, he was a complete mystery.

If nothing else, Elvis was multifaceted and multisided. Lester Bangs once concluded that Elvis' physical body housed both a plain and simple Southern boy destined to be a truck driver and an entity that became the most exciting performer in American history. Dr. Vernon Chadwick saw that he "performed in song what Martin Luther King Jr. proclaimed in sermon." Author Stanley Booth wrote that "Elvis has fulfilled the American dream."

Since Elvis revealed no major personal insights and walled off his personal life so effectively, much has been compiled *about* him and many "facts" have been widely disbursed. Most of what the public knows about Elvis has come from the authors of more than four hundred books (according to my research and listings from the Library of Congress). Reading those books has always been the primary means for discovering as much insight into or specific information about the King as possible.

Even more than twenty years after Elvis' death, books and papers have continued to proliferate. Both scholars and collectors alike, from their own unique perspectives, have tried to make sense of and evaluate each one. Though many books have proven to be very worthwhile, some were not even collectible or worth reading, especially those put together with little preparation, research, or familiarity with the subject.

What resources have been made available to help a fan, student, or collector discern the worthwhile and valuable Elvis material? Beyond listings compiled from Library of Congress holdings that have been circulated on the Internet (without valid critical commentary), the most useful critical appraisals of Elvis books, to date (1998), came in an all-too-limited twenty-five-page entry done by Gary Krebs as part of his *Billboard* book, *Rock and Roll Reader's Guide*. It was a plausible starting point. So was the listing of some 150 Elvis books on a 1998 CD-ROM entitled *The Elvis Files*.

Another excellent critical compendium of Elvis books (almost twenty pages worth) appeared in the 1985 book by Paul Taylor, entitled *Popular Music Since 1955: A Critical Guide to the Literature* (published in London by The H. W. Wilson Company). Along with its comprehensive listing of Elvis books were entries for just about every major music star from Petula Clark to Willie Nelson. As far as Elvis books were concerned, not even all the ones available at the time were critiqued (though whatever criteria Taylor may have had for including or excluding a particular book was never disclosed).

Additionally, a large-scale Elvis fan and collector, Maria Columbus, has reportedly been in the process of compiling an "Elvis in Print" compendium covering hundreds of books she has collected along with her opinions about their relative merits. That book was due out in early 1999 through the very small Ann Arbor, Michigan press, Popular Culture, Ink. Columbus once wrote, in the Gail Brewer-Giorgio book alleging Elvis did not die, that she still hoped "we can find out what really happened on August 16, 1977."

As the sheer number of books has mushroomed, the need has likewise skyrocketed for a much more detailed, complete, and extensively critical *comprehensive guide* to cut through the pages of all the books on Elvis and present an in-depth analysis of the relative values of each publication. The terminology, "all the books on Elvis," had to encompass much more than just complete books on him. Books that substantially and uniquely focused on Elvis and his associates (or just his associates as well as other parts of his "world") had to be included as well.

Thus, Scotty Moore's autobiography (which had much to say about his perspective on Elvis) was every bit as critical an entry as was Priscilla Presley's account of her life with Elvis (and afterwards). Just as essential was J. D. Sumner's life story which substantially covered his years with Elvis. Even Wayne Newton's autobiography was as valuable (for a different perspective on Elvis) as any of the Stanley brothers' books. Any book not covered by this guide was simply not worthwhile in any unique way (which is why *Alien Pregnant by Elvis* as well as the Japanese book, *Guts: Elvis*, were left out).

Analytical and informative insights into each critical book compiled or written about all or some facet of Elvis' life and career, including his memory and impact, have finally been brought together in this guide, *The Printed Elvis*. Each book included has been assessed according to its fan, collector, historian, or scholarly value, and what it offered relative to understanding Elvis' way of life, thinking, values, accomplishments, and any regrets. Having such an all-encompassing guide will make it considerably easier and less time-consuming to construct the most accurate and revealing conclusions about Elvis and his world. Collectors will also have the guide available to consult when planning acquisitions.

Anyone who so desired could, from this point forward, thoroughly study Elvis or simply ask questions about him. If, for example, someone wanted to locate only those books written by Elvis' close associates or perhaps wanted the most informative chronological overview of Elvis' life, that person would need only to consult this guide. Even if the request were to be able to read as many books as possible about Priscilla Presley, this guide would be the best source for information.

No book by itself, or even several taken together, could ever hope to contain every facet of his complex life and the phenomenon he became. To truly understand Elvis, it would take all the pertinent contents of books devoted to him along with all the insightful commentary found in books only partially dealing with him. This guide has brought all those books together. As a bonus, "The Notes on Sources" (Addendum III) listed those publications from which specific quotes were taken (when the quotes came from material not covered within the context of this guide).

Tracking down all the books that comprised this guide was an interesting endeavor. At one point, I ran across a friend of a friend who had a cousin whose last name began with a "K" (she thought) who had written a book that compiled every offbeat or weird story attributed to Elvis. The book may or may not have been published but if a copy were available, I was promised one. That was months ago. The idea sounded, to me, like a winner and if Mr. "K" did not finish such an endeavor, I'm sure someone will, probably sooner than later. I'm equally positive that when this guide hits the bookstores, twenty more books on Elvis will have been published.

Prior to Elvis' death in 1977, the most exhaustive study of his life came in the form of Jerry Hopkins' biography. As of 1977, critic Robert Dahlin noted, in an article for *Publisher's Weekly*, that the "unique appeal" of Elvis' music was carrying over to "books about him." Since then, several exhaustive biographies have come into existence, along with bibliographies, discographies, and even dictionaries.

Overall, the most complete understanding of Elvis came from authors with access to major primary source material and interviews. Some studies, based on a serious scholarly commitment, did appear and began to illuminate this worshiped but largely unknown enigma. The emergent pictures of Elvis revealed a multitude of surprises. Although most studies were based on well-researched and unique perspectives, all of them had built-in biases and interests that couldn't help but cloud the reality being discussed. Even those authors who worked hard to eliminate previous myths and biases ultimately created new ones.

In addition to the most comprehensive books, somewhere around fifty books on Elvis have been written by family members, friends, and associates. Actual authors included his Memphis Mafia, hairdresser, photographer, and on-and-off nurse. The people with firsthand exposure to Elvis, who saw, knew, or worked with him, could only present, in their books, the side of Elvis they witnessed.

The literature about Elvis has also included books on impersonators, anthologies of drawings, some well-intentioned university studies, glossy fan panoramas, and various beautiful photography collections. Elvis books have even been published in Russia and Japan. Because so much has been written, Booth wrote that "one day there will probably be an Elvis Presley Library, devoted to nothing else." Elvis has literally become the most written about performer in the history of the Western world.

Given the fact that Elvis' name could sell almost anything, several books have been marketed using his name in the title but having only a passing reference to him in the text. For example, professional football coach Jerry Glanville, who used to leave tickets at the box office for Elvis (symbolically done after Elvis died) wrote his memoirs and entitled them *Elvis Don't Like Football*. An English writer, Colin McEnroe, wrote a diet spoof (published by Dolphin Doubleday) that he called *Lose Weight Through Great Sex with Celebrities (the Elvis Way)*. Though quite funny, it was not really about Elvis.

Professor Karal Ann Marling, author of one of the best books about Graceland, has concluded that "the Elvis book industry shows no sign of slowing down." She wrote, in a lengthy article in the June 22, 1997, issue of the *New York Times*, that "just the opposite may be true" because there is "still enough stray data circulating in print and in cyberspace to support amateur Elvis Studies for years to come." In fact, "everybody in America probably knows enough to write a major Elvis book."

One such individual is a private investigator named Billy Miller. Perhaps before the beginning of the next century, Elvis readers will have the chance to read his "memoirs," which are being shopped, according to an article in *Variety*, to various publishers because they contain recollections of "work" he did for Elvis. It seems that Miller was retained by Elvis, starting in 1957, to do some detecting.

Some of the bombshells planned for the book were revelations of Elvis' illegitimate children, having impersonators appear instead of him, installing listening devices in cars he gave to friends so he could monitor their conversations (and discover what they said about him when they thought he couldn't hear). Why did it take Miller until the late 1990s to author such a book? He said he had to wait until his "confidentiality" agreement with Elvis ran out.

In her article, Marling went on to write that there are any number of "would-be best selling authors" hanging around Memphis "clutching huge, dog-eared manuscripts that prove amazing theses." Some of the theses, as far out as they may seem, have covered "how Elvis was killed by the C.I.A. on secret orders from the White House, how Elvis was an alien sent among us to foster world peace, how the letters in his name can be numerologically decoded to predict the exact moment of his once-upon-a-time son-in-law Michael Jackson's demise." Elvis has definitely become, according to Marling's assessment, "the subject of more books than O. J. Simpson."

Even with all the Elvis books potentially on the horizon, could there ever be a resolution as to his death, real or supposed? By the late 1990s, a consensus seemed to be shaping up that Elvis really has gone on to a spiritual world of some kind. Indeed, one of his most devoted fans, Wanda June Hill, who professed a long-term "platonic" relationship with the star, revealed that Elvis had always been a "starman."

Hill disclosed, according to authors Sherry Hansen-Steiger and Brad Steiger (writing in their book *Hollywood and the Supernatural*), that Elvis told her "his true home was from the stars." The phrases he used, according to Hill, to describe his origins were "out of this world" and "from up there." Specifically, he claimed to have come from the "Blue Star Planet" as well as "a base on the ninth moon of Jupiter."

In the same book, the Steigers quoted a spiritual medium named Clarisa as saying she has "seen Elvis on the Other Side. He is no longer in the physical." He has not come to rest there because, as the medium discovered, "the long-term, intense emotions about him by his millions of fans keep pulling his spirit body back to Earth." The sightings of Elvis on Earth, then, have really been, according to Clarisa, the appearance of "his ghost."

Reports of Elvis' spiritual comings and goings have not been surprising to his former companion Charlie Hodge. Hodge told an interviewer (Valerie Jones) that when Elvis was alive, "he had so much love in him. He helped everyone in need that he possibly could; if he could figure out a way to come back, he'd do it." After extensively researching numerous psychic encounters ordinary people have experienced with Elvis, Dr. Raymond Moody concluded that "as a people and as a culture, we can't let go of Elvis."

The Main Texts

But it was style as much as repertoire that made Presley:
his style was nothing like earlier white blues styles
(such as Jimmie Rodgers') but was characterized by
Presley's trembling, emotional voice which at times
seems barely under control.

−Charles K. Wolfe,
Tennessee Strings

That's All Right, Mama:
THE BOOKS ON ELVIS BY HIS FAMILY

> I learned from Elvis, often-sadly-from his mistakes.
> I learned that having too many people around can
> sap your energies. I learned the price of trying to
> make everyone happy.

> -Priscilla Beaulieu Presley,
> *Elvis and Me*

The Books by Relatives

The best relative books would have been ones by Elvis' father or mother. Neither even attempted such an undertaking and both were such private persons that they probably would have revealed little or nothing. Instead, we have Uncle Vester's book. Vester was Elvis' father Vernon's brother and worked at Graceland. He was too private and lacking in the personal depth to have seen Elvis in a critical light. The other relatives were cousins not close enough to have seen very much. Their books had value because they presented family background and communication.

Early, Donna Presley, and Edie Hand, with Lynn Edge. *Elvis: Precious Memories.* **Foreword by James Blackwood. Birmingham, Alabama: The Best of Times, 1997. 311 pp.**

Pritchett, Nash L. *One Flower While I Live: Elvis As I Remember Him.* **Memphis, Tennessee: Shelby House, 1987.**

Elvis' cousin, Donna Presley Early, was born the daughter of Elvis' father's youngest sister. Her book was written for several reasons, the foremost of which was to relate her mother's memoirs of the Presley family and their relationships with Elvis. Her mother, Elvis' Aunt Nash (his father's sister), had been in the process of writing the memoirs when she died, so interspersed throughout this book (in italics) were those remembrances.

Aunt Nash had served much of her adult life as an ordained minister (pastor), principally at the First Assembly of God in Walls, Mississippi. Her church was built with the help of large donations given by none other than Elvis himself. That's probably why she had earlier written a very non-critical book on her nephew, entitled, *One Flower While I Live: Elvis As I Remember Him.* It was published through the Memphis-based Shelby House in 1987. Since it had nothing insightful about Elvis, we can only be thankful that authors Early, Hand, and Edge finally brought out some of the more substantive writing Pritchett did but never released.

In a recent interview with Mary Anne Cassata, Early passed on that she (along with another cousin) wrote the book to expose people to the "private Elvis with his family, the Elvis having a meal, or Elvis just talking with his family and friends." Early also wanted to relate, through the book, the suspicions Elvis' father had about his son being murdered or at least killed through possible physician negligence or cover-up. Only in the areas of the Presley family relationships and the death suspicions did Early give unique views. So, even twenty years after the fact, the book won't open doors to redoing the official account of Elvis' death, but it will raise questions that should be more thoroughly researched.

Greenwood, Earl, and Kathleen Tracy. *The Boy Who Would Be King: An Intimate Portrait of Elvis Presley by His Cousin.* **New York: Penguin, 1990. 310 pp.**

Greenwood, Earl, and Kathleen Tracy. *Elvis: Top Secret: The Untold Story of Elvis Presley's Secret FBI Files.* **New York: Penguin, 1991. 340 pp. Copies of FBI files, last will and testament.**

Earl Greenwood was also a (distant) cousin to Elvis. For a time he was Elvis' press agent. His first book, the "intimate portrait," attempted to trade in on personal photographs and memories from family gatherings and visits. The more interesting disclosures centered on Elvis' mother's alcoholism, father Vernon's prison term, as well as some "orgies" Elvis filmed. Did Elvis inherit his sexual appetite from Grandma Dixie, who was sent to an institution suffering from an untreated case of syphilis? Greenwood did use the homosexual word relative to Elvis and his cohorts.

He also concluded that Elvis was deathly afraid of Frank Sinatra, based on comments Sinatra made to Elvis when Elvis was fooling around with Sinatra's girlfriend, Juliet Prowse. Nancy Sinatra, in Greenwood's mind, desperately wanted to have an affair with Elvis. Elvis also very much wanted to work with Barbra

Streisand in the movie, *A Star Is Born*. It was Colonel Parker who prevented Elvis from appearing in the film by demanding too much, top billing and too much money.

Greenwood obviously got interested in his cousin, so for a follow-up, he obtained a number of documents pertinent to Elvis, the most interesting of which were the FBI files. The most intriguing aspect of the files were the "blacked-out" parts, which were numerous (blacked out for "national security" reasons). Beyond the question of why so many was why there had to be deleted parts at all. What could Elvis have been into? Judging from the rest of the files, probably nothing. The entries were mainly bureaucratic language that attempted to cover the FBI's interest in Elvis.

Loyd, Harold (Elvis' Cousin and Gatekeeper). *Elvis Presley's Graceland Gates.* **Photos by Jimmy Velvet and Fans Everywhere. Franklin, Tennessee: Jimmy Velvet Publications, 1987. 126 pp.**

Harold Loyd, the son of Elvis' mother's sister (thereby making him one of Elvis' first cousins), was an older man, unassuming and content to be a security guard at the gates of Graceland. Loyd did live with the Presleys briefly when Elvis was quite young so he did pass on some views about how Elvis behaved as a boy. Otherwise, he had little to reveal but some intimate anecdotes about Elvis and the boys, including one where Elvis hurt his backside in a go-cart accident. Loyd was always there when fans were let in and Elvis came out to meet them.

The most fun parts of the book were the descriptions of Elvis' fans and some of the strange things they did. Loyd hooked up with Memphis entrepreneur Jimmy Velvet, who supposedly knew Elvis since 1955, to bring this book to the public. The photos from Velvet's collection were unique and worth seeing because of their largely unposed nature. Velvet was said to have been a friend of Elvis. In 1974 he got a Mercedes limousine from the King. After Elvis died, Velvet put together a touring memorabilia show.

In 1978, Loyd had his first run at telling about the "Graceland gates" in a book written with George Baugh, who was also a security guard at Graceland. The title was *The Gates of Graceland*, published in Memphis by Modern Age Enterprises. After that, he "authored" another book, this time with Lisa DeAngel, entitled *Elvis and His Fans*. Published in Memphis, its major purpose was to profile the kinds of fans who came to visit Graceland. The most recent book, the one done for Jimmy Velvet, was the most useful and informative.

Presley, Vester, as told to Deda Bonura. *A Presley Speaks.* **Memphis, Tennessee: Wimmer Brothers, 1978.   Reprinted 1981, 1982, 1985, 1987.   149 pp.   List of records, movies.**

Uncle Vester was a relatively uneducated older relative who worked for Elvis doing minimal tasks like watching the gate and tending the grounds. He traced the family history very loosely (and often too superficially) from the 1930s through the early 1970s. His insights were largely anecdotal and brought out the fun side of Elvis and his family circle. He did give us a good idea how everyday life at Graceland proceeded, what kinds of things Elvis and the boys did when at home, what kind of man Elvis' father was, and even various different Elvis eating habits. Interestingly enough, Vester actually collaborated on a Presley family cookbook.

Beyond Presley's reminiscences, there was a lengthy section on "the people who worked for Elvis." Actually there were only three people profiled, but their words provide perhaps the best insights into everyday life around Graceland. Interestingly, all of them could not profess enough "love" for their boss, Mr. Elvis. Mary Jenkins, his cook for fourteen years, disclosed that during that time, he bought her five cars. He also bought cook Nancy Rooks the first car she ever owned. Rooks stayed close to Presley, collaborating on that cookbook with him in 1980.

Smith, Gene. *Elvis's Man Friday.*   **Nashville, Tennessee: Light of Day, 1994.**

Here is another first cousin writing many years after the fact. He said, after the book was published, that he wrote it to "let the world know the whole truth." Smith made it appear, in his writing, that Elvis used him as a confidant. He passed on such information as Elvis once telling him, "I don't like being 'Elvis Presley'!" Smith also confided that Elvis would either carry his own knives, forks, and spoons with him when he ate out or he would obsessively polish the ones he was given.

The revelation about how much Elvis suffered from a severe sleepwalking disorder in his younger years was one of the few more enlightening bits of information.   Otherwise, Smith enjoyed discussing such details as telling Elvis how beautiful Priscilla was by equating her figure to a coke bottle. He purposely mumbled his words so she couldn't possibly understand.

About 1963 was when Smith "left Elvis," though he did reveal that Elvis would still call him. According to Marty Lacker (as quoted by Alanna Nash in the book, *Elvis Aaron Presley: Revelations from the Memphis Mafia*), "Elvis said he never wanted to talk to Gene [Smith] again after that incident over the jewelry in the early sixties." After that, Smith was said to have tried to visit Elvis at Graceland, even asking Elvis to purchase a motorcycle for him. Elvis never relented as far as ever seeing Smith again and never bought him the requested motorcycle. Given this insight from Lacker, one would have to wonder just how much Smith had to reveal about Elvis.

The "Stepfamily" Books

Elvis' mother, Gladys, died on August 14, 1958, about a month before Elvis was sent, by the Army, to Germany. Although Elvis, then only twenty-three, was able to be at her deathbed and funeral, he never really got to say goodbye. His tearful goodbye at her coffin has been duly recorded by a number of authors. How her death affected him could never really be known, but has often been speculated upon.

On July 3, 1960, Elvis' father, Vernon, married the former Mrs. Dee Stanley. He was forty-four and she was ten years his junior (making her about nine years older than Elvis). She had been married when she met Vernon in Germany (though that marriage to a decorated World War II veteran, Bill Stanley, appeared to have been all but over). Their affair resulted in a stormy marriage that for a while gave Elvis a "stepmother" and "stepfamily." Elvis did not attend the wedding, feeling it was inappropriate for his father to remarry so soon after Gladys' death. In fact, the twenty-five-year-old Elvis vowed he would never accept Dee nor would he treat her with respect.

At first, the new Mr. and Mrs. Presley lived with Elvis at Graceland, which Mrs. Presley found to be, as she told one interviewer, "a nightmare of all nightmares, with Elvis parading all his women, people with drugs by the bagfuls, and odd friends in and out of the house every night." Soon, they moved to a house nearby in Memphis. For approximately thirteen years, the Stanley brothers called Vernon their "daddy." They eventually lived with and worked for Elvis.

After Elvis' death, the "stepfamily" did not hesitate to reveal to the world their time with him. How believable they were could only be left to speculation, but at some time or other one or more has somehow discredited, disparaged, or contradicted another. Still, their reminiscences had value because they appeared to have accurately captured the turbulence surrounding Elvis. For a somewhat different slant, check out the elder Bill Stanley's 1987 book, *Living in the Shadow of the King*, published by the New York-based vanity house, Vantage Press.

Presley, Dee, Billy, Rick, and David Stanley, as told to Martin Torgoff. *Elvis: We Love You Tender.* **Note by Martin Torgoff. New York: Delacorte, 1979, 1980. 321 pp. Index.**

The book by the second Mrs. Vernon Presley and her boys (Elvis' stepbrothers), the Stanley brothers, about loving Elvis "tender" was fascinating, not only for their self-serving perspectives but their attempts to portray themselves as integral to Elvis' life. Though Dee (Davada) Presley obviously lived with Vernon (for about seventeen years) and moved through a part of Elvis' life, she still saw him from a distance. Nevertheless, the tabloid press, at one point, interpreted some of her comments as tantamount to saying that Elvis and his mother (Gladys) had a series of affairs. Dee also alleged that drugs so destroyed Elvis' body that he was forced "to wear diapers" during the final years of his life.

Much of her part of the book offered a singular view of how Elvis was handled or mishandled. She speculated on how he eventually fell apart. Also revealed was the stormy side of her marriage to Elvis' dad, which eventually ended in divorce in 1977, only some four months before Elvis died. Elvis was said to have been extremely pleased. During the course of the marriage, Vernon appeared to have had a number of affairs, specifically in 1974 with a nurse named Sandy Miller. Dee was always convinced that Vernon was "overdoing" sex. An interesting fact was that Elvis might have had another half brother but Dee had a miscarriage with Vernon's baby. When Elvis died, she was convinced his father also died, at least in spirit. She said she was amazed at how long he lived with his immense grief for his dead son.

The book was written with Martin Torgoff, who wrote about writing it. He claimed to have relied heavily on the insights from the brothers. He said that, for him, they clearly illuminated Elvis. On the other hand, when Dee first made her views public, they were so negative even her boys came forward and denied much of what she claimed. That didn't stop her. In spite of remarrying, she managed to turn her remote view of Elvis into another book. No major publisher would touch it. Completed in 1995, the new book supposedly presented, in even greater depth, Elvis' numerous problems. Since then, stepmother Dee has revealed that she has held at least two seances with Elvis. During one, she saw him in heaven with his mother (not his father!). His twin, Jesse, was the "guiding spirit that helped him there."

Stanley, Billy, with George Erikson. *Elvis, My Brother: An Intimate Family Memoir of Life with the King.* **New York: St. Martin's, 1989. 296 pp. Index.**

Stanley, David, with David Wimbish. *Life with Elvis.* **Old Tappan, New Jersey: Fleming H. Revell, 1986. 223 pp.**

Stanley, Rick, with Paul Harold. *Caught in a Trap: Elvis Presley's Tragic Lifelong Search for Love.* **Dallas: Word, 1992. 232 pp. List of albums, top-ten hits, films, concert tours, television and club appearances.**

Stanley, David E., with Mark Bego. *Raised on Rock: Growing Up at Graceland.* **Edinburgh, England: Mainstream Publishing Projects, 1996. 189 pp. Bibliography and list of sources.**

The boys have since written their own separate stories. In 1986, David, the youngest, led off with what he called "a Christian book," *Life with Elvis,* published by the New Jersey-based religious company, Fleming H. Revell. Right at the beginning he quickly went from his biological dad leaving to being introduced to his "new father, Vernon Presley." That started his tumultuous life as Elvis' "brother," a life that culminated in his realization that "if Elvis hadn't died, Rick [one of his two brothers] and I would have."

Ten years later (1996) he dropped his "Christian" point of view and wrote, with Mark Bego, a detailed insider's account that surprisingly came out only in England. In it he revealed a much more human side of his whole relationship with his older stepbrother. Perhaps the most touching story was the piecework recounting of how their mother and Vernon Presley began the affair that led to their marriage and the whole displacement of the three boys away from their biological father.

The elder Presley came across as a man without morals who would stop at nothing, not even lying to a supposed friend, to get what he wanted. By 1996, David no longer seemed interested in judging Elvis but in understanding what led him to such excesses. It became clear that through explaining Elvis' problems, David was able to come to grips with his own.

Prior to 1986, Billy did a quick book about Elvis' final tour, which was marketed in 1977 to play off Elvis' death. Entitled *Elvis: The Last Tour,* it was put out by the very small Star Fleet Publishers. Finally, in 1989, Billy published a major book about Elvis, which he called *Elvis, My Brother*. It came out via St. Martin's Press of New York. It was difficult to believe very much of Billy's account because the anger he felt toward Elvis came through consistently. The anger was genuinely based on the fact, in Billy's mind, that Elvis had an affair with Annie, Billy's young wife.

In 1992, Rick added his own memoirs, concentrating on Elvis' "tragic" search for meaningful love (which he probably did not get from his stepfamily). A Dallas-based religious publisher, Word, got the book, poignantly entitled *Caught in a Trap*, to market, primarily through Christian bookstores. To his credit, Rick also focused on many of the fun activities he was able to do by virtue of growing up in Graceland, such as being taught to box by the members of Elvis' inner circle. Prior to 1992, Rick did write *The Touch of Two Kings*, a relatively insignificant book, published in 1986 by T2K, Inc., which discussed the lights of his "new" life, Elvis and Jesus.

The brothers offered many insights, but knowing how Elvis protected and isolated himself through his manager, Colonel Parker, and the Memphis Mafia, one must take their claims of closeness with some skepticism. Yet their stories of drugs and sex did not differ markedly from other insider revelations. Were they in relative agreement because they knew or wanted to look like they knew? At least brother David claimed he did try to intervene, writing in his 1996 book that he told Elvis in 1977, "This is chicken shit. Dr. Nick is killing you with all those drugs."

David also went beyond the others in claiming that Elvis used cocaine, though medicinally only, of course. He was the source for Albert Goldman's later claims that Elvis committed suicide. Though he failed to discuss it in his 1986 book, David began conjecturing, in 1989, that not only was Elvis a suicide victim, he had even disposed of evidence that pointed to the suicide. The alleged evidence consisted of four syringes and at least three "attack envelopes," which were used to hold Elvis' nightly doses of drugs.

Elvis' stepbrothers, who were each born again, professed only to want to tell the truth about Elvis' need for love, his loneliness, and his self-abuse. They professed to have a Christian attitude toward wanting to bring out the real Elvis to help others. The financial rewards they gained as a result of their association with Elvis' legacy have certainly been substantial through book royalties and personal appearances. In their views, however, that was not their primary motivator. Had the boys not been Elvis' stepbrothers, judging from their own testimony, they would have been destitute children with numerous psychological problems.

There were interesting insights into the management of Elvis' life and tours, but too much of the text seemed unsubstantiated, even though Torgoff has said he was convinced. Not content with telling all he could about his own experiences with Elvis, David and a co-writer, Frank Coffey, marketed what Larry King called "a definitive womb-to-tomb time line on the King," an Elvis encyclopedia. It has been reviewed in the "The Elvis Reference Books" section.

The Ex-wife's and Ex-wife's Ex-partner's Books

For Elvis, there would always be the former Priscilla Beaulieu, with whom he fell in love when she was fourteen. He was twenty-three when they met in Germany, where she was living with her Army family. After Elvis returned to Memphis, she joined him, very quietly. In her twenty-second year, 1967, they were married. Then they had a child, Lisa Marie.

By 1972, their marriage was in serious trouble. It ended in divorce in 1973 with Priscilla romantically involved with karate instructor Mike Stone. It has been speculated that the marriage broke up because Elvis could not have sex with a woman who was a mother. Priscilla did say Elvis received therapy for that. Other conjectures about the reasons for the divorce ranged from Elvis' flings to Priscilla's inability to tolerate the men constantly surrounding Elvis. Mostly, Priscilla just grew up and away from Elvis.

Priscilla went on to become quite successful. Since publishing the book, she has edited a We Remember Elvis Newsletter, done considerable acting (in movies and on television), and turned the Elvis fortune from near-bankruptcy to riches. What was she really like? What was Elvis really like? What was their marriage really like?

These and so many other other questions were both touched on and skirted in her book. After Elvis, Priscilla lived with Michael Edwards, an aspiring model and actor. In the tradition of tell-all books, he went on to write about himself and Priscilla, and because she was famous and linked to Elvis, his book got published. The public failed to read it and it quickly appeared in cutout bins priced below a dollar.

According to one of the tabloids (The Enquirer), Elvis remained secretly in love with Priscilla and "all his girls had something in common–they were all like Priscilla in some way." Some of Elvis' closest friends, like J. D. Sumner, were also convinced that Priscilla was truly the love of Elvis' life. Sumner believed "Elvis loved Priscilla until he breathed his last breath."

Though Elvis "loved" Priscilla even at fourteen, he had to keep her under wraps because of what had happened to Jerry Lee Lewis after it became known he had married his thirteen-year-old cousin,

Myra Gale (Brown). When the English press discovered the real age of Lewis' bride, they literally crucified him. The flak spread to America, where Hollywood columnist Louella Parsons speculated that "Jerry Lewis may take legal action against Jerry Lee Lewis, the latter a singer who was booed off the stage after he married his thirteen-year-old cousin. Our Jerry is sick of being confused with this 'kissin' cousin.' "

When Elvis was asked about Jerry Lee's marital woes, he replied that he would "rather not talk about his marriage, except that if he really loves her, I guess it's all right." Years later (1982), when Myra Gale Lewis wrote about her life with Jerry Lee (in a book entitled *Great Balls of Fire*), she observed that when Elvis made that statement, he was about to become "enamored of his future wife, Priscilla Beaulieu, though having learned a valuable lesson from Jerry's experience, Elvis would wait ten years to marry her."

Priscilla once made the mistake of suggesting that Elvis style his hair like Ricky Nelson's. The remark was made innocently enough; she had seen a billboard portraying Ricky with his slightly wavy hair and Elvis had expressed concern over what to do with his styling. He screamed at her, "Are you goddamn crazy? After all these years, Ricky Nelson, Fabian, that whole group have more or less followed in my footsteps, and now I'm supposed to copy them? You gotta be out of your mind, woman." She also quickly learned not to truthfully critique his records.

He certainly was determined to follow what he believed, even if it meant no longer having sex with Priscilla after Lisa Marie was born. He told her his personal belief system kept him from sleeping with the mother of his child. "It just isn't right," he told her after she reportedly pleaded with him to make love to her. It was unfortunate Elvis didn't respect Priscilla enough to stay faithful and married. Her portrayal of herself and her inner growth revealed an admirable woman of fortitude and conviction.

Presley, Priscilla Beaulieu, with Sandra Harmon. *Elvis and Me*. New York: G. P. Putnam's Sons, 1985. 320 pp.

Priscilla's book was obviously the cream of the crop of books by family members. She had previously written about Elvis in a revealing magazine article. Her co-author did an excellent and skillful writing job. The perceptions Priscilla formed of Elvis ranged from a young girl idolizing him to a growing female molded by him. She was finally able to break free as a grown woman and stand on her own, but it took an affair with another man to begin the process. At the beginning of her relationship with Elvis, she did what she was told, including taking pills and being there for him (even tolerating some physical and emotional abuses).

There were no scandalous revelations though she did assert that Elvis was about to break up with live-in girlfriend, Ginger Alden. Unfortunately, he died and Alden has since claimed Elvis was about to marry her. Priscilla more than touched on their drug problems (a subject into which she delved much more deeply during subsequent interviews). To her credit, she focused primarily on the ins and outs of the relationship. Overall, she painted a picture of a very moody Elvis who had less and less control over his anger and outbreaks as he grew older. He also had a major problem with her getting pregnant, at one point telling her he had to have space from her. From all of her revelations the reader was able to piece together how Elvis thought and how he viewed the world around him, as well as his relationships with others, including his entourage of paid friends and his manager, Colonel Parker.

At the end of the book, after she discussed Elvis' passing, she observed that Parker was "from the old school," and though he seemed like a coldhearted businessman, in truth, "Elvis had been like his own son." In her words, the Colonel "had stayed faithful and loyal to Elvis, even when his career began to slip," though he, like Priscilla, did not like seeing Elvis read so many spiritual books. At the funeral, he was "already planning ways to keep Elvis's name before the public." Some critics would say that was proof of his interest in Elvis stemming solely from a business perspective. Priscilla concluded that Parker was "fearful" that Elvis' father, Vernon, "would be too distraught to handle correctly the many proposals and propositions that would be in the offing." Of Elvis, she concluded, "he was, and remains, the greatest influence in my life."

Edwards, Michael. *Priscilla, Elvis and Me: In the Shadow of the King***. New York: St. Martin's, 1988. 279 pp.**

The Edwards book, about Elvis and his "shadowy influence," was written by a man who never really knew Elvis but who lived with Elvis' ex-wife Priscilla for approximately eight years. The most revealing part of the book was Edwards' infatuation with a "very" young Lisa Marie, Elvis' daughter. There were also some interesting insights into Priscilla's character, her vanity and immaturity, which would surely have been factors in her failed relationship with Elvis.

One of the most interesting passages on Priscilla discussed the night she spent with actor Richard Gere. According to Priscilla, she "found herself in his car." After that, she couldn't "remember anything very clearly." The gist of the situation was that she woke up the next morning "naked in bed beside him, my clothes and his scattered all over the floor." Edwards' reaction was that "the princess I'd put on a pedestal came tumbling down." Though he said he tried to pull their relationship back together, she remained determined to finally end it. When he asked her what they would do "if we meet on the street some day," she replied, "Don't worry. We'll never meet."

Love Me Tender:
THE BOOKS ON ELVIS BY HIS FRIENDS AND ASSOCIATES

> Although Elvis was very human, and certainly a person who
> not only inspired, but who earned much devotion, his phenomenon
> follows the same mythic pattern as other dying gods and mythical
> figures, including Osiris and Quetzalcoatl.
>
> –Clarissa Pinkola Estes, Ph. D.,
> *The Soul of Popular Culture: Looking at*
> *Contemporary Heroes, Myths and Monsters*

The Memphis Mafia Books

Throughout his life, Elvis had a reputation for being as uncompromising in his loyalty as any human being could be. He entrusted many of his important business and personal decisions to his father, who had only a third-grade education. He surrounded himself with a coterie of companions, his Memphis Mafia, and kept most of them on his payroll no matter what. When, in his opinion, several turned on him, he was heartbroken. Some of the group who stayed to the end felt that the book (reviewed in this section) by former friends Red and Sonny West hastened Elvis' demise.

According to Alanna Nash, the Memphis Mafia was merely a group of young men "who traveled everywhere with him as both companions and quasi-bodyguards." They were somehow equivalent to Sinatra's Rat Pack. To Elvis, they were "a buffer zone-the one group of people with whom he could be himself." Hollywood reporter Sheilah Graham saw them as "the eight or ten men he always carried with him." Another Hollywood columnist, Hedda Hopper, claimed they "jealously seal him off from all intruders."

What did having such an entourage say about Elvis and what did it say about those men who devoted their lives to him? Dr. Peter Whitmer, in his book, *The Inner Elvis*, saw the Memphis Mafia as a cult, which served, for Elvis, as "a coping mechanism that allowed Elvis to reenact many of his childhood behaviors." Whitmer also concluded that Elvis needed "their adulation."

Revelations about Elvis from members of his entourage have given the world some of the best insights into what he was really like. The first came from the West cousins, of whom Red was one of Elvis' oldest friends and protectors (dating from their days in high school together). Since their devastating book, other "members" have gone public to create together a fascinating litany on all the aspects of Elvis' life as they saw and understood them.

Esposito, Joe, and Elena Oumano. *Good   Rockin'   Tonight: Twenty Years on the Road and on Tour with Elvis.* **New York: Simon & Schuster, 1994.   268 pp.   Index.**

Esposito was more than a friend, he was road manager and the unacknowledged leader of the Memphis Mafia. The two buddies met while both were in the Army. The book Esposito has finally written chronicled the road trips, the relationship between Elvis and the Colonel, and the vaunted drug usage. The final chapter dwelled on Esposito's views of Elvis' death. He kept to the facts as he saw them, from his pulling up Elvis' pajama bottoms to his informing others such as the Colonel and Priscilla.

He did not speculate on causes, conspiracies, or possible complications. Once he commented that Elvis died of a heart attack and from his point of view that was it. Overall, he acknowledged that Elvis became loathsome in his final years yet somehow remained the wonderful human being he portrayed him as throughout the book. Previously, Esposito tackled the Elvis legacy by compiling a short book on the performing Elvis, entitled *Elvis: A Legendary Performance.* It was published in 1990 by the Buena Park, California-based West Coast Publishing. In 1997, with assistance from Darwin Lamm, he released a book featuring his Elvis photographs.

Fortas, Alan. *Elvis: From Memphis to Hollywood: Memories From My Twelve Years with Elvis Presley.* **Ann Arbor, Michigan: Popular Culture, 1992.   322 pp.   Index.**

Fortas also produced an excellent, detailed book. He was one of the long-term Memphis Mafia members. Even though he did not harbor any resentments toward Elvis, he did candidly reveal the problems Elvis had with eating, prescription drugs, and living what essentially became a life "late at night." Fortas told how Elvis kept his friends involved by rewarding them extravagantly yet paying them little. Fortas also detailed the jealousy between group members competing for Elvis' time and their influence with him (which he claimed was not a competition for affection).

Hodge, Charlie, with Charles Goodman. *Me 'n Elvis.* **Memphis, Tennessee: Castle Books, 1988.   204 pp.**

Hodge's relationship with Elvis was explored in Esposito's book. In his own book, Hodge imparted his account and the the two sets of views largely coincided. Esposito only observed the interactions while Hodge analyzed his relationship with Elvis in terms of what Elvis thought, what made him happy, and what kind of character Elvis had. Hodge also seemed to have had more involvement with Elvis' music. There were many jam sessions in which Hodge played guitar while Elvis sang.

Hodge discussed what he believed to be indisputable evidence that Elvis never had a "love" child. He also went into considerable detail on the effect Elvis' mother's death had on Elvis. At the beginning of the book, Hodge assured Lisa Marie that her daddy was not what people said he became. That set the book's tenor.

Lacker, Marty, Patsy Lacker, and Leslie S. Smith. *Elvis: Portrait of a Friend.* **Foreword by Leslie S. Smith. Memphis, Tennessee: Wimmer Brothers, 1979.   New edition 1980.   369 pp.**

The Lackers portrayed a kinder, gentler Elvis, one who was always a good friend. They wanted the world to see Elvis as they saw him, through a "close" friendship. Leslie S. Smith, a former war correspondent, who has become a publisher and editor, assisted the Lackers in pulling together their story.

Though the Lackers did acknowledge some of Elvis' overindulgences, they did not see him as far out of control or as physically sick as others have portrayed him. In fact, they included moving passages about his legendary generosity, as well as great descriptions of building the Graceland garden. To Marty Lacker, Elvis was both an "impulsive man" and "a man of routine." His seemingly contradictory images of Elvis did not mean he was being inaccurate, it meant that Elvis truly seemed like two people.

The book was written in three parts, the first by husband Marty, who stopped working for Elvis after the party lifestyle became too much for him (and wreaked havoc on his marriage). His part was relatively free of personal animosity, though he did reveal that Vernon Presley made antisemitic remarks toward his (Marty's) mother. Wife Patsy wrote the second part as a spouse embittered by the hold Elvis had over her husband. Her story culminated in a discussion of Elvis' drug habits, blaming his physician for overprescribing drugs. She viewed Elvis' doctor as a pusher. The third and final part came from Smith and emphasized an "outside" view. Smith focused closely on two doctors associated with Elvis and his vaunted prescription drug use. He also discussed the effects of the drugs that Elvis was said to have been taking over a period of time.

Nash, Alanna, with Billy Smith, Marty Lacker, and Lamar Fike. *Elvis Aaron Presley: Revelations from the Memphis Mafia*. **New York: HarperCollins, 1995. New edition 1996. 947 pp. Index.**

The ultimate Memphis Mafia book was the one Alanna Nash put together by inter-weaving snippets of interviews with three inner circle members, Billy Smith, Lamar Fike, and Marty Lacker. Lacker's insights stuck pretty close to those he revealed in his book, co-written with his wife, Patsy. Fike, the "hidden" source for Albert Goldman's vitriolic diatribe against Elvis, gave a much more even-handed, detailed insight into his years with "the boss."

Smith, an Elvis first cousin, had never before talked at any length, so his views became doubly important, largely because he reinforced the pictures that Fortas, Esposito, and Hodge already created. He was also supposed to have been the one person for whom Elvis cared deeply, almost as deeply as he cared for his mother. The worst trashing Elvis got this time was the impression given of him as a devoted watcher of pornography.

Thompson, Sam. *Elvis on Tour: The Last Year*. **Introductory by Colonel Tom Parker. Memphis, Tennessee: Still Brook, 1992. 44 pp.**

Thompson, a former personal bodyguard to Elvis and brother of the one-time Miss Tennessee and live-in lover to Elvis, Linda Thompson, did what no one else has done. He chronicled, from a firsthand perspective, Elvis' later live performing efforts. Unfortunately he concentrated on Elvis' worst year, the one before he died, when Elvis was "fat" and falling apart. The presentation was useful nonetheless and, though it was not in-depth, it did show what it was like to be with Elvis, back stage, practicing, and setting up.

The text was mainly Thompson's personal memories of working for and traveling with Elvis. There were also six pages of informal pictures, along with copies of tour sheets for each of Elvis' final ten tours. Did Thompson as a bodyguard qualify for membership in the Memphis Mafia? He certainly hung around to the bitter end. Better yet, he was able to begin the book with an introductory letter from Colonel Parker.

West, Red, Sonny West, and Dave Hebler, as told to Steve Dunleavy. *Elvis: What Happened?* **New York: Random House, 1977. 332 pp.**

Robert "Red" West's relationship with Elvis began when he protected Elvis from a bully during high school. He and his cousin, Sonny (Delbert), were original members of the group surrounding Elvis. Red also wrote or co-wrote a number of songs for Elvis and other singers. Hebler was a karate champion who was hired by Elvis as a bodyguard. Not long before Elvis' death, they were all fired by Vernon Presley for various reasons. The "true" reasons fluctuated, with Elvis' father, Red, and Sonny espousing different versions.

Nevertheless, soon after they were dismissed the brothers wrote a venomous tell-all book (in tone and in terms of charges leveled). They detailed Elvis' secrets, his drug addiction, his mental phobias, and his strange habits and behaviors. They wrote in conjunction with *Star* editor/columnist Steve Dunleavy, who wove together "the experiences of three Presley bodyguards who were there partying with him, womanizing with him, worrying with him." According to an article in *Star*, the three Elvis bodyguards (as they were called) "had come to *Star* because they were terrified the King was destroying himself through his drug use." The same article went on to note that "in a bizarre coincidence, *Star*'s serialization of the story went on sale the very day Elvis died."

Author Robert Ward, a *Crawdaddy* contributor, revealed that he had been initially "offered a chance to co-author" the book, but had "instantly turned it down because it smelled of shit." Elvis tried to buy them back but they refused. Their book was said to have destroyed him and precipitated his death. Others, of course, have said that Elvis' health was already destroyed. Regardless, the book detailed some fascinating insights. The accusatory nature did make the most sensational revelations seem suspect. According to their observations, Elvis once held a gun to Jimmy Dean's head and chided Tom Jones for sticking a "damn sock down his pants." They said it hurt them "to see someone you love change so very much."

The Books by Former "Girlfriends"

It was a given that Elvis had many intimate female friends. That said, how could anyone know who was special and who was merely casual? After his divorce from Priscilla, Elvis had two highly visible and long-term love affairs. It has become a matter of record that neither of the girlfriends, Linda Thompson and Ginger Alden, ever wrote anything of import about Elvis.

Elvis' first post-Priscilla lover was Thompson, a former Miss Tennessee. She had considerable impact even if only judging by the amount of money he spent on her (a $30,000 credit card bill around the time they split up). Elvis actually began dating her as his marriage to Priscilla was falling apart. Subsequently, she lived at Graceland from 1972 through 1976, the year he met Ginger Alden. A movie, *Elvis and the Beauty Queen*, was based on their romance.

She once confided to an interviewer from *People* magazine that they "often thought it would be fun to just go away and live in a little shack on a farm, and forget fame and fortune and all the craziness that goes with it. I guess some people think that's what he's done." But it didn't happen that way, or as she admitted, "that's not how it was supposed to be." Still, had she had been there the night Elvis died, "it might have been different," because she was "so protective" of him. Unlike many of his most dedicated fans, she has acknowledged that her former lover has "left this world."

The second and last girlfriend was Alden (she was with him when he died). She first met Elvis at a fairground in Memphis when she was five years of age. It was her father who actually inducted Elvis into the Army in March 1958, after he was drafted in 1957. She said, "He just patted me on the head." At twenty-two, she was nineteen years younger than Elvis when they began dating in 1976. Their age difference once caused Vernon Presley (soon after Elvis died) to insinuate to Billy Stanley, Vernon's stepson, that perhaps Billy (very close in age to Alden) was having an affair with her.

Alden claimed Elvis proposed to her in the bathroom at Graceland and even bought her a $12,000 ring. They were to have been married Christmas Day, 1977. Unfortunately, Elvis died in August. According to Alden and her mother, Elvis remained close, even in death. In fact, they regularly communicated (through seances?) and each has seen his "ghost." The mother once sued the Elvis estate, claiming he promised to pay off her mortgage, among other things.

J. D. Sumner did write that Elvis told him, "J. D., I want you to be the first to know. I'm gonna marry Ginger. I've always wanted a boy, and Ginger's gonna have me a boy." Ginger was there with Elvis when he made that statement to Sumner. However, Sumner also wrote that "before he died, Elvis changed his mind. He told me he was not going to marry Ginger because he still loved Priscilla."

Though both Alden and Thompson have had little publicly to say about their times with Elvis, an earlier girlfriend has more than made up for their reluctance. June Juanico, who knew, dated, and fell in love with Elvis as he was gaining fame in the mid-fifties, published her memoirs in 1997. She turned down his proposal of marriage and went on to wed (and eventually divorce) Fabian (Taranto), though she stayed in touch with the King over the years, right up to his death. Her memoirs revealed a young girl who both adored and was in awe of the star that Elvis became. Another early girlfriend, Dixie Locke, simply recalled Elvis as just "a guy who played the guitar."

After Elvis became very famous and reclusive (and married), he supposedly had a number of female lovers who were carefully kept under wraps. Two of them, Lucy De Barbin and Joyce Bova, have gone public with highly publicized memoirs. Their alleged romances with Elvis were so secret that little if anything was known about them prior to Elvis' death. Still the two women created complete books chronicling their times together with Elvis. Even if they were only love-smitten fans, their tales of devotion were at least important testimonies as to how much a woman could "love" Elvis.

Actress Ann-Margret was very special to Elvis judging from their phone calls and acting sequences. She and Elvis worked together in *Viva Las Vegas*. They became an "item," discussed in depth in the gossip magazines. According to Ann-Margret, they lunched almost every day while Elvis was filming *Girl Happy*. When Ann-Margret told "the press" they were about to get married, one source stated that Elvis broke it off.

In her view, she grew away from him and when she realized she was thinking of him in the past tense, she broke it off. From there, she went on to meet and marry actor Roger Smith. When Elvis died, Colonel Parker had her do a eulogy. She did finally go public about Elvis, but only for a few tasteful pages in her autobiography.

Bobby Darin, legendary singer and, at the beginning of his career, co-writer of the novelty song, "I Want to Spend Christmas with Elvis," commented that "there have been two cosmic happenings in this century–Presley and Kennedy." He also revealed that "Elvis Presley confided in me soon after he did *Viva Las Vegas* with Ann-Margret that he was considering marrying her." Darin added that, not long after, Elvis heard Ann-Margret called a "female Elvis." According to Bobby, "Elvis reacted negatively. To his mind, it was vaguely homosexual! Whether that's what cooled his feelings for Ann-Margret or not, I don't know."

Though Elvis probably loved Priscilla the rest of his life, he had a penchant for casual sexual activity. According to many sources, he had all the women he could have wanted, even while married to Priscilla. The pool service man disclosed that whenever Elvis was at his "fabulous estate" in Palm Springs, "the girls draped around the pool were outstanding and always different." According to Ray Mungo, author of *Palm Springs Babylon*, one "unbridled" party ended with a dead party girl in the pool. Her body "was spirited out of the gated complex and clear to Los Angeles," with no follow-up police investigation.

Elvis' entourage, the Memphis Mafia, often procured hookers for him. Supposedly, Elvis would say, "Let's have a party tonight. Call down for a bunch of hookers." Sometimes he would say he didn't want to join in, he only wanted to "watch." The boys were quite relieved when he did take a hooker to his bed. Joe Esposito observed that Elvis didn't really like the hookers because "they weren't pure enough for him. Elvis romanticized sex." Yet he couldn't remain faithful.

Early in their relationship, Priscilla discovered that Elvis lied to her about how deeply involved he had gotten with Ann-Margret. Even after he swore he would never do it again, she said she knew "the future would bring more temptations for him." Actress and dancer Susan Schutte was one of those temptations.

In 1968, Schutte had a bit part in his movie, *Live a Little, Love a Little*. Three months later (after Elvis had barely been married to Priscilla for a year), he asked Schutte to meet him in Arizona, even offering to send his jet for her. Though Schutte was engaged at the time, she went without hesitation, telling her fiance (according to *People* magazine), "If it doesn't work out, I'll come back to you."

Schutte said she spent three days with Elvis and they rarely left the bedroom. Though he recited the Lord's Prayer to her at least once (and talked with her a lot), Schutte said Elvis was no saint. She did admit that she very much "loved our time together." Supposedly the one topic that didn't come up was Priscilla.

Bova, Joyce, as told to William Conrad Nowels. *Don't Ask Forever: My Love Affair with Elvis: A Washington Woman's Secret Years with Elvis Presley.* **New York: Kensington, 1994. 386 pp.**

Bova could well have been just another obsessed fan, just as De Barbin could be viewed that way. Bova, however, did present some compelling pictures and some equally compelling corroborating words from her sister. It's quite possible that Elvis had an affair (even a lengthy one) with Bova, a former congressional aide, just as he could have had one with Lucy De Barbin and another with a backup singer, Kathy Westmoreland (see her book under books by musicians).

One thing in Bova's favor, she did look, at the time, a lot like Priscilla. Not much verifiable information about Elvis was presented in her book, unlike the book by Westmoreland, who discussed at length Elvis' medical theories. Bova detailed her position in Washington and outlined how she managed to spend so much time with Elvis (even after he was married).

Otherwise, her book mainly consisted of recollections about their trysts and their feelings about each other, especially hers for Elvis. She tried very hard to explain how they kept everything so hushed up. Additionally, she claimed that Elvis got her into pills and even "made" her have an abortion. Overall, the presentation was compelling but the substance was too often less than believable, like her memory of Elvis saying he never touched two hookers he hired, he just watched them make love.

De Barbin, Lucy, and Dary Matera. *Are You Lonesome Tonight?: The Untold Story of Elvis Presley's One True Love and the Child He Never Knew.* **New York: Random House, 1987. 294 pp. Bibliography.**

De Barbin claimed to have been Elvis' "true" lover and would have married him had she not been prevented from doing so by his family and protective business management. She also claimed to have given birth to Elvis' daughter, Desiree. Little proof was offered and one had to take much at face value. Private detective John O'Grady "proved," according to Charlie Hodge, that Elvis did not father the child.

The scant evidence De Barbin provided, specifically a handwritten love poem, was given a handwriting analysis and judged genuine by a handwriting expert, Charles Hamilton. Some members of Elvis' inner circle, Joe Esposito for one, claimed that the affair certainly couldn't have lasted as long as De Barbin claimed. Even Geraldo Rivera got into the act with his own investigation, after which he said he had not been convinced.

Ultimately the question became, "why her?", when Elvis had so many well-known trysts. Judging from all that has been chronicled about how Elvis spent his time, there seemed to be little opportunity for him to spend so much time with De Barbin (and profess so much love). At the very least, this book was an excellent chronicle of fan obsession with a superstar. As Charlie Hodge revealed, all the Graceland telephones were carefully monitored and Elvis rarely, perhaps just once or twice, went anywhere by himself.

Ann-Margret, with Todd Gold. *My Story.* **New York: G. P. Putnam's Sons, 1994. 336 pp. Index.**

Van Doren, Mamie, with Art Aveilhe. *Playing the Field: My Story*. **New York: G. P. Putnam's Sons, 1987. New edition 1988. 310 pp. Filmography.**

Ann-Margret's book, though really her story, contained more than twenty pages dedicated to Elvis and her "relationship" with him. They did fall in love and they did a wonderful movie together, *Viva Las Vegas* (about which she detailed the behind-the-scenes parts). She eventually got married and did stay with her husband, actor Roger Smith, through sickness and health. That essentially summarized her revelations concerning herself and Elvis. Three months after Elvis' death, Colonel Parker asked her to host a televised Elvis tribute show. At the end she revealed she was, like everyone else, "a fan."

Ann-Margret was not the first Hollywood starlet with whom Elvis supposedly fell in love or who fell in love with him. In *Love Me Tender*, Debra Paget was Elvis' first leading lady and was said to have given him his first on-screen kiss (though she really didn't). Richard Egan, star of the movie, recalled that Paget "was crazy about him [Elvis]." Paget said that "I find something especially sexy in the features of his face, something very American about the rich expression of his eyes." Even more pointedly, she added that "the electric ecstasy Elvis stimulates in women is unbelievable! I learned this when we made *Love Me Tender*. What is that something Elvis has? I'm not sure I can explain. As Louis Armstrong once said about jazz, 'If it's gotta be explained to you, you'll never understand it.' "

Elvis' involvement with another young Hollywood starlet, Natalie Wood, did not end well. In a 1956 interview, Wood (then eighteen) confided that Elvis "surprised" her because he lived "by a rigid set of rules," yet he was "also tough and virile and full of fun." Things did get serious and Elvis asked her "to come on down to Memphis and meet my mother." Once there, however, he seemed interested only "in exhibiting her like a kewpie doll to an endless array of kissing cousins and high school cronies." After two days in Memphis, according to Warren G. Harris, author of the "bio-book," *Natalie & R. J.*, Natalie called home to her mother (in Los Angeles) and pleaded with her to "get me out of this and fast. Ring me right back and pretend somebody's dying or something."

Could Wood and Elvis have lasted? Natalie told her sister, Lana, that Elvis "can sing, but he can't do much else." At least their tryst had the effect of making Robert Wagner, whom Wood had also been seeing (and whom she would later marry), quite jealous. Upon her return to Hollywood, R. J. (as Wagner was fondly known) "wanted to know if she was really serious about 'that creep.' "

Elvis was also involved, for short spells only, with starlets like Mamie Van Doren and most of his leading ladies. He did not seem to want a career-minded woman for very long, however. Actress Gail Ganley revealed, after she dated Elvis for a while, that he had a "tough time understanding women and careers." She said he often wondered why she didn't just "get married and have kids."

The Van Doren book, like the one by Ann-Margret, was not wholly about Elvis. The part that did cover the relationship between Elvis and Van Doren, obviously seen from Van Doren's perspective, had to be an invaluable insight into Elvis' effect on women, especially famestruck, vain starlets. Beginning on page 149, Van Doren unraveled her Elvis entanglement.

She wrote that Elvis called her first (in Las Vegas), seemingly out of the blue. Though he wasn't married then, Van Doren was (and a mother to boot) and Elvis knew it. In her autobiography, she wrote that he asked her, "Would you like to come back to my hotel?" He then kissed her passionately and tried again, saying, "Are you sure you don't want to go back to my place?" At one point he even wanted to know if she was "wearing anything under" her dress.

She finally went out with him after he so determinedly asked, later kicking herself "for not succumbing to Elvis' magnetic sexuality." She claimed that she did turn him down and they parted. In 1971, in Las Vegas, she said she saw him again. This time he was polite and distant and she sensed his "internal struggle with forces beyond his control."

One other famous woman who claimed to have had a short but spectacular intimate relationship with Elvis was stripper Tempest Storm. She wrote in her 1987 autobiography, entitled *Tempest Storm: The Lady Is a Vamp*, that after he came into her room (in a Las Vegas hotel where she was doing a revue) through a back entrance (after climbing a fence at three in the morning), he grabbed her and, in her words, told her, "I'm as horny as a billy goat in a pepper patch. I'll race ya to bed." She even disclosed that her little dog got quite upset from "their heated cries" during one "marathon" session of making love. Of their 1957 romance of a week's duration, one columnist labeled it a "seven day whirl." After that, their paths didn't cross until he came to see her in 1970 while both were performing in Las Vegas.

Bette Davis' daughter, B. D. Hyman, a Hollywood personality, wrote briefly about Elvis in her biography of her famous mother. Hyman was not someone Elvis dated. In 1961, when Davis filmed *Pocketful of Miracles*, Hyman visited the set of *Blue Hawaii*, where she was able to meet Elvis. At fourteen, she developed a crush on him but stopped visiting the set when she felt her mother was making too much of her infatuation with the King. In her "candid portrait" of her famous parent, *My Mother's Keeper*, she revealed that Elvis was "moody as all-get-out but sweet."

Other starlets have given, over the years, fleeting insights into their affairs with Elvis. Actress Connie Stevens happily admitted that, after a brief romance with Elvis, "he was the best kisser ever." Former Elvis co-star Anne Helm told writers Peter H. Brown and Pat H. Broeske that Elvis "really liked sex. A lot of nights I didn't go back to my own bungalow. I felt a little ashamed about it the next morning, because I knew that the people on the set realized what was going on. I have to tell you, I had fun. And it was special."

Country star Skeeter Davis wrote of a very different Elvis in her memoirs, *Bus Fare to Kentucky*, published in 1993 by Birch Lane Press. After they had finished a performance at Silver Springs, she and Elvis took a ride on one of the glass-bottom boats. Later, on an elevator, as Davis recalled, "Elvis tried to kiss me. I resisted him, saying that I was not going to be another one of those silly girls who fell all over him." Then the elevator doors opened and she got off. From that point on, she "remained a friend to Elvis forever."

Juanico, June. *Elvis: In the Twilight of Memory.* Introduction by Peter Guralnick. New York: Arcade, 1997. 319 pp.

The title of Juanico's book came from a passage in Kahlil Gibran's book, *The Prophet*, a copy of which Juanico said she gave to Elvis while they were dating in the mid-fifties. Juanico was a native of Biloxi, Mississippi, who, in June 1955 went to see Elvis at the local Airman's Club. Author Peter Guralnick wrote, in the introduction, that one of the things "that makes June Juanico's book different" was the fact that she "reflected upon her experience, fleshed out her story with three-dimensional portraits," and above all "provided a structure which, far from distorting the experience, defined it."

What was that story? The first show led to a date which led to "being in love." That took the pair to a marriage proposal which led to a "no," even though Elvis' mother "wanted" the two to get married. After the refusal, there were only occasional encounters up until Elvis' death. The encounters sometimes read like two old friends getting together. All too often they came off as meetings where June seemed to treat Elvis like she was a hero-worshiping fan.

As Guralnick wrote, when it comes to personal accounts of Elvis, it's "hard to scrutinize" which ones are "spurious" and which ones looked at the situation "realistically." The intense times Elvis and Juanico spent together in 1955 and 1956, before Elvis became a "mega star," were recalled in human terms, two people who laughed, joked, met parents, planned for the future, and played at sex. No view like this has ever been painted of Elvis. After she turned down Elvis' proposal, she never let him go, despite a marriage of her own.

She went as far as speculating on why Elvis bought Graceland. In Elvis lore, Graceland, with its appearance so strikingly similar to the Mississippi mansions Elvis' mother had swooned over, was supposedly bought for her. Juanico thought differently. She even wrote that just before she turned down Elvis' proposal of marriage, he asked her to come "home" with him, that he had a "surprise" for her. She left without going to his home and on the way to her home in Biloxi the next day, she saw the headline, "Elvis Buys Graceland!" She wondered if he bought it as a surprise for her. We'll never know.

She did go to see him on occasion and once she tried to talk with him about her concerns over his lifestyle. After one such talk, she was supposed to see Elvis again. Abruptly, Elvis couldn't see her, he had "personal problems." She didn't realize it at the time, but she was effectively shut out. That rejection affirmed so many other views of Elvis, that he was isolated, that he was removed from anyone who would be frank and realistic with him. Producer Chips Moman was realistic with Elvis over his music and brought out of Elvis some of the best recordings Elvis ever did. Elvis never worked with Moman again. Jerry Lee Lewis said that he tried to "help" Elvis a couple of times, but Elvis "didn't wanna accept it." Juanico, through her view of Elvis, hit the nail on the head. Elvis wasn't forced into isolation. He chose it.

The Books by Peripheral Associates

How many people who knew Elvis in some way would eventually come forward and write books about him? Too many has to be the operative answer. Over the years some of the most peripheral people, including a nurse, a publicist, a fan turned secretary, a hairdresser, a maid/cook, and a trainer, have been able to market entire books devoted to their views on him.

The accounts by both the publicist and the secretary generated particular interest among those who wanted to know every possible detail about Elvis. Tucker, the publicist, worked directly for Elvis' manager, Colonel Tom Parker, not Elvis. He began his musical career as a bassist and opening comedian for Eddy Arnold. After Arnold became a Parker client, Tucker got to know the Colonel quite well.

Yancey, the fan turned secretary, provided the earth-shattering news that one of Elvis' girlfriends, Linda Thompson, was "bolder than Priscilla." Thompson was also the one who "talked baby talk to him when he was dejected." Fortunately, Marge Crumbaker (an award-winning newspaper columnist), the person who co-wrote Tucker's book, had the sensibility to add a great deal of insight about Colonel Parker, giving it a more than worthwhile edge. She researched back to when Parker was a Tampa, Florida, dogcatcher.

The nurse's book gave some insight into Elvis' medical problems and did present a chilling picture of the emergency room on the night he died. It was amazing that the hairdresser's book attempted to reveal more about Elvis' spiritual life than any other book. Together, all of these books can only be taken as the writings of people who did profit by their brief encounters with a very famous individual.

Cocke, Marian J. *I Called Him Babe: Elvis Presley's Nurse Remembers.* **Memphis, Tennessee: Memphis State University, 1979. 159 pp.**

Marian Cocke was Elvis' personal nurse on several occasions at a Memphis hospital and also his private nurse when needed. When they met (in 1975), she was the Administrative Supervisor of Nursing Services at Baptist Memorial Hospital in Memphis. When she served as his private nurse, he called her his "security blanket." Much of her book discussed her affection for Elvis brought on by his generosity. She disclosed not only getting a car from him, but how he gave it to her.

Her book was definitely not written to make money because all of the royalties went to charity. Her obvious affection for Elvis prevented her from imparting much in-depth material about his life. His ability to move people to absolute devotion, however, was well chronicled. The valuable parts of the book were Cocke's disclosures concerning Elvis' many health problems. She also gave a firsthand account of the events that occurred in the emergency room where Elvis was pronounced dead.

According to Joe Esposito, Cocke has put on yearly events to raise money in Elvis' name for many charities. He said that though "she's no youngster," she "works her heart out." During "Elvis Week," August 1997, she hosted a silent auction and dinner during which she honored those who assisted her in past fund-raising efforts.

Crumbaker, Marge, with Gabe Tucker. *Up and Down with Elvis Presley: The Inside Story.* **New York: G. P. Putnam's Sons, 1981. 256 pp.**

Gabe Tucker was associated with Colonel Tom Parker for years and through him, Elvis. It was Tucker who convinced Parker to book Elvis with the Hank Snow show, when Hank was the Colonel's client. Tucker was then an independent publicist, though he often served Parker in the press relations area, enabling him to witness a lot of the inside business dealings. His co-author, Crumbaker, a longtime journalist, added relevant detail about the Colonel's background.

Her investigative approach brought out, for example, the darker side of Parker's dealings with the Hill and Range publishing company. The picture she painted of Elvis showed him needing considerable prodding to do much more than hang out with his "group." She disclosed that Elvis stopped doing interviews because the Colonel became afraid of what Elvis might say. The Colonel also wouldn't let Elvis go overseas because he was afraid customs might find the many drugs Elvis and his boys were consuming.

One very informative chapter began by focusing on the efforts of private investigator John O'Grady to intervene in the out-of-control drug consumption Elvis got into after his divorce from Priscilla. O'Grady went directly to Elvis after trying to get Priscilla to convince Elvis to check into a hospital. Elvis brushed off O'Grady's concerns and attributed his problems to the higher altitude of Tahoe, Nevada.

In 1974, O'Grady wrote a tantalizing but relatively unrevealing autobiography (with ghostwriter Nolan Davis) entitled *O'Grady: The Life and Times of Hollywood's No. 1 Private Eye* that discussed, but never dug deeply into, some of his work with Presley. It was published in Los Angeles by J. P. Tarcher. In 1981, Tucker worked with Elmer Williams to publish (out of Houston) a collection of Elvis photographs under the title *Pictures of Elvis Presley.*

Geller, Larry, and Joel Spector with Patricia Romanowski. *"If I Can Dream": Elvis' Own Story.* New York: Simon & Schuster, 1989. 331 pp. List of spiritual books.

Geller was Elvis' hairdresser. He had previously "dressed" the hair of other Hollywood stars, such as rock star Johnny Rivers. Beginning with the first time he cut Elvis' hair, Geller became much more to him, eventually serving as unofficial spiritual adviser. By the end of their first talk, Geller said there were tears running down Elvis' face because he had finally found someone with whom he could discuss the ideas he had been afraid to reveal to anyone else.

The time Geller spent styling Elvis' hair and being his spiritual guide lasted a few short years until Colonel Parker effectively had him removed from Elvis' inner circle of friends. Soon after Geller was ostracized, Priscilla revealed that she and Elvis burned all the books Geller had helped Elvis acquire. They did the book-burning at three o'clock in the morning. However, Geller's influence never went away. At the time he died, Elvis was said to have been reading a spiritual book Geller had recommended. Geller had last seen Elvis at about 1:30 a.m., less than twelve hours before he died. He said Elvis looked worse than he had ever seen him.

The writings for this book were supposedly taken from a diary kept by either Elvis or Geller (or both), hence the subtitle, "Elvis' Own Story." If the contents were taken at face value, the insights into Elvis' spiritual and philosophical changes would prove invaluable to understanding the man. He went from his Fundamentalist upbringing to what some Fundamentalists would now label as "New Age" teachings, including the theories of numerology.

The problem with this book (and others like it) was that it was almost impossible to substantiate. Nonetheless, it was compelling and did appear to accurately chronicle Elvis' growing isolation and physical changes brought about by the deterioration of his health. Geller, in great detail, described the creation of the Graceland gardens. He also disclosed that Elvis had a fetish for female feet.

Parker, Ed [Edmund K.]. *Inside Elvis.* **Foreword by Mills L. Crenshaw. Orange, California: Rampart House, 1978. 197 pp.**

How many books by someone's trainer would ever get published? Even though Parker covered a relatively microscopic part of Elvis' life, his insights revealed a very unique working relationship, especially the part about Elvis wanting to create a martial arts movie with Parker as the star. The movie became very important to Elvis (late in his life) but was killed (behind the scenes) by Elvis' manager Colonel Parker.

Elvis had a favorite nickname, "Kahuna," for Ed Parker, a native Hawaiian (and cousin of singer Don Ho). Key segments of the book centered around specific discussions Parker said he had with Elvis. Parker also did considerable "railing" against the book written by the West cousins. As far as political leanings, Parker could only conclude that Elvis was a "gung ho, America first, flag-waving kind of guy."

Rooks, Nancy, and Mae Gutter. *The Maid, the Man, and the Fans: Elvis Is the Man.* **New York: Vantage, 1984. 51 pp.**

Rooks, only three years Elvis' junior (from Fayette County, Tennessee), was hired in 1967 by Elvis' stepmother, Dee Stanley Presley, to serve Graceland as both cook and maid. As of 1980, she was still there. She once wrote that "at times, Mr. E. P. might put a $100.00 bill into my pocket and smile." Elvis also gave her her first new car, a 1974 Pontiac. She was able to play herself in the 1981 movie, *This Is Elvis*. In 1980, she co-authored, with Vester Presley, *The Presley Family Cookbook*.

She limited most of her writing to some funny anecdotes and an insider's view of the day-to-day operations of Graceland. Some of her information was incorrect, especially part of the entry on Bob Neal. It was the endless line of fans that amazed her the most. With little unique information to offer, the book wound up being published through a vanity press (Vantage).

Though Rooks' name appeared first on the credits, two of the three sections were written by Gutter, the first of which discussed the relationship between Elvis and his upbringing in Memphis. She offered little factual support for her assertions. Next Gutter viewed Elvis from a fan's vantage point. Her involvement with the Oklahoma Elvis fan club was detailed, as was her "big" trip to Graceland.

Finally, in the third section Rooks took over. One fascinating revelation was forthcoming, that she was one of the last to see Presley alive. She wrote that "on Elvis's last day, it was as though he had nothing wrong with him at all. I asked him that morning, 'Mr. Elvis, do you want any breakfast?' He said, 'No, Nancy, I just want to sleep.' " She had little else to say except that he was a womanizer and addicted to prescription drugs.

Yancey, Becky, with Cliff Linedecker. *My Life With Elvis: The Fond Memories of a Fan Who Became Elvis' Private Secretary.* **New York: St. Martin's, 1977. 360 pp.**

Yancey came as a fan and ingratiated herself well enough to become a "private" secretary to both Elvis and his father. She saw Elvis' odd tastes, his strange relationships with his Memphis Mafia, and his many women. She had much to say about how the business was run and how Elvis was kept in a protective world. Her adamant belief, that "Elvis wasn't a drug addict," was based on comments from George Klein, a longtime Elvis friend, who said that "during a friendship of more than twenty years," he never knew Elvis to abuse drugs.

Yancey also delved into her encounters with Elvis' religious beliefs, noting that he became involved with the teachings of Yoga.

Her Baptist upbringing made her uncomfortable with his new outlook, no matter how hard he tried to explain that it paralleled Christianity. At one point, she wrote that Elvis' father had her hide Elvis' religious mail, which led her to observe that "Elvis's life was manipulated by his relatives and his friends more than he realized."

One of her financial revelations disclosed the amount Elvis' live-in lover (from 1972 to 1976), Linda Thompson, spent on her wardrobe. She also disclosed that when Ann-Margret called (after Elvis and Priscilla got married) she used the code name "Bunny" so Priscilla would not get suspicious. Later, that code name became "Thumper." At the end of the book Yancey observed that Elvis "never forgot the death of his mother." She died in 1958.

Author Peter Guralnick, in the second of his two books on Elvis, *Careless Love: The Unmaking of Elvis Presley*, would elaborate a similar thesis. In an interview with *Goldmine* he explained, concerning Elvis' growing isolation in the sixties, that "it's almost as if he had lost his way. I think it would be over-simplifying to say that his mother's death alone created that feeling, but I think it certainly contributed to that feeling. Because he saw his success as being, in a way, for his mother. Everything he had ever dreamt of had come true. And then the very reason for dreaming it was taken away. I think that caused a real crisis of faith."

Stuck on You:
THE BOOKS ON ELVIS BY HIS MUSICAL PEERS AND FANS

> We Elvis fans have truly loved a human being
> with the depths of our hearts and souls.
>
> –Sue Wiegert,
> *Elvis: For the Good Times*

The Books by Musicians

Elvis was so isolated that he rarely worked with peer musicians, except for early in his career when he did sing with Jerry Lee Lewis, Johnny Cash, and Carl Perkins. Perhaps that was why so much of his music (beyond those early recordings that fused the blues with country music) seemed not to be in touch with the times and often sounded as if it had been recorded in a vacuum (without concern for what else was happening musically). Only Perkins and Scotty Moore (one of the two players who backed Elvis early in Elvis' career) wrote significantly on the Sun years.

Lewis had his memoirs of the era collected into a book credited to Charles White and Jerry Lee as co-authors. Moore kept letting it be known in late 1996 and early 1997 that he planned to complete his autobiography. Then in late 1997, the book finally appeared, written by Moore, as told to James Dickerson, the author who previously wrote, on his own, the definitive story of contemporary Memphis music, entitled *Goin' Back to Memphis*. What a tale Scotty had to tell, especially about Colonel Parker's determination to get rid of him and bass player Bill Black.

In later years, the artist to whom Elvis seemed closest was Liberace and that was more due to their tastes in clothes and home furnishings (see the Bob Thomas biography of Liberace for more detail). When Elvis first played Vegas in the fifties and was bombing, the Colonel asked Liberace for advice and help, which

Liberace freely gave.   Together they posed for a unique picture showing Elvis on piano and Liberace playing guitar.

Elvis did meet The Beatles on August 27, 1965, at his place in Beverly Hills (on Perugia Way) but they did not hit it off musically or otherwise.   Supposedly, John Lennon revealed years later that meeting Elvis was like meeting Engelbert Humperdinck.   Elvis expressed disdain for Bob Dylan, yet did a version, in 1966, of one of Bob's songs ("Tomorrow Is a Long Time," included almost as an afterthought on the *Spinout* album) that Bob recalled as his favorite interpretation of any of his songs.   Elton John and Bernie Taupin met Elvis in late summer 1976, after which Elton told Bernie, "He's not long for this world."

Otherwise, there was little contact with fellow musicians. When Tom Jones first met him (they did see each other after that), he merely told Elvis, "I was influenced by you."   Little Richard met him and all he got out of Elvis was, "Man, I love your act."   Richard said Elvis was about to make a comeback and was making the rounds, "picking up ideas."   On the other hand, former Sinatra wife, actress Mia Farrow, once passed on to Elvis that Frank could not stand being in the same room with him, in spite of their working together on a 1960 TV show.

A particularly brief interaction was described by Neil Sedaka in his autobiography, *Laughter in the Rain*.   Sedaka recalled going to see Elvis with his wife, Leba, when both he and Elvis were working Las Vegas.   He remembered that although Elvis "was bloated and obviously in trouble with his life, he put on a big show," although right in the middle of the show, he had "to go the bathroom." Afterwards, Elvis and the Sedakas met and talked (the two singers were, according to Elvis, "on the same wave length and the same record label, RCA Victor") and sang "white gospel together for the good part of an hour."   Elvis gave Leba Sedaka a scarf to "match your gown perfectly."

The most unusual reminiscence on Elvis came from former Chicago Bulls center Dennis Rodman.   Although columnist Larry King once jokingly wrote (at least I hope he was kidding) that Dennis was planning to record with the Mormon Tabernacle Choir, Rodman, to the best of my knowledge, has not become a professional musician. Notwithstanding that he has been viewed primarily as a professional athlete, he has stood out, by his every twist in the media, as a polished performer, celebrity, and public figure (author of two books) almost to the extent that Elvis was.

Rodman, in his latest book, *Walk on the Wild Side*, wrote that some of his friends "think I am the second coming of Elvis."   He saw "some similarities" between himself and Elvis, specifically that they were both Southern boys who lifted themselves "out of a poor upbringing and hit the big time." More than that, Elvis was proof "that anyone with the right combination of flair, talent, drive, and luck can become important in America."

Just as Rodman has seen himself, Elvis was "into taking care of business." They have both "been able to transcend race in America." Elvis "hung out with lots of black people." Therein, from the words of one who has been through the worst of times, lay perhaps the best insight into Elvis' character; he "didn't give a shit what color you were." Rodman "saw Elvis bring all different types of people together because he was a damn good singer." He also understood that Elvis made it as an actor "by acting like himself."

Of the musicians with lengthy insights into Elvis, June Carter Cash wrote specifically of her memories of touring with and seeing Elvis perform early in his career. Carl Perkins also briefly discussed, in his first autobiography, the early Elvis. In his second, he got a little more personal about seeing the deteriorated Elvis shortly before he died. Hank Snow told of how he helped Elvis get started. Wayne Newton wrote about their parallel careers in Las Vegas.

June Carter Cash's later-in-life husband Johnny Cash did not delve into Elvis in his first autobiography. In his second, published in 1997, he finally opened up, albeit just a little. In one part, he told how "fabulous" a rhythm guitar player Elvis really was. In another, he told of a show where Carl Perkins actually did "outshine" Elvis. Cash also revealed that "contrary to what some people have written, my voice is on the tape." He was referring to the tape made at Sun Studio of the Million Dollar Quartet (Elvis, Cash, Jerry Lee Lewis, and Perkins). According to Cash's recollections, Elvis was the first to leave the studio that day.

Only backup singer Kathy Westmoreland and gospel singer J. D. Sumner (who also backed Elvis quite often) offered their views on Elvis in any detailed way. The most fascinating peer musician insight into Elvis was the one by the writer of "Heartbreak Hotel," Mae Boren Axton. She worked a long time for Colonel Parker and thus saw a lot of the business aspects few others saw.

Axton, Mae Boren. *Country Singers: As I Know 'Em.* **Introduction by Biff Collie. Austin, Texas: Sweet, 1973. 384 pp. List of fan club presidents and artists.**

Axton was a schoolteacher and part-time songwriter in Jacksonville, Florida. Slowly she worked herself further into the business. She first met Elvis before he became "big star Elvis," when he was just beginning to tour the South as booked by Colonel Tom

Parker. She helped promote that and other early tours and became familiar with Parker, who went on, of course, to exclusively manage Elvis. After informing Elvis he needed both Colonel Parker and a million-seller to launch his career, she proceeded to write (with Tommy Durden) that million-seller.

In the thirty-page section of her book devoted to Elvis, she recalled how she wrote that song, "Heartbreak Hotel," how she got it to Elvis, and what her relationship with Elvis was like for the rest of his life. Areas of his life she discussed included his marriage, his visits with her family, and his Las Vegas shows, some of which she witnessed. The one overriding theme she stressed was how important Colonel Parker was to Elvis' continuing success. Her assessment of Elvis, musically, was that "he could take any decent song (even Axton rejects) and sell a million."

Cash, June Carter. *From the Heart.* **New York: Prentice-Hall/Simon & Schuster, 1987. 197 pp.**

Newton, Wayne, with Dick Maurice. *Once Before I Go.* **New York: William Morrow, 1989. 269 pp.**

Pearl, Minnie, with Joan Dew. *Minnie Pearl: An Autobiography.* **New York: Simon & Schuster, 1980. 256 pp.**

Snow, Hank, the Singing Ranger, with Jack Ownbey and Bob Burris. *The Hank Snow Story.* **Note on the recordings by Charles K. Wolfe. Urbana, Illinois: University of Illinois Press, 1994. 555 pp. Photo album, index.**

June Carter Cash came from a long line of musicians (the Carter Family) and, though never romantically linked with Elvis, she got to observe his musical talents early in his career. She presented her firsthand insights in her first autobiography. The picture she unveiled was one of a very talented, shy, soft-spoken singer who had a way of innocently appealing to the women in the audience. She was very taken by his soft mannerisms and his gentle nature.

Other country and gospel artists have expressed their thoughts on or recollections of Elvis. For example, Gordon Stoker, leader of the Jordanaires, expressed some eyewitness recollections to writer Paul Hemphill that were captured in Hemphill's book, *The Nashville Sound: Bright Lights and Country Music.* He said Elvis was "an unhappy, unsatisfied man."

Years later, Stoker opened up about Elvis with interviewer Sandie Johnson (in the August 1994 issue of *DISCoveries* magazine), saying that Elvis' voice "was really a gospel voice." Hank Snow once told Stoker that he "wouldn't follow Elvis on to the stage." Yet the Grand Ole Opry turned Elvis down after he auditioned there. Stoker's opinion was that Opry manager Jim Denning [Note: though the interviewer spelled the name "Denning," the reference was most likely to Jim Denny, then head man at the Opry] turned Elvis down based on looks, not talent. Stoker said Denning "took one look at Elvis' long sideburns, and he said, 'I'm afraid you don't have it, boy.' He told him to go back to driving his truck."

Several things went wrong with Elvis, as Stoker saw it. First there was the Colonel. Elvis "wanted love, but the Colonel could never express anything close to it. He was a cold, indifferent man." To compensate, Elvis leaned on the Jordanaires "as family." Then there was the death of Elvis' mother. After that, Elvis became "more and more moody, and more difficult to work with." Elvis was, however, always complimentary of the Jordanaires' work, telling Stoker that "if there hadn't been the Jordanaires, there wouldn't have been a me."

Finally, Stoker appraised Elvis' drug usage. He recalled that Elvis "really only started using them [drugs] when he went to Vegas." The drugs were mostly "uppers and downers." He never used any of the "heavy stuff like cocaine or heroin." He took prescription drugs mainly "because he wanted the second show to be as good as the first." Stoker also said Elvis "never ate proper." Therefore, with his eating habits, "the pills he was taking did far more damage to his body."

Minnie Pearl recalled Elvis in chapter 24 of her autobiography. She was impressed by his "good manners" and his "quiet, almost shy, personality" and his "charisma in action." She once traveled with Elvis and his entourage and did a Hawaiian benefit show with him soon after his stint in the Army. There she saw "firsthand what was meant by Elvis driving an audience wild."

The country singer, Hank Snow, a Canadian, had a flourishing career when he found a new manager, Colonel Tom Parker. Parker, of course, became famous for managing Elvis. Parker brought to Snow, in 1955, the idea of bringing a young, relatively unknown Presley on as part of Hank's shows. That was how Snow came to help launch Elvis' career and lose Parker as manager in the process. In the end, he had nothing positive to say about the Colonel.

The details of all this were laid out by Snow in his autobiography, *The Hank Snow Story*, and it made for fascinating reading. For instance, he said he spoke to Steve Sholes of RCA Victor about signing Elvis. Sholes eventually did. Though not many pages were spent on Elvis, knowing the Elvis name always favorably impacted sales (of anything), the legend, "Here Hank reveals his role in launching Elvis Presley's career," was printed across the bottom of the book's dust jacket.

Wayne Newton was often billed as Elvis' successor as top Vegas performer. He regularly performed there when Elvis was headlining and thus got to know the King quite well. He even once referred to him as his friend Elvis. In chapter 18 of his autobiography, *Once Before I Go*, Wayne discussed, in depth, the relationship he built with Elvis. So deep was Elvis' admiration for Newton, he would often come out and introduce himself as Wayne Newton.

By the end of the chapter he informed his readers that Elvis has been reaching out to him from the afterlife because he passed his legacy on to him. Newton did not like Priscilla at all, feeling that she mistreated Elvis badly. He saw Elvis, at the time of his death, as a performer who was too sheltered and devoid of "feedback."

Fontana, D. J. *D. J. Fontana Remembers Elvis.* **[n.p.]: [self-published], 1983.   [unnumbered].**

Hill, Ed, as told to Don Hill. *Where Is Elvis?* **Atlanta: Cross Road, 1979.**

Matthew, Neal. *Elvis: A   Golden   Tribute.* **Memphis, Tennessee: [n.p.], 1985.**

Sumner, J. D., with Bob Terrell. *Elvis: His Love for Gospel Music and J. D. Sumner.* **Foreword by Bob Terrell.   [n.p.]: Gospel Quartet Music, 1991.   104 pp.**

Sumner, J. D., and Bob Terrell. *Gospel Music Is My Life.* **Introduction by James Blackwood.   Nashville, Tennessee: Impact, 1971.   208 pp.**

Elvis utilized many backing musicians, beginning, of course with Scotty Moore, the guitarist. Among the more famous names were drummer Hal Blaine, Bill Black (who had later fame with the Bill Black Combo), James Burton, and Tony Brown (later a prominent music executive in Nashville). As far as drummers went, not only did Elvis work with Blaine, he also, beginning with his 1954 Louisiana Hayride appearances, worked with another great one, D. J. Fontana.

After Elvis died, Fontana put out a self-published book (marketed with an album of Elvis' Louisiana Hayride recordings) which, other than the first page of writing, mainly consisted of historically valuable but not well-done black-and-white photographs. Fontana disclosed that he was with Elvis from 1954 until 1968, and that, in his opinion, "we were the inventors of what became 'Rock-a-Billy' music." The most interesting document in the book was a 1961 letter from Tom Diskin of the Twentieth Century Fox Film Corporation to Scotty Moore about a session for a picture called *Hawaiian Beach Boy*. The tentative start date was to have been March 20.

The Jordanaires and the Stamps (both gospel music groups) were the backing groups most often used by Elvis. On most of his early RCA records, the Jordanaires were harmonizing right behind him. Neal Matthew was the second tenor. He was also well known in rock and roll lore as being the man who taught Ricky Nelson how to play guitar. In 1985, he poured all of the Elvis memories (at least all of the good ones) he wanted made public into his book.

For his book, Ed Hill "told" Don Hill (no relationship) all about his experiences working with Elvis. Ed was a member (the baritone voice) of the Stamps Quartet from 1973 to 1978, during which time they regularly backed Elvis. Since the book was published in 1979, Ed not only wrote about his encounters with Elvis, he speculated on what happened to the very spiritual Elvis after his death.

J. D. Sumner's oddly titled book, *Elvis: His Love for Gospel Music and J. D. Sumner*, was actually a valuable documentary on Elvis' tours, his feel for gospel music, and his overall musical tastes. Sumner, leader of the Stamps, has long been a gospel music icon who backed Elvis on numerous tours, practices, and recordings. According to Sumner, Elvis came to know him almost as a father figure.

The hard work Elvis put into his act and the respect other musicians had for him came through clearly in Sumner's discourse. Elvis was a solid musician with a studied background in many musical genres. He was no musical flash in the pan. Beyond the music, Sumner detailed Elvis' religious background and beliefs, essentially contradicting Larry Geller's views (and others who have portrayed Elvis as a New Age religious icon). Sumner was quite believable.

Sumner's book on himself (also written with Bob Terrell) was obviously primarily devoted to his own life story. It was important for Elvis students, however, because it had an excellent section on the relationship between Elvis and Sumner. There was also a discussion of Sumner's influences, including everything from phrasing to interpretation, along with an assessment of how much Sumner's sound contributed to Elvis' later successful concert years.

Lewis, Jerry Lee, and Charles White. *Killer!: The Baddest Rock Memoir Ever.* **Discography researched and compiled by Peter Checksfield. Bibliography by Charles White and B. Lee Cooper. London: Arrow Books, 1995. 372 pp.**

During the time Elvis recorded for Sun Records, some of his fellow artists at the label were Johnny Cash, Carl Perkins, Jerry Lee Lewis, Roy Orbison, and Billy Lee Riley. When Cash wrote his first life story, he spent little time on Elvis, preferring to speak mainly about his own drug years and long recovery. In his second autobiography, published in 1997, he did dig into his relationship with Elvis, even telling the real truth about the Million Dollar Quartet.

There were two books on Orbison, neither of which delved into any substantial reflections or thoughts on Elvis. Riley has never written about himself nor has anything of any depth been written about him. Perkins did write two autobiographies, and, since both contained a good deal on Elvis, they have been reviewed separately.

Lewis has maintained a long-standing love-hate relationship with the Elvis persona. In his "autobiography," many of those feelings about Elvis surfaced, interspersed between major explanatory sections on his life and career, written by co-writer White. Along with the quotes from Jerry Lee came reminiscences from people such as his sister Linda Gail; Sam Phillips; Roland Janes, one of Jerry's early backing musicians at Sun Records; Myra Lewis, his third wife; and even British singer Tom Jones, who was heavily influenced by Jerry.

Despite the fact that Lewis was a pioneering American rocker, the book was published only in Great Britain. White is British and has almost exclusively worked in Britain, consulting for *Mojo* magazine and broadcasting for BBC Radio, while teaching an occasional university course. In 1984, White did a similar book on Little Richard, which did get published in the United States. Richard had relaunched his career at that time. As of 1995, when this book came out, Lewis was virtually gone from the American musical marketplace.

Though Lewis was not an analytical sort of person, in the parts of the book that quoted him, there were some very poignant and pointed reflections on Elvis. He felt that "people didn't know Elvis like I knew him." Based on that, he still concluded that "Elvis was a good person." He went further, saying that "Elvis Presley was rock 'n' roll to me." Beyond that, he had some great Elvis quotes. For example, Elvis told him that "you've got more talent in your little finger than I've got in my whole body." There were also some great anecdotes, like the time he and Elvis "rode our motorcycles down the street. Buck naked."

Ultimately, Lewis saw Elvis' decline in a different light. He said "I knew him very well and the books you read about him that his so-called friends put out on him and stuff like that, I think most of it is a bunch of baloney. He had a weight problem, he may have taken some diet pills or something to lose weight, but that's not what killed Elvis. What killed Elvis was loneliness and friends that he thought he had around him weren't friends–they got to him. I could see it happening."

He was right; Elvis was taking something. At one point, Lewis wrote about a "Doctor Painless," who "prescribed drugs for Elvis and just sent 'em off all the time." Former girl friend June Juanico described, in her book on Elvis, a time when "Elvis was hyped up on something," so much so that "his legs were bouncing under the table so fast you could feel the vibrations through the floor."

Moore, Scotty, as told to James Dickerson. *That's All Right, Elvis: The Untold Story of Elvis's First Guitarist and Manager, Scotty Moore.* **New York: Schirmer, 1997. 271 pp. Notes, list of recordings, list of guitars, select bibliography, index.**

This was the story of Scotty Moore, one of a trio of musicians, along with Elvis and Bill Black, whose sound broke open the music world in 1956. His guitar sound was as much a part of Elvis' early success as was Elvis' unique style. Of course, it was Elvis who went on to fame and riches while Moore made a mere total of $30,000 from his association with the King. The background on Moore reached back to his Tennessee boyhood, his naval service, and his marital discords.

It became the history of Elvis and Scotty after their first meeting and the breakthrough of the Sun Records single, "That's Alright (Mama)." A week after the session that produced the single, Moore became Elvis' exclusive manager ("complete management," as Moore referred to their agreement). Unfortunately, Elvis signed with Colonel Tom Parker and Parker began earnestly trying to replace Moore and Black, first with members of Hank Snow's band. Moore and Black stayed, but were reduced to being paid low salaries. Moore said he received only $235 out of the $50,000 Elvis got for appearing on "The Ed Sullivan Show."

Then Elvis joined the Army and the pair were let go. The association sort of ended and the reader was able to look inside the parts of Moore's life into which no one has really ever been interested, the parts without Elvis. He had done some musical work before Elvis, and after Elvis he did some very significant studio work. He played on a number of the Elvis soundtrack albums and visibly rejoined his old boss for Elvis' 1968 comeback special, then settled completely into studio work.

At one point, he said he didn't play guitar "for 24 years." The parts about Elvis co-author Dickerson coaxed from Moore included how Elvis lost his virginity, his hygiene problems, and his dedication to pulling pranks. The hardest aspect for Moore was "the fact that Elvis didn't keep his word." Beyond the Elvis memories, there were also myriad details about the early Sun sessions.

Moore talked recently with *DISCoveries* editor Jeff Tamarkin to drum up interest in both his book and a recording, *All the King's Men*. About the split with Elvis, he told Tamarkin, "It was strictly bottom line. We wasn't getting paid enough. We'd reached the point where the crunch had come on. We couldn't afford it."

What was Elvis like as a player, not just a singer? Moore told Dave Kyle of *Vintage Guitar* that Elvis "wasn't proficient, as far as knowing a lot of chords." One thing Elvis did have in his guitar playing, though, was "great rhythm." He had that same rhythmic feel in his voice. Moore explained that was what "impressed me about his voice, too-the rhythm he had with it. He might jump a bar on you or something, but he would still be there."

After that, Moore and Elvis lost touch with each other. When they finally got back together, he clearly saw that Elvis was in trouble. Elvis was having more than just problems with his weight. As Moore recalled, "I knew that something was desperately wrong." He added that "because of his vanity," Elvis could not have "grown old gracefully, like Sinatra has. He wouldn't have let himself grow old." Observing what had happened to Elvis, Moore was not surprised by Elvis' untimely death.

Perkins, Carl, with Ron Rendleman. *Disciple in Blue Suede Shoes.* **Foreword by Johnny Cash. Grand Rapids, Michigan: Zondervan, 1978. 146 pp.**

Perkins, Carl, and David McGee. *Go, Cat, Go: The Life and Times of Carl Perkins, The King of Rockabilly.* **Discography by Jim Bailey and David McGee. New York: Hyperion, 1996. 437 pp. Bibliography, notes, index.**

Perkins' two autobiographies contained some significant material about Elvis. The first account was woven around Perkins' religious conversion. In it he remembered longing to rock like Elvis, regretting that he was relegated to singing ballads. He recalled his devastating accident, discovering that even though he hit it big with his own song, "Blue Suede Shoes," Elvis took the song over. In fact, it was several months (well after the song had fallen off the sales charts) before Carl could go out and perform the song again. By that time the song was inextricably linked with Elvis.

To show no animosity lingered, Perkins closed with a poignant poetic reaction to Elvis' death. It ended with his statement that "a part of me and America died–when you passed away today." From his religious vantage point, though, he was hurt to "see how the world cries with the passing of a 'superstar' like Elvis" when "only a few" showed up for Jesus' funeral. Perkins concluded that "though Elvis was idolized, and fussed over," he was still "only a man."

The second autobiography, published in 1996, went into much more detail musically, leaving out most of the religious zeal. In it, Perkins delved into his feelings not only about Elvis, but Colonel Parker and Sam Phillips, the owner of the Memphis-based Sun Records. He gave details on how Elvis started, on some of the early tours they did together, and how he first met the King.

He told how Elvis' quick success hindered his own efforts. He unmasked the Million Dollar Quartet (really a trio) and revealed his feelings about his own composition, "Blue Suede Shoes" and what Elvis did with it. Recently, for example, the Rock and Roll Hall of Fame offered a "Blue Suede Shoes" doormat for sale. Perkins' name was not the one associated with the song title on the mat, but Elvis Presley's. At the end of the book, he did give a moving testimonial on his feelings about the very fat Elvis. He also expressed how he might have saved him had he put forth the effort to visit him.

Westmoreland, Kathy, with William G. Quinn. *Elvis and Kathy.* **Editorial supervision by Lawrence E. Crandall. Glendale, California: Glendale House, 1987. 312 p.**

Westmoreland was a classically trained singer who wound up singing backup to Elvis. He taught her to sing with emotion. For years she was also his lover, even during the time he was married to Priscilla. She concluded that Elvis could never belong to one person. She also revealed that Elvis' health had been deteriorating for years and he had been into self-medication for a long time before Dr. Nick (Nichopoulos) came into the picture. According to her, Elvis said, "I'm going to sing until the day I die."

She contended that Elvis' prescription pill usage actually prolonged his life. It was her understanding that Elvis had cancer before he died (a view shared by Larry Geller and Charlie Hodge). She said the autopsy never revealed what in her mind was a "fact." His medical intake (he "never took street drugs") was to help him overcome illness, sleep problems (insomnia), and inherited heart disease. Her account was believable yet naive. She believed Elvis was her "soulmate." She wasn't the only one. Ginger Alden once said Elvis told her he felt they were soulmates.

The "Fan" Books

To say Elvis had fans everywhere was almost an understatement. Actor Jim Hutton disclosed that Cary Grant admitted to him when they were working together on a film that he had a "crush" on Elvis Presley. John Lennon, who said he got started in music because "I heard Elvis Presley," also commented that Elvis "was not a deep thinker. He went by stereotypes. He thought blond hair belonged to girls, and dumb girls at that, so he changed his hair color. Dyed it black, to be somewhat more macho and intelligent."

Though Elvis began heavily greasing his hair in high school, its natural color has been characterized as "blondish-brown" (as opposed to "honey-blond"). Because Elvis dyed his hair black, a seventeen-year-old Ricky Nelson had his girlfriend, Sharon Sheeley, do the same to him. Elvis influenced people in the strangest ways.

Not only did Elvis have some incredible fans. he was a fan himself. Brenda Lee told interviewer Neil Pond (for *Country America*) that "when I was 14 and had out "Sweet Nothin's," which happened to be his favorite song at the time, he called my office and asked for an autographed picture." The "he" was, of course, Elvis.

Lee was both an Elvis fan and personal friend, saying they "remained friends throughout the years." Fellow fifties singer Pat Boone was not only a fan and friend, he always believed in both the greatness and basic goodness of Elvis. He believed that Elvis and he "shared a common deep belief in God and Jesus as the Messiah." To him, Elvis was always "a Christian, but he was cut off from Christian fellowship."

Boone had much more to say about Elvis, especially their so-called rivalry, or how he was "being pitted in the fan magazines against another young Tennessean, Elvis Presley." In his book, *Together: 25 Years with the Boone Family*, Pat wrote, "Elvis had come roaring out of the Southland in the fall of '55 and spring of '56. I had only a six or eight month head start on him, and we rode into the national limelight together. We were both from Tennessee; we were both from lower-to-middle class economic backgrounds; we both grew up in church. But there the similarities stopped. I was salt, and he was pepper. I was the conformist, and he was the rebel. I wore a tie, and he wore a wiggle."

Boone and Elvis did meet "a number of times during our early careers, usually in Hollywood after I had moved there." Though Boone noted the sharp contrasts in their lifestyles, there were some very "deep-rooted similarities," which centered around God, family life, and growing up in the South. As they both continued to live within a "mile or two" of each other, the magazines continued to treat their rivalry as "hot copy." Elvis had become, in Boone's eyes, "very mysterious," while remaining "still single." Boone had been married since 1953. Every so often, Boone would show up for an impromptu Elvis football game somewhere in the area. Otherwise, the two went their separate ways, the only similarity being their burgeoning movie careers.

The fan clubs for each star had a field day with playing the two idols off against each other. As Boone noted, he and Elvis "seesawed up and down the record charts, bumping each other out of the number one spot time and again, launching our movie careers at just about the same time, and our fan clubs reached mammoth proportions simultaneously. As a result, every fan magazine in America ran contests: 'Who's your favorite? Elvis or Pat?' The circulation of all the magazines soared, while teenagers from every part of the nation flooded their offices with thousands of mailbags full of votes. Sometimes I won, but usually Elvis did. I have no doubt that being a sharp contrast to Elvis actually was a help to my career."

Elvis was not often a fan of the musical groups who came to prominence after he did. Most of them were linked in his mind to "the drug culture, the hippie elements, the SDS," as he phrased it in a long rambling letter he wrote to then-President Nixon. However, his stepbrother, David Stanley, did turn him on to Led Zeppelin.

One night, when both Elvis and the group were in Las Vegas, Elvis had them invited first to his show then to his hotel suite. At the end of an evening "filled mostly with small talk" (in the words of Led Zeppelin's manager, Richard Cole), Elvis not only offered the group his autograph but said, "I want you to sign some for me, too." As one of the group members was signing his name, he whispered to Cole, "Can you believe it? Elvis wants my autograph."

Many of the musicians who worked with Elvis so often over the years, like the Jordanaires and the Stamps, developed deep-seated feelings for him, and he for them. The feelings were much stronger than those most people ever have for each other, even married couples. In fact, J. D. Sumner of the Stamps wrote that the last words Elvis spoke to him were, "J. D., I love you."

Frank Sinatra definitely was not a fan. Though he hosted the 1960 ABC-TV *Frank Sinatra's Welcome Home Party for Elvis* television show (to welcome Elvis back to civilian life), Sinatra consistently expressed disdain for the rocker, saying that "his kind of music is deplorable, a rancid-smelling aphrodisiac." Sinatra did mellow enough toward Elvis to say, upon hearing of Elvis' death, that he had lost "a dear friend."

More than twenty years after his death Elvis still had one of the most avid and loyal fan bases of any performer, dead or alive.

The dedicated fans, people who have become enamored with and deeply feel the memory of Elvis, are not crazy, love-starved, or otherwise demented people. They are ordinary people, who for personal reasons, have been instilled with a powerful emotion about an artist they consider to be more than just the best of his time. They will always be loyal to a fault, putting emotions about, devotion to, and memories and thoughts of Elvis above even a spouse. Elvis earned their devotion because he was the one star who was never too busy to give fans a "Kodak moment" whenever they asked.

Professor of Fine Arts Erika Doss wrote in her 1999 book *Elvis Culture: Fans, Faith, & Image* (published by the University Press of Kansas) that "Elvis fans have constructed what may amount to a quasi-religion." In preparing her treatise, she spent a vast amount of time and effort interviewing fans, observing fan clubs, and even attending some of the huge extravaganzas such as Elvis Week in Memphis. Throughout her research, she found dedicated fans like Joyce Noyes (from Minnesota), who told Doss that "Elvis taught me how to feel. Everything about him excited me. Elvis influenced my taste in men, as I fell in love with two men who had similar characteristics and who also loved Elvis."

Even men were adoring fans, as Doss discovered, especially Ron Graham (from Ohio), who informed Doss that "Elvis has done so much for so many, he has brought joy where there was sadness, those that were sick he has helped feel better, he has helped so many of us thru some bad times. I feel that God blessed Elvis in a very special way." The religious basis for Elvis adulation came through clearly in the words of Gloria Winters (from Tennessee) who explained to Doss that "God looked down on him and saw the unselfish heart and smiled on him, making him the ultimate king of all time, except for Jesus Christ himself."

Elvis treated his fans in a uniquely special way. Sue Wiegert, in her book *Elvis: For the Good Times*, concluded that "Elvis seemed to truly enjoy the exchanges with his fans, and it certainly gave them precious memories." Based on what appeared to have been a visible mutual affection between himself and his fans, Elvis reached and maintained a level of mass popularity beyond any other entertainer (even Marilyn Monroe). His fans have remained loyal to him (to the extreme). Worldwide, they have established in excess of four hundred fan clubs, many of which have a higher charitable purpose in keeping with Elvis' spiritual karma of giving and receiving.

Many fans have turned their deep loyalties into concerted efforts to keep their idol's name and memory alive. For example, Sue Mueller of Baraboo, Wisconsin, revealed to the Elvis world that she and a friend were in the process of writing a book about Elvis that would be entitled *Why I Liked Elvis*. She was asking all those who had any contact or connection with Elvis to send her their stories.

One of Elvis' former secretaries, Becky Yancey, told of the female fan who was so loyal she kept a picture of Elvis in her wallet but not one of her husband. The husband happened to be a marine and supposedly Elvis had to defend himself against this man, who became more than a little enraged over his wife's feelings toward Elvis. Yancey also reminisced about the many female fans who loved to send Elvis nude photos of themselves.

Elvis engendered some pretty deep feelings in people who were lucky enough to get to know him, even briefly. Columnist Ripley Hotch of the *Jacksonville Times-Union* wrote about a man named Harry Smith who refused to sue Elvis over a failed business venture because Elvis "was just too nice." In fact, Elvis "was the most hospitable man" Smith had ever met.

Actually, Smith clearly saw Elvis' biggest problem: "he was badly served by his advisers, who were just members of his family, and cronies who hung around." Of course, they were all people to whom Elvis maintained a deep loyalty. How well did Smith get to know Elvis? They communicated long enough, according to Smith, for Elvis to disclose that the "TCB" logo on his private plane stood for "Take Care of Booze and Broads."

Was that what "TCB" really meant? Elvis' girlfriend June Juanico wrote, in her memoirs, that she surmised from Elvis it stood for "The Cherry Busters," an affectionate nickname he had for his friends. She added that "I knew it couldn't stand for 'Takin' Care of Business,' because if it had he would have included the 'O.' "

Devoted fans would most likely have joined a fan club to communicate with other fans via newsletters and personal correspondence. Through fan clubs an entire pipeline of souvenirs and memorabilia became available for either sale or exchange. The biggest club was likely the British one spearheaded by Todd Slaughter. The other major fan organization was Blue Hawaiians for Elvis. Beyond that, fan clubs have sprung up in places like Defiance, Ohio, Antwerp, Belgium, and Elsternwick, Victoria, Australia.

How many fan clubs are still in existence? Patricia Jobe Pierce, in her 1994 book, *The Ultimate Elvis*, listed over 125 Elvis fan clubs nationally and worldwide. Timothy Frew, with an updated 1997 list, narrowed that number a little, listing only eighty-eight, including one in Japan. In his 1997 publication, *The Rock and Roll Reader's Guide*, Gary M. Krebs listed fifteen major clubs around the globe. One organization, the Elvis International Forum, publishes a quarterly magazine sold at retail nationally and internationally. It has also published two glossy books intended for collectors, *Elvis 15th Anniversary* and *Elvis 60th Birthday*.

Bill E. Burk, writer of more than half a dozen Elvis books, has been the head of the Memphis area club for close to a dozen years. Some fan clubs have chosen specific worthwhile causes beyond just remembering Elvis. The Ohio fan club, for example, supports a trauma center while one in Belgium supports several medical causes.

Most clubs consistently mail out some kind of regular publication. The English fan club has regularly compiled *The Official Elvis Presley Fan Club Magazine*. Along with news about Elvis, it has featured interviews with Elvis-like celebrities such as Cliff Richard. The Blue Hawaiians published the first of several books by club president Sue Wiegert.

Since most fans have consistently been enthusiastic followers and admirers in awe of someone they perceive worthy of adulation, they could be expected to write about their hero or heroine but only in the most glowing terms. Additionally, their purpose in writing would center around their feelings for that icon. Exactly that type of writing has resulted in the "fan" book.

A fan book was written with the intention of praising an idol, not delving into him or her from all appropriate considerations. While a biography has built into it the investigation, evaluation, and presentation of all facts and opinions, regardless of what may be discovered, the fan book would tend to exclude almost every aspect of the subject save those items or views that uplift or glorify. The Elvis "fan" books have almost exactly followed such a formula.

People who write from an adoring or worshipful perspective would likely have had nothing but the most impersonal of encounters. An autograph, a seat at a concert, an after-performance sighting would have meant the world to them but have little significance to anyone else. So while fan books may not be considered objective biographical works, the views presented on an idol like Elvis would still be integral to understanding the phenomenon surrounding the idol and give insight into why that person became so venerated.

Of all the fans who have written about Elvis, Wiegert has done the most credible job. The least credible was Boen Hallum's *Elvis the King*. Overall, the average fan came nowhere near being an accomplished writer. Despite that, more than a few have had something worthy to say or present.

In the early 1990s, the Alva, Oklahoma-based fan and writer, Jim Hannaford, self-published three volumes of clippings about and photos of Elvis entitled *Elvis: Golden Ride on the Mystery Train*. Since then, Hannaford put together a far more valuable work (with co-author Ger Rijff of Holland) on the Elvis movie *Jailhouse Rock* (see the section covering books about Elvis' movies). The now-deceased Albert Hand, part of the late fifties and early sixties English Elvis fan club domain, may well have pioneered fan-driven publications with several such notable efforts as a "handbook" (which featured studio-quality photographs as well as numerous stills from the movie *Flaming Star*) and the first crack at an encyclopedia.

Unfortunately, too many fan books could be seen in no other light but having been written for the benefit of one fan, the writer. In her undated self-published book, *Elvis: He Touched My Life*, Sharon Fox related just how Elvis "touched" her, in a strictly inspirational way, of course. Over the years, Fox has built a large and quite unique photo and clipping collection. In 1989, she self-published a major part of that collection in a "scrap" book entitled, *Elvis, His Real Life in the 60s: My Personal Scrapbook*. Hopefully, she will someday share more. Another fan, Karen Loper, circulated her scrapbook (out of Houston) as *The Elvis Clippings*.

Some fans' books had such a limited circulation that not only were they difficult to find, the authors remained almost completely anonymous. For example, the team of Grandlund/Holm contributed *Elvis–As We Remember Him*, in which they glowingly expressed their adulation of Elvis. Additionally, an "author" named Goodge paid a vanity press, Carlton, to publish a tribute entitled *We're So Grateful That You Did It Your Way*.

Still others had singular points of interest. Sara Erwin captured a neighbor's point of view (complete with a picture taken through a hole in the fence) in *Over the Fence: A Neighbor's Memories of Elvis* (a 72-page self-published book). It contained a section on "horseback riding with Elvis" as well as "other heartwarming stories." In 1994, Vera-Jane Goodin published her fan tribute under the title, *Elvis & Bobbie: Memories of Linda Jackson* (as a Limited Star Edition from Branson, Missouri). The title of Darlene Watkins' book, *Elvis–We Still Love You Tender*, sounded like a fan's reaction to stepmother Dee Presley's diatribe, *Elvis: We Love You Tender*.

When Robert M. Eversz wrote about "shooting Elvis" (the title of his book), was he referring to Elvis being shot as in making a movie or simply shot, as by a bullet? Anyone interested in finding out could obtain the 1996 book from Grove Press and read it. Finally, a "new" book, from Busted Burd Productions, was advertised for quite a while as "coming soon" (they must have been taking advance orders). It was projected as the first of four publications based on the diaries of superfan Donna Lewis, begun when she was only eleven years old.

Another 1997 book came from a superfan with the pseudonym of "Baby Jane" (formally known as Frances Keenan), who marketed her memories of Elvis as *Elvis, You're Unforgettable*, published by

Axelrod Publishing of Tampa, Florida. She was supposed to have been related to Colonel Tom Parker, though she offered no revelations about her alleged relative. Her book totalled 391 pages and was as much about her as it was about Elvis. It sold initially for the grand sum of $32.

Adler, Bill. *Bill Adler's Love Letters to Elvis.* **New York: Grosset & Dunlap, 1978. 96 pp.**

McLemore, P. K., editor. *Letters to Elvis.* **New York: St. Martin's, 1997. 109 pp.**

In 1978, not long after Elvis died, Adler collected a cross-section of letters from Elvis' younger fans. While some of the letters were quite bright and filled with "fun" memories of the King, too many were sad, almost morose. All of the letters (taken from various stages of Elvis' life as a star) expressed strong emotional ties to their idol, a major reason why Elvis has stayed so popular, even in death.

Since Elvis' death, the number of dedicated fans has grown significantly, as have their regrets, despondencies, and heartbreaks. McLemore captured many such feelings in the book he edited for St. Martin's Press. Initially, he sent a form letter to thousands of fans, in which he spoke of his devotion to Elvis and asked each person to respond with his or her own personal thoughts.

Surprisingly, the most heart-felt reminiscences focused on Elvis' music. One fan thanked Elvis "for the music you've brought to my life." Many expressed sentiments like Michele, who revealed that "I usually go home and put on one of your albums and listen to some of my favorite songs."

Linda (from Ohio) even sent in a copy of original artwork entitled "The Sun Never Sets on a Legend." Betty's devotion to Elvis began when she was twelve and went to school with him (in 1947). Another fan, Ann of New York, saw him in a dream: "handsome, strong, and innocent of what lay ahead."

Anonymous. *Elvis Presley: El Re Del Rock.* **Italy: [n. p.], 1963. [unnumbered].**

Bagh, Peter von. *Elvis! Amerikkalaise Laulajan Elama Ja Kuolema.* **Helsinki: Love Kustannus, 1977.**

Berglind, Sten. *Elvis: Fran Vasteras till Memphis.* **Stockholm: Askild & Karnekull, 1977.**

Brown, Christopher. *Elvis in Concert*. Ontario, Canada: Ajax, 1993.

Brown, Christopher. *On Tour with Elvis*. Ontario, Canada: Ajax, 1991.

DeWitt, Simon. *King of Vegas*. Rotterdam, Holland: [self-published], 1994.

DeWitt, Simon. *Auld Lang Syne: Elvis' Legendary New Year's Eve Show in Pittsburgh, Pa., 1976*. Rotterdam, Holland: [self-published], 1995.

Fraga, Gaspar. *Elvis Presley*. Madrid: Ediciones Jugar, 1974.

Grust, Lothar, F. W., and Jeremias Pommer. *Elvis Presley Superstar*. Bergish Gladbach, Germany: G. Lubbe, 1978.

Hansen, Mogens. *Elvis: Er Ikke Dod*. Copenhagen: SV Press, 1978.

Langbroek, Hans. *Hillbilly Cat*. Holland: [self-published], 1970.

Lohmeyer, Henno. *Elvis Presley Report: Eine Dokumentation der Lugen und Legenden, Thesen und Theorien*. Frankfurt: Ullstein, 1978.

Petersen, Brian. *The Atomic Powered Singer*. Sweden: [self-published], 1994.

Skar, Stein Eric. *Elvis: The Concert Years, 1969-1977*. Norway: Flaming Star, 1997.

Streszlewski, Leszek C. *Elvis*. [n. p.]: [n. p.], [n. d.].

Svedberg, Lennart, and Roger Ersson. *Aren Med Elvis*. Soderhamm, Sweden: AB Sandins Tryck, 1992.

Taterova, Milada, and Jiri Novak. *Elvis Presley*. Prague: Supraphon, 1969.

Tello, Antonio, and Gonzalo Otero Pizarro. *Elvis, Elvis, Elvis: La Rebelion Domestica*. Barcelona: Bruguera, 1977.

Verwerft, Gust. *Elvis, de Koning die Niet Sterven Kon*. Ghent, Belgium: Het Folk, 1977.

Many international fans as well as writers targeting their works at the growing coterie of non-American Elvis aficionados have contributed interesting and useful publications. Most were intended to stress pictorial spreads while imparting only a surface amount of information on Elvis' life (and quite a bit on his death if published after 1977). The major interest that most of the publications, such as the one by Streszlewski, have generated came from collectors (who wanted as complete a collection of Elvis books as possible) and fans who loved the pictures and the printed words that imparted no negatives relative to their hero.

The works by Fraga and Taterova were among the earliest published fan oriented works of any merit put out within the borders of a foreign country. The anonymously published 1963 Italian book, subtitled *El Re Del Rock*, characterized the typical fan book intended, during the 1960s, for the vast legions of foreign Presley devotees; the design appeared careless and hurried while the inexpensive paper was not meant to stave off deterioration. Though Elvis was not personally visible throughout most of the decade, fan books, especially overseas, were needed to keep his name and image out there.

The 1977/1978 works by Bagh, Berglind, Grust (and Pommer), Hansen, Lohmeyer, Tello (and Pizarro), and Verwerft all concentrated on presenting a memorable publication suitable for grieving fans (1977 was, after all, the year Elvis died). Even throughout the 1990s, fans from European countries, especially Norway and Sweden, kept the books coming. From Canada in the nineties came Brown's two self-published works which unfortunately turned out to be poorly designed and thought-out tribute/souvenir books. That was not to imply that there wasn't a continuing stream of publications coming out of other countries like Russia and China because there definitely was. The ones listed above had the most to offer and appeared like some amount of creativity and effort went into their creation.

A good bit of Elvis interest must have existed in Holland because Ger Rijff was not the only writer there to focus on him. Because several of Rijff's books were published in America and because he heavily researched Elvis, he did become the most well-known Dutch author on Elvis. His books were discussed in the section on reference books devoted to Elvis.

In 1970, Hans Langbroek (a self-proclaimed expert on Elvis' Sun recordings, he even claimed to own a 1954 cut of Elvis singing the Bill Monroe song, "Uncle Pen") marketed his Elvis booklet entitled *Hillbilly Cat*, which revealed that the Colonel was from Breda, Holland. In 1994, Simon DeWitt self-published his pictorial-based work, *King of Vegas.* The following year (1995), he came out with *Auld Lang Syne: Elvis' Legendary New Year's Eve Show in Pittsburgh, Pa., 1976.*

Canada, Lena. *To Elvis With Love.* **New York: Everest House, 1978. 126 pp.**

Carson, Lucas. *Elvis Presley.* **[n.p.]: Taco, 1989.**

Cogan, Arlene, and Charles Goodman. *Elvis: This One's For You.* **Memphis, Tennessee: Castle Books, 1985.**

Green, Margo Haven, Dorothy Nelson, and Darlene M. Levenger. *Graceland.* **Michigan: Trio, 1994.**

Greenfield, Marie. *Elvis: Legend of Love.* **Mountain View, California: Morgan-Pacific, 1981. 154 pp.**

Hallum, Boen. *Elvis the King.* **[n.p.]: [self-published], 1987.**

Harms, Valerie. *Tryin' to Get to You: The Story of Elvis Presley.* **New York: Atheneum, 1979. 175 pp.**

Hegner, Mary. *Do You Remember Elvis?* **[n.p.]: Tech Data, 1980.**

Hill, Wanda June. *We Remember, Elvis.* **Mountain View, California: Morgan Pacific, 1978. 86 pp.**

Hill, Wanda June. *Elvis Face to Face.* **[n.p.]: [self-published], 1985.**

Canada chronicled a special pen pal relationship Elvis had with Karen, a young cerebral palsy victim. Canada was the nurse who took care of Karen until she died in 1963. Her story showed a relatively unexplored area of Elvis' life, where he reached out to people and became personally involved, while choosing to remain unpublicized. In 1980, the book became a movie, *Touched By Love.*

Cogan, a teenage friend of Elvis, wrote solely from the point of view of "saluting" him while Hegner brought out all the reasons why "you" should remember Elvis. Cogan's co-writer was Charles Goodman, a reporter for the *Memphis Press-Scimitar.* She revealed that Elvis taught her and some friends how to put on makeup and told them white panties were best. She also described one of his early eating disorders, gulping down an entire coconut cake.

Greenfield and Carson attempted to show how they, as fans, felt about their King, but failed because they inevitably turned their efforts into tributes and not insights derived from their own unique perspectives. Greenfield was not only never critical in her appraisal of her idol, she approached his legacy as if he were on the level of being like a messiah. Carson simply concentrated on his glorified memories of being a long-term fan.

In her first book, Hill recounted everything about Elvis that was important to her. Her second book had to be "privately published." She worked as a secretary (not for Elvis), yet claimed to have been Elvis' confidante (she was once described as his "friend") for over fifteen years. In that first book, *We Remember, Elvis*, she revealed that Elvis talked with her by phone only hours before he died. He supposedly paid her way to Graceland and offered to buy a house for her and her daughter. He never did.

Hill professed to have been close enough to Elvis to have been told by him that, afterdeath, he would visit many people in the spirit. According to Maia C. M. Shamayyim, Hill "contributed the transcribed material for my book, *Magii from the Blue Star-The Spiritual Drama and Mystic Heritage of Elvis Aaron Presley*." The transcribed material came from tapes Hill made of Elvis talking to her over the course of their fifteen-year friendship. For more on Shamayyim's book, see the Elvis spiritual books.

The trio of fans, Margo Haven Green, Dorothy Nelson, and Darlene M. Levenger, created something no one else ever tried, a description of Elvis' home, Graceland, as seen by adoring visitors. A scholar, designer, or even newspaper columnist could only give a brick and mortar view of the mansion. The three fans/authors, through their glowing and excited prose, imparted a unique romantic splendor to the entire aura of the grounds and the building. Their book on Graceland has been, to date, the only one with feeling.

Harms claimed to have started the first Elvis fan club back in 1955. She was not the only claimant. Charles Lamb, who published the *Music Reporter* magazine for quite a few years, also tried to take credit for the first fan club. Even though Harms observed Elvis for over twenty years, her book contained a host of small mistakes, such as Elvis singing "Blue Suede Shoes" in 1952 instead of 1956. In 1952, he was still in high school.

Hand, Albert. *A Century of Elvis.* **Heanor, England: Albert Hand, 1959.**

Hand, Albert. *The Elvis They Dig.* **Heanor, England: Albert Hand, 1959.**

Hand, Albert. *The Elvis Pocket Handbook*. Heanor, England: Albert Hand, 1961. 100 pp.

Hand, Albert. *Meet Elvis*. Manchester, England: An Elvis Monthly Special Publication, 1962.

Barlow, Roy, David T. Cardwell, and Albert Hand. *The Elvis Elcyclopedia*. Heanor, England: Albert Hand, 1963.

Leigh, Spencer. *Elvis Nation*. Heanor, England: Albert Hand, 1963. 24 pp.

Saville, Tim, compiler. *International Elvis Presley Appreciation Society Handbook*. Heanor, England: Albert Hand, 1970.

In the fifties, Albert Hand became the founder and president of what was reputedly the first major British Elvis fan club. From that position, he self-published five of his own short (the longest was about one hundred pages) "booklets" intended mainly for noncritical reading by other fans. He also published a twenty-four-page effort by author and superfan Spencer Leigh, who would later co-edit (with Alan Clayson) the 1994 English compendium entitled *Aspects of Elvis*. Hand's original "Handbook" was the first of its kind, though it has certainly been outdone by Saville's 1970 effort.

The *Elcyclopedia* was notable for having been the first effort at compiling major Elvis "facts" into one easy-to-read volume. It was updated regularly throughout the seventies, as was the Leigh piece. The only value the Hand books (including the Leigh one) have retained in the nineties has been their worth to collectors, currently about (for the originally published volumes) $100 each for a relatively clean (and complete) edition.

Leigh, Vanora. *Elvis Presley*. New York: Bookwright, 1986.

Maliay, Jack. *Elvis: The Messiah?* [n.p.]: TCB, 1993.

Marino, Jan. *The Day Elvis Came to Town*. New York: Avon, 1993.

Olmetti, Bob, and Sue McCasland, editors. *Elvis Now–Ours Forever*. San Jose, California: [self-published], 1984.

Panta, Ilona. *Elvis Presley: King of Kings: Who Was the Real Elvis?* Hicksville, New York: Exposition, 1979. 248 pp.

Pierson, Jean. *Elvis: The Living Legend*. New York: Carlton, 1983.

Prince, James D. *The Day Elvis Presley Came to Town*. Lexington, North Carolina: Southern Heritage, 1995

Thompson, Patricia, and Connie Gerber. *Walking in His Footsteps*. Maryland: Towery, 1981.

West, Joan Buchanan. *Elvis–His Life and Times in Poetry & Lines*. Norris, Tennessee: Exposition, 1979.

West, Joe. *Elvis: His Most Intimate Secrets*. Boca Raton, Florida: Globe Communications, 1993. 64 pp.

Woog, Adam. *The Importance of Elvis Presley*. San Diego: Lucent Books, 1997.

All seven of these books undoubtedly got published because they referred to Elvis Presley, yet each work did have some merit by documenting the unique devotion Elvis' fans had for their object of worship. Leigh's book was the most evenhanded, giving a good account of how and why the author came to be so enamored of the King. Panta (who became a resident of Ontario, Canada) supposedly heard spirit voices who informed her Elvis was the greatest prophet ever. Originally from Hungary, where she was a milk-processor, she came to view Elvis as a "king of kings" and saw his hometown, Tupelo, as a holy place.

Actually, she was more than an Elvis fan, she was a "visionary," a self-professed prognosticator who claimed to have foreseen Elvis' death. She even wrote him and tried to visit him to warn him. The high point of her devotion to Elvis came when a very mild and beautiful male voice actually told her that "you just had brain surgery" and "your spirit and Elvis's spirit" have become "united."

Published in the same year and by the same small press as Panta's book, Joan Buchanan West's literary contribution was a book of poems on Elvis from a fan's point of view. It was dedicated "to the Living Memory of Elvis Aaron Presley." The dates on Elvis' life span were listed as "1935–NEVER." Her poem titles clearly revealed her sentiments: "Elvis and His Guitar," "Elvis, We Miss You," and "There Will Always Be an Elvis Presley."

The book by McCasland and Olmetti turned out to be an extensive set of emotional fan essays. Not only did the fans write, they sent in personal snapshots featuring the King. Some of the chapter titles told the story very well: "On the Bathroom Floor," "My Elvis

Blackout," and "Elvis in the Snow." The book was self-published but worth procuring if only for the experience of reading the depth of emotions some people professed toward Elvis. McCasland has, for some time, headed up the Elvis Now Fan Club of San Jose.

While Prince simply wrote about viewing an Elvis performance, Thompson and Gerber described walking where their idol had once walked, Memphis, Graceland, and elsewhere. Maliay saw Elvis as a likely messiah and Woog similarly tried to establish just how important Elvis really was. Marino remained content to merely discuss seeing Elvis whereas Pierson went to great lengths to show him as a legendary figure whose persona will never die.

Was the other West, Joe West, a fan? He certainly wrote for fans in his tabloid-style compendium of so-called secrets that were not really secrets at all. The book was very small (size-wise) and was originally intended for exclusive sale in supermarkets. The contents depicted Elvis as an actor, an animal lover, a womanizer, and a very secretive individual.

Page, Betty. *I Got Ya, Elvis, I Got Ya.* **Edited by Rechey Davidson. Memphis, Tennessee: Pages' Publishing, 1977. Reprinted 1978. 72 pp.**

Betty Page's book read like a diary focused solely on following Elvis. Her objective always seemed to be to get one more glimpse of Elvis and when she failed she would write something like, "Damn! Missed him again." Once she thought she had a great picture of Elvis leaving a concert when she discovered it wasn't Elvis but someone named Al. Actually, "Elvis had just left with Dick."

Page was the consummate fan who could wait "hours and hours and hours" to see Elvis "for two seconds." In her opinion, it was Elvis' "majesty on stage" that made him so revered by his other fans. Editor Rechey Davidson closed with a touching eulogy, in which he observed that "the Heavenly choir has added a great lead singer."

Roy, Samuel. *Elvis: Prophet of Power.* **Brookline Village, Massachusetts: Branden, 1985.**

Roy, Samuel, and Tom Aspell. *The Essential Elvis: The Life and Legacy of the King as Revealed Through Personal History and 112 of His Most Significant Songs.* **Foreword by Gordon Stoker (of The Jordanaires). Nashville, Tennessee: Rutledge Hill, 1998. 205 pp. Discography.**

In his first book, Roy saw in Elvis not a mere entertainer but an individual of enormous power. He did acknowledge that Elvis looked bad at the end of his life, but before that Roy saw him filled with "residual energy." For his second book, Roy, a rock music columnist, joined with University of Pittsburgh popular culture instructor Tom Aspell to produce a book that built a picture of Elvis based heavily on their interpretations of how and why he recorded or sang specific songs. Though the point of view was unique, the analysis was too subjective.

Wiegert, Sue. *Elvis: For the Good Times*. Los Angeles: The Blue Hawaiians for Elvis, 1978. 178 pp.

Wiegert, Sue. *Elvis: Precious Memories*. Contributions from Elvis friends and fans. Los Angeles: Century City, 1987.

Wiegert was a devoted fan who got heavily involved in one of the largest Presley fan clubs (she became president). In her view, "Elvis was a gift from God." Her first book was published thanks to that fan club and can still be ordered through it. In addition to her own insights, she covered the activities of other fans like the extremely aggressive California woman who asked Elvis what kind of toilet paper he used. Elvis told her he used "real soft Aurora."

There was a special Elvis medical "report" from a nurse, Carole Neely, and numerous Elvis tidbits. For example, he loved to play with song lyrics. Once he improvised a verse of "It's Now or Never," singing, "Now that you're here, too bad you're queer, my dear." During one performance, a female fan reached up to kiss him and grabbed his necklace as well. It broke off in her hand and she refused to return it. A disgusted Elvis said to the fan, "You son of a bitch."

The second book, also available through the Blue Hawaiians, was similarly heavy with views and insights from other fans and some supposed friends of Elvis (people who knew him when he was growing up). A couple of years later, that book was joined by a second volume. In volume 2, more than fifty celebrities (of varying levels of fame) shared personal memories of encounters with Elvis, mostly gained from working with him in some manner.

An interesting episode Wiegert told about in the first volume came from a fellow fan. It had to do with the four days Cybill Shepherd took off from filming *The Last Picture Show* to be with Elvis in Palm Springs. Supposedly Elvis and Shepherd were lounging at the pool when Elvis began kissing her quite intimately. The fan's observation was that Cybill never moved nor did she open her eyes. Later (March 1997, to be exact), Cybill would tell Oprah (Winfrey) that "there were a few things that, you know, Elvis didn't know."

Flaming Star:
THE BOOKS ABOUT ELVIS' CAREER

> Elvis was a mystery –
> his life baffled even him.
>
> –Charlie Hodge,
> *Me 'n Elvis.*

The Books on Elvis' Movies

Most fans saw Elvis most often in the context of his movies. Thus, the images presented in those films have become not only the lasting ones, but have formed the major public perception of Elvis. Sadly, there has been no definitive work done on his films. Only the book by Eric Braun came close but it was too adulatory in tone to be considered critical. Braun came up short by not bringing in historical facts behind the creation of the movies or other people's opinions about their quality. Instead, he relied on his own delineation of storylines and plots as well as his personal opinions about their relative merits.

The next best book was by Peter Guttmacher, who did bring in some public statements by people like Paul Nathan and Hal Wallis, but was mainly content to project his own conclusions and thoughts. His pictures were lavish, ranging from theater lobby posters to elegant stills. His text contained errors, unfortunately, from quotes applied to the wrong movies to misplaced reviews. Beyond his book, the others were too adulatory to be of much value.

The definitive text must be written because the movies have been too harshly viewed for too long. Critics like Ethan Mordden have pointed out that his films were the only major consistent musicals during the sixties. Greil Marcus had the foresight to anticipate that sometime in the future when the world has gotten far enough away from denigrating Elvis, there may well be a class taught on his films, though it will probably have to be given in France.

Since most Elvis films were shot primarily to feature him, they never became classics. Most obviously did not challenge Elvis the actor and were evaluated by many critics as being downright awful because they lacked plot and featured trite scriptwriting. On the positive side, both *King Creole* and *Wild in the Country* might have been great with more work. Others, like *Change of Habit, Girls! Girls! Girls!*, and *The Trouble With Girls* were filled with surprisingly subtle nuances, philosophical issues, and creative depth in the storylines as well as in the plots.

Elvis never did act in what might have been, for him, a major critical role, though he certainly portrayed some off-beat characters, like the ones in *Charro!, Change of Habit*, and *Wild in the Country*. Mostly he played himself. The fact that he never tried such a role kept his Hollywood career from being perceived as anything but a huge moneymaker. That's what the Colonel wanted, to have Elvis on top, taking no risks and raking in piles of cash. That assessment has been reiterated in some of the more incisive critiques on Elvis' movie career.

Aros, Andrew A.   *Elvis: His Films and Recordings*.   Diamond Bar, California: Applause, 1980.   64 pp.

Though the word "films" came first in the title, the main emphasis was on Elvis' recordings, in the form of a comprehensive and chronologically-ordered discography that fully listed songs and their writers as well as where individual recordings took place. In addition, the author provided detailed notes on each major recording. As far as the films were concerned, there were only brief synopses and limited credit information.

Bartel, Pauline.   *Reel Elvis!: The Ultimate Trivia Guide to the King's Movies*.   Dallas: Taylor, 1994.   184 pp.   Bibliography.

Though Bartel did write from a thirty-plus-year perspective, there was no cogent film criticism or presentation of theory in her book about Elvis' film career. Instead, she was content to present interesting and often obscure facts about the making of the various movies, what happened on the set, or nuances about the other performers. The easy-to-use layout made the book an excellent reference source.

Ultimately the book was marred because of its emphasis on presenting trivia questions and answers with the approach of "see how much you don't know." After completing the book, readers could say they discovered the fate of co-star Judy Tyler and learned that exotic dancer, Little Egypt, sued because of the unauthorized use of her name in *Roustabout*. The author's uncritical points highlighted "facts" about the Elvis persona and cinematic work but provided very little insight.

Bowser, James W., editor. *Starring Elvis: Elvis Presley's Greatest Movies: Stories and Photos.* **New York: Dell, 1977. 255 pp.**

Bowser's book presented synopses of the stories behind each major Elvis film. The text should be treated as prerequisite reading prior to delving into any critical analyses of Elvis' film work. In the introduction, Bowser discussed the best and worst aspects of films like *Kid Galahad, Jailhouse Rock,* and several others. For example, he wrote that in *Wild in the Country*, Elvis actually seemed to be having fun. The *Viva Las Vegas* pairing of Elvis and Ann-Margret reminded him of the magic between Fred Astaire and Ginger Rogers. On the down side, even Bowser had to admit that "I never could believe him as a prizefighter in *Kid Galahad*."

Braun, Eric. *The Elvis Film Encyclopedia: An Impartial Guide to the Films of Elvis.* **Woodstock, New York: Overlook, 1997. 191 pp. List of movies, fan clubs, bibliography.**

Who is Eric Braun and why should his book on Elvis films become the premier available reference source for students interested in Elvis' film history? As an author, he did an in-depth analysis of the life and career of Doris Day. Using Glenn Mitchell's *Laurel and Hardy Encyclopedia* as a guide and inspiration, Braun consulted numerous private collections of Elvis film memorabilia and sifted through some very extensive scrapbooks devoted to Elvis cinematography. His starting point for reference was the now outdated guide, *The Elvis Presley Pocket Handbook* from 1964 (it was first self-published in 1961 by the author, Albert Hand).

It was what Braun accomplished that should be the ultimate focus of judgment, critical or otherwise. Alphabetically, he captured entries for just about every aspect of Elvis' moviemaking. For example, because Mae West turned down the opportunity to star as Elvis' mother in *Roustabout* (indignantly, Braun added), she rated an entry. Detailing that relationship added something, albeit not highly significant, to the understanding of what was behind at least one Elvis film.

As far as the entries for each film, Braun unfolded his views on the storylines and plots, beginning with the major credits and followed intermittently by some critical appraisals that at times proved helpful in understanding the relative merits of each film. In *Viva Las Vegas*, he stated that "the plot is sheer tired formula." Was that merely opinion? Yes, it was, but it did have some factual basis and concurring criticisms to the same effect.

As an added value for each film entry, Braun listed and discussed each song associated with the soundtrack. Beyond the films, he chronicled interesting and in-depth facts on people associated with Elvis, especially relative to the King's movie career. The entry under the Memphis Mafia consisted of a list of people loosely associated with that designation, such as Nick Adams, Elvis' first actor friend, Sonny West, who had bit parts in a number of Elvis flicks; and even Larry Geller, whom the Colonel despised but who tried to help Elvis contact his dead twin, Jesse.

This has become perhaps the most useful and detailed book on Elvis in Hollywood and related aspects of his career because one could look up a person like Elsa Lanchester, who worked with Elvis on *Easy Come, Easy Go*, and not only discover what she did in that movie, but how her film career evolved. I never really knew who Margrit Buergin (seventeen-year-old German girlfriend) was until I read this book. The depth of detail, extensiveness of the entries, and the relative tightness of the writing has made this book valuable but by no means the definitive work the Elvis films deserve.

Doll, Susan. *The Films of Elvis Presley*.   Lincolnwood, Illinois: Publications International, 1990.

Doll, even though writing from a 1990 perspective, was content to give the reader an uncritical overview. That was surprising given that she earned a Ph.D. degree in Radio, Television and Film from Northwestern University. Additionally, she has taught film courses at several Chicago universities. Nonetheless, the book was useful as a reference for time, place, cast, and other general information on each film.

Editors of *Consumer   Guide*. *Films of Elvis Presley*. New York: Smithmark, 1991.

The *Consumer Guide* magazine editors have become known for informing shoppers of the best and worst in consumer goods, from appliances to automobiles. They have tackled the film industry, telling parents what movies would be suitable for children and sometimes for adults as well. In this book, they analyzed Elvis films from a subjective viewpoint. Their comments proved interesting, if only from the perspective of remaining relatively untouched by any

Elvis hype. In 1989, the editors compiled another Elvis book entitled *Elvis: The Younger Years*. It was published by Dutton/New American Library of New York.

Guttmacher, Peter. *Elvis! Elvis! Elvis!: The King and His Movies*. **New York: Friedman/Fairfax, 1997. 128 pp. Bibliography, index.**

Boasting an "incredibly cool and collectible, exclusive soundtrack CD," Guttmacher's book stood out among its competitors pictorially. The CD wasn't bad either, with songs like "King of the Whole Wide World" (from *Kid Galahad*) and "There Ain't Nothing Like a Song" (a duet with Nancy Sinatra from the film, *Speedway*) to go with the best of early Elvis soundtrack songs, including "King Creole" and "Mean Woman Blues." The reproduction of movie stills had to be the best ever done in book format.

There were lots of little offbeat parts in the book to make it of interest to fans and researchers alike. For example, a quote from an internal memo by producer Paul Nathan stated that (concerning the movie *Blue Hawaii*) "we were not making Jimmy Dean in *East of Eden*." A coffee vendor on the set of *It Happened at the World's Fair* remembered that "Elvis includes you in the conversation."

There was also a section of excerpts from letters sent by Elvis fans to Hal Wallis. Two of the letters found fault with Elvis' leading ladies while one saw a Catholic conspiracy trying to hold down a good protestant boy. Beyond those little surprises, for such a heavily and lavishly illustrated book, there was a lack of depth as far as historical information on what went into the making of each film. There was simply too much reliance on a subjective analysis of each movie's plot.

Hannaford, Jim, and Ger Rijff. *Inside Jailhouse Rock*. **Holland, Michigan: Jim Hannaford Productions, 1994.**

In 1994, Hannaford wrote an article in *DISCoveries* to explain the point of the book. He wrote that it contained "a host of unpublished photos from the movie, interesting notes from the script, letters of correspondence from the producers, and other choice tidbits of information." Also featured, according to the write-up, were "photo copies of many official documents from the movie," as well as "sheet music, letters, and much more." That summarized the book. It did contain a lot of interesting background information, some of it valuable primary source material. There was no critical commentary about the movie itself; that was never part of the author's scope. For what it set out to accomplish, it became an extremely valuable resource.

Lichter, Paul. *Elvis in Hollywood.* **New York: Simon & Schuster, 1975. 188 pp. List of movie music.**

It took Paul Lichter to compile one of the most complete film studies on Elvis. Lichter, who also wrote in detail on Elvis' music, tackled Elvis' film career with the enthusiasm of a fan and a critic, all in the positive sense, of course, because he, in reality, adored Elvis. Still, the wealth of detail, on each film especially, more than made up for any lapses in critical analysis.

On Tour was the final film to be documented in this book, which was published in 1975, two years before Elvis' death. Lichter would have nominated the film for an Oscar in the documentary category. Where Lichter presented useful and unique information, he excelled. The part on Elvis' movie music listed not only the songs in each movie, but which songs were released and which ones were excluded. Lichter even noted which songs were intended (actually recorded) for a specific movie but were deleted as of the final cut.

This and his book on Elvis' music (*Elvis: The Boy Who Dared to Rock*) were Lichter's two best and most worthwhile works. He put out four quite unsatisfactory books through Jesse Books of Huntingdon, Pennsylvania, from 1983 through 1992. They were essentially "fan" paeans (thin books with lots of photos) boasting the following titles, *Elvis: All My Best* (1989), *Elvis: Behind Closed Doors* (1987), *Elvis Memories: A Love Story* (1985), *Elvis: Rebel Heart* (a 1992 deluxe hardback edition with glossy, flamboyant photos). If nothing else, Lichter was the consummate fan.

McLafferty, Gerry. *Elvis Presley in Hollywood: Celluloid Sell-Out.* **London: Robert Hale, 1989. 240 pp. Filmography, index.**

Schuster, Hal. *The Magic Lives on: The Films of Elvis Presley.* **Los Angeles: Movie Publishers, 1989.**

If one was seeking a negative perspective, McLafferty's book, published in England, was the one. His perspectives did cause a rethinking of possible kindly thoughts toward Elvis' acting abilities, but did not allow for objective analysis of the films, because the author saw no basic artistic merit in them. The better movies weren't *Casablanca*, but they were not abject failures.

Schuster's book simply presented basic facts on each film. It was more of a retrospective with little analysis and no behind-the-scenes stories. Though not negative in tone, it offered nothing of value, save for some professional pictures.

Pond, Steve. *Elvis in Hollywood: Photographs from the Making of Love Me Tender.* **New York: Penguin, 1990. 108 pp. Filmography.**

Pond did the text for a collection of photographs from the archives of Michael Ochs. The photographs were taken on the set of Elvis' first movie role, *Love Me Tender.* The young Elvis could be seen with all his pouting charisma. Explanatory notes detailed how Elvis' finest natural and unencumbered acting job came to be. Pond understood Elvis as a "commodity" but recognized "the talent that made that exploitation possible to begin with." The filmography in the back proved useful in pinpointing the co-stars, producers, and directors involved in all of Elvis' subsequent films.

Wallis, Hal, with Charles Higham. *Starmaker: The Autobiography of Hal Wallis.* **New York: Macmillan, 1980. 240 pp. Inter-office communications, index.**

Hal Wallis produced some of Elvis' better early movies, such as *Loving You, King Creole,* and *GI Blues.* He later returned to produce slicker efforts like *Paradise, Hawaiian Style,* and *Easy Come, Easy Go.* In his book, he devoted a complete chapter, entitled "Elvis," to his entire history of working with Elvis. Given the close relationship the two men had, Wallis supplied very little detail, nowhere near as much as he presented, for example, on Bette Davis. He did discuss the Colonel, saying that "Elvis was a delicately tuned engine. Colonel Parker supplied the fuel."

Not only was Wallis a pivotal figure in Elvis' career, he figured prominently in the destinies of other major stars, such as Edward G. Robinson. Robinson wrote in his memoirs that Wallis was "perhaps the least known of the movie moguls because actually he is not a mogul at all." In Robinson's opinion, Wallis was not very well recognized because he went "from pictures about Becket and Queen Elizabeth (historically accurate and beautifully devised) to Elvis Presley and Martin and Lewis." The closest Robinson could come to understanding the Wallis/Presley association was that "maybe he saw in Presley a *Nouvelle Vague* (which he most certainly was)."

Weisman, Ben. *Elvis Presley: "The Hollywood Years."* **Secaucus, New Jersey: Warner Bros., 1992. 88 pp.**

Weisman wrote fifty-seven, mainly movie, songs for the King (more than any other songwriter), songs that had to contain elements of rock, country, blues, and pop. He noted that Elvis copied his demos almost exactly, so he not only used "the same type of rhythm section," he hired singers "that could copy Elvis' sound." Some of the demo singers he used were Otis Blackwell, Glen Campbell, P. J. Proby, and Ray Peterson, who had the first hit recording on "The Wonder of You," which Elvis took top-ten in early 1970. Leon Russell and James Burton were among the talented musicians used to create instrumental tracks for Weisman's demos.

Though most of Weisman's book consisted of sheet music, the few insights were priceless. He recalled that Elvis "would get so carried away [in the studio], he would forget to sing directly into the mike." After meeting Elvis in 1957, he recalled that "in my wildest dreams, I never imagined the impact he was about to make on the world."

Zmijewsky, Steven and Boris. *Elvis: The Films and Career of Elvis Presley.* **Secaucus, New Jersey: Lyle Stuart, 1976. 224 pp. Discography of million-sellers.**

The Zmijewsky brothers did a more than satisfactory job of presenting critical and informative detail, making this book one of the best unbiased works on Elvis' cinematic output. In addition to film synopses, they devoted an entire section to his moviemaking history. Their recounting of the making of the first Presley movies was very thorough. They quoted Director Don Siegel's criticism of the studio that put out *Flaming Star*, when he said, "They should have put on a campaign emphasizing that Elvis emerged as an actor in the film."

As a bonus, the authors went beyond the movies to capture highlights of Elvis' recording and performing career. They interwove his life story, at least as much as they knew from popular sources, around movie and career critiques. For some of his best movies, they included a short but incisive review. Also included was a partial discography that stopped at 1970, though the book came out in 1976.

The Books on Elvis' Music

The Elvis legend began with the music. The sound consisted of a raw, raucous Elvis, backed by Scotty (Moore), playing some great guitar "riffs," and Bill (Black), the bass player. There was no drummer, only Black, who could, according to drummer D. J. Fontana, "slap the fire out of a bass. No notes, just wood." It ended with Elvis telling Kathy Westmoreland, "I've never sung a lasting song."

In between he developed a voice that renowned music critic Henry Pleasants assessed as, "in a word, an extraordinary voice." So, whatever Elvis may have come to mean to people, it was his musical talent, especially his interpretive skills, that attracted most fans to him in the first place Some of his recordings went beyond great while many were substandard. Until the final year, Elvis in person was as exciting as any rock act, even The Rolling Stones.

He definitely was never a songwriter–not ever, not even one time. During an early (albeit brief) interview, he even sheepishly confessed that he had "never written a song in my life. It's all a big hoax. It makes me look smarter than I am."

Country artist Hank Thompson recently recalled that when Elvis was opening for him, he came to Hank asking for "advice about some country songs Elvis had written." Thompson looked at the songs and concluded "they weren't very good songs." In fact, he said, "Elvis would never have made it doing songs like the ones he sang for me that night." Nonetheless, Elvis' name appeared on quite a few songs as co-writer. It was strictly a business practice, insisted upon by either him or Colonel Parker or both.

Many of Elvis' biggest hits were published through Hill and Range, a music publishing company run by Freddie Bienstock and Jean and Julian Aberbach. Much of the time, but not always, before Elvis would record a song, especially a new one, at least some part (usually half) of the rights would have to be assigned to the company (or to Elvis Presley Music or Gladys Music, both of which were publishing entities managed by Hill and Range). That's why Elvis' name was on "Love Me Tender," for example.

One of the few times that didn't happen involved Tony Joe White, who hit it big in 1969 with his own composition "Polk Salad Annie." According to Phil Sutcliffe (writing in *Q* magazine), when Elvis was looking for material in 1969, White got a call directing him to the studio where Elvis was recording. There he was pulled aside by the three head honchos from Hill and Range. They decided Elvis should record three of White's songs, including "Polk Salad Annie," but only after White signed the rights over to their company.

White objected and was preparing to leave when Elvis came out of the control room. He recognized White and hollered, "Hey, Tony Joe!" The two men went out for beers and White explained to Presley what had taken place. Elvis said he would take care of the problem, which he did. When he finally recorded four of White's songs, "Polk Salad Annie" and "Rainy Night in Georgia" (both done live in 1972), and "For Ol' Times Sake" and "I've Got a Thing About You, Baby" (1973 studio recordings), both the writer and publisher retained their full and rightful copyrights.

The great songwriters like Johnny Mercer didn't have to give Elvis writer's credit or any part of the publishing, so Elvis didn't, as a rule, record their material. Dolly Parton recalled the time Elvis wanted to record a couple of her songs. She said that he "was here in Nashville" and wanted to cut "I Will Always Love You." Felton Jarvis, Elvis' producer, called Dolly and told her, "Elvis has to have half the publishing on the song. Everything he records, unless it's already a standard, Elvis has to have half the publishing." Dolly wouldn't agree to that and, as a result, Elvis never recorded her song.

Whether he consistently recorded great songs or not, Elvis touched millions through his music, even though critically he was said to have had a thin, weak voice, to have sung flat too many times, to have had a limited range, and to have recorded some of the most inane songs ever. Elvis never recorded "The Times They Are A-Changin'." He never got funky with "Sex Machine," nor did he ever get soulful with "Land of a Thousand Dances." He did his own brand of rock and roll with "Good Luck Charm" and "Viva Las Vegas."

When it came to the creation of his music, Elvis could waver between caring very much and not caring at all. At times during his career he was involved, creative, and committed, while at other times, especially toward the end of his life, his approach was chaotic at best. British songwriter and "A&R" (artists and repertoire) man Bunny Lewis (composer of the song, "Girl of My Best Friend") got the opportunity to watch Elvis record in the early sixties and came away impressed by how hard the King worked at making his music. Lewis said that "Elvis was working on a three-day session, sweating it out from noon to midnight." It wasn't just the long hours of dedication that Lewis saw. Elvis "completely controlled" the session. He "altered things, tried new sounds and okayed all the takes."

James Burton, who once played guitar for Ricky Nelson, began regularly backing Elvis during the seventies. He recalled Elvis telling him, "I can afford the best and I will definitely have the best." His work with Elvis brought Burton a deep respect for the man as an innovative musical force, who "had such a fantastic ear for music it's unreal." In sessions, according to Burton, Elvis "listened to the songs and put them together with the musicians." He also "definitely felt what he liked," and had "what you might almost call perfect pitch."

In contrast, piano player (and by the nineties, MCA Records executive) Tony Brown recalled a much different, lackadaisical, unorganized approach when he joined Elvis' band in the mid-seventies. On his first night, Brown had to go on and play because there had been "no rehearsal." In his view, "those were wild days.

Elvis was usually zonked on pills and might call songs the band had never rehearsed." For even some of the biggest shows, Elvis "used to come in just before we'd go onstage. We'd be leaving the dressing room and he'd come in with that huge entourage." One night, Brown said Elvis looked his way and slurred, "Hey, Tony." When Brown turned around, Elvis just said, "Er, damn, I forgot what I was going to say."

Has anyone ever really understood what Elvis' music was all about? Conway Twitty did, especially when Elvis first hit big. He said, "This Presley sound was something else–like millions of other listeners, I was totally consumed by it. There just had never been anything like it before." What did Conway mean, like nothing before? It was the same sets of chords in front of a basic beat with lyrics about love, good or bad.

Twitty continued: "We had all listened for many years to the blues, and of course Gospel music and country music, and here was something totally different. Yet what I didn't realize at the time was that it was actually a blend of all three of those kinds of music. So what my ears heard was something I thought I'd never heard before." To Conway, that first Elvis record "was an approach and rendition that no other singer had done before. It was a brand-new sound, a brand-new feel, it came out of left field. It took this country by storm, and it's hard to describe all those feelings."

Elvis never let on publicly, in any depth, what he thought about his musical accomplishments. Internationally famous Welch singer Tom Jones, who saw himself as a friend of Elvis', once revealed, according to his biographer, Colin Macfarlane, that the only thing Elvis "liked about his later records was the cleaner sound and production." Jones also said Elvis privately confessed he didn't have "copies of his old Sun records because he 'hated the rotten sound.' "

Only half a dozen books devoted themselves entirely to Elvis' music. Of those books analyzing his music, two were written mainly to chronicle and praise it, while three others limited themselves primarily to his live shows, performances, and tours. Only one was an in-depth analysis covering every major facet of the music. That was the one by Robert Matthew-Walker, published in England.

The best analysis of Elvis' music and its context came as a section in a 1975 Greil Marcus book, *Mystery Train*. Marcus presented his view of the best American innovation in music over an approximate twenty-year span. Elvis was at the forefront. The next best partial analyses of Elvis' music came from authors Stanley Booth and Henry Pleasants.

Elvis' music also rated chapters in other rock and roll music books. Unfortunately, they did not possess or offer any special or unique insights beyond a historical perspective. Primary examples of such accounts were Mike Jahn's *Rock from Elvis Presley to the Rolling Stones*, Arnold Shaw's *The Rockin' 50's*, Jon Landau's *It's Too Late to Stop Now*, and Gene Busnar's *It's Rock 'n' Roll*. *Rock of Ages: The Rolling Stone History of Rock and Roll*, by Ed Ward, Geoffrey Stokes, and Ken Tucker, unquestioningly rehashed Elvis in a fifties context, an analysis done more effectively in several of the Elvis biographies.

Booth, Stanley. *Rhythm Oil: A Journey Through the Music of the American South*. New York: Random House, 1991. 254 pp. Index.

Clark, Alan. *Legends of Sun Records: Number One*. West Covina, California: The National Rock 'N Roll Archives, 1992. [unnumbered].

Clark, Alan. *Legends of Sun Records: Number Two*. West Covina, California: The National Rock 'N Roll Archives, 1992. [unnumbered].

Dickerson, James. *Goin' Back to Memphis: A Century of Blues, Rock 'n' Roll, and Glorious Soul*. New York: Simon & Schuster Macmillan, 1996. 276 pp. Chart information, notes, selected bibliography, index.

McNutt, Randy. *We Wanna Boogie: An Illustrated History of the American Rockabilly Movement*. Hamilton, Ohio: HHP Books, 1988. New edition 1988. 285 pp. Bibliography, index.

Parish, James Robert, and Michael R. Pitts. *Hollywood Songsters: A Biographical Dictionary*. New York: Garland, 1991. 826 pp. General index, song and album index.

Pleasants, Henry. *The Great American Popular Singers: Their Lives, Careers, & Art*. New York: Simon & Schuster, 1974. 384 pp. Glossary, index.

The set of books by Booth, Clark, Dickerson, Pleasants, Parish and Pitts, and McNutt offered snippets of important insights into Elvis' music. None had anything extremely substantial to offer, but none could have been left out because their perspectives offered fringe views of Elvis' career. Booth's book looked back, from a 1967 perspective, on Elvis and his first professional musicmaking for Sun Records. He quoted at length, Dewey Phillips, a Memphis disc jockey, who told how hard Sam Phillips worked to get Elvis "on the blues thing."

Booth also wrote a near eyewitness account of the death of Elvis' mother. From that, he concluded Elvis never got over her death. Going beyond 1967, another chapter, albeit a short one, discussed the women in Elvis' life, especially Priscilla. The shortcomings in the Elvis and Priscilla marriage were succinctly summarized.

Clark's two books were both short efforts, crammed with copies of clippings that chronicled the careers of all the major performers on the Sun Records roster. Elvis' two sections presented his rise from regional flash to superstar, as documented by charts, newspaper releases, and other items. There were similar great sections on fellow stars such as Jerry Lee Lewis and Roy Orbison. In the early eighties (1981 and 1982), Clark had focused two pictorial books specifically on Elvis, *Elvis Presley Memories* and *The Elvis Presley Photo Album* (both were self-published out of West Covina, the first by Leap Frog Productions and the other by Alan Clark Productions).

Dickerson, a magazine and newspaper editor, offered firsthand accounts of contemporary Memphis music, especially the Stax sound. He knew producer Chips Moman, as he did so many of the movers and shakers of Memphis music production. He clearly saw where the musical Presley was in the late sixties, an insulated man surrounded by people afraid to tell him even when he was singing flat.

It was a beaten Elvis that Dickerson observed, a man reeling from his divorce and without musical direction. He saw Moman come in and very carefully handle Elvis to get the best out of him for perhaps the last time. Interestingly, when the opportunity came for the two of them to work together again, Presley declined, showing perhaps that by the seventies, before he died, he no longer wanted to work hard to bring out his best musical self.

Pleasants' book uniquely examined Elvis as a serious singer. His technique and recordings were contrasted with those of Frank Sinatra, Ella Fitzgerald, and Ethel Merman, who have always been presented in a more favorable light, talent-wise, than Elvis. This time Elvis was viewed as both an outstanding interpreter and musician. Pleasants understood that not only did Elvis have a great voice and art (he reminded us that "no singer survives for nearly twenty years without them"), he was also able to sound "like a country boy singing for friends and neighbors on the front porch. That was part of his appeal."

McNutt explained Elvis' true place in the development of that wild artform, rockabilly, a musical genre somewhere between country music and rhythm and blues. He presented two great perspectives, the first focusing on the rise of Sun Records. Then he led off with Elvis as the first great "rocker" among all the many rockabillies, who, if he couldn't keep his hips moving, was dead. To McNutt, it was Elvis, not Bill Haley or Carl Perkins, who was "destined to be favored by history" as rockabilly's main leader.

The book by Parish and Pitts was intended as an encyclopedia on performers with success as both singers and film stars. Thus, there was a strong section devoted to Elvis. The seven-page entry presented plot overviews of his movies and observations on the ups and downs of his musical sales. It also speculated on his private life and the problems he had at the end of his career. In spite of all the purported problems, Elvis earned approximately $816,000 for a 1975 one-night concert in Detroit. The authors concluded that "of all the movie singers, Elvis alone, has remained constantly in the public view."

Cotten, Lee. *Did Elvis Sing in Your Hometown?*   Sacramento, California: High Sierra Books, 1995.   278 pp.   City index.

Cotten, Lee.   *Did Elvis Sing in Your Hometown, Too?* Sacramento, California: High Sierra Books, 1997.   336 pp.

This book was uniquely illustrated with copies of programs from various shows Elvis did in various venues. It presented a detailed chronology of his live shows (every known performance) over many years across the country (up to 1968). Beginning with Elvis' childhood, it culminated with the benefit he did in March 1961 in Honolulu.

Cotten presented useful biographical clips on musicians such as Scotty Moore and offbeat background on some of the stranger places Elvis entertained. A city-by-city index helped pinpoint specific tour stops. Why the book was marketed by such a small publisher (though Popular Culture Ink has taken up distribution) has to remain a mystery since its unique subject matter would rank it high on any list of important Elvis reference material.

The follow-up (with the word "too" at the end of the title) began with the videotaping in June 1968 of Elvis' "comeback" special. It covered nine additional years ending with Elvis' final performance in Indianapolis, Indiana (June 26, 1977). In between were all the large and small venues Elvis played as he declined into a mumbling parody of his once great persona.

Gordon, Robert. *The King on the Road: Elvis Live on Tour: 1954 to 1977.*   New York: St. Martin's, 1996.   Simultaneously published in England by Hamlyn, an imprint of Reed Consumer Books Ltd.   208 pp.   Concert log.

Gordon's book, long overdue, immediately became the best book on the live, touring Elvis. It featured great pictures, reproductions of reviews, clippings, advertisements, and posters. Each year was encapsulated as to the details of tours, live shows, and appearances.

The section on the Louisiana Hayride was especially well chronicled with many exceptional and unique pictures. At the end of the book, the author included a precise concert log. One of the factors that made this book definitive was the author's exclusive access to the files of the Elvis estate and the papers of Colonel Tom Parker.

Gray, Michael, and Roger Osborne. *The Elvis Atlas: A Journey Through Elvis Presley's America.* **New York: Henry Holt, 1996. 192 pp. Listing of live appearances, bibliography, general index, index of places.**

Gray's book was quite imposing, in both content and scope. It effectively focused on Elvis' life and career by presenting more than 150 unique maps and detailed descriptions, along with glossy pictures, of places where Elvis recorded, performed, made movies, and sometimes lived. Each section was broken down chronologically into what Elvis did, where he performed, and how he lived (when it was possible to know).

Entire sections covered Elvis' 1955 tour through the South, his Army days, and Las Vegas shows. The chronological listings in each section were amazingly specific. The part on the death of Elvis intricately tied together everything going on in his life, his activities, his recordings, and especially the aftermath of his death. Another quite unique part focused, in detail, on Elvis' frantic first year of touring, especially his demanding schedule.

James, Antony. *Presley: Entertainer of the Century.* **New York: Tower, 1977. 224 pp.**

Rubel, David. *Elvis Presley: The Rise of Rock and Roll.* **Introduction by Eric Hirsch, Assistant Professor of Sociology, Providence College. Brookfield, Connecticut: Millbrook (distributed by Houghton Mifflin Company), 1991. 96 pp. Notes, suggested reading, index.**

Though the James book did delve into Elvis as a live entertainer, it basically rehashed what other books, based on original research, had already presented. James also accepted, without question, previous statements made by others, such as the claims by Dr. Francisco and Dr. Nichopoulos that when Elvis died, he had no drugs in his system except "those he was taking for his hypertension and for a blockage of the colon." Important crises in Elvis' life were often glossed over, such as his mother's deteriorating health and subsequent death. The author simply mentioned she had hepatitis and died relatively quickly.

Rubel's book went back to the early history of rock and roll and attempted to show Elvis' part in it. Though the book was pegged as a biography, its analytical parts concentrated mainly on Elvis' music. The ideas were solid but depended too much on quotations excerpted from Jerry Hopkins' original and detailed 1971 Elvis biography. In an attempt to lend the book a scholarly air, it was presented as part of a "New Directions" series with an introduction written by sociology professor Eric Hirsch.   Hirsch's unique view was that Elvis' "outrageously expensive lifestyle" was responsible for sending "the message that teenagers should spend money and have fun."

Lichter, Paul. *Elvis: The Boy Who Dared to Rock.* **London: Sphere Books, 1980.   Reprinted 1981.   304 pp.   Live appearances, recording sessions, discography, films.**

Lichter (who edited the *Memphis Flash*, a bimonthly Elvis fan magazine) took a view toward Elvis' music similar to that of a fan because he was, ultimately, a "super" fan. His view was therefore informative but uncritical and noninterpretive. The book was well organized into four "books," one on Elvis' life, one on his major live shows, the third on recording sessions, and the fourth presenting a lengthy discography. The transcript of Elvis' 1971 New York news conference was presented intact.

The live show section was a fan's view of watching Elvis in performance from 1970 until his death. Lichter closed by revealing he had seen over eight-hundred shows. To him, they were all simply great.   The listing of live shows stood for years as the best documentation of its kind.

The recording session documentation was complete and without commentary. The discography was exhaustive as far as listing titles of singles, albums, and even bootlegs. Where the contents of albums were listed, they were often incomplete. As complete, factually, as this book was, Lichter was content to follow it up, in 1985, with a tribute-style book entitled *Elvis: A Portrait in Music.*

Marcus, Greil. *Mystery Train: Images of America in Rock 'n' Roll Music.* **New York: E. P. Dutton, 1975, 1976.   New edition 1982.   320 pp.   Notes and discographies, index.**

Only part of the Marcus book was on Presley, but what a part it was. As an incisive analysis of the development of Elvis' music, it had probably more value than any other, except for Escott's work on Sun Records. Marcus traced Elvis' usurpation of the blues and the mixing of country music into his early style. From there, he analyzed every aspect of a music that "excludes no one." Elvis was not an accident. He was not someone who sat on a street corner and waited for success to snatch him up. Marcus clearly saw that in Elvis "the will to create himself, to matter, was so intense and so clear."

Presley's career was the embodiment of "success in a democracy." He impacted American style, ideology, and mores. The Presley part of the discographies section was an insightful appraisal of his recorded output through the mid-seventies. One of the best critical discussions of Elvis books came in a section entitled "Elvis In Print and in the Grave." Randy Newman, Robert Johnson, and Sly Stone were among the other luminaries covered in this book, placing either them or Elvis in select company depending on one's point of view.

Matthew-Walker, Robert.   *Elvis Presley: A Study in Music.* Kent, England: Midas, 1979.   Reprinted 1980.   154 pp. Filmography, select bibliography, select discography, index.

The Matthew-Walker book attempted to seriously study Elvis' music. The only problem was that the author did not understand what made the music both great and appealing to millions of fans. By attempting to divorce the Elvis phrasing and presentation from the musical study context, Matthew-Walker failed to consider two key ingredients that caused the music Elvis developed to stand out relative to what his contemporaries created.

He somewhat redeemed himself by analyzing the songs Elvis chose to record, though this was marred by the praises he had for some of the filler songs on various albums. For example, he felt that the title song for the movie, *Charro*, was "unusual and dramatic." Sometimes his comments were right on target. He perceptively explained how the song, "Devil in Disguise," had its guitar and piano introduction "contradicted by the subsequent cha-cha rhythm."

Elvis' musical repertoire did not stand up to disciplined musicological analysis because, as music, it was formulaic and not often out of the ordinary. What it had was a certain built-in phrasing, specific accents, and a dominant rhythm and simplicity that made it easily memorable and unchallenging to both the singer and the listener, which allowed the physical presence of the singer to be the primary focus. Any study of Elvis' music had to incorporate the context in which the music was made in order for the study to impart a valid understanding. The author only did that sporadically, rendering his conclusions incomplete at best.

The "Army" Books

When Elvis reported for Army duty in March 1958, he took a bus from Memphis to Fort Chaffee, Arkansas, where he was given a military haircut. He began his service as a private E-1. By the time he was discharged, he had been promoted all the way to the rank of sergeant. Going into the Army forever changed Elvis and the direction of his entertainment business career.

It was not so much what happened to Elvis there, but that it showed the heights to which Elvis could grow in the public mind by his being unavailable. The Army years began the isolation of Elvis. Yet, those years also matured Elvis and taught him responsibility and pride in what he did. What else happened in those years has become the subject of a number of fascinating books.

Burk, Heinrich. *Elvis in Der Wetterau: Der "King" in Deutschland 1958-1960.* **Frankfurt: Eichborn Verlag, 1995.**

Cortez, Diego, editor, with Duncan Smith. **Photographs by Rudolph Paulini.** *Private Elvis.* **Stuttgart, Germany: FEY Verglas, 1978.** **199 pp.** **Index to photographs.** **New edition, 1979, Omnibus Books, London.**

DeVecchi, Peter. *The Sounding Story.* **Germany: [n.p.], 1959.**

Mansfield, Rex, and Elisabeth Mansfield. *Elvis the Soldier.* **Bamberg, West Germany: Collectors Service, 1983.**

These four books on Elvis in Germany all came from that country over a thirty-five year period. DeVecchi's book may have been the first that "covered" some part Elvis' stay in Germany (as well as his career to date). Unfortunately, it was not the most detailed because the author never got close to Elvis for any length of time. It was one of the first books a specific author "wrote" on Elvis (as opposed to those books that were compilations of material already released in magazines). As such it has maintained a high value (about $200 for a clean used copy). Its German origin (and the fact that it was written in German) helped increase its worth to collectors.

The best part of Cortez' book (written in German and English) turned out to be the Rudolph (or Rudolf) Paulini photographs, shot during Elvis' 1959 leave in Paris. He was captured with beautiful girls (often local hookers), fellow diners, kitchen staff, and a few of his "mafia." Beyond the unique photos and some interesting reproductions of various clipping, it boasted what Greil Marcus called "a probing text by Duncan Smith." Otherwise, it had very little scholarly or research worthiness, which probably explained why it was never made widely available in the United States.

Mansfield came from Dresden, Tennessee, and did some service time with Elvis up to the point where he almost became a hired associate. He revealed that Colonel Parker advised him not to take the job, though the Colonel said he would deny that advice if Mansfield ever spoke of it to Elvis. Mrs. Mansfield (maiden name Stefaniak) was a native German girl who briefly served as Elvis' "live-in" secretary in Germany (she also dated him and by her own admission had a physically intimate relationship with him).

Mansfield, the soldier, told how he once stood guard duty for Elvis. He also claimed that Elvis gave him amphetamines and bought pills from a soldier working at the base dispensary. The Mansfields were married after Elvis left Germany. Their book, a slim but personal look at Elvis' Army tour, was one of three similar pieces the pair wrote about Elvis in Germany, all published only in Germany.

The most recent book to come out of Germany was Burk's 1995 work. Written and published in German, it was a good general overview but added little to the literature already in print about Elvis' time overseas. Michael Gray and Roger Osborne did reference it in their book, *The Elvis Atlas: A Journey Through Elvis Presley's America*.

Corvino, Nick. *Elvis: The Army Years: 1958-1960.* **Nashville: Green Valley Record Store, 1978. 93 pp.**

Corvino's book was basically without value, as far as presenting facts, but was quite interesting in its speculation on how Elvis' Army life might have been. Unfortunately, it was a "fictionalized" account, though there was a factual basis built on the accounts reported in the media. Of what value was Corvino's book? Not much except for its usefulness in ordering Elvis' time as a chronological foundation for a biography.

Hatcher, Harley. *Elvis Disguised: The "John Crow" Recordings: A Remarkable Personal Experience.* **Beverly Hills, California: C.M.I. Books, 1980. 238 pp.**

The Hatcher book was undoubtedly the most implausible of all the Elvis "Army" books. The author claimed to have been a soldier during the time frame of Elvis' service tenure. He related that while at a U.S. base, he spent a great deal of time with someone who certainly appeared to be Elvis, but who would not admit it (he called himself "John Crow"). Supposedly, Elvis was in the United States at the time, due to Army needs and his mother's illness and death.

They sang together and had many long conversations, most of which were detailed throughout the book. Hatcher even came forth with tapes he said he made at some of their jam sessions. The problem with the book was that Elvis' time and whereabouts in Germany have been minutely chronicled in detail and so well documented that it would seem to make any lengthy time elsewhere next to impossible.

If true, though, the book would definitely put a whole different slant on Elvis' time in the service. The author likely ran across a very convincing impersonator (Orion?). The arguments and coincidences presented along with personal characteristics and singing abilities were compelling. Hatcher took the tapes to a number of people, including record executive Mike Curb, who became convinced, according to Hatcher, that the voice on the tape belonged to Elvis.

Jones, Ira, as told to Bill E. Burk. *Soldier Boy Elvis.* **Memphis, Tennessee: Propwash, 1992.**

Jones' account was published in 1992, thanks to Bill Burk, Memphis newspaperman, who marketed a number of his own Elvis books (see the section on Elvis biographies). It gave a glimpse by someone who was there as Elvis' sergeant and observed much of what Elvis did. Jones was integral to Elvis' Army tour and duty.

His account was doubly important because it showed what Elvis faced as a "plain" soldier overseas. A major portion was chauffeuring Jones around parts of Germany in a Jeep. The main question concerning the book's credibility would have to be how much of the tale was either lost or embellished because it took so long for it to surface.

Levy, Alan. *Operation Elvis.* **Illustrated by Dedini.   New York: Henry Holt, 1960.   New edition 1962.   117 pp.**

Levy's work was also both a true and fictionally enhanced narrative. It was mainly a fun-loving presentation of the Elvis "romp" through the service from a publicist's point of view. Actually, Levy was a Manhattan-born reporter for the Louisville, Kentucky, *Courier-Journal.* In 1958, he won *The New Republic*'s "Young Writer Award." To hear Levy tell it, Elvis' company and their activities were akin to Sergeant Bilko and his men.

Beyond Levy's original writing, there was an excerpt from the *TV Star Parade* interview with former Presley girlfriend Anita Wood, as well as the obituary of Gladys Presley (Elvis' mother) from the September 1958 edition of *Movie Life*. Wood said she was "proud of the way Elvis has done in the Army." The original price of the book was $2.95. Few copies have remained in circulation, so, as a collector's item, it has commanded upwards of $50 for a clean used copy. A near mint first edition copy recently sold for over $200.

Osborne, Jerry P. *Elvis: Like Any Other Soldier.* **Port Townsend, Washington: Osborne Enterprises, 1988.   148 pp. [unnumbered].**

Osborne's account was true but was mostly a pictorial and clipping work. More than half the book fell under the section "The Candid Elvis," which consisted of informal shots of Elvis, mostly in fatigues. Before that, there was a detailed history of the 2nd Armored Division, into which Elvis was drafted.

There were pictures of other soldiers, with some of them doing the tasks to which Elvis was assigned. Most interesting, there did not appear to be any shots of either Colonel William Taylor or Sergeant Ira Jones. The book ended with Elvis, still in uniform forty-two hours after his discharge, saying, "I'm kind of proud of this uniform. If I weren't, I wouldn't be wearing it now."

Schroer, Andreas. *Private Presley: The Missing Years–Elvis in Germany.* **Foreword by Gordon Stoker of the Jordanaires. New York: William Morrow, 1993.   Originally published in 1993 in England.   158 pp.**

It took Schroer to present an accurate and complete overview of Elvis' army years, especially the time spent with Priscilla. He unfolded a fascinating look at how a twenty-one-year-old dated a fourteen-year-old and subsequently convinced her parents to allow her to move into Graceland with him. By Schroer's account, Elvis was a competent and intelligent soldier, who did not want or get any favorable treatment.

Even in Germany, Elvis had a huge record collection, to which he regularly listened, either with Priscilla or other friends. His favorites were ones by black artists. While in the Army, Elvis did some publicity work, but by and large, he was "just a soldier." The book came with a compact disc of early Elvis recordings that had not been previously released by his recording company, RCA.

Taylor, William J., Jr. *Elvis in the Army: The King of Rock 'n' Roll as Seen by an Officer Who Served With Him.* **Novato, California: Presidio, 1995.   169 pp.**

During Desert Storm, the American military incursion into the Middle East in the early nineties, Colonel William Taylor appeared regularly on ABC Television as a consultant to explain troop actions to viewers. He seemed to be a highly believable expert. In 1958, Elvis served in Taylor's unit in Germany. Supposedly, Elvis sought out the superior officer, Taylor, as both friend and mentor. On the basis of that relationship, Taylor said he got to know Elvis very well.

So he surfaced in 1995 with a book that detailed everything about what Elvis did as a soldier, a mechanic, a tankdriver, and a combat-ready infantryman. Once, according to "Lootenent" Taylor, he and Elvis picked up a couple of girls together. In 1998, Taylor, Joe Esposito, and Sergeant Jones accompanied a tour of German sites "where Elvis lived, worked and played." The tour, dubbed the "Elvis Presley G.I. Commemorative Week," was licensed by Elvis Presley Enterprises.

Devil in Disguise:
THE BOOKS ABOUT ELVIS' SOCIAL AND HOME LIFE

> Elvis, for instance, if you believe what you read,
> ate more food than any other man who ever lived.
>
> -Jane and Michael Stern,
> *Elvis World*

The Culinary Books

Eating was quite important to Elvis. Was he, as some therapists might conclude, stuffing his feelings? Andy Warhol, in his diaries, wrote that Elvis threw one big dinner party while he was in Las Vegas. According to Warhol, Elvis had quite a few of his Memphis Mafia at the party in addition to two invited guests, Truman Capote and Doris Duke. What an unusual guest list!

Capote wrote that "Elvis Presley gave me the only dinner party I've ever heard of his giving, in Las Vegas." How did it come about? Capote added that after he saw Elvis' opening show, he was invited down "to this apartment he had there in the hotel, and the dinner party consisted of about eight young men and one old friend of mine, Doris Duke. This table was full of orchids up and down, and everything looked very fancy in a gauche, peculiar way." What was served? To the best of Truman's recollections, the dinner consisted of "fried pork and fried chicken and fried catfish."

Not only was Truman Capote an interesting choice for a dinner guest, so was Doris Duke. Duke, the daughter of a wealthy tobacco magnate and twenty-three years older than Elvis, was said, by more than one "friend" to have been very attracted to him. She even had him out to her home in Hawaii. According to her biographer, Stephanie Mansfield, Duke and Elvis were both members of the Self Realization Fellowship in Los Angeles and disciples of the Paramahansa Yogananda. They also had a shared belief in reincarnation and were "world-class shoppers." An acquaintance, Leon Amar, revealed that Duke was "madly in love with Elvis."

The cuisine served at the Capote/Duke dinner party underscored how much Elvis' prodigious appetite was centered around fried foods, huge portions, and fats and more fats. His eating habits were as much to blame for his death as any overmedication or dependencies. According to Tom Jones' biographer, Colin Macfarlane, Jones revealed that Elvis told him "he was having trouble keeping his weight down and was resorting to 'medical measures' to help him."

Jones also observed that "towards the end it looked like nobody had any control over him. He just got bigger and bigger. I'd been seeing Elvis since 1965 and every time I saw him he was never the same weight. He would either be thin or heavy. He only seemed a normal weight once, around 1969 to 1970." Macfarlane commented that Elvis "had a strange diet. His favourite food was hamburgers and it was nothing for him to consume dozens of them during the course of a day. He also tended to drink large quantities of Coca-Cola."

In the summer of 1998, columnist Andrea Billups wrote (for a Gainesville, Florida newspaper) that a "new offering from Courtesy Books, *The I Love Elvis Cookbook*," brought "painfully into focus" the whole "sad issue of Elvis' frightful eating habits." She commented that most of the recipes were "loaded with shortening, bacon grease, eggs or oil" and that "after years on this diet you gotta figure the fat's gonna curl up in your arteries and send you on your way to your creator." To her, that had to explain "Elvis' affinity for gospel music." In fact, when Billups ran a few of the recipes by a noted dietician, that food expert's professional opinion was "now we know why Elvis is no longer with us."

Elvis' tastes in food were the culmination of generations of Southern cooks, who, by necessity, had to find ingenious ways to present tasty dishes incorporating inexpensive foodstuffs, such as gravies, the fattier parts of meats, and starchy ingredients. Not surprisingly, the Elvis dietary disasters have spawned some intriguing cookbooks, wherein lie recipes for banana fritters, bacon and potato soup, sausage spoon bread, and, of course, chicken a la king. So glory in the tastes but be wary of the life-threatening excesses.

Adler, David. *The Life and Cuisine of Elvis Presley.* **New York: Crown, 1993. 159 pp. Index.**

Anonymous. *The Wonder of You Elvis Fans Cookbook,* **Volumes 1 and 2. [n.p.]: R & M Crafts Reproductions, 1985.**

Adler was also the author of a book on Lisa Marie Presley. This time he put together a book that was much more than a collection of recipes. It tied all phases of Elvis' life with his food intake, especially hamburgers, even his diets and the final years of "tragic" dinners.

The "tragic" dinners section incisively explored the role that Elvis' "overeating" and dieting may have had concerning his heart problems and death. Another section featured amphetamines washed down by Shasta soda. To prepare this book, Adler consulted with a host of people close to Elvis, from actress Barbara Eden to the former night cook at Graceland, Pauline Nicholson.

The uncredited *Wonder of You* cookbook was not a presentation of Elvis recipes but of Elvis fan recipes. There was "Don't Be Cruel Cauliflower" and "Change of Habit Butternut Squash." But, why wasn't there an "All Shook Up Shake" or a "Love Me Tender Steak"? The book was fun and showed once again how unique and creative Elvis fans could be, especially relative to their King.

Butler, Brenda Arlene, editor. *Are You Hungry Tonight?: Elvis' Favorite Recipes*. Avenel, New Jersey: Bluewood, 1992. 64 pp.

There were no culinary wonders in Butler's book, rather an insight into the eating habits of a poor, white Southern male. In the introduction, she wrote that although Elvis may have lived like a king, "he ate like his subjects." Only the section on the wedding cake (and wedding breakfast) with preparation instructions was filled with intricate directions. Most of the time, his food had to be overcooked, plain-textured, and not fancy. His true love was a fried peanut butter and banana sandwich.

One aspect of Elvis' culinary tastes that this book presented (unlike many of the others) was that although Elvis preferred Southern cooking, he did develop a taste for Oriental cooking. His two favorite eating places in Memphis were The Gridiron (a "burger" diner) and Chenault's Restaurant, which specialized in biscuits and sorghum syrup. In spite of the fatty foods featured in the recipes, the accompanying pictures always showed a young, trim Elvis.

The most important aspect of the book was Elvis' domination over what was served and eaten wherever he lived or stayed. He dictated what was to be stocked and the details of preparation. He even told Priscilla not to eat fish around him. So the man who sang about the rolling sea actually hated fish. A close associate of Andy Warhol backed the fish-hating conjecture. Bob Colacello, in his book, *Holy Terror: Andy Warhol Close Up*, wrote that when he interviewed Priscilla (for *Interview* magazine), she blurted out during the conversation that "Elvis hated fish."

Jenkins, Mary, as told to Beth Pease. *Elvis: The Way I Knew Him*. **Memphis, Tennessee: Riverpark, 1984.**

Jenkins, Mary, as told to Beth Pease. *Memories Beyond Graceland Gates*. **Buena Park, California: West Coast, 1989. 101 pp.**

Jenkins cooked for Elvis for fourteen years, beginning in 1963. Her real name was Mary Fleming. She knew a lot about his eating habits and chronicled them here, including his love for her homemade vegetable soup. She also observed his living habits and likewise divulged them. The details she gave were never hurtful, but more based on her awe of the man who lived his life by night.

Her hours were from 7:00 a.m. to 2:00 p.m., so how much could she have seen? The two often did have breakfast together and listened to the "Gospel Jubilee." She claimed to have been visited by his spirit in a dream. Her memories of redecorating Graceland were fascinating. She also knew each of the boys who hung out with him.

Though not easily obtainable, her two books made for interesting reading, especially her Elvis, Priscilla, and Lisa Marie anecdotes. There were some great shots of Lisa as a young girl as well as more than a few taste-tempting recipes. Most of her pictures came from a scrapbook she compiled on Elvis. Elvis rewarded Jenkins' service by buying her a home and a Cadillac and six other cars while she worked for him. She played herself in the 1981 movie, *This Is Elvis*.

McKeon, Elizabeth, Ralph Gevirtz, and Julie Bandy. **Foreword by Alvena Roy (Elvis' California cook).** *Fit For a King: The Elvis Presley Cookbook*. **Nashville, Tennessee: Rutledge Hill, 1992. 240 pp. Glossary of cooking terms, index.**

McKeon, Elizabeth. **Foreword by Wayne Newton. Introduction by Alvena Roy (Elvis' California cook).** *Elvis in Hollywood: A Cookbook and a Memory Book*. **Nashville, Tennessee: Rutledge Hill, 1994. 237 pp. Filmography, index.**

The McKeon et al. book was approached more like a conventional cookbook though it did contain interesting informal pictures from all phases of Elvis' life. There were hundreds of recipes placed in such categories as "The Gladys Special" and "Garden Party" (not Ricky Nelson's). Many recipes were easy to fix, but many were quite complex, especially the Christmas ones.

Just how tied Elvis' life was to food was captured in a Lisa Marie quote. Lisa recalled that when the maids "are cooking corn bread and black-eyed peas for us like they always did–it feels just the way it used to, when my dad was alive." McKeon's follow-up book centered around recipes and food preparation utilized for Elvis while he was making movies.

A brief filmography was presented but little else that gave any new insights into Elvis' habits. The second book was merely an extension of the first. A considerable number of photos from his moviemaking days (and nights) as well as some intriguing anecdotes from people about his Hollywood days and nights were interspersed throughout. The photos were interesting but poorly reproduced.

Presley, Vester, and Nancy Rooks. *The Presley Family Cookbook.* **Memphis, Tennessee: Wimmer Brothers Books, 1980.   178 pp.**

Uncle Vester, with his co-writer, presented the world with favorite recipes from the Presley clan. They, like most Southerners, liked fried foods and simple recipes. Some of the better recipes covered how to cook mashed sweet turnips, fried squash, and ham hocks with pinto beans. Vester's insights effectively completed one of the best pictures the world could obtain of the Elvis culinary habits and how they came to be. Co-author Rooks served at Graceland as both maid and cook. She later published her own recollections of Elvis, from an insider's point of view.

Wolf-Cohen, Elizabeth. *The I Love Elvis Cookbook: More Than 50 Hit Recipes!* **Philadelphia, Pennsylvania: Courage Books, 1998.   80 pp.   Index.**

Given the newspaper columnist's comments on this book, I approached it with great anticipation. Though short (in number of pages), it did not disappoint. Even the trivial facts the author pointed out (for example, Elvis' famous banana pudding recipe came straight from the box of Nabisco's Vanilla Wafers) helped add to the understanding that Elvis' cuisine never rose above the ordinary.

Beginning with a very informative and analytical introduction by Mick Farren, "Elvis Has Left the Kitchen," Wolf-Cohen wove her way from Elvis' mother's earliest spreads to the description of the Graceland kitchen as being the one place in Elvis' life that "never faltered, never closed." Farren relied heavily on the memoirs of Memphis Mafia personnel like Lamar Fike and Marty Lacker to make points about how much Elvis loved bacon and could only eat meat that was almost burnt. He also wrote about some of the crash diets.

The Social and Political Books

We do not know Elvis' political persuasion. The best guess would have him being a Nixon Republican, given his expressed admiration for and ultimate success in obtaining an audience with the then-president. May Mann disclosed that she tried to convince Elvis to run as Nixon's vice president. Socially, we do know Elvis was very charitable, especially when he was in the position to surprise someone in need (or someone he liked) with a very expensive and improbable gift.

How much Elvis gave away can only be speculated. He was certainly generous to a fault. How socially conscious was he? He didn't seem to get involved beyond charitable performances, probably because his famous stature prevented him from becoming too visible.

Just how much of a problem was public visibility to Elvis? At first, Elvis could not go anywhere without causing a riot. He kept that opinion of himself for a long time and because of it only went out at night. As author Sharon Urquhart observed, "because of his fame, Elvis was unable to attend movies during regular show times." So he often rented entire movie theaters or fairgrounds after hours to enjoy himself with friends while not attracting curious crowds.

Later in his career, while recording in Hollywood, an individual at the session told Elvis he would not attract any attention if he went out in public during the day. Elvis did not believe him. So they went out around Sunset Boulevard. No one noticed. Elvis was out of touch and had become dated. It was not until his death that he again gained the level of public adulation he had enjoyed early in his career.

Given his celebrity status, Elvis' life was about as abnormal as a life could be. How abnormal? In his 1990 autobiography, Ronnie Milsap explained that the enormous load Elvis carried was driven home to him "on New Year's Eve, 1970, the second time I played a private party for him at T. J.'s." That was the night Milsap was told "each time Elvis went to the men's room, he was escorted by four bodyguards-one in front, one behind, and one on each side."

Finding that peculiar, Milsap asked Elvis' buddy, Alan Fortas, why. Fortas replied, "That's where he gets hit up, man." According to Fortas, "Elvis was generous to a fault. When he'd go to the rest room, he was an involuntary captive of people who would ask him for money," even at his own private party. As Milsap observed, Elvis' "popularity, and character, were actually haunting him to where he couldn't even go to the men's room without being hounded."

From a personal interview with Barbara Pittman, who knew Elvis since his days at Sun Records, writer Ellis Amburn disclosed that Elvis had told Pittman in 1977, "I'm bored. The only time I feel alive is when I'm in front of an audience, in front of my people. That's the only time I really feel like I'm human."   Did his strange, demanding lifestyle drive Elvis over some kind of edge?

When actor Elliott Gould was still married to Barbra Streisand, in 1971, he appeared to have "flipped out" while filming a movie called *A Glimpse of Tiger*.   Although he denied it, his problems seemed to have stemmed from drug usage. Because of some allegedly bizarre behavior by Gould, Warner Brothers canceled the film and sued him for production costs. Gould remembered it as "a difficult time. To be considered mad was an unnerving experience." The capper, to him, was when "Elvis Presley, who'd said he was an admirer of mine, sat down in front of me, a gold forty-five in his belt, and told me, 'you're crazy.' "

A year earlier, at Elvis' private New Year's party, Ronnie Milsap stated that Elvis "was acting a little strange. He carried two loaded six guns inside cowboy holsters strapped around his waist." Though not a therapist, Milsap saw that Elvis' life "had to be a psychological ambush for him." He put it bluntly that "formally educated people from economically and psychologically stable backgrounds" could not "have carried the burden of fame that clobbered Elvis."

Hazen, Cindy, and Mike Freeman. *The Best of Elvis: Recollections of a Great Humanitarian.* **Memphis, Tennessee: Memphis Explorations, 1992. 185 pp. Bibliography.**

Preserving the legend of Elvis in the face of sordid accounts of drug abuse and personality disorders has been difficult. Yet there was a contrasting picture, one that was thoroughly presented in the Hazen and Freeman book. Where other books portrayed Elvis as obsessed with sex and a lover of pornography, Hazen and Freeman claimed that Elvis often read the Bible to his female friends. On the benevolent side, prior to his TV and Vegas comebacks, Elvis' only live shows were done as charitable affairs.

He did much to personally help individuals and worthy causes. The Jaycees named Elvis one of the outstanding young men in America. In a ten-year span he contributed over half a million dollars to charity with little or no fanfare, because he wanted it that way. Through a benefit performance, he helped his hometown of Tupelo create a park for kids. This kind of information on Elvis' charitable nature has gone a long way to dispel the growing suspicions that he spent his days sleeping and nights drugged and overindulging.

Krogh, Egil "Bud." *The Day Elvis Met Nixon.* **Bellevue, Washington: Pejama, 1994. 61 pp.**

Krogh, a former member of Richard Nixon's inside staff, gave a short but intricate look at the December 1970 day when Elvis asked for and got a personal audience with then-President Nixon. His book detailed, minute by minute, what happened and what was said as well as what Elvis left the meeting with, a "special assistant" badge from the BNDD (the Bureau of Narcotics and Dangerous Drugs). The accompanying photographs were priceless, as was Nixon's "letter to fans of the King." Overall, the book provided a great insight into the kind of person Elvis became in his later years.

Elvis did not go into politics nor did he lend his name to political causes. His endorsement could have swayed thousands of votes in any given campaign. That Elvis would go to such extremes to see Nixon and desperately wanted to fight drugs spoke volumes on the contradictions of his final years. Krogh found it "incredible" that Elvis' White House visit was not discussed in the press "for over a year." In January 1972, it was columnist Jack Anderson who first wrote of the meeting.

Krogh did an excellent job recalling the manipulating that went into getting Elvis his special badge. The events, set against the backdrop of a Watergate-dominated White House, revealed as much about presidential politics as it did about Elvis. Krogh's book has become an essential Elvis document, succinctly but knowingly written, because it presented a side of Elvis never revealed quite so publicly. Nixon even sensed that Elvis "was a very shy man." The cover picture of Elvis and Nixon shaking hands has become a classic, available even through the Nixon library.

The Graceland Books

Graceland was named by the family of publisher S. E. Toof, who established the acreage as a farm during the Civil War. Toof named the land after his daughter, Grace. The estate home into which Elvis eventually moved was built in 1939 by Dr. Thomas Moore and his wife, Ruth Brown Moore. Toof's daughter, Grace, was her great aunt.

The fourteen-acre estate, dominated by a twenty-three-room colonial style house, became Elvis' home on April 10, 1957. The sale price was $100,000, which astounded Elvis' realtor because the next highest bid, from the Memphis YMCA, was only $35,000. Elvis wanted the place that much. He had told his mother he would buy her the finest house in Memphis. At the time, Graceland was on

Bellevue Road, a stretch of Highway 51. That stretch became Elvis Presley Boulevard.

The house was completely redecorated, utilizing heavy drapery, shag carpeting, and Naugahyde. The emphasis was placed on splashy colors, jungle themes, and, most of all, indulgence and extravagance. A soda fountain was even installed in the game room. It wasn't until 1982, five years after Elvis died, that the mansion was opened for tours.

Before then the public could only conjecture what life was like there for Elvis. Stanley Booth, a Memphis writer, had a unique opportunity to get a glimpse inside during Elvis' lifetime and, in an article entitled "A Hound Dog, to the Manor Born," wrote about it. He described the house as being "crowded with friends and friends of friends, all waiting for old El to wake up, come downstairs, and turn them on with his presence. People were wandering from room to room, looking for action, and there was little to be found. That was the gist of the scene, scattered groups of people lounging around waiting for Elvis at Elvis' house.

When Elvis finally appeared, according to Booth, the entire group focused all their attention on him. He disclosed that a "sensation" ran through the place and a few minutes later, "the entire company" moved out to the lawn, where Elvis was trying to start "a big blue model airplane." When Elvis was there without a crowd, a different picture unfolded. As Booth remembered one particular afternoon, he wrote that "you would have seen Elvis, all alone for a change, riding his motorcycle around the pool, around and around and around."

Once Graceland was open to the public, a fee was charged for a tour. That entrance fee currently amounts to $16 per adult. Approximately 650,000 people have visited every year since it opened to the public (or about 2,000 to 2,500 per day). Countless more have come to the gates to stand and view the grounds and the large iron gate with an embedded musical insignia. Elvis Presley Enterprises has also become headquartered there.

The best way to begin viewing Graceland would have to be through *Elvis Presley's Graceland: The Official Guidebook*, especially the updated and expanded second edition. Both the updated and first editions were put together by Laura Kath and Todd Morgan. From a "double" welcome to Graceland by Priscilla and Lisa Marie Presley to photographs featuring the significant parts of and surroundings adjacent to the mansion, the lavish colorful booklet almost substituted for a full tour (but not quite, of course).

Booth, Stanley. *Elvis Presley's Graceland.* **New York: Aperture, 1986.**

Brixley, Ken, and Twyla Dixon. *Elvis at Graceland.* **Photographs by William Eggelston. Memphis, Tennessee: Cypress, 1983.**

Ken Brixley's book was the first to focus exclusively on Graceland. Booth's was the second. They were both superseded, pictorially and analytically, by Chet Flippo's opus. It was surprising that Booth created such a forgettable book, because he has done great writing in the popular music field, especially in the book *Rhythm Oil.* But forgettable it was because it limited its scope to some superfluous background and ordinary depictions.

The compendium by Brixley and Twyla Dixon with photographs by Memphis photographer William Eggelston was an interesting and rich creation but paled in comparison to the larger, more intensely photographed work Gil Michael did with Flippo. Brixley's text contained little not covered in more intimate detail by Flippo and Michael. The pictures were still fabulous and one of a kind. They showed Elvis relaxing, playing, and just plain hanging out at home.

Even though the writing was limited, it still contained some interesting anecdotes, such as Elvis and Priscilla picking Noritake (Buckingham pattern) as their wedding china. This was the book that discussed Elvis' pet turkey, Bow Tie. It was also the one that told us that even though Graceland was centrally air-cooled, Elvis ran a wall-unit air-conditioner in his bedroom at all times. Unfortunately, the book, when it first came out, was available only through mail order.

Flippo, Chet. *Graceland: The Living Legacy of Elvis Presley.* **Foreword by Todd Morgan for the estate of Elvis Presley. Edited by Mike Evans. Special photography by Gil Michael. San Francisco: Collins, 1993. 256 pp. Index, list of gold and platinum certifications.**

Graceland defined Elvis as much as anything else because, as many books have shown, it was the end result of Elvis' sense of fashion and taste. To really see Graceland short of a trip there, one would have to peruse the Flippo book. The former senior editor and feature writer for *Rolling Stone* magazine wrote the text for this coffee-table extravaganza. That text pushed the book into a category of greatness.

Flippo's words offered a one-of-a-kind perspective that significantly stood above much of the known body of Elvis writing.

His insights into the creation of modern-day Graceland added an essential dimension to the Elvis persona. The narrative aspect of the writing was dry and pedantic, as if constrained by being commissioned.

Flippo could not be totally held in check, however, indulging in self-deprecating wit when least expected. Complementing the text were magnificent, flawless photos, most of them taken by Gil Michael, Director of Photography at Memphis State University. There was an emphasis on the interior and grounds of Graceland with two pictorial tours of Elvis' automobiles and airplanes, notably the *Lisa Marie*.

The early pictures of Elvis and the photos of the Audubon Drive house highlighted the first part of the book. The combined pictorial study of "The Jungle Room" best exemplified the unique decor that filled every room at Graceland. Until one spent considerable time absorbing the contents of this book, one could not understand the opulence with which Elvis surrounded himself.

Hazen, Cindy, and Mike Freeman. *Memphis Elvis-Style Rock Music Anthology.* **Winston-Salem, North Carolina: John F. Blair, 1998.**

Urquhart, Sharon Colette. *Placing Elvis: A Tour Guide to the Kingdom.* **New Orleans, Louisiana: Paper Chase, 1994. 112 pp. Sources, index.**

Graceland exists in Memphis, a city whose inner workings greatly affected Elvis, from Sun Studios to Humes High. Hazen and Freeman authored, in 1998, a book that explored the complex relationship Elvis had with Memphis. It delved into the historical aspects of Memphis, especially the musical roots. For each place in Memphis they discussed, they offered interesting facts or anecdotes. They also attempted to set some records straight, specifically that Elvis never attended any other school in Memphis but Humes High. Prior to this book the authors had written about Elvis' charitable side (that book was reviewed in the part of the social and political aspects of Elvis).

Urquhart went further than Hazen and Freeman, by assembling a richly detailed overview of almost every aspect of Memphis (and Tupelo, too) relative to "placing" Elvis (as she put it). She also contradicted their claim that Elvis only attended Humes High in Memphis. She had him briefly attending Christine School.

Her book was broken into two major sections, the first discussing Tupelo and Memphis as they were during Elvis' stays at each place. In Tupelo, she took the reader to obscure places such as Riley's

Jewelers (where Elvis' attending physician, at his birth, hung out). In Memphis, the reader toured the halls of Priscilla's high school (Immaculate Conception) and got a view of the inside front door at Lauderdale Courts, where the Presleys lived from 1949 until early 1953. There was also a picture of the first house Elvis bought for his family in 1956, where they lived until moving to Graceland.

The other part of the book presented the current status of both locations, making it possible to juxtapose, for example, the different looks taken on by Elvis' favorite record store in Tupelo. The routes to take to each residence in Elvis' life and a host of other places were also mapped out. There were even more striking photographic views, such as the inside of the Tupelo Hardware Company, the Elvis Presley seat in the Memphian Theater, the auditorium stage at Humes High, and the close-up of the Libertyland roller coaster.

Her reason for compiling this book was an interesting one. She wrote that "the question may arise as to whether an individual who had little or no contact with Elvis can actually come to know him." Her answer formed her purpose, that there was a way for a person "to come closer to Elvis, especially now that he is no longer with us in body: by making the pilgrimage to his Graceland mansion in Memphis and by standing near his final resting place in the Meditation Garden." Much of her book was designed to assist in making that "pilgrimage."

In conclusion, Urquhart wrote that the reason "we travel to Elvis' place" is to "come closer to him." That was her approach to understanding the man "more fully," to travel "into his time." Poetically, she quoted a Joe South song, which requested potential abusers, criticizers, and accusers to "walk a mile in my shoes."

Marling, Karal Ann. *Graceland: Going Home with Elvis.* **Cambridge, Massachusetts: Harvard University Press, 1996. 258 pp. Sources.**

Marling has taught Art History and American Studies at the University of Minnesota for years. She has also written a number of books, all published through Harvard University Press. This, her latest, analyzed every aspect of the Elvis mansion, Graceland. She put the mansion in the context of the "American dream of home" at its most decadent yet opulent extreme.

She discussed how it came to be and how it changed as a reflection of Elvis' fashion sensibilities, and most of all, its place in Southern mansion-building. She also investigated Elvis' life and where he lived prior to Graceland. Her account of transforming the mansion from gaudy palace to tourist shrine was spell-binding.

In a recent article written for the *New York Times*, she added her account of how Elvis and his then live-in girlfriend, Linda Thompson, "in a momentary fit of exuberance, circa 1974," purchased "acres of crimson shag carpeting from a startled local dealer" and proceeded "to slather it everywhere," to the point where they "even had squares of the stuff glued to the woodwork," was hilarious. According to Marling, no less a public figure than Caroline Kennedy visited Graceland and walked away in revulsion at the decor.

Kennedy later wrote, in a *Rolling Stone* article, her assessment of what she saw, beginning with "the wookie-fur lampshades in the aptly named den." Marling similarly described Graceland, at the time of Elvis' death, that it "seemed just fine on the outside, all columns and spurious dignity, but on the inside horror lurked." Priscilla (who as trustee for daughter Lisa Marie, took control of Graceland) redid the mansion's decor after Elvis died and by the time it was opened for tours in 1982, it was "a far more subdued place, a home befitting a personage of substance and significance," albeit "kind of bland."

Winegardner, Mark.   *Elvis Presley Boulevard: From Sea to Shining Sea, Almost*.   New York: Atlantic Monthly, 1987.

Winegardner complemented Marling's ideas by creating not only a portrait of the "real" Graceland but an accompanying view of how those outside Graceland saw it. His writing came from the trip he actually took to Graceland, where he viewed the *Lisa Marie* (Elvis' airplane), the tear in Elvis' pool table (caused by a friend attempting a trick shot), the trophy room, and the various different motorcycles Elvis owned. He even purchased a cheap gift shop souvenir. His final assessment was that the house "could easily be mistaken for a dormitory at a Midwestern women's college. It could, except for the steel bars covering all the windows."

Wright, Daniel, with contributions from Mark Landon Smith. *Dear Elvis: Graffiti from Graceland*. Foreword by Vernon Chadwick, Founder and Director of the International Conference on Elvis Presley at the University of Mississippi. Introduction by Robert Gordon, Author of *It Came from Memphis*. Memphis, Tennessee: Mustang, 1996. 95 pp.

Graffiti is a depiction of feelings, in this case, feelings relative to Elvis. The author of this book, Daniel Wright, lifted what he considered the best writings that have appeared on the walls of Graceland. They were fun, mostly lighthearted in an ironic sort of way, and quite picturesque. The writers came from places like

Holland and Australia, with an Aloha from Israel for good measure. One writer wrote as "E" and told people to quit writing on his wall.

In addition to the "best" graffiti, the author disclosed that the current Graceland management team has occasionally hired a firm to use a high-powered water wash to clean away objectionable writings. They haven't sandblasted, painted, or used chemicals. When Elvis was alive, they worked very hard to keep the walls clean at all times. After he died, they pretty much let nature keep them clean.

To introduce the book, Dr. Vernon Chadwick, who put together the first annual Elvis conference at the University of Mississippi, gave his views on the Elvis phenomenon. Robert Gordon, author of *It Came From Memphis*, wrote a provocative introduction. This book was a further illustration that every conceivable topic related to Elvis has come out somewhere in book form. At the end, the author noted that he would like to receive "good graffiti" from Graceland for a sequel.

Crying in the Chapel:
THE BOOKS ON ELVIS' DEATH, AFTERLIFE, AND SPIRITUALITY

> Elvis always referred to death
> in terms of going home.
>
> –Larry Geller,
> *"If I Can Dream": Elvis' Own Story*

The Books on the Death of Elvis

The death of Elvis was one of the most traumatic pieces of news this country has heard in modern years. It ranked with the assassination of JFK as the day when people could remember where they were and what they were doing when they heard the news of the tragedy. The aftermath has become every bit as important as the death itself (perhaps even more so).

Though doubtless completely discredited, the intriguing possibility that Elvis did not die has lingered, fueled by several books. How Elvis died and who was responsible still fascinates and has been the subject of at least one exhaustive study. For some, conspiracy theories have abounded. The literature on his death and the aftereffects has taken over as one of the fastest growing areas of published Elvis materials.

Brewer-Giorgio, Gail. *The Elvis Files: Was His Death Faked?* **Foreword by Raymond A. Moody, Jr., M.D., and Detective Monte W. Nicholson. New York: Shapolsky Publishers, 1990. 275 pp. Selected bibliography/sources for books and other materials.**

Nicholson, Monte W. *The Presley Arrangement.* **New York: Vantage Press, 1987.**

Brewer-Giorgio was back with a new book (in 1988 she wrote a book questioning whether Elvis was still alive), this time raising the specter of Elvis' death being faked. Nothing was new, however, except for the book being published and a video becoming available. No controversy was to be found in spite of the hype. Even her "catching" Joe Esposito speaking of Elvis in the present tense (well after his death) did not prove Elvis was living and Esposito knew that, unless someone desperately had to believe otherwise.

Though she provided more documentation than before (she claimed to have extensively read hundreds of FBI files), much of the contents duplicated her other Elvis books. She wrote that Elvis worked for the Drug Enforcement Agency (DEA) and as such should not have died of an overdose of prescription drugs. She also felt that the Kalamazoo sighting of Elvis and the fact that Muhammed Ali's mail went to Kalamazoo were not merely coincidences, meaning that Ali, suffering from Parkinson's disease and unable to care for himself alone, could have been hiding Elvis.

Brewer-Giorgio concluded that Elvis and his father were victims of some kind of extortion plot. Other sources have shown that, towards the end, Elvis was very paranoid and delusional. Tanya Tucker wrote in her autobiography that she "knew from firsthand experience that Elvis had been in very bad shape." T. G. Sheppard, who had seen Elvis just before he died, told author James Dickerson, "I wasn't surprised. He was huge. I knew something had to give. I could see him deteriorating, with his weight and all that."

Too many people said they saw Elvis dying, they saw him dead, and they saw him buried. They would all have had to have been in on a very large and involved conspiracy and not one, in twenty years, has confessed to any kind of cover-up. All those people with the same basic lie, that Elvis died, is too much to believe.

Brewer-Giorgio did produce a "survey" showing more than eighty percent of Americans believed Elvis still lives. No methodology, statistical background, or sampling controls were offered. Her other major pieces of evidence, the pictures of sightings, have been discredited elsewhere as being obviously doctored.

Before Brewer-Giorgio got her book published, Los Angeles Sheriff's Department Detective Monte W. Nicholson paid, in 1987, the vanity press, Vantage, to put out his book, which was based on unsubstantiated allegations about "cover-ups" surrounding Elvis' death. No major publisher would touch a collection like this, intended for those fans with a need to believe Elvis "lives," which probably accounted for why the detective wrote (on Brewer-Giorgio's behalf) that he thought she "left no stone unturned." Recently I interviewed an individual who published his book through a vanity press. When I asked why, he said he had "no other choice."

Goldman, Albert. *Elvis: The Last 24 Hours.* **New York: St. Martin's, 1991. 192 pp.**

Goldman was back to disparaging Elvis (see the review of his Elvis biography, which he authored prior to this book, in the section on Elvis biographical material). This time he didn't hide behind Lamar Fike. He came right out and said Elvis' death was a suicide. His major source was none other than David Stanley. Goldman wrote that David's "intimate knowledge" was "the basis for the whole endeavor." Other than David's allegations, Goldman offered little else to back up his conclusions.

Major portions of the book were initially presented in *Life* magazine. The hype surrounding the issue sounded like there was new and startling evidence proving Elvis killed himself with an intentional overdose. In reality, the evidence turned out to have been some syringes and packets Stanley claimed to have hidden the night Elvis died. Stanley said he had forgotten about getting rid of the items. Much of the rest of the book was little more than a reworked prejudicing of the "facts."

Gregory, Neal, and Janice. *When Elvis Died.* **New York: Simon & Schuster, 1980. New edition 1982. 404 pp. Selected editorials, sources, bibliography, index.**

The Gregorys (formerly research and legislative assistants in Washington, D.C.) compiled their book to focus on what happened the day of Elvis' death. Newspaper clippings, photos, and reminiscences by affected people were all brought together in an attempt to make Elvis' death date stand out with regard to how people remembered it and associated it with other facets of their lives. They succeeded in preserving some of the original accounts of Elvis' death as well as tributes, such as the one from James Brown who asserted that Elvis did indeed have a following among black Americans. The personal memories gave a moving insight into the impact Elvis had on his fans.

Grove, Martin A. *The King Is Dead: Elvis Presley.* **New York: Manor Books, 1977. 252 pp.**

Hollywood Reporter columnist Grove tried to accomplish a feat similar to the Gregory book, but failed because he put the book out to quickly. Elvis died in 1977 and the book was published the same year, allowing no substantial research time. As a result, the first chapter concentrated on simply recounting what had been revealed, up to that point, about the sequence of events the day Elvis died.

Further into the book, Dr. Jerry Francisco (Shelby County Medical Examiner) was quoted about his thoughts on what caused Elvis' death. It was "cardiac arrhythmia." He found no evidence of any "pills" that caused any problems. From Dr. Francisco, the book turned to quoting Ginger Alden's mother, who revealed that Elvis was about to announce his engagement to her daughter, Ginger.

After that, the rest of the book turned largely to filler, with an entire chapter devoted to record releases and another to Elvis' movies. There were also movie reviews from various newspapers and trade publications. In reality, the book gained value by being a souvenir commemorating "that" day. Fans and souvenir collectors came to value the book, which has accounted for sales of near-mint copies, long out of print, at twenty times the original purchase price.

Mann, May. *Elvis: Why Won't They Leave You Alone?* **New York: New American Library, 1982.   214 pp.**

Zeller, Alexander. *The King Lives On.* **[n.p.]: Zeller Books, [n. d.].**

As far as Mann went, one had to believe her contentions that she had secret and previously unknown interviews with Elvis, that she knew he knew he was dying, and that she was one of a very privileged few to have known Elvis very well. Her *Elvis and the Colonel* book (covered in the section on Elvis biographies) was filled with conjecture that had to be taken on faith. So was this one. Unfortunately, she was often reluctant to verify what she said she was told.

In chapter 7, a starlet friend of Mann's, who spent a "night of love" with Elvis, disclosed to her that "nature" had endowed Elvis "with a tremendous physical sex organ." While that may have been of some interest, it was difficult to decide the authenticity of the claim because the starlet remained anonymous. Mann seemed to realize that she might have had a credibility gap because, as she revealed in her other book, she often had her picture taken with Elvis so people would know she really did see him.

The most useful parts of Mann's book were the reprints of some of Elvis' public interviews. Otherwise, she was content to take him at face value and recommend that his fans believe him when he made statements like "I've never been strung out on drugs." He told that to Mann in the mid-seventies.

To her credit, she quoted him numerous times from face-to-face talks they had. She did make the effort to seek him out. Zeller, on the other hand, presented nothing new and didn't really have any contentions except that Elvis will really never die because he made such a positive impact and became so loved by so many.

Parker, John. *Elvis: The Secret Files*. **London: Anaya, 1993. 272 pp. Index.**

Parker's book, with a title similar to the one by Brewer-Giorgio, actually contained, occasionally, the type of revelations that she only promised (but failed to deliver). The most surprising revelation came from Elvis' "drug" doctor (Dr. Nick), who claimed that Elvis was killed by a blow to the neck. Parker titled the book as if it were taken from recently revealed files, especially government ones.

There were quite a few FBI documents and a whole lot of speculation about FBI knowledge of Elvis and Mafia links. Parker also claimed to have conducted interviews with some pretty incredible figures, even the Colonel himself. Additionally, he included excerpts from some rarely-heard tapes Hal Wallis recorded before he died. In them, Wallis was more than blunt about his opinion of Elvis' acting abilities (or lack thereof).

Parker did assess various "death" theories, focusing heavily on a possible Mafia "hit." He gave plausible reasons for any conclusions he drew. However, he did not have any convincing reasons why either the U.S. government or the Mafia would want Elvis dead. Nonetheless, because of its revelations about the contents of FBI files, this book and the one by Charles Thompson (discussed next) became the "must read" books of the "cause of death" genre.

Thompson, Charles C., II, and James P. Cole. *The Death of Elvis: What Really Happened*. **New York: Bantam Doubleday Dell, 1991. 407 pp. Bibliography, index.**

The best insight into how and why Elvis died was offered by Thompson and Cole. They actually dug into original source material and talked to people involved, conducting numerous in-depth interviews. Their investigation into the coroner's report and prior activities was detailed and painstaking. They did not see the death as suicide and presented documents and logical arguments making it almost impossible to come to that conclusion.

They also discussed much of what led up to Elvis' demise, such as overmedication by Dr. Nick and Elvis' own fad diets, which obviously stressed his heart. Finally, they presented a number of medication-related theories and wound up concluding Elvis likely died from a codeine reaction. They certainly discredited Albert Goldman's suicide theories and impressed CBS newsman Mike Wallace enough for him to write that the book was "a superb reporting job." Previously, in 1979, they had produced a program for ABC's *20/20* show entitled "The Elvis Cover-Up," which exposed Elvis as being addicted to prescription drugs, no thanks to Dr. Nick.

The Books on Elvis after Death

Did Elvis die? Did people see his "spirit" soon after he died? Did he fake his death so he could walk away from the hardships and isolation of fame? Was he murdered? Was his death from a heart attack or from the ravages of abusing medication? The questions relative to Elvis' death have been endless and have come from many perspectives. Many Elvis after-life scenarios have also appeared.

Each "death" perspective had an advocate who either believed Elvis didn't die or was convinced the circumstances surrounding the death could have been more fully investigated. Sensation-hungry tabloids initially fueled many rumors. In turn, those rumors were given further credence by people who sounded convincing, like an ex-Army officer who claimed to have discussed Elvis' whereabouts with him for years following his "faked" death.

That individual, Bill Smith, was a retired Air Force major and Texas record producer. He claimed, in a book he wrote, *Memphis Mystery*, that he spoke to Elvis (by phone, of course) in 1980 and in 1983 he received a copy of a tape containing a monologue by Elvis. That was supposedly the same tape that Gail Brewer-Giorgio used as the basis for her similar claims. Smith also said he received a tape containing ten new Elvis recordings. Why he waited until 1988 to tell the world all of his wonderful news has never been disclosed.

It only took until 1979 for Richard H. (Dick) Grob (then Graceland security chief) to lay out his thesis of a conspiracy surrounding Elvis' death. It took less time (one reading) to see the blatant holes in his theories. That's probably why his book, *The Elvis Conspiracy?*, only got published by a small Nevada-based press, Fox Reflections. Faced with such allegations, one has to recall the statements by J. D. Sumner and Charlie Hodge, that Elvis died and his body was in the casket.

Still, even twenty years after, in 1997, doubters remained, specifically Tanya Tucker, who expressed on a Nashville Network talk show that she was convinced it was not Elvis in that coffin. Tanya's words had to open more eyes than an unknown, uncredited Gail Brewer-Giorgio. Tanya had no evidence either. While she did write, in her autobiography, that it didn't "look like him," she seemed upset mostly by his being "buried in a cheap polyester suit."

Another doubter, Bill Beeny, opened the "Elvis Is Alive Museum" in Wright City, Missouri, a few years after what he called Elvis' "so-called death." Beeny told *People* magazine that "there's no other museum that purports Elvis is alive." To document the continued existence of Elvis, Beeny has been marketing a $10 pamphlet entitled *DNA Proves That Elvis Is Alive*. In support of his conclusions, Beeny created a "satin-lined open coffin" complete with a mannequin that had no resemblance to the King. He did it because it reflected the fact that "the individual in the casket" at Elvis' real funeral didn't resemble Elvis.

Anonymous. *Elvis the Other Side: World Spirit Message from Edie (Spirit Guide).* **Houston, Texas: Golden Rainbow Press, 1980. 96 pp.**

Hatcher, Holly. *Elvis Is That You?* **Edited by Terry Sherf. Beverly Hills, California: Great American Books, 1979. 240 pp.**

Many people, Wayne Newton included (see the chapter in his autobiography), have claimed to talk with Elvis' spirit. Edie, a spirit guide, accomplished that feat not long after Elvis died and in a 1980 book those conversations were chronicled. The messages from Elvis imparted no Earth-shattering revelations; they were meant to comfort people, especially those who had been close to him.

Hatcher's book was much longer primarily because she talked to him longer and he seemed to have had much more to say, though again there were no major utterances. Primarily, the reader was able to find out that Elvis was doing well in the afterlife, especially in a musically creative sense. These two books have become the most notable examples of spirit contact with Elvis. Other people around the world have talked at length with him. One man even relayed the message that Elvis has begun writing songs. Another claimed to have specific lyrics written by Elvis after death.

Chanzes, Steven C. *Elvis . . . 1935 - ?: Where Are You?* **Epilogue by Steve Crown, Executive Coordinator, Eternally Elvis. Wilton Manors, Florida: Eternally Elvis/Direct Products, 1981. 128 pp.**

Chanzes' book was one of the strangest ever written. It alternated between speculating on the reality of Elvis' death and attempting to deify the legend. The book was published through an organization known as Eternally Elvis based in Wilton Manors, Florida. Ultimately, the author brought the reader to the unavoidable conclusion that Elvis' death was faked. Why did Elvis fake his own death? The answer was just too obvious: Elvis lacked freedom! He obviously couldn't obtain freedom without "dying," then running away.

How that faked death might have occurred was presented through a supposed unwitnessed conversation between Elvis and Charlie Hodge and then one between Hodge and Enos, the man whose body allegedly came to rest in Elvis' coffin. Perhaps that's why, at the beginning of the book, the author hinted his work could be considered fiction. A later tabloid piece echoed the claims of this book, telling the story of a devoted Elvis double who died for him so he could live in peace and anonymity. After the book's publication, Hodge filed a million-dollar libel suit against the author.

Cohen, Daniel. *The Ghost of Elvis and Other Celebrity Spirits*. New York: G. P. Putnam's Sons, 1994. 100 pp.

Holzer, Hans. *Elvis Speaks from the Beyond and Other Celebrity Ghost Stories*. New York: Dorset, 1993. 210 pp.

Moody, Raymond A., Jr., M.D. *Elvis After Life: Unusual Psychic Experiences Surrounding the Death of a Superstar*. Atlanta: Peachtree, 1987.   158 pp.

The Moody, Cohen, and Holzer books didn't dispute Elvis' death. Instead, they built on that fact, purporting to present information on Elvis' whereabouts and situation after death. Most of what Moody discussed came from people who claimed to have encountered Elvis through some psychic visitation, experience, or dream. The subjects then went on to tell what Elvis supposedly divulged and give their descriptions of what he had gone on to look like. Moody visited one subject in person and discussed at length her conviction that her son was the reincarnation of Elvis.

Holzer approached his disclosures in more of a ghost story manner. The chapter on Elvis was just one of many celebrity ghost sightings. Cohen covered much the same ground as Holzer, except that he did it for a preteen audience. That these types of after-life books on Elvis should crop up was not surprising as they have also surfaced relative to other celebrities, notably John Lennon.

How could anyone ever validate Holzer's claims of Elvis speaking from beyond the grave through the body of a New Jersey housewife? Cohen wrote that none of what he discussed, such as the ghost of Elvis hitchhiking to Memphis, could be substantiated, so one needn't look to him for claims to that effect. Both books went on to cover other undocumentable celebrity ghost stories.

Giorgio, G. B. (Gail Brewer-Giorgio). *The Most Incredible Elvis Presley Story Ever Told*.   **Atlanta: Legend Books, 1988. New edition published as** *Is Elvis Alive?: The Elvis Tape*, **New York: Tudor, 1988.   196 pp.**

For quite some time, Brewer-Giorgio hyped the story that Elvis did not die, first for Legend Books, then for Tudor, in a mass distribution paperback version (that supposedly sold over a million copies). She even attached, to the paperback, a tape of what was supposed to be Elvis' voice, answering questions after he had supposedly died. The statements on the tape unfortunately did not contain anything to prove they were recorded after Elvis' death.

They could have been Elvis musing over his long and successful career. The words could have been spoken by an imitator. In fact, it was alleged that Eternally Elvis, Inc., did hire an Elvis vocal imitator, David Darlock, to recite the words on the tape. Eternally Elvis was the group behind the Steven Chanzes' book.

The rest of Brewer-Giorgio's book was little more than speculation, mainly based on the supposed misspelling on the gravestone of Elvis' middle name, Aaron. That misspelling has been accounted for elsewhere. J. D. Sumner, in his book on Elvis' love for gospel music, completely discounted all the "Elvis lives" hype by saying he was there and saw the "dead" Elvis. Elvis really did die. Interestingly, Brewer-Giorgio wrote and marketed a novel, *Orion*, a tale about a rock star who faked his death.

Harrison, Ted. *Elvis People: The Cult of the King*.   **London: HarperCollins, 1992.   188 pp.**

Harrison, instead of denigrating those who idolized Presley, sought to understand and tell about them. His descriptions of the rituals fans performed at the gravesite were presented and analyzed without prejudice. Ultimately, he raised the devotion for Elvis to a near-religious level by wondering if the phenomenon were akin to the birth of a religious movement.

Could people actually worship Elvis or were they just exceptionally fanatical?   Harrison was once the religious commentator for the BBC so he already had a tendency to interpret aspects of the Elvis "cult" in spiritual terms. Then again, how else could one view the holding of services for an icon raised to a deity level?

Harrison also discussed various shrines and ceremonies dedicated to Elvis, even describing how people now pray through Elvis as if he were a saint. Elvis as King would be one thing but Elvis as religious icon on the par with Christian leaders had to be quite incredible. Harrison found such a movement and did an incisive job of investigating it without condemning or approving it. Instead, it could be seen as a logical extension of Elvis' own deeply professed faith.

Marcus, Greil. *Dead Elvis: A Chronicle of a Cultural Obsession*. **New York: Bantam Doubleday Dell, 1991. 233 pp. Citations, index.**

The Marcus perspective read as if it emanated from someone completely sick and tired of all the hype over the "deification" and "resurrection" of Elvis. Marcus had a place for Elvis based on his living contributions and artistic merits. There was more to Marcus than a distaste for Elvis fantasies as he extended his critique to a society that has become obsessed with death and overly willing to treat its entertainment stars as if they were royalty.

The book, because it cut to the heart of societal foibles, became required reading for many college courses on social issues. There was no major extant or unique Elvis information provided, but a real context for the Elvis legacy, which has become an "obsession with his memory." Marcus claimed he didn't write about "a real person," instead he presented "an exemplar of the American dream."

Elvis became "Elvis Christ, Elvis Nixon, Elvis Hitler, Elvis Mishima." Ultimately, he turned into "Elvis as godhead." Marcus analyzed a number of critical portrayals of the artist, from Lester Bangs' conclusion that Elvis gave his generation "a sense of itself as a generation" to Simon Frith's view that Elvis "dissolved the symbols that had previously put adolescence together." In the end, Marcus saw Elvis' story shrink "down to the size of your favorite song."

O'Neal, Sean. *Elvis Inc.: The Fall and Rise of the Presley Empire*. **Rocklin, California: Prima, 1996. 242 pp. Bibliography, index.**

Before O'Neal wrote his book, he was primarily a collector of Elvis products and memorabilia. He happened upon a treasure trove, an acetate of an unreleased Elvis Sun Records master. When he tried to negotiate the release of the acetate with various record companies, he ran into the specter of the Elvis Presley estate, or Elvis Presley Enterprises (EPE).

The intimidating nature of the organization so intrigued O'Neal that he began to investigate it, the results of which were presented in this volume. Among the highlights were an in-depth investigation of the problems between Colonel Parker and estate representatives. The major insights centered around how the net worth of a "dead" Elvis increased from almost nothing to hundreds of millions of dollars.

In between, the author exposed questionable business units established by Parker to profit from the Elvis persona. He showed how Priscilla took control after Vernon's death and turned a young "in-his-prime" Elvis into a merchandised figure on a par with Mickey Mouse. Perhaps the most shadowy set of activities O'Neal unraveled were the agreements forged between EPE and the United States Postal Service.

Rodman, Gilbert B. *Elvis After Elvis: The Posthumous Career of a Living Legend.* **New York: Routledge, 1996. 231 pp. Notes, sources, index.**

Scholarly study of Elvis continued unabated with this book, which concerned itself with the entire cultural phenomenon of Elvis after death. The chapters were cleverly titled after Elvis song titles that revealed little of each chapter's scope, yet each one unfolded brilliantly. The author, a professor from a small Florida university, has to rank as one of the premier Elvis analysts. He has so far put forth the best and most complete understanding of the American fascination with a dead idol.

Rodman, the scholar and author, analyzed the Elvis posthumous career from several vantage points, such as the link between the Elvis myth and larger controversial cultural areas, specifically race and sexuality. He theorized a commonality between Elvis fans and detractors that was curious but understandable, that both groups could not exactly know why Elvis mattered. In between, numerous Elvis fables and foibles were examined, from fan behavior to the controversial choice of a picture for the Elvis stamp. He concluded that our "reinvented" culture "belongs to Elvis," not just to us.

The Elvis "Sightings" Books

If Elvis did not die, then where could he be? If he did die, he certainly left behind a great deal for people to see (as in souvenirs and monuments). So, Elvis sightings have two perspectives, one being the sightings of Elvis mementos while the other was the possible "physical" sightings of an Elvis who did not die (or who visited in a spirit or "ghostly" form). Either way there was plenty to view, as the books in this section do not hesitate to point out.

Barth, Jack. *Roadside Elvis*. **Chicago: Contemporary Books, 1991. 184 pp. List of fan clubs, bibliography, index.**

Pollard, Mark, editor. *Elvis Is Everywhere*. **Photographs by Rowland Scherman. New York: Clarkson N. Potter, 1991. 78 pp.**

Yenne, Bill. *The Field Guide to Elvis Shrines*. **Los Angeles: Renaissance Books, 1999. 251 pp. Index.**

Barth and Pollard both captured odd occurrences of Elvis memorabilia, road signs, and interesting references to the King. Barth's pictures may not have been as eye-catching, but his written views about the various phenomena were much more humorous. The person reading Barth's book was not told about sightings of Elvis after death because the author was convinced Elvis had really died.

Pollard's book was a photographic journey through America that was constructed by photographer Rowland Scherman. It took the reader to many locations where some recollection or evocation of Elvis could be found. The focus was not on physical sightings but views of Elvis items, such as pictures, signs, memorabilia, decanters, tattoos, and anything that evoked the memory of Elvis.

Yenne, who also authored a book on Elvis collectibles (specifically covering one of the finest personal collection of Elvis artifacts), created a book that listed every physical location that was important to Elvis in some way and called each one a shrine. For example, the Hilton Hawaiian Village was listed because Elvis stayed there while shooting *Girls! Girls! Girls!*. There were also some shrines listed that Elvis did not necessarily visit but which had a relationship to him anyway. The various Nevada wedding chapels were, of course, never attended by Elvis, not even in his most religious times. They were listed because they each have an Elvis impersonator present to participate in any wedding ceremony.

Brown, Hal A., editor. *In Search of Elvis: A Fact-Filled Seek-and-Find Adventure*. **Illustrated by Rick Sales. Copy written by Leslie Senevey. Ft. Worth, Texas: The Summit Group, 1992. 45 pp.**

Eicher, Peter. *The Elvis Sightings*. **New York: Avon, 1993. 209 pp.**

Holladay, John. *Where's Elvis?* **New York: Checkerboard, 1992. [unnumbered].**

Klein, Dan, and Hans Teensma. *Where's Elvis?: Documented Sightings Prove That He Lives.* **New York: Penguin, 1997.**

Eicher's book presented all the sightings of Elvis since his "death." Some of the sightings were real, at least in the eyes of the beholder, but most were discussed in a tongue-in-cheek fashion. The book was meant as humor but in a roundabout way it chronicled a phenomenon of the eighties and nineties, the reports of Elvis living in some unexpected locale, far from fame and its burdens.

Brown approached his search for Elvis as a kid-style game (patterned after "Where's Waldo?"), in which the participant was supposed to find a "tiny" Elvis amidst hundreds of other tiny people. Holladay also took a "Where's Waldo" approach to possible Elvis sightings, though his drawings were not as intricate. Both books aimed for a younger audience that would enjoy searching hundreds of faces to find that one Elvis profile in some very strange location.

Klein and Teensma produced photographic evidence that Elvis showed up in the most unlikely places, even at the million man march on Washington. The photos, humorously doctored, even captured Elvis at his own funeral, where he said he just came by to pay his respects. The authors claimed Elvis could be found in each picture even though, in some, he was but a tiny face in the crowd.

Van Oudtshoorn, Nic. *The Elvis Spotters Guide: The King Lives! Here's How to Find Him.* **Springwood, Australia: Take That Books, 1992. 96 pp. Chronological listing of record releases, terms and conditions of reward offer.**

Van Oudtshoorn's book was filled with wonderful tongue-in-cheek humor bordering on absurdity, though it began with straightforward accounts of Elvis "sightings." The tip-off to the direction the author planned to take came with his copies of newspaper clippings detailing the more ludicrous incidents of running into Elvis. One amazing tale that complemented the religious overtones surrounding his myth had him secretly working at a Bolivian leper colony and performing miracles.

The guide began with the premise that you "gotta" be more than a "hound dog" to track down Elvis. You would need "facts" to find him, so more than three hundred important clues were given. Some recalled humorous incidents from the start of Elvis' career. The Graceland phone number was included "in case you want to check if Elvis has come home." Quite a bit of useful information was also listed in the form of a lengthy compilation of Elvis' most successful recordings. On the final page was the posting of a reward for anyone who could bring in Elvis Aaron Presley.

The Elvis Impersonator Books

Beyond the physical remains of Elvis in his grave (along with alleged sightings), the next-best-thing to "live" physical Elvis appearances and performances had to come from impersonators. That explained their tremendous popularity. With his untimely death and limited performances over the years while alive, impersonators ultimately became the closest many people got to their King.

According to author Tom Graves, a young Southerner named Bill Haney "was the first and certainly most influential" Elvis impersonator. When Haney stopped doing his Elvis act in 1982, Graves estimated there were some "two thousand people doing the same thing Bill Haney did for a living." Haney said he quit because "there are too many bad Elvis acts out there stinking things up for the rest of us."

Recently on the Maury Povich daytime television talk show, a man appeared, ostensibly as part of a reunion of old high school friends. This particular man had spent twenty-four years as an Elvis impersonator. His comments about how he made a living were very enlightening. He said, "It's a good living. You can grow into the part. A few extra pounds are no detriment at all in this branch of show business. People always love to see Elvis." That was the magic of Elvis; people took him to heart no matter how he looked.

Cabaj, Janice M. Schrantz. *The Elvis Image.* **N o r r i s , Tennessee: Exposition, 1982.**

Kelly, Joe. *All the King's Men.* **Berkeley, California: Ariel Books, 1979.**

Kelly's 1979 book was one of the first to delve into a phenomenon that started even before Elvis' death, the Elvis impersonator. He used words and photos to present people like El-Ray-Vis, Little El, and Big El. In those days there were limited numbers of impersonator acts, not the thousands there are today. Kelly even had the foresight to present several female Elvis impersonators, who strapped down their breasts and donned the Vegas-style jumpsuits.

In 1982, Cabaj covered similar ground but in a more unorthodox way. She didn't just present the acts, she went into all the trials and tribulations she experienced in her search for the really good ones. Along the way she passed on such observations that the wax Elvis figure she viewed in Nashville actually looked like Glen Campbell.

Cahill, Marie, editor. *I Am Elvis: A Guide to Elvis Impersonators.* **Production direction by Bill Yenne. New York: Simon & Schuster, 1991. 128 pp.**

The book edited by Cahill was essentially a photobiographical journal of more than fifty people who made their living looking, acting, and trying to sing like Elvis. There were young, old, black, Oriental, and even female look-alikes. The number of impersonators documented an effect no other entertainer (save Marilyn Monroe) ever had, a host of people who wanted not just to be like him but to own that spotlight the same way he did.

The evocation of the music certainly transported the fans. Many of the performers portrayed exaggerated moves and routines, thereby adding a probably unintended but nonetheless humorous perspective on the King's stage antics, especially the karate moves. The tendency to portray the Las Vegas Elvis showed that maybe that was the side of Elvis that stood out in the memories of many fans.

Pritikin, Karin. *The King & I: A Little Gallery of Elvis Impersonators.* **Photographs by Kent Barker. San Francisco: Chronicle Books, 1992. 95 pp.**

Text author Pritikin, in the "little gallery" book, wrote a lengthy exposition about the various worlds of Elvis impersonators. She especially captured the seamier side of making a living imitating Elvis. Most performers revealed how much of a "dress-up" effort impersonating Elvis has become.

Barker, the photographer, presented miniature pictures of each performer. Alongside the pictures, most performers disclosed why and how they've done what they've done and, even more important, what kind of hold the Elvis mystique has had over them and when they first realized it. One spoke about Elvis' vibes coming though him when he put on the jumpsuit. Another said that the only thing he couldn't stand in the world was people making a mockery of Elvis. Didn't he ever hear of the 1974 Boxcar/RCA Records album, *Having Fun With Elvis on Stage?* Even Elvis spoofed Elvis.

Rubinkowski, Leslie. *Impersonating Elvis.* **Winchester, Massachusetts: Faber & Faber, 1997. 301 pp.**

Rubinkowski began by telling about the first time she witnessed a performance by an Elvis impersonator (as a newspaper reporter). Instead of it being some laughable kick, she sensed it meant much more to the audience, especially the women. That began her fascination with a movement that keeps Elvis alive for thousands of fans. She said she logged thousands of miles to attend shows by leading impersonators and interview them.

In her descriptions, she captured minute details of their lifestyles. The most convincing was Dennis, who wouldn't hang an Elvis clock on his wall because it was too gaudy. From a lengthy overview of Dennis, she took us to the finals of a "contest," where fans were told not to get out of their seats to pick up a scarf. If they did, they would be told to leave. Dennis wore a black jumpsuit but didn't win. Nonetheless, a fan called him Elvis, which made his night.

Such was the world of the impersonator, to perform like Elvis, but not necessarily become him or live like him. The author took for granted that Elvis adulation has not become a religion, but more a time and place for fans to just remember the King and think about what had been and what might have been. As for the impersonators, they were finally able to be just like him, a dream that began, for at least one, all the way back in childhood.

The Elvis "Spiritual" Books

Elvis' family, like so many Southern families, was heavily tied to and involved with its church. Elvis grew up singing gospel music. When he was nine, he was baptized with "the holy spirit." As he became increasingly famous, he developed a view of himself as a very special gifted person with some unique spiritual significance.

Elvis' dad, Vernon, claimed "a mysterious blue light appeared over and around the place where Elvis lay as a newborn baby struggling for life." Once a star, Elvis radiated an undeniable aura and charisma. That presence translated into a belief, for some (including Elvis), that he had spiritual healing powers. The spirituality surrounding Elvis has recently fostered a view that he should be the basis for a new religion.

Elvis was raised a staunch Southern Baptist, but according to many sources, he became involved in a variety of religious circles. The ironic twist to Elvis' religious convictions was that, in the words of the Everly Brothers, "they used to hold revivals whenever Presley came to town, because they figured he was the agent of the devil." Joe Esposito wrote in his column for *Pop Culture Collecting* that "Elvis did delve into the occult and Eastern religions" because he was trying "to figure out why he was the person that God picked to be who he was." Esposito emphatically stressed that Elvis never "believed in any of those religions." Was that another way of saying that religion, like food, became just another excess in Elvis' life or was it one of the few aspects of his life about which he cared deeply?

Spiritually, Elvis appeared to be, at times, a born-again Christian at peace with his God and singing His praises through his many gospel albums. At other times, he was fascinated by the occult and non-born-again concepts, studying UFOs and reincarnation. He actually predicted he would not live longer than his mother, who also died at forty-two (but as it turned out, she was really forty-six). Because of his connections to otherworldly activities, psychics and clairvoyants have claimed to often channel his spirit.

In 1987, psychic Bill Falcone, who worked out of the Berkeley Psychic Institute (aka The Church of the Divine Man) claimed to have regularly communicated with Elvis in the spirit world. Falcone's take on Elvis' life struggles was that they stemmed from two spirits (the spirits of the twins Elvis and Jesse) who continuously battled for the one surviving body. Elvis was the good spirit, the religious one who adored his mother and respected all women. Jesse was the bad or rebellious one, who took drugs, participated in orgies, and became a gun fanatic and recluse.

One psychic claimed that Elvis revealed he had become, in the afterlife, a songwriter. That went along with another psychic, from Europe, who has actually tried to publish the many compositions Elvis has supposedly written since dying. Even in death Elvis has added another dimension. So, a mere paradigm of good or evil or even the juxtaposing of the two could not suffice to explain the man or the persona. Nor could the views of drugged or clean, moneymaking versus critical acclaim, or even born again as opposed to New Age do the job. In many ways Elvis was everything everyone said he was, no matter how diametrically opposed, and more.

As many fans have become wrapped up in the spiritual aura surrounding Elvis' memory, some books have taken a near ludicrous turn on the subject. The low point came with a book entitled *God's Works Through Elvis* (available from Exposition Press). The author seriously saw Elvis as God's messenger. At least when A. J. Jacobs created his book, *The Two Kings: Jesus, Elvis*, he approached it with a debunking sense of humor.

Jacobs, A. J. *The Two Kings: Jesus, Elvis*. Illustrated by Eric White. New York: Bantam, 1994. [unnumbered].

Ludwig, Louie. *The Gospel of Elvis Containing the Testament and Apocrypha Including All the Greater Themes of the King with an Introduction, Commentaries, the Complete Notes of St. Cliff, and Illuminations.* **Arlington, Texas: The Summit Group, 1994. 179 pp. Bibliography.**

Noting that Elvis "once confided to a friend that he thought he was the Messiah," Jacobs humorously compared Jesus and Elvis. Along with pictures by Eric White, he made such comparisons as "Jesus was a healer," while "Elvis passed out prescription drugs to friends and family." The rest of the book showed similar far-fetched parallels between the King and the Christ, such as Jesus being the Lord's shepherd as opposed to Elvis dating Cybill Shepherd. The end result after all the unlikely comparisons was an obvious conclusion that Elvis was no more "otherworldly" than anyone else.

Louie Ludwig delivered a more humorously offbeat approach than even the one taken by Jacobs. He created satirical biblical passages to make fun of the emerging Elvis religious cults. He also portrayed (tongue-in-cheek, of course) Priscilla as the Virgin, Hank Williams as "St. Luke," and Bob Dylan as the Woodsman.

Colonel Parker became "the Snake," while Fats Domino wound up as "the Fat Man" and Chuck Berry "the Duck." In a deceptively clever "Commentary on the Gospel of Elvis," the trend to view Elvis as a religious icon was traced from "three known churches of Elvis" to "countless buttons, stickers, graffiti, and T-shirts proclaiming the King's divinity." Given the book's satirical flavor, it was interesting to read that Ludwig equated rock and roll to a "call to arms."

Long, Marvin R. *God's Works Through Elvis.* **Hicksville, New York: Exposition Press, 1979. 32 pp.**

Mann, Richard. *Elvis.* **Foreword by George Otis. Van Nuys, California: Bible Voice, 1977. 186 pp.**

Thornton, Mary Ann. *Even Elvis.* **Harrison, Arkansas: New Leaf, 1979. 188 pp.**

Writing two years after Elvis' death, Reverend Long attempted to rewrite Elvis' life as one without debauchery and excesses and one with religious commitment. God not only sent Elvis, he worked through him, putting him on Earth to be an example to others. The orientation of the book is Fundamental Christianity and as such, portrayed Elvis as a Fundamentalist, as well.

Mann's book examined, also from a conservative entrenched religious point of view, not only Elvis' beliefs but how "the church" viewed Elvis. It tended to degenerate at times into a diatribe against modern pop music, especially rock and roll. Other times it meandered into lengthy explanations of religious doctrine.

If the book hadn't focused on Elvis' life story, it would have been just another fundamentalist diatribe. By the end of the book, Mann was off into a full analysis of Paul, who used to be Saul. Elvis' problems stemmed from his getting off into "hocus-pocus-dominocus." Not only that, but toward the end, Elvis had "retreated more and more into the fantasyland of popcorn and cotton candy."

Thornton's book was "a religious book of sorts." She came from Missouri believing God told her to find Elvis and help him reclaim his spiritual destiny. Her perspective wasn't exactly Fundamentalist in tone though it did speculate on the disposition of Elvis' soul from a doctrinal religious standpoint. Without the religious overtones, this book would have had no place in an Elvis book collection.

Shamayyim, Maia C. M. (Linda Christine Hayes). *Magii from the Blue Star – The Spiritual Drama and Mystic Heritage of Elvis Aaron Presley.* **Crestone, Colorado: Johannine Grove, 1996.**

Tanner, Isabelle. *Elvis: A Guide to My Soul.* **Dobbs Ferry, New York: Elisabelle International, 1993.**

Shamayyim started out life as Linda Christine Hayes. Her spiritual changes resulted from her work with Thoth/Tehuti and the Ultra and Inner Terrestrials. She saw in Elvis, during the course of thirty-six concerts, "miracles of the spirit that would be difficult to put into words." According to her eyewitness report, "the interaction between Elvis and his audiences went far beyond entertainment, and into the realm of mystical communion." She said she began writing about Elvis' spirituality (his "true life mission") as he "shared" it "with his phone friends, who were people from ordinary walks of life with whom he developed close friendships over the telephone."

Her picture of Elvis was of a man cut off from the world, living at night, surrounded by a twelve-man group of friends, dominated by Colonel Parker, spending a great deal of time on the telephone with ordinary people to discuss some significantly different non-Christian religious viewpoints. I point out the non-Christian aspect because Elvis was raised in and followed a very Fundamentalist approach to Christianity. It wasn't until later in life that Larry Geller said he got Elvis into books on Eastern religions. Elvis supposedly kept his "special friends" confidential because "he feared that had the forces who controlled his outer life known about them, even those precious contacts would have been snatched from him."

Nonprovable telephone contacts and secret talks with people who had no way of physically interacting with Elvis would be almost impossible to evaluate. If they were true, it would show a side of Elvis so much bigger than the superstar persona he was when he died. If not true, such reports of such contacts would still be valuable to illuminate not Elvis but the kind of people who have continued to idolize him so long after his death.

Shamayyim's book was based to a large part on "transcriptions" (from tapes) maintained by a fanatical Elvis fan, Wanda June Hill, the one who claimed Elvis even offered to buy her a house. The fact that he never did must mean something. Remember, too, that Brewer-Giorgio depended on a "tape" to unfold her proof that Elvis did not die. At any rate, Elvis had numerous conversations with Hill because he "wanted someone outside the crazy atmosphere in which he lived to tell his spiritual truth to the world."

Hill claimed that Elvis discussed spiritual beings who came to him "as light forms" and "showed me the future." They always came to him when he was alone, specifically several times "when I was in the . . . closet." Maia concluded based on her own observations and all that Hill told her that Elvis was one of those "human beings who were destined as spiritual leaders in various degrees of brilliance." She made her observations both in her book and in an article she wrote for *Angel Times* (Volume One, Issue Four), entitled "Elvis and His Angelic Connection."

Tanner's piece was even more ominous, seeing salvation in her devotion to Elvis. She wrote of Elvis, that he "was not just an entertainer, he was a chosen artist with the gift of a giving soul and a supernatural talent." She went on to say that he "had to walk a path existing on a higher frequency level, where he searched for his own spiritual self." Why did he fall apart? It was because "many who could not reach as high found it easier to pull him down to their level." In reality, though, Elvis did not fall like it appeared he did.

His perceived fall "only happened in the minds of others" who wanted to create a "false image." Elvis took a lot of drugs, not because he was "a drug addict" but because he had to be heavily medicated "to ease his tremendous physical pain due to cancer." Backup and sometime girlfriend Kathy Westmoreland also claimed that. The only medical person who ever said Elvis had cancer was Dr. Nick (Nichopoulos), the same doctor who was said to have overprescribed prescription drugs for Elvis. Was it true or did Dr. Nick say it to cover up his excessive prescription writing?

Tanner was both a super Elvis fan and a self-proclaimed religious expert. She once said that "my poems and portraits of him are based on the precious spiritual experience I had with him." Her other occupation has been to create, on commission, spiritual Elvis paintings for private collectors.

Stearn, Jess. *Elvis: His Spiritual Journey*. Norfolk, Virginia: Donning, 1982. Reprinted 1982. Originally published as *The Truth About Elvis*, New York: Jove, 1980. 253 pp.

Stearn's book was written in tandem with Larry Geller, Elvis' former hairdresser. Eventually, much of what was written here became Geller's own co-written book on Elvis, *"If I Can Dream": Elvis' Own Story* (reviewed in "The Books by Peripheral Associates"). Stearn has had a continuing fascination with delving into out-of-body experiences and life after death, so it was only natural for him to delve into Elvis after death.

What did Stearn and Geller say that was interesting? Geller divulged how he got Elvis into studies of Zen and started him meditating, although his perspective of patiently teaching Elvis became quite tedious. Beyond the serious spiritual tone of the book, the authors did paint a humorous side to Elvis, such as the time he was smitten by a young Southern belle who turned out to be a hooker. The Elvis that emerged was also quite self-important. He had come to believe he had a great spiritual importance for the world.

On the sexual side, Stearn's picture of Elvis emerged as a very confusing one. He had a "virginal" idealization of women while viewing them largely in terms of lust. For example, Elvis had periods during which he would have sex with every possible woman and then turn around and live without sex for lengthy periods of time.

Strausbaugh, John.   *E: Reflections on the Birth of the Elvis Faith*. New York: Blast Books, 1995. 223 pp. Bibliography.

The reassessment of Elvis following his death may well result in a new religion based on Elvis as some sort of saint or go-between with God. Strausbaugh has emerged as one of the first authors to thoroughly investigate the growth of a belief system centered around Elvis as a spiritual God-like individual. Some of his disclosures were humorous and some were downright scary, especially the parts about spiritual possession.

The examination of Elvis as religious icon contrasted the Elvis faith with beliefs held by similar "millennial" cults. In the author's words, the growth of an Elvis "religion" was "consistent with contemporary trends in American religious expression." By placing "Elvism" in the context of modern cult activity, the author may have foreshadowed the actual deification of Elvis by an Oregon church.

Wilson, Charles Reagan.   *Judgment & Grace in Dixie: Southern Faiths from Faulkner to Elvis*.   Athens: The University of Georgia Press/Brown Thrasher Books, 1995.   202 pp. Notes, index.

Wray, Matt, and Annalee Newitz, editors.   *White Trash: Race and Class in America*.   New York: Routledge, 1997.   272 pp. Notes, index.

These two books devoted sections to Elvis in order to explain him as an icon. Conceptually, for Wilson, icons were maintained and promoted by religious leaders as visual images of a particular movement. In the South and in terms of mass culture, Elvis was the most visual. In fact, he became the most photographed person in history.

There were three parts to the Wilson view of Elvis iconography, the wild and rebellious (the father?), the fun-loving (the son?), and the fantasy image (the holy ghost?). Though Elvis has been intertwined with hero-worship and religious devotion, this author saw Elvis the icon as primarily a secular object. Religious overtones encompassed Elvis the Pentecostal but only as an underlying mover of societal images. Though the analysis of Elvis relative to religion was brief, it still accomplished its task of placing Elvis and his context within a broader societal framework.

Gael Sweeney, in her section entitled "The King of White Trash Culture" (in the book edited by Wray and Newitz), saw Elvis as an icon that represented everything garish, flashy, and inappropriate for what became labeled White Trash culture, a Southern-based rural aesthetic that was often politically incorrect. She traced Elvis through his excesses, from his gyrations, outfits, and performances, to the political arena and his encounter with then-President Nixon. She explained the phenomenon he portrayed as a product of the low-class culture from which he sprang.

In her view, it has been the fans of Elvis, also products of White Trash culture, who have taken their image of Elvis and turned him into a "saint of White Trash." From the Pentecostal basis of Southern religion, Elvis has become "The King" or "a spiritual guide and savior to believers." Elvis died and whatever he may have been long ago disappeared. It has been replaced by a quasi-religious veneration that buys large quantities of Elvis products and delights in having his spirit rechanneled to them through impersonators. The author concluded that "Elvis has left the building, but the King remains."

I Was the One:
THE ELVIS BIOGRAPHICAL MATERIAL

I doubt that there's another human being who could
have stood the pressure that Elvis Presley had on him.

-J. D. Sumner,
Elvis: His Love for Gospel Music and J. D. Sumner

The Elvis Biographies

Elvis did not come close to either writing or in some way telling his
complete story. Many people close to him tried to do that in his
place. They told partial stories, fraught with their own prejudices
and agendas. Other people, far removed from Elvis, tried to piece
together detailed and complete accounts, based on press reports,
interviews, and secondary material. Given the enormity of compiling
the definitive picture of Elvis, some books have focused on just the
early years.

The most complete effort so far, encompassing two full length
books, was written by Jerry Hopkins. The first of the Hopkins' books
was, in fact, the only credible biography of Elvis published prior to
his death. Otherwise, every biography published before 1977,
especially those released in the late fifties and early sixties, had
only two redeeming values: they were intended for fans and they
have become prized collector's items.

It was not until Hopkins put together his comprehensive story of
Elvis' life, gleaned from hundreds of personal interviews, including
some with individuals extremely close to Elvis, that serious
biography on the man began. Peter Guralnick completed a two volume
Elvis biography, the second installment coming in early 1999. The
first volume, which appeared in 1994 and limited itself to the period
in his life that concluded with his army induction in 1958, was an all-
encompassing work, one that brought in details from the man who

taught him to play guitar and many of his girlfriends, even the not so serious ones.

In Guralnick's first volume, he interviewed literally hundreds of people, many who had not talked before or who had not been emphasized as major players in Elvis' development. One such person was Memphis native Jesse Lee Denson, or simply Lee Denson, as he now calls himself. Denson and his brother Jimmy, a former Golden Gloves boxer, were quite instrumental in teaching Elvis the rudiments of music, especially guitar-playing. Later, Lee wrote "Miracle of the Rosary," which has been included on several Elvis albums and anthologies.

I recently had the pleasure of interviewing Lee, a talented writer and one of the best rockabilly musicians who has remained undiscovered and unappreciated by American audiences. Though Guralnick referred to Denson quite a bit and did credit him as the man who taught Elvis to play guitar, Denson felt that not enough was presented about those early Elvis years, or as he called them, "Elvis' lost years." As a result, Denson (hopefully in collaboration with his brother) was writing his view of Elvis beginning with Elvis' move to Memphis in September 1947 up to his gaining national prominence.

[Lee] Denson acknowledged that the September 1947 date was sooner than most researchers have concluded but said he was there when Elvis and his family moved into Grandmother Minnie Mae Hood's house at 572 Poplar. The Densons and the Presleys immediately met at the Poplar Street Mission, run by J. J. Denson (Lee's father). The Densons later helped the Presley family obtain a $35 a month two bedroom apartment at Lauderdale Courts.

Woody Deegan, writer for a Memphis publication, *Dateline: Memphis*, previously interviewed Denson at length. Most of Denson's reminiscences centered around jam sessions at Lauderdale Courts beginning in 1947. Along with Lee, the Burnette brothers, Johnny and Dorsey, were major contributors to the musicmaking, as was Bill Black, who was later to back Elvis when he recorded for Sun Records. In fact, it was at one of the jam sessions that Elvis and Black first met, much earlier than the 1951 date given by author Elaine Dundy.

Deegan wove an entire article around his talk with Denson. One point he made was that the little money Vernon Presley earned "didn't seem to stretch much further than the corner liquor store." In my discussion with Denson, he acknowledged that Vernon had quite a drinking problem in those days. Because of the poverty caused by the waste of their meager finances, Gladys, according to Denson, worked hard to make life as "pleasant as possible" for the teenage Elvis.

Deegan's article was quite comprehensive and unique, discussing aspects of the early Elvis rarely touched upon by other writers. For example, through his research he discovered that "many of the graduates of the Humes High Class of 1953 say that Elvis never graduated Humes and never walked across the stage to receive his diploma at the commencement exercises." Although further research did produce a picture of a high school diploma with Elvis' name on it, Deegan could not verify when or how it was awarded.

There were more missing pieces of documentation on Elvis' early life. For example, Deegan found that the records on the Presleys' stay at Lauderdale Courts were missing. All the other records on people who stayed at the Courts during that time period were found intact, but not the Presleys'. He discovered that many people "believe" Colonel Parker "made arrangements to purchase, alter, or destroy those records to protect the privacy, or shortcomings of the Presley family." According to Deegan, the family was "evicted" from the Courts. In spite of all the comprehensive (and frivolous) Elvis books, Deegan's article showed once again that there is still much to learn about Elvis, especially "the lost years," as Lee Denson called them.

That first book by Guralnick and the first Hopkins volume quickly stood out among the best celebrity biographies done this century. In 1997, the Guralnick and Hopkins books were joined by the exhaustively researched and conversationally written biography from Peter Harry Brown and Pat H. Broeske. Some critics have called the Brown and Broeske book the best single-volume Elvis biography.

The book garnered such acclaim because it offered, as critic Edward Morris wrote, "a more thorough and up-to-date account of his death and a more charitable assessment of Presley's personal physician, the much vilified George 'Dr. Nick' Nichopoulos." Some overwhelming logic and evidence was cited to definitively demonstrate that Elvis died of heart failure. On Dr. Nick's behalf, the authors noted, in their acknowledgments, that he was "one of the most misrepresented names in the Presley saga."

During the past decade, the psychological biography has become popular. The author of such a work not only delved into a person's life but attempted to depict possible states of mind and motivational analyses. The best previous celebrity ones were done on Leonard Bernstein and George Gershwin. In 1996, Peter Whitmer's psychological investigation into Elvis became available. In the evaluation of Elvis biographies, it has attained a rank just below the Hopkins and Guralnick works.

Even after reading the psychological profiles, the nagging question remained: Who was Elvis? He was a human being who somehow transformed himself and transformed others. Bob Neal, a Memphis deejay in the fifties who became involved business-wise with Elvis before Colonel Parker took over, said that "Elvis was very shy and unassuming–very pleasant and quiet. But when he went on stage, he was like dynamite. He stole the show."

He was also two entities when he should have been one. Neal remembered that the country station disc jockeys would say Elvis sounded "too black," while the black stations thought him to be "a damn hillbilly." Dr. Whitmer would explain that in terms of Elvis being a twinless twin. He wrote that "understanding the complexities that shape a twinless twin is the key that unlocks the mystery of Presley's motivations, his behavior, and his special powers."

Adair, Joseph. *The Immortal Elvis Presley, 1935–1977.* **Stamford, Connecticut: Longmeadow, 1992.**

Covey, Maureen. *Elvis for the Record: The Story of Elvis Presley in Words and Pictures.* **Compiled by Todd Slaughter. Designed by Michael Wells. Cheshire, England: Stafford Pemberton, 1982. 96 pp.**

Doll, Susan, contributing author. *Elvis: The Early Years: Portrait of a Young Rebel.* **Lincolnwood, Illinois: Publications International, 1990. 128 pp.**

Haining, Peter, editor. *Elvis in Private.* **Foreword by Todd Slaughter. New York: St. Martin's, 1987. 175 pp. Chronology, family tree.**

Slaughter, Todd. *Elvis Presley.* **London: Wyndham, 1977. 128 pp. Discography.**

The books by Adair and Doll were intended as colorful overviews of the life of the King. As such they were paeans for an adoring, uncritical mass of fans. Doll's book, though available in paperback only, attempted to be as visual as a coffee table book by including glossy color photos and a reasonably accurate though unquestioning overview. Adair's book did hit all the chronological highlights.

Haining's book took a major departure. It included twenty-nine articles about Elvis that had previously been available only through the magazines in which they were originally published. The authors included Vester Presley, Johnny Burnette, Rufus Thomas, Scotty Moore, Chet Atkins, John Lennon (on the meeting between Elvis and The Beatles), Juliet Prowse, Linda Thompson, and Elvis, himself, among other famous people.

The so-called article by Elvis was actually a piece intended to tell fans he was doing great (he "dropped a few pounds") and expected his career to resume once he left the Army. All of the pieces came from the collection of British Elvis fan club president Todd Slaughter, who also wrote the introduction. Haining has since followed up with a newer book entitled *The Elvis Presley Scrapbook: 1955-1965*, published in 1991 in Philadelphia by Trans-Atlantic (and in London by Robert Hale). It was primarily a series of reproductions of items about Elvis.

The two publications in which Slaughter was involved presented little in the way of insightful understanding or analysis of why Elvis did what he did, although they did serve as vehicles that gave the fan a set of who did what, where, and when. The best Slaughter effort was the adulatory work he wrote, by himself, *Elvis Presley*. The high points were the appendices, which included statistics about Elvis' record sales and information about the British fan club.

As one of the main organizers of Elvis' official British fan club (he actually took it over from Albert Hand, when Hand died in 1972), Slaughter got a lot of exposure to Elvis' organization. Unfortunately, he never took the time to ask critical questions. He had already completed half of the book when Elvis died, so in parts it came across like Elvis was very much alive, then at times it read like the King was quite dead.

Slaughter merely participated in the creation of the book, *Elvis for the Record*, published in Great Britain only. Maureen Covey and Michael Wells (the designer) were the primary movers, with Slaughter's more famous name needed to appeal to Elvis fans everywhere. The book was primarily a set of fan club-style pictures with accompanying text. In addition to these two books, Slaughter also compiled two tribute books honoring his idol.

Alico, Stella H. *Elvis Presley-The Beatles.* **Illustrated by E. R. Cruz and Ernie Guanlao. West Haven, Connecticut: Pendulum Press, 1979. 63 pp.**

Anonymous. *Elvis Lives!* **London: Galaxy, 1978. 49 pp.**

Jones, Peter. *Elvis.* **London: Octopus, 1976. 88 p.**

Three British books came out in the latter part of the seventies, from presses that specialized in brief, quickly written bios on celebrities. The first, by Peter Jones, appeared the year before Elvis' death (1976). It presented a brief biographical text with many lavish pictures, concentrating significantly on stills from Elvis' films. The anonymous Galaxy publication appeared the year following Elvis' death hoping to cash in on still-grieving fans and their desire to purchase anything Elvis. The photos, though in no way out of the ordinary, should have been at least somewhat satisfactory.

At Pendulum, the idea must have been if a book about one superstar could sell respectably, why not hit a much larger audience by covering, albeit even more hurriedly, two superstar entities, one from America and the other from England? That's about all Alico's book did, illuminating neither Elvis nor The Beatles (although it was targeted at school libraries, containing questions and recommended writing exercises). It's 1979 date played off the growing demand for books on Elvis after his death. The Beatles were by then accorded legendary status because of their lengthy split and many solo projects.

Anonymous. *Elvis Presley: His Complete Life Story in Words and Illustrated with More Than One Hundred Pictures.* **London: Illustrated Publications, 1956.   64 pp.**

Editors of *TV Radio Mirror Magazine. Elvis Presley.* **New York: Bartholomew House, 1956.**

Though the "anonymous" book (from Illustrated Publications) wound up with an overly long subtitle, it was a short and simplistic work. It stood out, however, as the first of the heavily illustrated Elvis biographies (compiled though it was). The pictures came from *Photoplay* magazine. Though it had no credited author, a clean copy has gained enough value to be currently worth in the neighborhood of $200. It has become quite coveted by fan and collector alike, partly because of its age and partly because of the photographs. Incidentally, *Photoplay* issued a paperback-only tribute in 1977 to commemorate the death of Elvis. Published through Cadrant Enterprises of New York, it was a 128 page overly sentimental work that featured many stills from Elvis' movies.

The book from the editors of *TV Radio Mirror Magazine.* had all the appearances of being literally thrown together in 1956 to take advantage of Elvis' seemingly overnight rise to national prominence. It followed soon after the "anonymous" book from Illustrated Publications and, because of its age and pictures, it too has become a sought-after collector's item worth in excess of $100. Because they had been part of a magazine, the articles at least had fan appeal.

Anonymous. *Elvis: The Man and His Music.* **Manchester, England: World International Publications, 1981.   92 pp.**

Anonymous. *The Elvis Story.* **London: Orbis Books (Rockups Series),   1985.**

Charlesworth, Chris. *Elvis Presley.* **London: Telstar, 1987.**

Nixon, Anne E., and Todd Slaughter. *Elvis: Ten Years After.*
London: Heanor Record Centre, 1987.

Of these four British works, the two anonymous ones were the
least valuable. World International's publication emphasized Elvis'
early years and was targeted at a young (pre-teen to early adolescent)
audience. The Orbis book was part of a series that included rock stars
from all eras. Nixon's book (written with Todd Slaughter and
released only in England) was intended to view the Elvis phenomenon
from a perspective ten years after his death. Its value was its
understanding of the fan worship that grew so incredibly over those
years. When read in conjunction with books on the religious fervor of
some Elvis followers, a deeper context for fan adulation can be seen.

Charlesworth was one of those British authors with a great
many rock music biographies to his credit, none of which have stood
out as great writing. Most of his information consistently came from
trade and daily newspapers and periodicals. Rarely did he gain a
unique interview of his own (or anything more in-depth than a brief
publicity talk). This book on Elvis was no different. The one unique
aspect was an accompanying cassette.

Black, Jim. *Elvis on the Road to Stardom.* **London: W. H.
Allen, 1988.**

Gelfand, Craig, and Lynn Blocker-Krantz. *In Search of the
King.* **New York: Putnam, 1992.**

Black's book, an English publication, was similar to the Howard
DeWitt and Peter Guralnick books because it focused on early Elvis
only, though it was rendered obsolete by those two more heavily
researched and detailed undertakings. Gelfand and Blocker-Krantz
went searching for the "real" Elvis by looking at all aspects of his
career. Though available through a major publishing company, it
lacked, as did the book by Black, the detail and introspection of the
more thoroughly researched biographical works.

Brown, Peter Harry, and Pat H. Broeske. *Down at the End of
Lonely Street: The Life and Death of Elvis Presley.* **New
York: Penguin, 1997.   524 pp.   Chronology, filmography,
television appearances, discography, bibliography, index.**

Brown and Broeske set out to accomplish what "no one had ever
attempted," namely to write a "traditional birth-to-death

biography" of Elvis. The "never attempted" claim could well be debated by some of the other authors cited in this section. Nonetheless, this may well prove to be the best and most in-depth single volume biography.

The list of Elvis associates they interviewed was massive, including co-stars from many of his movie projects. Much of the factual chronology came from detailed news accounts. Even though the authors used such a dichotomy of sources, their writing flowed and remained animated and interesting throughout.

For example, their recounting of the episode, during the filming of *Clambake*, in which a groggy Elvis fell and hit his head, raising a "festering lump," was reconstructed from several disparate interviews. They were able to make the story sound like one complete cohesive event. Through this incident and countless others, the two authors constructed perhaps the most complete picture of Elvis' drug abuse and the damage that abuse caused over time. They even detailed the first trip that Elvis, Priscilla, and others took on LSD, using a Timothy Leary primer as a guide.

One very scary overdose almost resulted in Elvis' death. From various sources, the authors detailed the manipulations used by Colonel Parker to keep Elvis' drug problems from being turned into a scandal, even to the extent of delaying some much needed medical help. The points of view on Elvis' musical skills were not as negative as in some past books. These authors very much admired the command Elvis had over his musical repertoire. They felt he constantly "reinvented" himself, especially through the context of his 1968 TV special.

More than anyone else, Brown and Broeske realized that one of the most unique reasons for Elvis' success was his relationship with his fans. They quoted Elvis as saying (about his fans), "It's only because of them that we're here in the first place." He became the most photographed celebrity ever by rarely hesitating to create a fan's "Kodak moment," even to the point of "climbing out of his limo" while heading from one gig to another.

Buckle, Philip. *All Elvis: An Unofficial Biography of the "King of Discs."* **London: Daily Mirror, 1962. 64 pp.**

Gregory, James, editor. *The Elvis Presley Story.* **Introduction by American Bandstand's Dick Clark. London: Hillman, Thorpe & Porter, 1960. 160 pp.**

Hamblett, Charles. *Elvis the Swingin' Kid.* **London: May Fair Books, 1962.**

Primus, Claire. *Elvis: "The King" Returns.* **New Hampshire: Edgar, 1960.**

Once Elvis left the Army, he was hot news again, picking up with his fans like he had never left. With his return the demand for any kind of story was overwhelming and authors like Buckle, Gregory, Hamblett, and Primus rushed to fill that vacuum with their publications. Buckle's book was billed as unofficial, which meant no one close to Elvis was consulted as a source. The only unusual point he made was his speculation that Elvis would visit England.

Gregory functioned as, at the time his book was published, the editor of *Movieland and TV Time.* The book was an edited set of information (with thirty-two pages of pictures and a color pinup) about Elvis with an introduction by American Bandstand's own Dick Clark. It purported to have "the whole story of Elvis in the Army." When it came out in 1960 in paperback only, it sold for a mere thirty-five cents. Its original availability was strictly through magazine advertisements. Currently, one of those original copies (in a clean, near-mint condition) would command around $50.

Hamblett, often tongue-in-cheek, tried to present Elvis as a "cool" rocker who was still "swingin' " even though he had just gotten out of the Army. There were some great "Elvis in the Army" pictures. Overall, none of the books had anything unique to reveal about Elvis because they were intended simply as standard fare for the average fan. Primus glossed over much of what Elvis had done in order to present her view that Elvis would pick up right where he left off.

Researchers would not find these books enlightening. However, collectors have already deemed them to be of considerable value (upwards of $30 for a clean used copy of Buckle's book) because of their scarcity after being out of print nearly thirty years. In 1997, a copy of Hamblett's comic book-like publication sold for $25.

Burk, Bill E. *Early Elvis: The Humes Years.* **Memphis, Tennessee: Red Oak, 1990.**

Burk, Bill E. *Early Elvis: The Tupelo Years.* **Memphis, Tennessee: Propwash, 1994.**

Burk, Bill E. *Early Elvis: The Sun Years.* **Memphis, Tennessee: Propwash, 1997.**

Burk, Bill E. *Elvis Memories: Press Between the Pages.* **Memphis, Tennessee: Propwash, 1993.**

Burk, Bill E.   *Elvis: A 30 Year Chronicle.*   **Tempe, Arizona: Osborne Enterprises, 1985.**

Burk, Bill E.   *Elvis Through My Eyes.*   **Memphis, Tennessee: Burk Enterprises, 1987.**

Vernon Presley once said that "Bill Burk wrote more good things about my boy than anyone." Burk was a journalist for about twenty-six years with the *Memphis Press-Scimitar.* He recalled that time period, saying, "It was my fate to be the lone reporter on duty during the night hours when Elvis would awaken." Of course, Burk had to witness him "cavorting around the streets of Memphis." After that, Burk published a regular Elvis periodical, *Elvis World.* He has not only written more than a few books on the King, he has published some four hundred articles on him as well. Burk met and talked with Elvis on several occasions.

As a result of the admiration he developed for Elvis, Burk published many tribute and commentary books on Elvis. If that were all he wrote, one could readily conclude that's how he made a living. It would be tempting to dismiss his work after perusing only the tributes. Of the three "Early Elvis" works, which stood out as his best and most insightful pieces on Elvis, the *Humes* book (Humes High School in Memphis) found Burk concentrating on Elvis' high school activities and credibly brought out the detail of those years.

Humes High was where Elvis was first protected by Red West (later a leading member of the Memphis Mafia) and where his dependence on and need to be surrounded by "friends" was established. Throughout high school Elvis stood out because of his outlandish clothing styles and longish (for the times) hair. Overall, this book was the most detailed insight into a specific time frame on early Elvis, based on views and insights from former classmates, teachers, and friends.

Burk continued his fascinating looks at Elvis' early years by releasing, in 1994, a book that focused on Elvis in Tupelo, and in 1997, a book about his Sun recording work. In the *Tupelo* book, as in the *Humes* book, Burk relied heavily on first person accounts from those who knew or remembered Elvis. He drew from neighbors, friends, and even people who only knew Elvis in passing.

There were many little known facts in all three books, like the one from an old newspaper that pointed out where Elvis really finished in a talent contest. Burk was among the first to reveal that Elvis once had a face lift. There were also many rare and never-before-seen photos. The remainder of the Burk books were basically tributes. Only in one was there something unique, the descriptions of

Graceland that appeared in *Elvis Memories*. For more photos from Burk, find his 1990 collection (published by his own Propwash Publishing) entitled *Elvis: Rare Images of a Legend*, as well as his 1996 compendium, *Elvis in Canada* (also from Propwash).

Danielson, Sarah Parker. *Elvis: Man or Myth.* **Lincoln, Nebraska: Bison Books, 1990.**

Kirkland, K. D. *Elvis*. **Preface by Sandy Martindale. Stamford, Connecticut: Longmeadow Press, 1988. 111 pp.**

As far as the books by Danielson and Kirkland, there wasn't much there. Danielson did present the facts and myths as she saw them, but it would have been helpful had she at least waded through the major myths and discussed the basis for their existence. The Kirkland book, published two years before the Danielson one, merely presented the basic Elvis story. The writer of the preface, Sandy Martindale, wife of renowned disc jockey Wink Martindale, had dated Elvis (quite often, she claimed) throughout the early sixties.

DeWitt, Howard A. *Elvis: The Sun Years: The Story of Elvis Presley in the Fifties.* **Ann Arbor, Michigan: Popular Culture, 1993. 364 pp. Bibliographic essay, sources, index.**

DeWitt's book was supposed to have been the work of a serious historian and though it focused on a subset of Elvis life and career, it was nonetheless a biography, albeit a partial one. The emphasis was on the years before Elvis signed with RCA. Was the book a serious, well-researched, scholarly work?

It read as if it were, but critics have since pointed out some basic holes in the research and logic. Colin Escott, for one, alleged major research flaws and problems in the discernment of what was fact and what was not. The parts about Elvis and Sun Records did seem to check out, based on comparisons with accounts by other historians.

Gehman, Richard. Edited by Mary Callaghan. *Elvis Presley: Hero or Heel?* **London: L. Miller & Sons, 1957. 66 pp.**

Holmes, Robert. *The Three Loves of Elvis Presley: The True Story of the Presley Legend.* **London: Charles Buchan's Publications (Hulton Press), 1959. 63 pp.**

Gehman put together one of the first souvenir Elvis "biographies" published in England, which concentrated mainly on whether or not Elvis was a virtuous person. Holmes' book was also a nonsubstantive book that presented Elvis' three loves as being "love" for the Church, his mother, Gladys, and his country. The triteness of the writing and information has become obvious, from a forty-year perspective. The major importance of both books would be their scarcity, making them currently worth (to the dedicated collector) in excess of $50 each for near-mint copies.

Goldman, Albert.   *Elvis*.   New York: McGraw-Hill, 1981.   598 pp.   Index.

Goldman purported to have written a complete biography of Elvis. The *Boston Globe* called it "the definitive biography of Elvis Presley." Actually, the only major unique and somewhat believable aspects of the book centered around Lamar Fike's view of Elvis. Fike (a longtime member of the Memphis Mafia) had many reasons to be bitter and thus he came across as frustrated and disillusioned.

Fike's recollections were valuable because they tended to mirror the problems presented by the West cousins. He also offered much more detail than Fortas. The problem was that Goldman interspersed too much of his own conjecture and unsubstantiated stories. For example, he couldn't just report that Elvis French-kissed a fan, he had to color the incident by saying Elvis stuck his "fat tongue" into the fan's mouth.

Such stories were included merely because they appeared to tie Fike's views with Goldman's conjectures. How could those conjectures be anything but suspect when Goldman started the book with a distinctly stated bias, that "Elvis fancied himself a glamorous latter-day pope?" Goldman did take the reader on a surprisingly valuable "tour" of Graceland and did present some interesting views of Elvis from his producer, Chet Atkins.

Atkins remembered being shocked when he first saw Elvis and not being able to "get over the amount of eye shadow he was wearing. It was like seein' a couple of guys kissin' in Key West." The reaction by Atkins was not nearly as graphic or biased as the one from Jim Denny, then the manager of the Grand Ole Opry. Grossman wrote that after Elvis appeared on the Opry, Denny disgustedly told Elvis, "We don't do that nigger music around here. If I were you, I'd go back to driving a truck."

On one of the few positive notes, Goldman appeared to have been the first to discover that Colonel Parker was an "illegal alien." Though this book was Goldman's "opus," he didn't stop writing about either rock music or Elvis. He took on the John Lennon legend with equal or greater bias, according to the perspective of many critics. He also wrote about Elvis' last twenty-four hours, stretching his interpretations to try and show Elvis committed suicide.   In a collection of his writings, entitled *Sound Bites*, Goldman wrote about his views of a 1956 Elvis.   As part of a July 1999 article for *Gadfly*, author Victor Bockris, reflecting on Goldman's 1994 death, quoted Goldman as saying, Elvis "put a bad taste in my mouth."

Guralnick, Peter. *Lost Highway: Journeys & Arrivals of American Musicians.* **New York: Random House, 1979. New edition 1982.   362   pp.   Selected   discography,   general bibliography,   index.**

Guralnick, Peter. *Last Train to Memphis: The Rise of Elvis Presley.* **Boston: Little, Brown, 1994.   560 pp.   Notes, bibliography,   brief   discographical   note,   index.**

Guralnick, Peter. *Careless Love: The Unmaking of Elvis Presley.* **Boston: Little, Brown, 1999.   766 pp.   Notes, bibliography,   brief   discographical   note,   index.**

In addition to the two books listed above, Guralnick authored another American music classic, *Sweet Soul Music*.   The 1979 work, *Lost Highway*, was in reality Guralnick's preparation for his first full volume on Elvis.   There he presented, in his section on rockabillies, three great pieces on Elvis, his background, and ultimate fame.   The pieces, "Elvis, Scotty, and Bill: A Sidelong View of History," "And the American Dream," and "Faded Love," presented thumbnail sketches of his early life, his rise to fame, and most of all, his beginnings with Sun Records.   Interspersed with these pieces were chapters on fellow-Sun artist Charlie Rich and another great purveyor of the Sun sound, Jack Clement, who was closely associated with Johnny Cash.

In 1994, Guralnick presented the first of a two-part biography of Elvis, entitled *Last Train to Memphis*.   That first installment quickly took the premiere place as the grand opus on early Elvis.   It was incredibly detailed, painstakingly accurate, and, surprisingly, imparted much new information, particularly the events surrounding the funeral of Elvis' mother.   The relationship between Sam Phillips, head of Sun Records, and Elvis was intricately portrayed as one between two men who came to grudgingly admire each other.   The respect started when Elvis sang the Arthur Crudup song, "That's All Right Mama."   Phillips "was amazed that the boy even knew Arthur 'Big Boy' Crudup."   In time he would come to realize that Elvis "damn sure wasn't dumb, and he damn sure was intuitive."

To achieve such detail and integrity, Guralnick conducted hundreds of his own interviews and referred back to many others, specifically those done by Jerry Hopkins for his earlier two volumes of Elvis biography. Guralnick's end result was to place Elvis in the context of his times, to cut away from the legend and see the incredibly complex individual, and finally to show why Elvis happened as he did. The notes and the bibliography of works on Elvis were the most detailed of any yet available.

The final Guralnick installment (also published by Little, Brown) appeared in early 1999 (actually very late 1998) bearing the title *Careless Love: The Unmaking of Elvis Presley*. He picked up with Elvis' return from his Army tour of duty in Germany. The years Guralnick had to cover were difficult years to explain. The sixties found Elvis isolated, acting in a long series of tedious films that he once called his "travelogues," and quite literally without direction except in the area of exploring his own purpose for living. That exploration led Elvis to a wide spectrum of religious thought, a topic which Guralnick explored and explained without prejudice.

When he approached writing this second book, Guralnick said that although he knew how the story ended, he still wanted to present it in such a way that it unfolded with anticipation and excitement. He wanted to give it a "condition of suspense," one which would make the reader want to tell Elvis to change, to not go back to his old life. With that approach, Guralnick made the second part of Elvis' life appear compelling. The stories behind his wedding to Priscilla, his comeback special, many of his movies, his buying a ranch, and even his final days came across with a freshness and clarity not achieved in any prior Elvis book.

Though Guralnick spent over 700 pages on this part of Elvis' life, there were still questions, gaps which other writers could and should fill in. Guralnick eloquently and thoroughly delineated Elvis the individual. The complete history behind his movies still remains to be analyzed and presented. Ernst Jorgensen has already completed the definitive look at Elvis' recordings. Both of Guralnick's books on Elvis have to be the model for any further serious writing about the greatest popular singer of all time. Gerald Marzorati wrote in the *New York Times* that "Guralnick wants us to understand that that song will never be over, and after reading him, we do."

Hanna, David. *Elvis: Lonely Star at the Top*. New York: Nordon, 1977. 224 pp.

Staten, Vince. *The Real Elvis: A Good Old Boy*. Dayton, Ohio: Media Ventures, 1978. 150 pp.

Tatham, Dick. *Elvis.* Film material written by Jeremy Pascall. London: Phoebus, 1976. American edition by Chartwell Books, Secaucus, New Jersey. 96 pp.

Tomlinson, Roger. *Elvis Presley.* London: [n. p.], 1973.

Trevena, Nigel. *Elvis: Man and Myth.* London: Atlantic Books, 1977.

Authors have always tried to find a new slant to take when exploring Elvis' life. The most useful and interesting ones have come about when the author has not only studied the subject in depth but the source material as well. That didn't happen with any of these five books, but two at least did try different perspectives. Hanna took the approach that Elvis was a star and stars are usually isolated and therefore lonely. Elvis, thus, was lonely, according to Hanna, who unfortunately offered no backing for such a position.

One-time television critic Staten tried to present Elvis as nothing more than a simple country boy, uneducated, from the poor rural South. Staten used that view of Elvis as a framework for discussing how Elvis fit into Staten's own unfolding life. It would have been an interesting approach had there been some detailed sources that Staten worked with. Staten did make a case for "Uncle Richard," a country music deejay at the Memphis station WMPS, being the first to play the Elvis single "Blue Moon of Kentucky." He also told us that Elvis was so upset after his appearance on the Grand Ole Opry that he left his stage clothes in a gas station restroom just outside Nashville.

At least Staten was able to form some interesting, sometimes fresh and unique, points of view, especially of Elvis in the fifties. Perhaps that ability enabled him to write his other book, *I Was a Teenage Teenager.* Staten's premise toward Elvis was that his basically good character counted for more in the long run than did his excesses, or even some of his poorer quality music. On the other hand, Tomlinson's 1973 book, published after Elvis hit the spotlight again, was merely a composite of every surface piece of information floating around about Elvis. His book literally gave new meaning to the words of John Means, Washington newspaper columnist, "Ho, hum. Another book about Elvis Presley."

Both Tatham's and Trevena's works merited the same critique leveled at Tomlinson's; they presented, with unimaginative prose, the "basic" story. Tatham's book did add a film-by-film chronology featuring both a synopsis and critical overview. A year later, Tatham rushed out a superficial sixty-four-page book through

Phoebus entitled *Elvis: Tribute to the King of Rock*. The concentration was on photographs, some of which were unusual non-posed items.

Hopkins, Jerry.   *Elvis: A Biography*.   New York: Warner Books, 1971.   New edition 1972.   Reissued 1975.   446 pp. Discography, chronological listing of films.

Hopkins, Jerry.   *Elvis: The Final Years*.   New York: Playboy, 1981.   304 pp.

The Hopkins books (one a continuation of the other) became the first definitive works on the overall life and career of Elvis. The only weakness proved to be the lack of citing of source material. No detailed notes or bibliography accompanied either of the texts. Hopkins could not have simply known all that he presented nor could he have been there when so many of the events transpired. Obviously, much was derived from newspaper accounts, periodical articles, and interviews. Both books lacked accountability.

Where did the wealth of firsthand information, the interview excerpts, and personal insights come from? Without being able to evaluate sources, the truth behind any book cannot be discerned. What was discussed was well written, in detail, and gave a clear insight into an Elvis who struggled to develop a serious, lasting career. Hopkins' most effective insight covered Elvis' transition from a Southern rock and roll idol into a polished movie star.

Together, the books established the complete Elvis metamorphosis from banging on an inexpensive guitar to making the best dressed lists in leading magazines. Hopkins analyzed the infamous Las Vegas concerts and the filming of the concert documentaries. He closed his first book around 1970, just after Elvis, in comeback, was solidified in the American mind. The sequel's focus went from 1970 to Elvis' death, following a lengthy deterioration. Hopkins saw Elvis' continued dominance as a product of both Colonel Parker's business acumen and audacity.

The second book, especially, chronicled the tours, the recording efforts, and the falling apart of the individual. Hopkins was less than gentle with the Elvis image, portraying his gun-toting episodes, diatribes against political "leftists," and his massive food and sex intake. The control that Colonel Parker "took" was also detailed. An interesting insight not often discussed in other books centered around the amount of control Vernon Presley exerted over his son.

Roberts, Dave.   *Elvis Presley*.   Miami Springs, Florida: MSI Corporation, 1994.   119 pp.   Discography, chronology, index.

The Roberts work was called a CD book because of its "CD-size" format. As a general overview it was useful though it had nothing new to add. The discography was extensive and formatted in such a way that were the book available on a CD-ROM, intricate searches could be conducted. Otherwise, it was just a compendium of known biographical points. The publisher, MSI, has also marketed more than thirteen similar books on such musical icons as Bob Marley, The Beatles, Jimi Hendrix, and Eric Clapton.

Tunzi, Joseph A. *Elvis: Encore Performance.* **Chicago: JAT Productions, 1990.**

Tunzi, Joseph A. *Elvis: Encore Performance Two: In the Garden.* **Chicago: JAT Productions, 1993.**

Tunzi, Joseph A. *Elvis Highway 51 South Memphis Tennessee.* **Chicago: JAT Productions, 1990.**

Tunzi, Joseph. *Elvis '68: Tiger Man.* **Chicago: JAT Productions, 1997.**

Tunzi, Joseph. *Elvis '69: The Return.* **Chicago: JAT Productions, 1991.   106 pp.**

Tunzi, Joseph A. *Elvis '70: Bringing Him Back.* **Chicago: JAT Productions, 1994.**

Tunzi, Joseph A. *Elvis '73: Hawaiian Spirit.* **Chicago: JAT Productions, 1992.**

Tunzi, Joseph A. *Elvis '74: Enter the Dragon.* **Chicago: JAT Productions, 1996.**

Tunzi, Joseph A. *Elvis Standing Room Only.* **Chicago: JAT Productions, 1994.**

Tunzi, Joseph A. *Photographs and Memories.* **Chicago: JAT Productions, 1998.**

One can only say that Joseph Tunzi (like Elvis biographer Bill E. Burk) has done a ton of work on Elvis. Unfortunately, none of it has been readily available in stores, but through mail order. Each book (all from a nineties perspective) has been limited to a specific time period in Elvis' career, concentrating on the music and performances. The pictures in *Elvis '74* stressed the "dragon-motif" costume Elvis wore that year. Taken together, they formed one of the most in-depth chronicles of the King's career from the late sixties forward.

While not strictly eyewitness accounts, the set of books did bring together material, especially some great documentary photographs, that imparted the tremendous reaction to the Elvis that fans saw and heard in a renewed form. The shows and the songs performed were given an especially detailed analysis. *Elvis '69*, for example, described (through photos, many of which were by Hank de Lespinasse) the stage (Las Vegas) and touring efforts of that year which was spotlighted by his best live work ever.

The second "encore performance" book dissected the Madison Square Garden show. Some of the perspectives, such as the one taken for the *Elvis '73* book, excluded a lot of other Elvis aspects of that year. It actually took until 1997 for Tunzi to present his pictorial account of Elvis' Christmas 1968 comeback television special, sponsored by the Singer Company.

TV Guide ranked the comeback show as one of ten most memorable moments in television history. By waiting so long, Tunzi, in *Elvis '68: Tiger Man*, was able to present many never before seen photos excerpted from the special. Late 1997 saw the announcement of yet another book (a limited edition carrying a fifty dollar price tag), entitled *Photographs and Memories*.

In that publication (which actually came out in 1998), Tunzi combined over one-hundred unpublished Elvis photos (interspersed among many others) with a text that featured the memories of people who worked with or were in some way associated with Elvis. For example, drummer Hal Blaine remembered how "very respectful" Elvis was of "the studio musicians." Gene McAvoy, Art Director for NBC-TV's 1968 Elvis special, shared that he "couldn't imagine Elvis with gray hair." He saw it as "kind of a picture that you don't see."

Gordon Stoker (of The Jordanaires) made it clear in the newest Tunzi book that Elvis had a "super, super nice attitude." What he said was hardly different from the comment he made to *Goldmine* in 1994, that Elvis, like Rick(y) Nelson, was "a very sincere person." In that same 1994 interview (with *Goldmine*), Stoker also revealed that Elvis did become "more and more moody, and more difficult to work with" because "he had financial problems, [and] health problems."

Wallraf, Rainer, and Heinz Prehn (co-author). *Elvis Presley: An Illustrated Biography.* **Translated by Judith Waldman. Design by Roland Siegrist. London: Omnibus, 1978. 199 pp. Chronology, discography, filmography.**

Originally published in German, the best parts of this book were the chronology, filmography, and discography. The discography went beyond the usual listings to include bootlegs and tributes by other singers. The filmography featured detailed synopses. Additionally, there was some great album art, posters, and press releases. Otherwise, the text was relatively superfluous, as far as telling Elvis' full story.

As a result of being long out of print, it has become a highly-prized collector's item, which was ironic, since the book itself contained a very interesting listing of Elvis collector items. While Wallraf has not been visible since in the Elvis publication circles, Prehn was credited with co-writing another book, this time with Bernard Kling. The book was simply entitled *Elvis Presley* and came out in the United States in 1979 through a New York-based organization called Music Sales.

Whitmer, Peter, Ph.D. *The Inner Elvis: A Psychological Biography of Elvis Aaron Presley.* **New York: Hyperion, 1996. 480 pp. Notes, index.**

Ultimately, Whitmer's book relied heavily on psychological interpretations, such as Elvis being a "twinless twin." He investigated just about everything credible written on Elvis and then proceeded to build, in terms of psychological concepts, a picture of what might have been going through Elvis' mind during the key points in his life. Ultimately, Elvis' life decisions were dictated by his emotional makeup.

Whitmer explained, for example, that Elvis' marriage may have broken up because Elvis did not want to have sex with a woman who had become a mother. That problem stemmed from the relationship he had with his mother, which may have stunted all other relationships with women. Elaine Dundy did a similar analysis in her book on Elvis and his mother and came to similar conclusions, showing that Whitmer was not offbase with his ideas.

Especially interesting was Whitmer's blow-by-blow account of the time Elvis took off alone, on a commercial flight from Memphis to Los Angeles. He had left Graceland after a fight with his father, Vernon. He met only one person in L.A., old friend Jerry Schilling. Then he went to Washington, where he finagled a visit with President Nixon and obtained a much sought-after narcotic's agent badge. Whitmer understood the psychological manifestations behind Elvis' quest for the ultimate badge of authority, that he always needed "some form of status to prove his 'specialness.' "

By the time of his actual death, Elvis had turned his preoccupation with death "into an obsession." He was having "nightly drug stupors" to return to a harmony he had long ago experienced with his mother at his twin brother's grave. Elvis needed to leave this life so the precise details of his death have never mattered. In Whitmer's view, Elvis died because his "last prayer was answered."

The movies Elvis did were the best he could do. Ultimately, he rose to the personal level at which he was comfortable, victimized by food phobias, distorted living habits, and sycophantic friends. He especially craved amphetamines because they gave him "the illusion of being more in control." In the end, Whitmer presented a uniquely insightful look into Elvis' life, quoting many people involved with Elvis but well outside the protective ring of friends and business associates. His view of Elvis was a dual view of Elvis, that "his 'powers' were often interpreted in spiritual terms and yet they were infused with the erotic politics of sexuality."

The Elvis Books for Kids

In 1978, following Elvis' death, RCA was busy mining its vaults to create albums that would appeal to everyone clamoring for more Elvis music. Given the demand, the company did not have to be too discerning about the quality of its output. One album they released was *Elvis Sings for Children and Grownups Too!*. The songs were among the silliest Elvis ever recorded, such as "Big Boots," "Cotton Candy Land," "Five Sleepyheads," and "Old MacDonald."

The cuts were taken off seven of Elvis' soundtrack albums, from *G.I. Blues* to *It Happened at the World's Fair*. Of all the posthumous compilations offered in the first few years, it was one of the poorest sellers. It did reflect, however, the Elvis had to children as well as women and men. Book authors also saw that appeal. The result was an interesting array of books intended for young readers.

Bowman, Kathleen. *On Stage: Elvis Presley.* **Mankato, Minnesota: Creative Education, 1976. 41 pp.**

Krohn, Katherine. *Elvis Presley: The King.* **St. Paul, Minnesota: Lerner, 1993.**

Taylor, Paula. *Elvis Presley.* **Mankato, Minnesota: Creative Education, 1974. 31 pp.**

The Mankato, Minnesota-based Creative Education press has long published books designed to present to juvenile readers the major issues and people of the day. With Elvis, they did it twice. The first time was to present a general biography that succinctly and superficially covered the high points of the King's life (for an age level of pre-teen. That was Taylor's book (in a nutshell).

The Bowman book (also targeted at pre-teens) appeared just before Elvis' death and not long after some of his best live work. The author took the approach of presenting what it was like to be part of an Elvis tour, as well as what it was like to see Elvis in person. The insight into putting on a major show was especially realistic for a young audience.

Minnesota has become one of the major centers for publishers specializing in child and juvenile literature. The St. Paul-based Lerner's has continually created above average publications for those two age groups. Krohn's book was no exception with its well-written prose and factually based approach that enabled it to appeal on a level that's both fun and encouraging to read. The focus was on Elvis the superstar, not the human Elvis, but then who has ever captured the human Elvis?

Daily, Robert. *Elvis Presley: The King of Rock 'n' Roll.* **New York: Franklin Watts, 1996. 144 pp. Index.**

Love, Robert. *Elvis Presley.* **New York: Franklin Watts, 1986. 128 pp. Index.**

In 1986, Franklin Watts published, as part of their Impact Biography series, the 128-page book by Robert Love. It was intended for a juvenile audience. A review from the *Library Journal* noted that "fans will enjoy the great variety of photographs spanning Presley's life in this sane and welcome book." Then in 1996, the same company published the Robert Daily book, also as part of their Impact Biography series.

The Daily book spanned 144-pages and was likewise geared for teenage readers. The "series," as of 1996, featured books about Aretha Franklin, The Beatles, and B. B. King, among others. The two books, published ten years apart, would appear to be part of an interesting turn of events. Could "Daily" and "Love" have been pseudonyms for the same author (or set of authors)? Both books did tackle some of the more controversial aspects of the King, such as his abuse of prescription drugs. Illustration-wise, they were limited to some interesting, but mainly publicity, photos.

Friedman, Favius. *Meet Elvis Presley*. **New York: Scholastic Book Services, 1971. New edition 1973. 128 pp. Chronology.**

Friedman put together, during Elvis' lifetime, the first view of Elvis for young adult readers. He purposely included a part about Elvis relating to a black teenager in order to make Elvis seem approachable by a younger age group. As such, it has stood as the premier work in this area. Given its age, it has also come to be worth a great deal as a collectible. In 1997, a mint to near-mint copy was valued at $50. As far as the content, the book was more than good because it interspersed some excellent quotes with detailed history.

Gentry, Tony. *Elvis Presley*. **Introduction by Leeza Gibbons of Entertainment Tonight. New York: Chelsea House, 1994. 127 pp. Discography, further reading, chronology, index.**

Gentry's biography was perhaps the most detailed Elvis book for younger readers, though it was uncritical and surface in its approach. It did, however, weave a very useful chronological path. It also placed Elvis in the context of the times, a rapidly changing postwar society. Though the discography was too general, the further reading list, albeit brief, was focused. The unfocused introduction by Gibbons never once mentioned Elvis by name as it rambled on about being a hero or heroine in the twentieth century.

Panter, Gary. *Invasion of the Elvis Zombies*. **[n.p.]: Raw Books, 1984.**

Pearlman, Jill. *Elvis for Beginners*. **Illustrated by Wayne White. London: Writers and Readers Cooperative/Unwin, 1986. 159 pp. Testimonials, bibliography.**

Pearlman's book was not in-depth or inclusive of new information or insight. It was great fun, though, with its wonderful black-and-white cartoon drawings and odd poses of Elvis. The parts on his Las Vegas shows were very much to the point. The main value it had was the context of the times that it built around Elvis, from what was happening in country music to events in the country as a whole. It also took the time and space to define many terms that, though peripheral to the Elvis world, covered concepts critical to understanding that world.

All Panter did was create a graphically bizarre comic book on a par with *Tales from the Crypt*. In this set of drawings, "the swamplike side-burned hip-slinging natureboy drags another crispy bicuspid girl through a quick boggy acre and into his smelly fortress of solitude." Such a view of Elvis should have appealed to a wide audience, everyone from hellfire preachers, who saw Elvis as pure filth anyway, to devotees of new-wave comic art, those whose imaginations know no bounds.

Wootton, Richard. *Elvis!* **New York: Random House, 1982. New edition 1985. Originally published as** *Elvis Presley, King of Rock and Roll,* **England: Hodder and Stoughton, 1982. 127 pp.   Index.**

Wootton's book was an encapsulated rehash of commonly known aspects of Elvis' life and career, although the author did chronologically order the career highpoints and add some surface analysis. Included were more than forty-five photographs, but most were recycled studio poses and movie stills. The final chapter, with its focus on Elvis' prescription pill usage, the ornate gravesite, and an updated status on the restoration of his Tupelo birthplace, offered the most useful information. Overall, the book was substantially superior to a cooperative work Wootton compiled with John Tobler the following year (1983), *Elvis: The Legend and the Music.*

The Biographies on Family and Associates

What were the people around Elvis like, especially those who have not chosen to tell their own stories, such as the Colonel, Elvis' mother, his daughter, and even Sam Phillips, the power behind Sun Records? Their stories did get told, though not directly, but in the form of biographies. Some authors did a thorough job while others chose to paint nothing more than a surface picture.

Lisa Marie's story told us nothing; neither did a quick one about Priscilla. Fortunately, Priscilla's story finally came out directly from her as well as from a former lover (Michael Edwards). In 1997, a full-blown biography was marketed. On the other hand, the story of Gladys Presley was both analytical and incisive, while Phillips' life account was interspersed with an excellent history of Sun Records. The other entries in this section offered much less.

Adler, David, and Ernest Andrews. *Elvis, My Dad: The Unauthorized Biography of Lisa Marie Presley.* **New York: St. Martin's, 1990.   179 pp.**

The Adler book, purportedly on Elvis' daughter, Lisa Marie, was essentially a thin paperback that shed no new light on either Elvis or his daughter. It merely chronicled the basic facts about her life and some of the more public aspects of Elvis' life. What its purpose was, other than to sell copies by seeming to offer information on a person integral to Elvis, remained anyone's guess. It certainly didn't cover Lisa's life in any deep biographical sense, though it did provide tabloidal stories of her drug abuse, dropping out of high school, becoming a Scientologist, and winding up as the twenty year old bride (of Danny Keogh or Keough) and, finally, the mother of Elvis' granddaughter, Danielle.

Dundy, Elaine.   *Elvis and Gladys*.   New York: Macmillan, 1985.   350 pp.   Bibliography, index.

The Dundy book was a fascinating account of Elvis' relationship with his mother, Gladys, and how much she affected all his other relationships and other facets of his life. It presented a surprisingly incisive account of her life, as close to a full biography as possible. The most helpful aspect of the book was the setting, in which Dundy juxtaposed the relationship between Elvis and his mother within a context of Southern mother-son relationships.

She offered some interesting revelations, asserting that Elvis knew Bill Black as early as 1951. Even then, they practiced long hours together. She divulged that Elvis hitchhiked to Meridian, Mississippi, to enter a Jimmie Rodgers festival singing contest. The young Elvis was more musically talented than previously thought.

On the other hand, there was too much speculation on how the various racial and ancestral mixtures made Elvis what he became. Her implication that part of Elvis' private persona was shaped by his love for Captain Marvel comic books seemed far-fetched. Dundy also suspected that Colonel Parker "blackmailed" Vernon Presley, using his knowledge of Vernon's imprisonment for check forgery. That's not to say there weren't moments of brilliance in the book.

In the twenty-first chapter, Dundy unfolded, in full detail, the death of Gladys, which was precipitated by hepatitis and a resultant failing of the liver, brought on by an ever-increasing intake of alcohol that was being kept even from her doctor. After she died, Dundy quoted one relative's observation that Elvis "didn't seem like Elvis ever again." That relative said Elvis threw himself on the coffin and no one could "get him to stop touching her." Finally, they had to cover the coffin with glass.

Gladys died in August and so did Elvis. Dundy wrote that August was a bad month for Elvis. The notice of termination of his marriage was filed August 1974. In August 1975, Elvis was hospitalized (after collapsing) in Las Vegas. August 4, 1977 was the day the book by the West cousins (and Dave Hebler) was published, and of course, less than two weeks later, Elvis was found dead.

Escott, Colin, with Martin Hawkins. *Good Rockin' Tonight: Sun Records and the Birth of Rock 'n' Roll.* **Foreword by Peter Guralnick. New York: St. Martin's, 1991. Originally published as** *Catalyst: The Sun Records Story,* **London: Aquarius, 1975, and revised as** *Sun Records: The Brief History of the Legendary Record Label,* **London: Omnibus, 1980. 276 pp. Sources, numerical listings of Sun records and affiliated labels, index.**

Floyd, John. *Sun Records: An Oral History.* **Editor's note by Dave Marsh. New: York: Avon, 1998. 191 pp. Bibliography, index.**

Vernon, Paul. *The Sun Legend.* **[n.p.]: Steve Lane, 1969. Also self-published by author, 1969, London.**

The Escott (and Hawkins) book was intended as a chronicle of Sun Records and as such it worked very well. But it offered so much more. It was truly the story of Sam Phillips, founder of Sun Records. As such it gave the best insight into Elvis' Sun days, how Phillips ran the company, what his attitudes were, and much more. In fact, the Phillips story went right up to the failure of Holiday Inn Records.

Overall, the book was very well researched and written but not the first to focus on the record company. That honor belonged to a little known work by Paul Vernon entitled *The Sun Legend,* which Escott's comprehensive work rendered obsolete. In 1993, Howard DeWitt wrote a book that paralleled Escott's by concentrating on the period Elvis was with Sun and first joined RCA. So did Peter Guralnick. Escott uniquely focused on Phillips and others at Sun and their relationships with Elvis.

The newest book on Elvis, Phillips, and Sun Records came out in 1998 as part of a series, For The Record, edited by Dave Marsh and published by Avon Books. It was billed as an oral history with an interspersing of reminiscences from artists like Scotty Moore, Little Milton, Roland Janes, Rufus Thomas, and many others. Through talks, historical facts, original documents, and internal records, Floyd told the company's story from its founding as a label devoted primarily to blues artists until its 1969 sale to Shelby Singleton.

Finstad, Suzanne. *Child Bride: The Untold Story of Priscilla Beaulieu Presley.* **New York: Crown Publishers, 1997. 387 pp. Sources, index.**

Latham, Caroline. *Priscilla and Elvis: The Priscilla Presley Story: An Unauthorized Biography.* **New York: New American Library, 1985. 189 pp. Bibliography.**

The Michael Edwards book about himself and Priscilla (covered in the first section) shed more light on Priscilla and her personality than did the Latham book. This was unfortunate, because Latham had been, until 1997, the only nonconnected (to either Elvis or Priscilla) writer to chronicle Priscilla. Currie Grant, who introduced Elvis and Priscilla (though it was not known on whose behest) was supposed to have been writing a "revealing" story on Priscilla (and Elvis). It has yet to materialize, though it has been advertised.

Latham's book was a hastily prepared paperback that presented already known "facts" about Priscilla and her marriage to Elvis as well as its subsequent failure. The author did speculate how Priscilla's emerging self-image doomed the marriage. Little else of substance was offered in that area, though there was some detail about what happened to Priscilla after the divorce. She became a successful and hard-working mother, actress, and business woman, a world away from that fourteen-year-old who first met Elvis.

Fortunately, Latham's book did not remain the only one that covered Priscilla's life. A bombshell book, *Child Bride*, appeared with much fanfare in 1997. Grant was cited as the source behind many of the key parts, even though he said he still hoped to get his own work published. The author, a lawyer by way of the University of Houston, claimed to have asked Priscilla and Grant key questions face to face. Their answers often came out as heated disagreements.

Priscilla has long claimed that Currie came up to her and in a display of braggadocio, offered to introduce her to Elvis. Currie remembered, just as adamantly, that Priscilla came to him and even had sex with him, a married man, in order to meet Elvis. Priscilla was fourteen at the time and newly arrived in Germany. Finstad, the author, drew her own conclusions, despite the lack of witnesses, that since Priscilla had appeared to contradict herself in this area on previous occasions, she must be lying and Currie, the man cheating on his wife with an underaged teenager, must be telling the truth. Interestingly, many of the pictures in the book came from Currie.

An even more interesting sidenote came via an August 1998, press release, which announced that Priscilla had been awarded "$75,000 in a defamation lawsuit against a man who claimed they had an affair before she married Elvis Presley." The news flash, datelined

Santa Monica, California, continued by stating that "Superior Court Judge Daniel A. Curry ruled August 19 that Lavern Currie Grant, a former army buddy of Presley's, made false statements that were repeated and used as the source for the book *Child Bride: The Untold Story of Priscilla Beaulieu Presley* by Suzanne Finstad." In closing, it was noted that "Ms. Presley had sued for at least $10 million."

Anyway, Finstad continued on to spin quite a tale on Priscilla and finally Elvis and Priscilla's daughter, Lisa Marie, including how Lisa really met Michael Jackson. Concerning Priscilla, she once dressed (after an outrageous makeover) just like Ann-Margret after she heard Elvis was having quite a time with the actress during the filming of *Viva Las Vegas*. Elvis and Priscilla even had an intense fight about Ann, during which Elvis confessed the affair.

The details of Priscilla's life and motivations poured out of the pages of this book. Discussed were the reasons why the relationship between Elvis and Priscilla slowly churned to the ending of Priscilla having an affair with Elvis' karate buddy, Mike Stone. Supposedly, "the straw that broke the camel's back" was Priscilla's discovery of a love note to Elvis signed by a "Lizard Tongue."

Many peculiarities about Elvis, such as his fascination with teenage girls, were discussed at length. Revealed was Priscilla's supposed admission that she had sex with other teenage girls after being urged to do so by Elvis, who filmed the encounters. The book continued through scandal after scandal, such as Priscilla's dalliance with British photographer Terry O'Neill, who, after two months, became the first man to ever dump her.

The book ended with Priscilla in a never-ending identity crisis, her reluctance to give up her famous last name, Presley, though she had been so long divorced and Elvis so long deceased. She was in love with a man named Marcos and even had his child. She would not take the step of marrying him because of self-proclaimed fears brought on by the hurts of her other relationships, with Elvis, Mike Stone, Mike Edwards, and others. Edwards concluded otherwise. The last page had him urging her to "give the fucking name up" and marry the guy (Marcos).

Gripe, Maria. *Elvis and His Friends*. Translated from Swedish by Sheila La Farge. New York: Delacorte, 1976. 224 pp.

Gripe, Maria. *Elvis and His Secret*. Translated from Swedish by Sheila La Farge. New York: Delacorte, 1979. 208 pp.

Gripe's 1976 book implied that the reader would get an insight into Elvis and all of his entourage. Instead, one got a superficial glimpse at any "associate" that could be "name-dropped." The main focus was on Elvis and his performing career. Refer to books by Hodge, Fortas, and Esposito, to gain any understanding of Elvis' friends.

Since Gripe did not succeed with her first book, she tried again, using a titillating title, *Elvis and His Secret*. After wading through some trite writing, it was very disappointing to discover that Elvis' secret was his deep spirituality. His love for his family and his home life as well as his generosity were the other well-known "secrets" mentioned by the author.

Hutchins, Chris, and Peter Thomson. *Elvis Meets the Beatles: The Untold Story of Their Untold Lives*. **London: Smyth Gryphon Ltd., 1994.   248 pp.**

By 1965, The Beatles were at the peak of the musical world and Elvis, in spite of his top ten hit, "Crying in the Chapel," was heading for a musical, artistic, and sales tailspin. Still, they had to meet, which they did, in 1965, a meeting at which The Beatles were supposedly so nervous not much was said right away and not much happened until they became involved in a jam session. For those first few minutes the English group sat and stared at Elvis. Finally Elvis said he was going to bed if that was all they were going to do. John Lennon eventually asked Elvis a pointed question: when was he again going to record the kind of music for which he became famous? That was about the extent of it, at least according to most accounts.

The authors of this book, though not involved, came up with a picture that was based mainly on after-the-fact rumor, hearsay, and speculation. They even questioned whether or not Elvis informed to the FBI on John Lennon's "drug" usage. A detailed account of this legendary meeting should have provided an insight into Elvis' attitudes and conduct around other musicians. This book did not provide that kind of insight. The two authors remarketed the book again in 1996 as *Elvis & Lennon: The Untold Story of Their Deadly Feud*, still published by Smith Gryphon.

Logan, Horace, with Bill Sloan. *Elvis, Hank, and Me: Making Musical History on the Louisiana Hayride*. **Foreword by Hank Williams, Jr.   Introduction by Johnny Cash.   New York: St. Martin's, 1998.   274 pp.   Index.**

O'Neal, Sean. *My Boy Elvis: The Colonel Tom Parker Story*. **New York: Barricade, 1998.   343 pp.   Bibliography, index.**

Rose, Frank. *The Agency: William Morris and the Hidden History of Show Business.* New York: HarperCollins, 1995. 532 pp. Notes and sources, bibliography, index.

Vellenga, Dirk, with Mick Farren. *Elvis and the Colonel.* New York: Delacorte, 1988. 278 pp. Recording sessions: 1954 to 1957, live concerts 1969-1977, discography 1954-1977, index.

Horace "Hoss" Logan was the man behind the fabled Louisiana Hayride, one of the premier showcases of country music, right behind the Grand Ole Opry. Located in Shreveport, Louisiana, the Hayride gave a major boost to the careers of performers like Jim Reeves, Webb Pierce, and most of all, Elvis and Hank Williams. Logan devoted a multitude of pages to Elvis, beginning with his first appearance, during which he "didn't exactly set the world on fire."

The most riveting parts of Logan's book detailed the manipulation and deviousness Colonel Parker employed against anyone who opposed him as he strove to take over Elvis. Even Logan was left realistic and bitter. It was that dislike and distrust of the Colonel that fueled his version of how Parker landed Elvis, from his first contracted role (through Elvis' parents) as "special advisor" to his "disgraceful" treatment of Scotty Moore and Bill Black.

Logan's view of Elvis was far more favorable. In fact, he admitted that "there's no way to exaggerate Elvis's contribution to the *Hayride's* national popularity. Nothing that ever happened to our show was more important than he was." When Elvis became too big for the Hayride and wanted to move on, Logan did not attempt to block him. He knew that "forcing Elvis to keep working for 200 dollars when he could make twenty or thirty or forty that much for a Saturday performance somewhere else would've been wrong." After Elvis put on his last Hayride performance, Logan wrote that "I had enough sense to know that nobody could really replace Elvis."

Logan and Presley kept in touch over the years and in 1977, when the two met for the last time, Elvis told him he wished he could go back and do the Hayride again. Logan said he detected a tremor in Elvis' hand and a detached, tired look in his eyes. Elvis reminded him of how Hank Williams had acted and looked the last few months of his life. In the end, he felt that it was Elvis' moviemaking that killed him, or as Logan phrased it, "the seductive influences of Hollywood and its atmosphere of make believe and unreality."

The Vellenga book was the only in-depth analysis of Colonel Parker (proclaimed a Colonel in Louisiana), until the O'Neal book came out in late 1998. O'Neal incorporated all previously known information and more. Even later in 1998, those two books were superseded by one from a Memphis-based writer, James Dickerson, entitled *Colonel Tom Parker: The Carny Who Managed the King* (published by Watson-Guptill). Dickerson had a few fireworks of his own on the Colonel he dug up after years of research.

O'Neal, author of a 1996 investigative book on Elvis Presley Enterprises, entitled *Elvis Inc.*, used his 1998 book on the Colonel to update material presented in the earlier work. In 1996, he was barely able to touch on the suit brought by the Elvis' estate against the Colonel. In 1998, he had learned enough to go into far more detail.

One of the more interesting aspects of the Elvis/Colonel Parker saga was the entire scenario that led to Elvis signing with his future manager. Supposedly, Gladys Presley was opposed to the deal and only toward the end did Hank Snow soften her up enough to give her approval to the deal. At least that's the way O'Neal explained it. Memphis-based writer Woody Deegan discovered another version, partially from Jimmy Denson, a close family friend to the Presleys.

Denson said that when Elvis signed a contract with the Colonel, "it was the most anguish" he had ever heard from Gladys. He added that "after that, none of Gladys' friends from church had much to do with Elvis. They thought he had sold out to the devil himself." According to Deegan, Gladys told Elvis, "If you sign with that man [Parker], it will kill me." Elvis went ahead and contracted with the Colonel on August 15, 1955, and as Deegan noted, Gladys died three years later almost to the day (August 14, 1958).

Throughout both his books, especially the newer one, O'Neal wrote well, almost spellbinding at times. What his works lacked (his 1998 book, especially) were unique disclosures (like the Jimmy Denson comments that Woody Deegan reported). He effectively updated the Parker story begun by Vellenga by pulling together the diverging paths of Priscilla and her eventual management of Elvis' interests after his death, the Colonel's life after Elvis, and many details of the posthumous Elvis business. At the end of the book, in rough form, the author presented a reconstructed plan put together by Parker to promote the movie *Spinout*.

Though the Rose book was about another promoter, William Morris, many of its pages were devoted to the Colonel, especially his history of show business hustling. It became an essential Elvis book for that reason alone. Fortunately, it had much more to offer. For example, did you know that Elvis watched a Las Vegas lounge act do "Hound Dog" in a style similar to the one he used when he made it so popular? Of course, the obvious question was how Elvis got involved with the Morris agency when he was tied so closely to the Colonel.

Vellenga's book was the one that most significantly blew the lid off the Colonel's masquerade and revealed his true identity as an illegal alien (though both Albert Goldman and Hans Langbroek had already made that disclosure). Once the revelation was made, the book turned into an enlightening account of the Colonel's business dealings. It painstakingly revealed how he controlled Elvis and why Elvis allowed it to continue.

Above all else, the book showed how the Colonel's manipulation of public perceptions may not have helped Elvis' career critically and artistically, but how it helped ensure Elvis' legendary and adulated status, especially after his death. The Colonel was quoted as saying that he thought he served Elvis well. Yet Elvis was never allowed to perform outside the U.S. supposedly because the Colonel was afraid his illegal alien status might be discovered. From there, the authors delved into allegations of complicity by Elvis' record label, RCA, in depriving Elvis and his estate of millions of dollars.

It took another writer, songwriter Phil Ochs, to summarize the essence of Colonel Tom Parker. According to biographer Michael Schumacher, Ochs concluded that the Colonel was extraordinarily successful because he "knows more about organizing America than Angela Davis or SDS. He understands the American mentality." In Ochs' view, Elvis was a Parker creation, "a giant commercialization of the working-class singer." The Colonel put Elvis in a gold suit because it "was Parker's idea of the super-gross carnival treatment, a cheap ikon [sic] of all America has to offer."

Mann, May. *The Private Elvis.* New York: Simon & Schuster, 1975. New edition 1977. Originally published as *Elvis and the Colonel*, New York: Drake, 1975. 294 pp.

As originally titled, *Elvis and the Colonel*, Mann's book gave the impression that a reader would gain insights into how Elvis and the Colonel worked together. If that were the intent, the book failed. It was reprinted and retitled in the wake of Elvis' death. Actually, the book was about Mann and Elvis. She claimed it came straight from a diary she kept exclusively about Elvis.

Mann claimed she tried to persuade Elvis to run as Nixon's vice president. That was one of countless personal encounters with him that propelled heavy sales of her book. On many occasions, she was granted private but "short" interviews with Elvis. Through the Colonel, she often gained access to Elvis' dressing rooms. Her questions were never deep or probing and her revelations often going only as far as what kind of flowers Elvis gave the young starlets he dated. That may have been why she was able to gain access.

Palmer, Robert. *Baby, That Was Rock & Roll: The Legendary Leiber & Stoller.* **Introduction by John Lahr. New York: Harcourt Brace Jovanovich, 1978. 131 pp. Recordings of works, chronological listing of records produced.**

When Robert Palmer died in 1998, America lost a great historian and meticulous storyteller. His tale of the writing duo, Jerry Leiber and Mike Stoller, went to the very soul of making catchy yet timeless pop music. The East Coast born and raised duo composed some of the most memorable Elvis hits, such as "Hound Dog" and "King Creole." They also wrote a lot of songs for him that wound up as either album filler or movie soundtrack selections.

Their story was integral to understanding both the music Elvis made and liked. Yet their creations didn't stop there. Groups such as the Coasters and the Drifters had great success with their material. Delving into their music and lives was a prerequisite for appreciating the musical milieu within which Elvis stood out.

Right away, they were "very impressed with him [Elvis]. We were impressed with how good he was. He would do a great take and then insist on another and another and still another." Elvis' work ethic was what they remembered: that "he never looked at the clock" and "when he was in the mood he could do fifty takes of a number and go on to the next tune without taking a break."

In another of his books, *Deep Blues*, Palmer briefly evaluated Elvis' blues roots, concluding that Elvis' Sun Records single "That's All Right" resembled "Muddy's earliest sides in its combination of a strong blues vocal with stark electric guitar and prodding string bass backing." Palmer also wrote that although rock and roll was inevitable, "it's difficult to imagine the music catching on the way it did in 1955 without [Sam] Phillips and Elvis Presley."

In a 1995 book, entitled *Rock and Roll: An Unruly History*, Palmer did a precise yet in-depth job of establishing Elvis' place as a first-generation rocker. He didn't do it by telling the reader what to conclude, rather he did it by quoting other musicians who knew and worked with Elvis. For example, he captured explanations by Rufus Thomas and Roy Brown on how they saw Elvis' relationship to black music. Brown's assessment disclosed Elvis' charitable donations to sickle cell anemia research, something that has been long overlooked in the face of rushing to judgement over his later excesses.

8

I Gotta Know:
THE ELVIS REFERENCE WORKS

The Elvis Universe is a place where individuals are
able to believe just about anything they want, and
Elvis Presley can be all things to all people.

-Mick Farren,
The Hitchhiker's Guide to Elvis

The General Reference Books

Biographies have always presented condensed views of their subjects
over time, taken from huge amounts of primary and secondary sources.
Thus, only parts of interviews and documents ever surface in a such a
work. Fortunately, for those who require additional detail, some
researchers have chosen to compile reference books filled with more
complete sets of source material, such as pictures, documents,
clippings, and complete interview transcriptions.

Sometimes reference books take an encyclopedia or dictionary
format, in which facts or dates may be looked up. Just as often, they
may appear as a collection of reproduced or newly published articles
about a particular subject. Sometimes, they are compendiums of
interviews, a most appropriate way to collect oral history.
Exclusively pictorial books could also serve as reference works because
pictures are the only means available to view the "body language" of
a subject.

Elvis himself always seemed to be trying to figure out why he
became who he became. So why shouldn't everyone else? Then again,
who or what did he become? There are numerous encyclopedia
entries, chronological lists, quotes, studio logs, newspaper clippings,
and much much more, more than enough to back up any conclusion.
Another opinion would simply take its place among the millions
already rendered. As Ronnie Milsap once observed, "opinions about
Elvis Presley are like noses-everybody has one." Milsap said that

what Elvis left us, "recorded songs that became standards" and "a memory that became a legacy," should be all that matters.

In Elvis' case, the reference books have abounded, yet too many contradictory explanations have been drawn from the same sets of original source material. It's all a matter of what meaning was derived from which specific pieces of information. Did the blue light that appeared the night of his birth have religious significance or was it merely a weather phenomenon? Even with all the information available on Elvis, most of the contradictory conclusions have remained hopelessly unresolved.

Choron, Sandra, and Bob Oskam. *Elvis!: The Last Word: The 328 Best (and Worst) Things Anyone Ever Said About "The King."* **New York: Carol, 1991. 103 pp. Index.**

Since the comprehensive interview with Elvis never existed and since the quotes from him were largely intended as publicity material, the next best set of quotes had to come from those who knew him best or worked closely with him. First, there was the book compiled by Choron and Oskam. Though it was comprised of uncited quotes, the anthology did have the value of presenting, uniquely, what others thought of or observed about the King.

There were insights, often contradictory, about Elvis' sexual prowess and orientations, his acting ability, and even what he meant to others who would later also become stars. The quotes ranged from a disparagement by Marlon Brando to an insight from Marty Lacker on how Elvis got started using certain drugs. Though most of the quotes were readily available elsewhere, it was most helpful to have them under one cover, especially the lengthy one by Willie Nelson about how Elvis affected his audience when he was "hot."

Clayton, Rose, and Richard M. Heard, editors. *Elvis Up Close: In the Words of Those Who Knew Him Best.* **Atlanta: Turner, 1994. 405 pp. Listing of "those who knew him best," index.**

The *Elvis Up Close* book, edited by Clayton and Heard, featured lengthy quotes about Elvis not only from famous people but from those who knew him best. There were quotes from army, musical, and business associates, as well as from admirers and former neighbors. Most of the quotes came from the editors' privately obtained collection done in the best traditions of oral history. Best of all, the quotes were arranged in chronological order over fifteen chapters. An observation from a friend, Mary Reeves Davis, came first.

Some of the people close to Elvis whose comments appeared in the book included Larry Geller (hairstylist and self-described guru), RCA record producer Felton Jarvis, recording artist T. G. Sheppard, and guitar wizard James Burton. The book was also a great source for discovering what other musicians, such as James Blackwood (gospel singer), Shaun Nielsen (backup singer, whose first name used to be Sherrill), Tom Jones, and even Faron Young recalled about Elvis. It was Young who was credited with telling the Colonel that "my damn kid could have handled Elvis Presley! Goddamn, Parker, you ain't that brilliant!"

Songwriter Don Robertson observed that Elvis could have recorded songs by great writers like Johnny Mercer, but writers of his caliber were "too successful to give up a share of their writer royalties just to get Elvis to record one of their songs." The much-maligned Dr. Nick (Nichopoulos) was quoted as saying that Elvis took steroids (along with other medications) for the last four years of his life. The steroids were said to have been for bowel problems.

Coffey Frank. *The Complete Idiot's Guide to Elvis: The King Lives On!* **Foreword by Dave Marsh. New York: Alpha Books, 1997.   348 pp.**

So many "Idiot's Guide to" books have been marketed over the past several years on subject matter ranging from computer software to classical music, that the one on Elvis by Coffey could easily have gotten lost in the shuffle. Fortunately, Coffey turned it into a humorous tour de force (or was that farce) beginning with Marsh's comment that "Elvis and idiocy go a long way back." The pointless "idiotic" facts that Coffey uncovered provided more laughs than Elvis' favorite Inspector Clouseau movie.

Some of those facts included the Sierra, Nevada, truck stop that featured a collection of Elvis "guns" as well as the tattoo art exhibit on the King located in Illinois. Otherwise, the book turned mundane when the author dwelled, almost too much, on the facts of Elvis' life and recording career. Most of that has been rehashed much too often. Even the chronology, though detailed, offered nothing new.

Collins, Lawrence. *The Elvis Presley Encyclopedia.* **London: Globe Communications, 1981.   64 pp.**

Gates, Graham, and John Tobler. *The A–Z of Elvis.* **London: Mason's Music, 1982.**

Along with Martin Torgoff's thorough work, these two books were among the earliest attempts to compile Elvis encyclopedias or dictionaries (the "Elcyclopedia" co-compiled by English fan Albert Hand was undoubtedly the first). Though they were admirable creations, they were rendered obsolete by Fred Worth's gigantic 1988 effort. Collins' work came out as a too-short (sixty-four pages) paperback. Because it was one of the first Elvis encyclopedias, its value to collectors has risen to double its original value, providing the copy is in mint condition. Gates' co-author, Tobler, previously wrote several superficial rock biographies, the best of which was on Elvis' peer, Buddy Holly.

Davis, Arthur. *Elvis Presley: Quote Unquote.* **New York: Crescent Books, 1995. 80 pp.**

Farren, Mick, and Pearce Marchbank. *Elvis: In His Own Words.* **London: Omnibus, 1977. New edition 1994. 123 pp.**

Farren, Mick. *The Hitchhiker's Guide to Elvis.* **Ontario, Canada: Collector's Guide, 1994. 178 pp.**

McKeon, Elizabeth, and Linda Everett. *The Quotable King: Hopes, Aspirations, and Memories.* **Nashville, Tennessee: Cumberland House, 1997. 173 pp. Bibliography.**

Rovin, Jeff. *The World According to Elvis: Quotes from the King.* **New York: HarperCollins, 1992.**

Elvis never did a probing give-and-take interview with anyone skilled at that undertaking, so the next best insight has had to come from books which compiled quotes by Elvis. Farren's Omnibus publication was the best such undertaking. It was comprehensive, compiling just about everything Elvis ever said publicly, ranging from press statements to offhand remarks.

It has been alleged that the Colonel did not like Elvis talking to the press because he was afraid Elvis might make a major gaffe. The quotes included here revealed no such tendency, indeed Elvis showed he could effectively spar with the media. As helpful as Farren's work appeared, the quotes were uncited and taken out of the context in which they were made. Co-editor Marchbank entered the Elvis publishing world the same year with a "quickie" tribute book published by Wise Books of London.

In 1992, Rovin had attempted to do what Farren did more successfully in 1994. Rovin and Farren did not always present the same quotes but Farren certainly presented a lot more. Rovin's quotes seemed like little more than asides spoken by the King and they were not dated or cited. Farren at least put his quotes in different subject areas, so it appeared like Elvis was answering his critics or commenting on Graceland, for example.

Elizabeth McKeon's previous published encounter with the Elvis legacy consisted of two excellent cookbooks. Here she presented every Elvis comment she could find on any subject, such as his personal life, his movies, life in the Army, and especially his music. Many quotes pinpointed the fact that Elvis had definite deep opinions, specifically on the media, that "a lot of these guys aren't reporters, they're marksmen." He was a dedicated mama's boy, saying that "I still think of her every single, solitary day."

The unfortunate part of the book was that no specific sources were given for any of the quotes. The bibliography showed that she must have relied on a lot of what Dutch collector Ger Rijff compiled over the years. In the end, McKeon showed that Elvis had a deep sense of self, that he knew it was his unique personality that made him so popular. She quoted him saying, about acting, that he was "not going to take lessons because I want to be me."

Farren's 1994 compendium turned out to be an encyclopedia of many little known Elvis facts (such as his love for peanut butter and jelly), attributes, and unusual quotes. For example, Farren discovered that musician Charlie Feathers claimed in a 1990 interview that "Gladys took a trip to Florida without Vernon and was carryin' on with a colored fellow down there and was pregnant right after. Nope, Vernon ain't his daddy. No sir." In addition to other items like Elvis trading cards, many worthwhile Elvis books were listed and intelligently critiqued.

Of the five books in this grouping, the one by Davis was the least satisfying. Published by Crescent Books, known for their odd-sized, hurriedly compiled coffee-table-like books, Davis compiled quote after previously published quote. Most of the quotes came from five books, *Elvis: A Biography* and *Elvis: The Final Years*, both by Jerry Hopkins, Richard Wootton's *Elvis Presley, King of Rock and Roll*, Wootton and John Tobler's *Elvis: The Legend and the Music,* and *Elvis: What Happened?*, by Red and Sonny West (the West cousins), Dave Hebler, and Steve Dunleavy.

The major eye-catching quote came from Colonel Parker soon after Elvis' death (see page 78). Parker felt that even though the King was gone, business would go on as usual. He said, "We're keeping up our spirits and keeping Elvis alive. I talked to him this morning and he told me to carry on." The "him" was Elvis' dad, Vernon, not Elvis himself.

Davis did take a stab at a short biography of Elvis to complement the large-type quotes. Nothing he presented went beyond any of the sources he used. His only personal analysis covered the aftermath of Elvis' death, specifically the criticism of Albert Goldman's biography of Elvis, about which he observed: "It destroyed the Elvis myth in far too convincing a manner for those who found him to be an inspiration, and appeared equally scathing about his admirers."

Higgins, Patrick, editor. *Before Elvis There Was Nothing.* **New York: Carroll & Graf, 1994.   127 pp.**

Higgins' book, *Before Elvis There Was Nothing,* was another example of books specializing in "quotes" famous people made about Elvis. Some of the statements used were crucial to telling Elvis' story, such as Stella Stevens disclosing that "on the set of *Girls! Girls! Girls!* he was drunk part of the time and showing me his pill book the other part of the time." The highlight of the featured photographs was the first publicity shot issued by RCA on Elvis.

Latham, Caroline, and Jeanne Sakol. *"E" Is for Elvis: An A-to-Z Illustrated Guide to the King of Rock and Roll.* **New York: Penguin, 1990.   New edition 1991.   301 pp.**

All Latham did was bring together known facts about Elvis. There was nothing new or in-depth. The main value was to have a lot of general facts and some interesting tidbits under one cover. She told us, for example, that co-star Debra Paget said she never dated Elvis. In addition to the entry on Paget, everything in the book was arranged in alphabetical order so one's curiosity was easy to satisfy as long as the question was not too intricate.

Moore, W. Kent, and David L. Scott. *The Elvis Quiz Book: What Do You Know About the King of Rock & Roll?* **Chicago: Contemporary Books, 1991.   131 pp.   Bibliography.**

Rosenbaum, Helen. *The Elvis Presley Trivia Quiz Book.* **New York: New American Library, 1978.**

Rosenbaum created the first major publisher trivia and quiz book on Elvis. It was inevitable and the only unexpected aspect of such a compilation was that it took until 1978 for it to come out. One would have thought fans would have demanded such a book long before that. Obviously Elvis' death opened the market up for anything on Elvis. As a first try, it was brief and simplistic.

Moore's effort, thirteen years later, was much more detailed and intriguing. It was also fun and informative in that it helped pin down areas where a reader may not have been as informed as previously thought. The book dared to ask the question, "what do you know about the King . . . ?", and through its answers it added minute facts but not much information. The lists that resulted from several of the questions were quite helpful in ordering aspects of Elvis' career, such as his film appearances.

Nash, Bruce, and Allan Zullo, with John McGran. *Amazing But True Elvis Facts.* **Kansas City, Missouri: Andrews and McMeel, 1995.   147 pp.**

The Nash book took an "amazing but true" approach to the legacy of Elvis, in that it compiled the most unbelievable and bizarre known stories about the King. For example, Elvis' last words to Ginger Alden were, "Okay, I won't." Unfortunately, it did not list sources. Nash previously compiled an Elvis quiz book, which was both too brief and too simplistic.

Pierce, Patricia Jobe. *The Ultimate Elvis: Elvis Presley Day by Day.* **New York: Simon & Schuster, 1994.   560 pp. Bibliography, index.**

Pierce has had her book billed as "ultimate" and it truly was. The chronology was detailed, factual, and thorough, going all the way up to 1993. That meant that all the postdeath controversy about Elvis was covered. Then there were the various discographies, video and film listings, information on "Elvis people," and more miscellaneous information than ever thought possible, down to a list of participants in football games, which included luminaries like television stars Lee Majors and Jack Lord as well as two fellow musicians from the fifties, Pat Boone and Rick Nelson.

The section on the friendship between Elvis and Liberace was unique to this book. To top it off, there was an amazingly rich bibliography, as well as sections on Elvis' statistics, the women in his life (beyond just the "girlfriends"), and considerable factual movie data, such as a list of films in which Elvis sang a duet. For collectors, there was information on the leading buyers and sellers of Elvis memorabilia. An incredible job was done in bringing all this material together, which has made acquisition of the book essential.

Rijff, Ger. *Elvis Presley: Echoes of the Past.* **Voorschoten, Holland: "Blue Suede Shoes" Productions, 1976.**

Rijff, Ger. *Faces and Stages: An Elvis Presley Time-Frame.* **Rotterdam, Holland: It's Elvis Time, 1986.**

Rijff, Ger. *Memphis Lonesome*.   Rotterdam, Holland: It's Elvis Time, 1988.

Rijff, Ger, and Jan Van Gestel.   *Elvis: The Cool King*. Photography by Bob Moreland.   Wilmington, Delaware: Atomium Books, 1991.   Originally published in Holland in 1989.

Rijff, Ger, and Jan Van Gestel.   *Elvis: Fire in the Sun*. Wilmington, Delaware: Atomium Books, 1991.   Originally published in Holland in 1989.

Rijff, Ger, with Bill DeNight and Sharon Fox.   *The Elvis Album*.   Lincolnwood, Illinois: Beekman House, 1991.

Rijff, Ger. *Long Lonely Highway: A 1950's Elvis Scrapbook*. Ann Arbor, Michigan: Popular Culture, 1992.   210 pp.

Rijff, Ger. *The Voice of Rock and Roll: Elvis in the Times of Ultimate Cool*.   Rotterdam, Holland: It's Elvis Time, 1993.

Rijff, Ger, with Gordon Minto.   *60 Million TV Viewers Can't Be Wrong: Elvis' Legendary Performances on the Ed Sullivan Show*.   Amsterdam, Holland: Tutti Frutti Productions, 1994.

Rijff, Ger, with W. A. Harbinson and Kay Wheeler.   *Growing Up with the Memphis Flash*.   Amsterdam, Holland: Tutti Frutti Productions, 1994.

Rijff, Ger, with Linda Jones and Peter Hann.   *Steamrolling Over Texas*.   Introduction by Kathy Westmoreland. Amsterdam, Holland: Tutti Frutti Productions, 1998.   120 pp.

Rijff, Ger, Michael Ochs, and Trevor Cajiao.   *Shock, Rattle & Roll*.   New York: Sterling, 1998.   96 pp.

Rijff, a Dutch citizen, published, through his own Holland-based Tutti Frutti Productions, a proliferation of Elvis books, most of which turned out to be similar to the one entitled *Long Lonely Highway*, published in 1992 by Popular Culture of Ann Arbor, Michigan. The first book he actually published was called *Elvis Presley: Echoes of the Past* and it was self-published (out of Voorschoten, Holland) in 1976. Some of his works have finally become available in this country and other parts of the world, specifically the one (credited to Rijff, Bill DeNight and Sharon Fox) entitled *The Elvis Album*.

Two more compendiums (both done with Jan Van Gestel), *Elvis: The Cool King* and *Elvis: Fire in the Sun,* were published in 1991 by Atomium Books of Wilmington, Delaware, after being originally put out in 1989 by Tutti Frutti (of Amsterdam). *Elvis: The Cool King* was an exceptional creation, featuring photography by Bob Moreland in the form of 170 never-before-published pictures of Elvis from a 1956 gig and another 1961 engagement in St. Petersburg, Florida. Even Colonel Parker was highlighted from the sidelines, ever-present cigar in mouth.

The other books Rijff published through his Tutti Frutti company were *Faces and Stages: An Elvis Presley Time-Frame* (1986) and *Memphis Lonesome* (1988). *The Voice of Rock and Roll: Elvis in the Times of Ultimate Cool* (1993) was available through It's Elvis Time (based in Rotterdam). 1994 was an extremely productive year for Rijff with *Inside Jailhouse Rock* (a photographic collaboration with Jim Hannaford, which was also published by Hannaford through his Jim Hannaford Productions of Holland, Michigan), *60 Million TV Viewers Can't Be Wrong: Elvis' Legendary Performances on the Ed Sullivan Show* (a lavish cooperative pictorial effort with Gordon Minto), and the work with W. A. Harbinson and Kay Wheeler on *Growing Up with the Memphis Flash,* another Tutti Frutti publication. The 1994 Hannaford/Rijff book on *Jailhouse Rock* was reviewed in the section on Elvis' movies.

Rijff also participated in a great cooperative work with photographer Jay B. Leviton entitled *Elvis Close-Up,* which was published by Simon & Schuster (and reviewed in the section on Elvis photograph collections). His finest accomplishment was *Long Lonely Highway* because it presented the highpoints of Elvis' career in a scrapbook format of clippings, photos, and images. The material emphasized the beginnings of the Elvis phenomenon. The accounts of growing crowd sizes and reactions heralded his meteoric rise. It was great to see the clips in original form as they shed a firsthand light on Elvis' activities.

Some of what Rijff showed the reader was also referred to in the various bibliographies listing Elvis source material. It was great to have so many copies of original documents in one place for easy reference. The way Rijff arranged the material helped recapture the excitement surrounding Elvis when he first started out. The book was closed with a great cross-reference to people, places, and specific items of interest.

In 1998 Rijff joined Michael Ochs of the Michael Ochs Archive and Cajiao to produce another pictorial spread featuring "dozens of behind-the-scenes photos" depicting Elvis as "he prepared for and performed in a 1956 *Milton Berle Show* on NBC." It was "loaded with 125 black and white illustrations taken in Los Angeles June 5, 1956." Most of them captured "a relaxed Elvis just being himself."

Along with the pictures, there were five pages of text that not only described the show but the overall public reaction, as well. According to the authors of this important historical document, "Uncle Miltie" received a huge number of letters that attacked Elvis' on-stage antics and gyrations. They described the letters as being largely negative and "charged with moral outrage."

Like Rijff, Cajiao was a Dutch Elvis fan who liked to write about his idol. In 1998 he came out with his own book, *Talking Elvis: In-Depth Interviews with Musicians, Songwriters, and Friends*, in which he compiled the results of interviews he conducted with people close to Elvis, most notably Red West. It was published by Rijff's Tutti Frutti Productions. Many of the talks had been previously published in *Elvis: The Man and His Music*, a periodical that emanated from the Rijff organization. Also published in 1998 (by Rijff) was the largely pictorial book entitled *Steamrolling Over Texas*, which captured Elvis touring through that state.

Stanley, David E, with Frank Coffey. *The Elvis Encyclopedia: The Complete and Definitive Reference Book on the King of Rock & Roll.* Foreword by Lamar Fike. Santa Monica, California: General Publishing Group, 1994. 287 pp. Index.

The same criticism leveled at the Latham book could be tendered toward David Stanley's "encyclopedia," though Stanley did present some unique (and never-before-published) photographs. There were more than three hundred in all. In fact, the most interesting aspect of Stanley's work was the resurfacing of Lamar Fike, through the brief foreword he wrote and some of the minute asides he offered during the course of the book.

To his credit, Stanley did present some new insights into Linda Thompson, one of Elvis' last involvements. He also told of a meeting between Elvis and Led Zeppelin. A special section, in which he discussed fifty of the most important people in Elvis' life, revealed, for the first time, some details on the backgrounds of lesser known Elvis associates. In 1997, co-author Coffey compiled the slyly humorous *The Complete Idiot's Guide to Elvis*.

Torgoff, Martin, editor. *The Complete Elvis.* New York: Delilah, 1982. 253 pp. Bibliography.

Torgoff's attempt to achieve an encyclopedic compilation of information about Elvis was not very useful nor was it any more inclusive than Latham's work. It was great for another reason, though, because it included lengthy well-written articles on various aspects of what went into the making of the Elvis phenomenon. Among the writers Torgoff tapped were Stanley Booth (two articles) and John Walker, who wrote at length on Elvis bootleg albums. Lenny Kaye speculated on what Elvis might have been like had he lived.

Additionally, Torgoff wrote about the book he did with Dee Presley and her sons, the Stanley brothers. The bibliography was lengthy and there were many great color photos not found in other sources. His "A to Z" on Elvis was quite inclusive but not very deep. Some obscure entries included the United Paint Company where Vernon had worked and the Patricia Stevens Finishing School where Priscilla learned to dance. The picture of Ed Hopper's black eye was quite interesting. He was the guy Elvis punched during a 1956 Memphis gas station altercation.

Worth, Fred L., and Steve D. Tamerius. *Elvis: His Life from A to Z.* **New York: Wings Books, 1988. New editions 1990, 1992. 618 pp.**

Worth and Tamerius succeeded where both Torgoff and Latham didn't, in the attempt to compile and order vast informative entries, because they came as close as possible to being exhaustive in their efforts to include, in one complete source book, every known fact and nuance about Elvis, especially his performances, recordings, films, and even television appearances. There were over six hundred pages of photos, dates, definitions, and details that were not as easily accessible elsewhere. The two writers had a 1981 414-page preview of this work entitled *All About Elvis*, published by Bantam.

The multitude of entries ranged from the only Andrew Lloyd Webber song Elvis ever recorded, "It's Easy for You," to an entry on the U.S. Army captain who recruited Elvis back in 1958. Every song that was ever recorded by Elvis was analyzed even if it only appeared on a bootleg. One of the most informative parts discussed records that featured a sound-alike, not Elvis.

As in any book that attempted to be exhaustive about too many topics, this one had its share of misinformation and errors. For example, Fred Rose would be a little unhappy to learn that Leon Rose, not himself, wrote "Blue Eyes Crying in the Rain." The "Leon" may have been a misconstrual of the name of Fred's wife, Lorene, who shared some songwriting credits with her husband and held some on her own, at least one of which was recorded by Hank Williams.

At the end of the book, the authors discussed the Million Dollar Quartet session and how it came about. Johnny Cash was at Sun studio for a Carl Perkins session. Jerry Lee Lewis was there, too, playing piano. Elvis stopped by. Pictures were taken, then Cash left (though Cash has claimed he did not leave), so a trio was (supposedly) taped that day, not a quartet. The rest, as they have said, was history.

The Bibliographies and Source Listings

Beyond books, there is still a vast wealth of information on Elvis, in periodicals, newspapers, and other documents. To find it all, one would have to spend hours looking in periodical indices, library card catalogs, online systems, where they exist, and combing through individual unreferenced publications. Fortunately, three authors, Lee Cotten, Patsy Hammontree, and Wendy Sauers, compiled extensive bibliographies that contained every conceivable piece of Elvis literature and documentation (up to the time they were published).

In 1998, a fourth researcher, Robert Gentry of the *Sabine Register* (Many, Louisiana), quietly offered, for $34.98, a two-volume compendium of local (Shreveport) information on the Louisiana Hayride, which featured a myriad of details on Elvis' appearances there as well as stories on Hank Williams, Johnny Horton, and Faron Young. The actual radio logs from station KWKH were reproduced. Being able to read news stories on early Elvis refocused attention back to the incredible energy and musical talent that was the bedrock of his extraordinary, but all-too-short run in the public spotlight!

Cotten, Lee. *All Shook Up: Elvis Day-by-Day*. **Ann Arbor, Michigan: Pierian, 1985. 580 pp. Bibliography, index.**

Cotten complemented the compilations by both Hammontree and Sauers by giving the most extensive day-by-day chronological look at Elvis ever attempted. Any need to investigate specific details, time frames, or events could be satisfied by the information in Cotten's book. The listings began with Elvis' birth and ended when he died, leaving out the events and controversy surrounding his demise.

The entries in between were fascinating. Then there were the appendices, one of which offered a detailed discussion on Elvis' place in the Memphis music scene prior to July 1954, focusing on Elvis' growing musical capabilities, a view not often offered. Usually Elvis was portrayed as a musically ignorant truck driver who happened to want to cut a record for his mother. New evidence offered by the compilers of an RCA box set disputed that view by showing that Elvis cut at least one other record having nothing to do with his mother.

Hammontree, Patsy Guy. *Elvis Presley: A Bio-Bibliography.* **Westport, Connecticut: Greenwood, 1985.   301   pp. Chronology, filmography, discography, index.**

The work by Dr. Hammontree, a professor at the University of Tennessee, was a combination biography, bibliography of major source material, and chronicle of Elvis' film work and recordings. It was a major work and one that has become an essential starting place for any Elvis researcher. The biographical part, though all too brief, was well written and accurate.

It was obviously well researched, especially her conclusions on the real makeup of the Elvis audience. She discovered that Elvis fans came from all walks of life and all parts of the economic strata. The sources listed were in-depth and the critiques were very useful, steering the reader to the most obviously valuable ones.

Sauers, Wendy, compiler. *Elvis Presley: A Complete Reference.* **Jefferson, North Carolina: McFarland, 1984.   194 pp.   Index.**

When comparing Hammontree's book to the one by Sauers, the Sauers book, in its listing of source material, had a great deal more to offer. Sauers presented and discussed every conceivable piece of writing done on Elvis, even the mainly "fan" pieces. Her compilations were not strictly listings of media articles or reports. Some consisted of event-oriented entries, though the attempt to chronologically order Elvis' life was too limited.

The Discographies

With the release of the 1997 boxed set, *Platinum: A Life in Music,* RCA and a few other companies (such as Time-Life) have now made available almost everything Elvis was known to have recorded. Six "unreleased bonus cuts" appeared as part of a 1998 Time-Life six double-CD collection. The extensive notes accompanying most of the collections of Elvis' recorded works have more than adequately informed the public about every detail of every recorded track. So, why would anyone need to have extensive discographies in book form? The most useful publications either presented systematic views of all the releases and re-releases of recorded Elvis product or extensive session data (or both).

Banney, Howard. *Return to Sender: The First Complete Discography of Elvis Tribute and Novelty Records, 1956 - 1986.* **Photographs by Charles Weitz. Ann Arbor, Michigan: Pierian, 1987. 320 pp. Index.**

A most unique addition to the various listings of Elvis recordings was this compendium of more than a thousand song titles, complete with factual details about each song, that were either recorded as tributes to Elvis, mentioned him in some way, used an excerpt from a record, or imitated his style. Included were narratives, novelties, and soundalikes cut between 1956 and 1986. Weitz's photographs captured Elvis in some very relaxed poses. Another Ann Arbor press, Popular Culture, subsequently obtained this book for its catalog.

Barry, Ron. *All American Elvis: The Elvis Presley American Discography.* **Phillipsburg, New Jersey: Maxigraphics, 1976. 221 pp.**

Tunzi, Joseph A. *Elvis Sessions: The Recorded Music of Elvis Aaron Presley, 1953–1977.* **Introduction by Recording Engineer Al Pachucki. Chicago: JAT Productions, 1993. New edition 1996. 346 pp.**

Tunzi, Joseph. *The First Elvis Video Price and Reference Guide.* **Chicago: JAT Productions, 1988. 192 pp.**

Whisler, John A. *Elvis Presley: Reference Guide and Discography.* **Metuchen, New Jersey: Scarecrow, 1981. 258 pp. Song title index, general index.**

Barry, Tunzi, and Whisler all compiled amazing amounts of worthwhile information. Their finished products were simply not as exhaustive as the one by Ernst Jorgensen. Still, each one had merit, especially Whisler's, because it featured a lengthy bibliography in addition to the discography. While Tunzi's book was the most inclusive, Barry offered some advice on how to collect hard-to-find items. Though he also featured some innovative artwork, Barry limited his listings to American releases only.

Tunzi had another claim to fame. In 1988, he compiled the first Elvis Presley video guide. It contained listings of movie prints, promotional tapes, and foreign releases as part of its lengthy presentations. It also had pricing information, which was especially useful for obtaining items with limited distribution. A lot of movie stills (mostly black and white) complemented the various listings.

Tunzi's 1993 "sessions" book first came out through mail order only. Recently it appeared in a revised edition (412 pages) that quickly became even more useful than the first. There were many great photos along with the endless appendices covering gold and platinum records, concert lists, and even a limited bootleg section. Elvis' recording engineer and friend, Al Pachucki, wrote an inspiring introduction. As an added bonus, the second edition contained over one hundred new and unpublished photos.

Carr, Roy, and Mick Farren. *Elvis Presley: The Illustrated Record.* **London: Eel Pie, 1982. 192 pp. Discography.**

Hawkins, Martin, and Colin Escott. *Elvis: The Illustrated Discography.* **London: Omnibus, 1981. Originally published as** *The Elvis Session File: 20 Years of Elvis***, 1974. 96 pp. Selected bibliography.**

The books by Carr and Hawkins, both published in England, presented some very complex and useful listings. The Carr book, part of a series presented by Eel Pie Press, unearthed considerably more detail. For example, while Hawkins and Escott listed the backing musicians for a 1965 (*Frankie and Johnny* soundtrack) session as unknown, Carr and Farren completely listed, by name, all musicians involved. Overall, the biggest weakness of the Hawkins and Escott book was its failure to more completely identify the session players.

Hawkins listed sessions first, then recordings, all in chronological order, while Carr compiled the sessions, recordings, and commercial releases together under each year. Carr also presented the best pictorials, showing Elvis on the cover of *TV Guide*, some great publicity shots of the King with Ann-Margret, and a whole slew of Vegas poses. Featured were clippings, commentary, and copies of ads that caught the rise and growth of the Elvis phenomenon, including a lengthy list of concerts. The discography of Elvis' British releases was one of the best ever done. Unfortunately, both books have been superseded by newest version of Ernst Jorgensen's book.

Cotten, Lee, and Howard A. DeWitt. *Jailhouse Rock: The Bootleg Records of Elvis Presley 1970–1983.* **Authorized by Elvis Presley Enterprises. Ann Arbor, Michigan: Pierian, 1983. 367 pp. Label index, personal name index.**

Cotten's work stood as the perfect complement to Ernst Jorgensen's discographical treatise because it presented details on recordings Jorgensen did not include, the bootlegs. They were unauthorized recordings, which usually consisted of live or demo cuts. Cotten only covered a fourteen-year period. Fortunately, that was the most productive span for illegal Elvis recordings. The first Elvis bootleg came out of Europe in 1970, under the title, *Please Release Me*.

Much of the fourteen-year period covered a time when Elvis was traveling extensively, which was right up until his death. Elvis' death and its aftermath, of course, generated so much more demand for product, especially concert material. The bootlegs, though subject to confiscation if discovered by legal authorities, have always been extremely valuable as insights into Elvis' concert work and the chemistry between fan and idol. Cotten's work has become the standard for bootleg discographies.

Dowling, Paul. *Elvis: The Ultimate Album Cover Book*. New York: Harry N. Abrams, 1996.

Though this book was intended to be one of those art books filled with pictures of Elvis as he appeared on a huge variety of album and other record covers, it turned out to be one of the best pictorial listings of his many American and foreign releases. It began with pictures of the "A" sides of his five Sun Records singles. The remainder of the book was devoted to the pictures used on foreign and American RCA LPs, EPs, and singles.

Foreign "various artists" releases were also depicted. Along with Elvis cuts (and his picture on the cover), there were cuts by such other RCA artists as Eartha Kitt, Harry Belafonte, and even "the female Elvis" Janis Martin. The last picture presented in the book was an especially poignant one, a somber-looking Elvis. It embraced the cover of the 1985 album, *Reconsider Baby*. The author, Dowling, has a collection of more than seven thousand Elvis recordings.

Jorgensen, Ernst. *Elvis Presley: A Life in Music: The Complete Recording Sessions*. Foreword by Peter Guralnick. New York: St. Martin's, 1998. 454 pp. Discography, outtakes, index. First published as *Elvis Recording Sessions*, Denmark, 1984. Published in the United States in 1993 by Popular Culture as *Reconsider Baby: The Definitive Elvis Sessionography, 1954-1977*, Ann Arbor, Michigan, credited to Ernst Jorgensen, Erik Rasmussen, and Johnny Mikkelson.

Jorgensen's work was, in a word, exhaustive. It has become the best public record of Elvis' sessions and subsequent recordings and told where and when Elvis did each specific recording. It tracked down the origin of each cut, which has been difficult to follow due to many recompilations. The level of detail was not intended for casual reading. Not only were the names of session players presented, for example, but the names of the recording engineers as well. Full reproductions of session sheets and notes were often included.

By the late 1990s, the small press that published the book, Popular Culture, had to tell customers the book had gone out of print and, though listed in their catalogs, was no longer available. The choice was not theirs, but Jorgensen's. He had parlayed his session knowledge into being given the job as producer of RCA's latest Elvis boxed set, *Platinum: A Life in Music,* which compiled, even after all these years, many unreleased recordings such as Bob Dylan's "Blowin' in the Wind" and a 1953 demo of "I'll Never Stand in Your Way."

That recognition enabled him to get his newest version (1998) as published by St. Martin's Press under the title *Elvis Presley: A Life in Music: The Complete Recording Sessions.* Jorgensen was listed as the only author and Peter Guralnick added a foreword. This newest edition was even more comprehensive and historically detailed. For example, Jorgensen compiled the first alphabetical cataloging of outtakes, in which he listed not only the takes but the albums on which the various completed (and edited) tracks could be located. All of Elvis' albums, even posthumous ones, were referenced in the session listings.

Any reader, casual or otherwise, could readily discover how Elvis learned about fuzz tone or how he was introduced to Bob Dylan's "Tomorrow Is a Long Time." Incidentally, he first heard it not as a Dylan recording, but as a track on the album *Odetta Sings Dylan.* The record belonged to Charlie Hodge and Elvis had become quite taken with that particular song.

Peters, Richard. *Elvis: The Music Lives On: The Recording Sessions, 1954-1976.* **London: Pop Universal/Souvenir, 1992. 144 pp. List of studio sessions.**

Peters has been a busy author, writing books on Frank Sinatra, Buddy Holly, and Barry Manilow. He had previously done an Elvis tribute book that was published through the British Elvis fan club in 1984, entitled *Elvis: The Golden Anniversary Tribute.* In 1985 it was published in the U.S. by Salem House.

This Peters book presented a great deal of historical discussion about Elvis' recording sessions. Considerable information came from the archives of the Official Elvis Presley Fan Club of Great Britain (the Todd Slaughter organization). While Jorgensen offered more detail, Peters presented more background material, down to a picture of Elvis playing drums. Some of the background was superfluous but fascinating, such as the description of the RCA Records office used by Felton Jarvis, one of Elvis' favorite producers.

The book began with a blow-by-blow depiction of the last recording session Elvis did. It was set up by Jarvis and held at Graceland in October 1976. Interestingly, the session ended November 1 when it became obvious that Elvis "had clearly lost interest." Jarvis recalled that the last topic he and Elvis discussed, during a visit at Graceland in early summer 1977, was Elvis' desire to tour Europe and Japan. Jarvis felt that Elvis' mood that day was such that he "didn't seem like he had a care or worry in the world."

Robertson, John. *The Complete Guide to the Music of Elvis Presley*. **London: Omnibus, 1994. 118 pp.**

Robertson's work was newer and more entertaining than the other discographies, especially in its written commentary about each recording, album, and collection. It was a perfect companion to Jorgensen's work, especially the section detailing Elvis' concert recordings. As an artist, Robertson concluded that Elvis "squandered his talent" largely because he did what he was told. Elvis "abhorred conflict," especially in dealings with the Colonel.

The main presentation of Elvis' recorded legacy began with the appraisal that Elvis had done about a hundred of the finest recordings ever, along with some of the most hilarious and inane mistakes any artist ever made. The detailed entry on Sun Records' Million Dollar Quartet has been, to date, the best and most informative explanation of that set of tapes. In his appraisal of Elvis' final years, Robertson felt that "in 1968 and 1969, Elvis made the finest records of his career." Overall, Robertson showed where various Elvis recordings have ended up especially on albums and collections, specifically compact discs.

Townson, John, Gordon Minto, and George Richardson. *Elvis UK: The Ultimate Guide to Elvis Presley's British Record Releases, 1956-1986*. **London: Blandford, 1987.**

RCA released Elvis albums worldwide. They did not, however, always release the same singles and albums in different countries, creating a vast collector's market for foreign Elvis recordings. Townson has compiled a complete listing of the releases RCA created specifically for Britain. Some of the American and British releases did overlap, but for the most part, especially on the compilations, there were wide-ranging differences. The pictures used by RCA specifically for England were fascinating.

9

A Mess of Blues:
THE ELVIS LITERATURE

Elvis was the last of our sacred cows
to be publicly mutilated.

−Lester Bangs,
Elvis Presley: The Rebel Years

The Elvis Commentaries

Several collections of Elvis commentaries have been compiled. Together, they have become essential items in that under a single set of covers they amassed some of the most diverse ideas about who Elvis was. Additionally, they delved deeply into the basis for his massive appeal, and the factors that have contributed to the cult-in-making situation evolving after his death.

From all the views presented, one could most readily understand Elvis' place in American pop culture and how he became such a factor. Could one understand Elvis, the human being? Elvis was no longer human, he had been elevated, in the words of the editors of the *Southern Reader,* to "the status of an academic discipline." Elvis' role in popular American culture became the basis for college courses.

Chadwick, Vernon, editor. *In Search of Elvis: Music, Race, Art, Religion.* **Boulder, Colorado: Westview, 1997. 294 pp. Notes, index.**

This book represents the results of the first annual international conference on Elvis, held in 1995 at the University of Mississippi. Elvis has now become an important enough factor in American popular culture to rate an entire conference centered around studying the phenomenon he has become. Chadwick, the editor, holds a doctorate in comparative literature. He set up, earlier in the nineties, a comprehensive-college level course to study Elvis (Elvisology).

In his view, Elvis was "a rebellious, radicalizing force of democracy, equal opportunity, and free expression." Viewing Elvis in that light, the conference examined his Southern background, place in popular music, and the religious aspects of his death. Contributors included Bill Malone, who wrote the definitive history of country music; Ernst Jorgensen, compiler of the definitive Elvis sessionography; Ger Rijff, who assembled an extensive Elvis "scrapbook" as well as more than a dozen other publications; and Neal and Janice Gregory, who extensively investigated Elvis' death.

There was nothing outlandish presented in this book. The writings were all done in a very serious, scholarly fashion. Overall, they made the case that the study of Elvis as a very serious force in shaping American popular culture was an area that needed to grow and generate much more research. Chadwick concluded that "Elvis names the funky intersection of music, race, art, and religion," because he was "the first full-fledged creation of modern media."

Not everyone in academia has agreed that the study of Elvis, as Chadwick and others have done it, has been an outstanding endeavor. Karal Ann Marling, a professor of Art History and author of the definitive book on Graceland, wrote recently, in the *New York Times*, about what she saw as "determined efforts on the part of academia to render him unappetizing and dull." To her, "the best known example of scholarship run amok in the name of the King came in August of 1995, at the first annual International Conference on Elvis, mounted at the University of Mississippi in Oxford."

Chadwick's reason for studying Elvis was that the King embodied rebellion and the undermining of the status quo. Dr. Marling saw a particular humor in the idea that an academician could ever hope to understand the Elvis phenomenon, noting that "professors are viewed as dull, long-winded, badly dressed and out of touch," while Elvis was "the most deeply cool human being who ever wiggled across this planet in spangles." That led her to ask how "could a professor in elbow patches and tweed ever hope to comprehend that profound, unspeakable state of grace?" She did have a point, which was "to be as cool as Elvis is to be beyond the scope of mortal discourse," meaning that if anyone were to ever understand the Elvis phenomenon, it won't be university scholars.

Clayson, Alan, and Spencer Leigh, editors. *Aspects of Elvis: Tryin' to Get to You*. Selective bibliography by Alan Clayson. Complete discography of official Elvis Presley recordings 1953–1977 by Peter Doggett. London: Sidgwick & Jackson, 1994. 346 pp. Index.

The discography by Peter Doggett was among the best done on "official" Elvis releases. As a British book, the focus was on the best of British rock and roll commentary. Among the highlights was an article by Todd Slaughter, president of the biggest Elvis fan club. In it he quoted the Colonel as saying Elvis would not appear in England because there were no "big venues." To counter the view that Elvis never left the country because the Colonel had to hide his illegal alien status, Slaughter claimed the Colonel had traveled outside the United States and "never hid his Dutch origins." The Colonel would even "talk with Dutch fans in their language."

Topics of other articles were the Elvis movie soundtracks, the greatness of his voice, Elvis relative to James Dean as an idol, Elvis' management, his family, and even a commentary on Albert Goldman's commentaries. Other insightful articles covered Elvis in Art and the Elvis stamp. The book was fully indexed, a very important plus.

Quain, Kevin, editor. *The Elvis Reader: Texts and Sources on the King of Rock 'n' Roll.* **Preface by Mojo Nixon. New York: St. Martin's, 1992. 344 pp. Filmography, documentaries, television specials, selected reading list, bibliography, index.**

Quain's book contained, in addition to a collection of some exemplary analytical works, detailed listings on other readings along with details about Elvis' films, documentaries, and television specials. It was introduced by Mojo Nixon, a performer who has done some of the most interesting and bizarre "tributes" to the King, including one that celebrated his being "everywhere." One of the pieces on Elvis' music, written by Charles Wolfe, squarely placed him in the gospel music tradition. Not only did Elvis' musical style derive from that form of music, he used his own popularity to promote it.

The best piece for placing Elvis' continued popularity in context was the one done by Nick Tosches, entitled "Elvis in Death." In it, he not only poked fun at the worshipful reverence accorded Elvis' legend, he pointed out how writers like Ilona Panta and Larry Geller have come close to insinuating that Elvis may have been the Son of God. To Tosches, "Elvis was the last great mystery, the secret of which lay unrevealed even to himself."

Tharpe, Jac L., editor. *Elvis: Images and Fancies.* **Jackson, Mississippi: University Press of Mississippi, 1979. Reprinted 1980. 179 pp.**

Tharpe compiled a very useful and incisive "reader" that contained some of the best nonfiction articles on Elvis. Some of the contributors completed their research thanks to funding from grants for the study of American culture. The article that analyzed Elvis' innovative vocal style brought back into focus the basis for Elvis' greatness. With all the hoopla surrounding Elvis' afterlife, his musical talents have too often been passed over.

One of the most in-depth studies analyzed the various views of Elvis found in national periodicals. Another thoroughly dissected the relationship between Elvis and his audience. Though there were views from Australia and Thailand, one of the most unusual articles was by Richard Middleton, which contended that Elvis' two contributions to rock and roll were "romantic lyricism" and "boogification." Since the book's initial publication as a university press hardcover book, it has been re-released as a trade paperback from Da Capo Press of New York.

The Literature and Humor Books

An icon as all-encompassing as Elvis had to become the subject of at least one novel not limited to perspectives based on fact but which could be as absurd or creative as possible. As it has turned out, Elvis became the subject of several very good fictional tales. The first of this genre was supposedly written in 1961 by Cleo C. Baker. As a seventy-two page book, the story line, about Elvis playing in a football game, was not developed very deeply. That was probably why the book wasn't published until 1978.

Overall, the literature books ranged from a novel featuring a pitiful impersonator known as the "big" Elvis to a fanciful tale in which a possible life story was constructed for Elvis' dead twin, Jesse, had he lived. Some very humorous takeoffs were also published, focusing especially on people's reactions to Elvis' death. Finally, two readers collected various literary works that centered on Elvis.

The fictional books chosen for this part had to be largely about Elvis or have Elvis, in some way, play a major part or impact the story in some grand way. Greil Marcus, in his book, *Mystery Train: Images of America in Rock 'n' Roll Music*, saw two novels, both written prior to 1977, as being largely about Elvis even if in a less obvious, more detached setting. The first novel he cited was Harlan Ellison's *Spider Kiss*, published by Pyramid (of New York) in 1975. The book was first marketed in 1961 with the title *Rockabilly*.

To Marcus, it chronicled "the rise-and-inevitable-fall of a Southern flash." The major characters included "a soul-searching flack (the narrator), a Col. Tom-style manager," and "a rockabilly hero who is not only a great big hype but a natural artist whose genius no evil, including his own, can ever quite snuff." Marcus' appraisal was that "out of these materials comes a story that makes sense, and an ending with some real tragedy in it."

The other novel Marcus singled out was Nik Cohn's *King Death*, published in New York by Harcourt Brace Jovanovich (also in 1975). In Cohn's book the main character was not only a pop star but a killer with the stage name King Death. By no accident, according to Marcus, the star/killer was from Tupelo, Mississippi. Marcus also advised that "the book's dedication makes it clear that King Death is none other than the risen ghost of Jesse Garon Presley, Elvis's dead twin: in other words, a version of Elvis himself."

While no other novels were noted by Marcus, he did especially praise the way in which a specific passage from William Price Fox's *Dixiana Moon* built Elvis' death into an ongoing narrative. The passage Marcus admired so much featured "a young New Yorker and an old-time Southern hustler" on a drive through the South when the New Yorker hears an old Elvis Sun Records single on the radio: "Wonder what he was like," he says to his tent-show mentor. "He wasn't like anyone," says the would-have-been Col. Parker. "You start trying to compare Elvis to something and you can forget it. . . . Bo, all you can do with a talent that big and that different is sort of point at it when you see it going by, and maybe listen for the ricochet."

Benson, Bernard. *The Minstrel.* **New York: G. P. Putnam's Sons, 1977. [unnumbered].**

Though nothing in the title or the actual story line specifically referred to Elvis, the dedication for, foreword to, and description of the book left no doubt as to its inspiration. The book was specifically dedicated "to the living memory of Elvis Presley." The foreword described the "great gift" that Elvis possessed. The jacket notes stated that Benson "wrote *The Minstrel* as a personal gift for Elvis." It came out initially in a leatherbound edition that sold for $250. Currently that edition, as a clean, near mint copy, would sell for at least $2,500.

Benson's wife introduced him to Elvis' music well after he had personally undertaken his own study of Tibetan philosophy. What really attracted Benson to Elvis was the statement by a Tibetan lama, made after the lama saw Elvis on television. He concluded after the show, that "there is a very good man." The actual book was a very general simplistic tale of a young troubadour who was reincarnated into different lifetimes several centuries apart, each time bringing inspiration, peace, love, and joy to people throughout the world. The writing was very uplifting and inspiring.

At the end, Benson explained the role of a peacock feather. He said not only did Elvis love peacocks, but the feather itself had strong esoteric value. It symbolized a creature that thrived on poisonous plants and transmuted them into something good and beautiful. In Benson's words, Elvis embodied the essential desire to do good.

If one merely read the text of the book and not the author's commentary, one might find nothing especially relevant to Elvis. Yet, one of Elvis' closest friends, Charlie Hodge, called it "the truest story about Elvis ever written." The security chief at Graceland, Dick Grob, concurred, saying "the book is probably the truest story of Elvis that could have been written, especially from a spiritual standpoint."

Bleasdale, Alan. *Are You Lonesome Tonight?* **Boston: Faber & Faber, 1985.   96 pp.**

Among the fictional works about Elvis, there have been several comic books (which have not been included) and one two-part play, *Are You Lonesome Tonight?* (the title taken from an Elvis single). Bleasdale's 1985 drama featured an older and younger Elvis, both of whose lives centered around the intake of food, from hash browns and bacon to numerous fried eggs and much more.   The script was heartbreaking because it concentrated on Elvis' decline; yet at times it was quite entertaining. The Colonel, Elvis' father, mother, and wife characters acted out lifelike supporting parts.   Interestingly, Elvis' Memphis Mafia companions were not written into the script.

Bourgeau, Art. *The Elvis Murders.* **New York: Charter Books, 1986.   216 pp.**

DeMarco, Gordon. *Elvis in Aspic.* **Portland, Oregon: West Coast Crime, 1993.**

The first premise of the Bourgeau novel was that Elvis did not die in 1977. As the fast-paced action got underway, a plot to murder the aging King of Rock and Roll unfolded. Beyond naming Elvis and describing his aging lifestyle, the book could have been about anybody and any murder. The twists and turns were contrived and the writing style was amateurish at best.

DeMarco's book, from a small Oregon press that specialized in "detective-type" novels, could only be assessed as ho-hum.   It probably sold some more copies by featuring Elvis' name than it would have without it. The story could have utilized any celebrity name and still have been as uneventful.

Charters, Samuel. *Elvis Presley Calls His Mother After the Ed Sullivan Show.* **Minneapolis, Minnesota: Coffee House, 1992. 104 pp.**

Charters has been known, over the years, for his nonfiction books on the blues. He has covered "race" music, country blues, and the "poetry" of the blues. While his grip on his subjects has always been incisive, his writing style was usually quite dry, analytical, and pedantic. Similarly plodding and slow, this book quickly dropped from the marketplace and went out of print.

The script concentrated on Elvis explaining to his mother how he felt about his life at the moment. Inserted where appropriate were answers from his mother and asides to allow for comments from other characters. The Elvis monologues were long and rambling and though they might have reflected the author's concepts of Elvis, they failed to capture the unusual bond between son and mother.

Childress, Mark. *Tender.* **New York: Harmony, 1990. 566 pp.**

The Childress book was inspired by real people, though it was intended solely as a work of fiction. The parallels were obvious. The lead character was a rock and roll star who was born in Tupelo, Mississippi. From there, the book was riveting, partly to see how close the parallels to real life were and partly because the inside story on rock and roll music was gripping and detailed.

The classic fiction writer, Stephen King, clearly understood that the Childress book was "more inside rock and roll than about it." Actually, Childress went deeper into the Presley musical world than that. As another writer pointed out, almost every musician had a Bill Monroe (bluegrass artist) song that inspired them. "Blue Moon of Kentucky," according to Childress, was Elvis' Monroe song.

Committee to Elect the King, the. *Elvis for President.* **New York: Crown, 1992. 60 pp.**

The impact Elvis' death had, and its aftermath, spilled over from recordings and serious non fiction writings to humorous pieces that tended to deprecate that impact. For instance, the "committee to elect the King" obviously poked fun not just at Elvis but at the whole political process by showing there were just as many reasons to elect a dead Elvis as there were a live politician. After all, Elvis already had a stamp, a distinguished (?) military career, and hadn't inhaled since 1977, so who better to run this country? Beyond similar sarcastic observations, this short book offered little else.

Duff, Gerald. *That's All Right, Mama: The Unauthorized Life of Elvis's Twin.* **Dallas, Texas: Baskerville, 1995.   278 pp.**

Maughon, Robert Mickey, M. D. *Elvis Is Alive.* **Kodak, Tennessee: Cinnamon Moon, 1997.   254 pp.**

Womack, Jack. *Elvissey: A Novel of Elvis Past and Elvis Future.* **New York: Tom Doherty Associates, 1993.   319 pp.**

Duff, Maughon, and Womack took off-the-wall approaches to their fictionalized accounts of some bizarre aspects of Elvis' life. Duff's main character was more than just an Elvis impersonator. He was secretly Elvis' twin, Jesse, believed to have died at birth. Though Duff's look into the world of Elvis impersonation was fascinating, his speculation on what might have happened had Elvis' twin lived was, at best, only mildly interesting. Actually, the idea of a secret life of an assumed-to-be-dead person worked better when seen as a way of poking fun at the growing number of "Elvis lives" theories.

Maughon's impersonator, found in Paris, turned out to be the "real" Elvis, who confessed to faking his death in 1977. The book's hero was Memphis coroner, Dr. Robert St. John, who went from exhuming Elvis' grave to searching for the "living" Elvis. The author's profession was listed as being in the medical arena, not the literary, which accounted for the book's interesting premise yet pedestrian writing style.

Womack satirized the idea that Elvis may have been a very special spiritual person. He created a couple that traveled through time to kidnap Elvis and make him into a near-deity. Did that sound implausible? It would be as good a way as any to explain the burgeoning growth of an Elvis religion and the near worship accorded his memory by his many fans. And, it was no more implausible than another, albeit very poorly constructed, novel, Jack Yeovil's *Comeback Tour*, which had Elvis fighting the KKK, swamp mutants, and voodoo practitioners.

Flinn, Mary C. *Elvis in Oz: New Stories and Poems from the Hollins Creative Writing Program.* **Charlottesville: University Press of Virginia, 1992.**

Gilmore, Brian. *Elvis Presley Is Alive and Well and Living in Harlem.* **New York: Third World, 1992.**

Flinn's compilation of writings from the the Hollins Creative Writing Program showed that although it turned out some very interesting and creative work, most of the writing was not done for the purpose of enlightening anyone about Elvis. Mostly, Elvis' name got invoked but other than that he was not the center of these inventive, creative short pieces. In another 1992 book, Gilmore wrote a poetic work that captured the racial dichotomies underlying the Elvis phenomenon. Born and raised in Washington, D.C., Gilmore was attending the District of Columbia Law School at the same time he was turning out some highly unique and racially incisive poetry.

Friedman, Kinky. *Elvis, Jesus & Coca-Cola.* **New York: Simon & Schuster, 1993.   256 pp.**

Shankman, Sarah. *The King Is Dead.* **New York: Pocket Books, 1992.   275 pp.**

The above two mystery novels touched on Elvis and his environment but did not specifically incorporate him into their tales. The first, from 1992, was by Sarah Shankman, entitled, *The King Is Dead*, the fifth in her series of Samantha Adams whodunits. The action took place in a world Elvis once inhabited, specifically Tupelo and other settings such as the Elvis Memorial McDonald's. Some strange, very Southern characters discussed Elvis a lot. One observed that he "went from poor white trash to rich white trash."

Singer/songwriter Kinky Friedman (composer of sarcastic gems like "Ride 'Em Jewboy") turned from composing and performing to writing mystery novels that starred his persona as a Greenwich Village detective. In late 1997, he authored a novel entitled *Road Kill* that turned a plot to kill Willie Nelson into the main story line. In 1993, he wrote *Elvis, Jesus & Coca-Cola*, a title that incorporated three major icons, from popular culture (Elvis), religion (Jesus), and the business world (Coca-Cola).

While Elvis himself was not central to the plot there were some hilarious asides involving him, such as the revelation by one of the characters, Ratso, that when Elvis' grandmother died, she revealed, "Ah'm a Jeeeeeeeewww!" That was right after Ratso let out that Elvis used to send Priscilla out at four in the morning for Polaroid film. Elvis has become such an icon that every conceivable weird foible about him has in some way permeated the fabric and folklore of our culture.

Grizzard, Lewis. *Elvis Is Dead and I Don't Feel So Good Myself.* **Atlanta, Georgia: Peachtree, 1984. 269 pp.**

Grizzard the columnist has written, over the years, many short pieces that he has then collected and issued as full-length books. Most of them were witty, insightful works that, though thought-provoking, did not necessarily fit together as a cohesive book. Although Elvis was mentioned in the title of this book, that didn't mean Elvis was the subject of the entire book. In the first article, "A Last Toast to the King," Grizzard ruminated on Elvis' death.

When he first heard about it, his reaction was that it had to be joke. Then after the reality sunk in, Grizzard said he was hit by another reality, that Elvis "died straining for a bowel movement." After that, he spent much of the next "seven years hoping against hope that it wasn't true." Read this book if you like Grizzard, not to learn about Elvis or find out very much of what Grizzard thought about Elvis.

Henderson, William McCranor. *Stark Raving Elvis.* **London: W. H. Allen, 1985.**

This was one of the first novels to involve Elvis in its story line. The lead character was a factory worker (on an assembly line) as well as a part-time Elvis impersonator. As the performances and the story evolved, sometimes in an amusing fashion, the impersonator began to believe that somehow Elvis had anointed him the heir apparent. In real life, Henderson has served as an English professor at North Carolina State University.

He has also performed (near where he lives) as a "gentler, noncompetitive" Elvis impersonator. He wrote a book about working as one of hundreds of such pretenders, entitled *I, Elvis: Confessions of a Counterfeit King* and published (in 1997) by Boulevard Books of New York. Two years later (1999), Henderson's wife, Carol, summarized (for *The Oxford American*) her views on her husband's appearances as an impersonator, saying, "I'm sorry – call me a snob – but I don't 'get' Elvis, even when he is my husband."

Kalpakian, Laura. *Graced Land.* **New York: Grove, 1992. 264 pp.**

While Elvis was central to this novel, he was not the main character. Joyce Jackson, a woman driven to an existence dependent on public assistance, was. She wanted to carry on for Elvis, not as a rock and roll star, but as a benevolent person. The welfare people considered her a fraud.

The newest social worker sent to work with her discovered not a corrupt person but an indomitable woman who had made it through life despite being abandoned first by her father then by her husband (on the day Elvis died in 1977). She rose above her traumas because Elvis' music not only kept her going, it inspired her. The regular interspersing of his songs into the story had a dual purpose of uplifting the main character and preventing the entire book from being weighted down by an excess of sentimentality.

Kluge, P. F. *Biggest Elvis*. New York: Penguin, 1996. 341 pp.

The Biggest Elvis was actually one of a trio of impersonators. Each impersonator represented one of three sides of Elvis, from Baby Elvis to Dude Elvis (the movie Elvis) culminating in the Biggest. Their performances took place, of all locales, near a large United States naval base in the Philippines.

Then something happened to the "Biggest" Elvis. For very specific reasons he had to be eliminated. That's when the mystery started, which consumed most of the rest of the book. All of it was intertwined with a societal fascination for the "dead" Elvis and the growing decadence of our culture from an overseas perspective.

Peabody, Richard, and Lucinda Ebersole, editors. *Mondo Elvis: A Collection of Stories and Poems About Elvis*. New York: St. Martin's, 1994. 228 pp.

Sloan, Kay, and Constance Pierce, editors. *Elvis Rising: Stories on the King*. New York: Avon, 1993. 262 pp.

Mondo Elvis and *Elvis Rising* were collections of fictional works about Elvis, his influence on people or their lives, and societal implications. Some works were duplicated across the two books, but by and large both collections were unique. There were poems, short stories, and book excerpts, all of which were critically excellent.

The folks who brought you *Mondo Elvis* previously brought you *Mondo Barbie* (the doll!). Some of the work was new and unique, including the writings of Nick Cave and Janice Eidus. Other excerpts came from works that were previously published, works by authors such as Greil Marcus and Mark Winegardner.

The selections included in *Elvis Rising* were bound by their attempt to explain the Elvis charisma. The two editors wrote in their introduction that "Elvis is a cultural phenomenon like none other." One story examined Elvis in the context of why people need larger-than-life heros. The story that best captured the hold Elvis had on some people was the one which centered around a ballplayer whose wife orgasmed based on a poster of Elvis on the bedroom wall.

Sammon, Paul M.   *The King Is Dead: Tales of Elvis Postmortem*.   New York: Dell, 1994.   380 pp.

Sammon's book was a collection of recent short fiction, many quite bizarre. One story had Elvis meeting Godzilla while another speculated on the life of his long-dead twin. All of the stories were well written, fun, innovative, and imaginative, especially David Morrell's, which delved into the absurdity of teaching Elvis at the college level. That would put Elvis right up there with "Victorian Culture" and "Nineteenth Century American Culture."

Some of the humor veered toward sarcasm, as in the story about "the sacred treasures of Graceland." On the other end of the spectrum Roger Ebert contributed a review on the only movie about Elvis worth seeing, *This Is Elvis*. In his opinion the film rated three and one-half stars (out of four). Overall, the effect and tone of this book were to poke fun at the "Elvis is alive" phenomenon, while delving into why there was such a phenomenon at all.

Follow That Dream:
THE ELVIS COLLECTIBLES AND VISUALS

> I once traded an Andy Warhol "Elvis Presley" painting
> for a sofa. I always wanted to tell Andy what a stupid
> thing I'd done, and if he had another painting he
> would give me, I'd never do it again.
>
> –Bob Dylan,
> *Yakety Yak: The Midnight Confessions and*
> *Revelations of Thirty-Seven Rock Stars and Legends*

The Guides to Collectibles

Elvis has survived, through books, fan clubs, recordings, and reruns of his various films. During his lifetime, he was so isolated from his public that, for almost everyone, access to him came only through those same venues. Maybe someone couldn't see or touch Elvis but he or she could own a hand-painted picture of him on a collectible plate, an Elvis clock, an Elvis reading lamp, or even an Elvis telephone.

Author Patricia Jobe Pierce put the Elvis collectibles phenomenon into perspective when she observed that "whenever a new product becomes available, devotees rush to purchase it." She was referring to Elvis products and "millions" of people purchasing them. Even in the nineties, she discovered that "millions of fans still flock to purchase items made with Elvis's image or name on them."

As far as the future goes, she wrote that "Elvis is a media sensation with no obvious saturation level." That would explain why, beyond those of other deceased public figures, Elvis items have gained an unprecedented place in people's lives. Elvis Presley Enterprises has done a great marketing job. Right from the start, of course, Colonel Parker's main thrust in marketing Elvis was through souvenir sales, all the way from concerts to drugstores.

However, the zealousness of collectors and fans cannot be underestimated. In a recent auction, a unique copy of *Elvis' Christmas Album* fetched a record-high bid (the most money ever offered for a Christmas record of any kind). Though he did not disclose the amount (in his statement), Gordon Wrubel, president of Good Rockin' Tonight, the company that held the record auction, observed, "Elvis remains the most avidly collected rock and roll artist."

Over the years many Elvis items have merited high bids at numerous auctions. In a book (entitled *Rock and Roll Memorabilia*) not exclusively devoted to Elvis, Hilary Kay pictured some of the items that attracted the most interest at various auction houses, like Sotheby's and Christie's. She captured busts of the King, an Elvis radio telephone, an original *Roustabout* poster, along with other collectibles that have rated top-dollar bids.

Many homes have a picture of John or Robert Kennedy or both. Even more have Elvis statues, records, magazines, and prayer mats. Elvis lives on, not in Kalamazoo or Alabama, but in memories, movies, music, and memorabilia. People drink their liquor, not from an old fruit jar, but from an Elvis statue decanter. They can even move their personal computer mouse on an Elvis mousepad after they have played Elvisopoly.

Elvis collectibles have not only spawned entrepreneurial ventures, but a whole host of Elvis collectibles experts. Some of the biggest names in the expertise area, who have compiled books on the topic, have been Steve Templeton and Jerry Osborne. They, first and foremost, became experts in collecting. Osborne has not only covered Elvis items, but rare and out-of-print recordings in all areas of popular music. Not one of the experts, except Osborne, has delved very far into Elvis book collecting, and he only did it as an adjunct to his more thorough presentations of the Elvis recordings.

Others, who have written books on collecting Elvis, started out as collectors only and got into writing books about collecting primarily as a means of sharing information with other collectors. The most well-known individuals in this category have been Rosalind Cranor, Pauline Bartel, and Joni Mabe. Bartel began as a member of a large Elvis fan club. Mabe's collection, complete with items she made, has grown into a traveling show.

In this section, the discussion of Elvis collecting has obviously centered on only the published books about the subject. There are also experts in the field who have not authored some kind of manual or guide. One such person initially gained fame as a member of the Elvis Memphis Mafia, the group about whom Elvis once said, "They aren't employees. These boys are my friends from down home." That person (or "friend") was Joe Esposito.

With such close access to Elvis, it was not a stretch for him to become an Elvis collectibles expert. Even though he has not authored a book on collecting Elvis, he has contributed a regular column, "Esposito on Elvis," to a collector's magazine, *Pop Culture Collecting: Memories & Memorabilia*. One of his best columns focused on the 1997 version of Elvis week in Memphis, where an estimated 25,000 people participated in a candlelight vigil at Graceland.

An earlier column was more representative of his message to collectors, however, its topic being Elvis' wardrobe and dressing habits. Not only did Esposito discuss "wearable" souvenirs, he gave a number of insights into Elvis' personal habits and assumptions. For example, Elvis liked boots because even though he was an even six feet tall, he aspired to be taller. He also abhorred blue jeans because "jeans were a sign of poverty to him."

As a celebrity, Elvis felt he should be like the old Hollywood stars, who, in his eyes, always maintained "a good image in public." Stars, in his estimation, were meant to be "good role models for kids to look up to." He was "an entertainer 24 hours a day." According to Esposito, Elvis would have been appalled by superstars who "walk around in T-shirts and shabby old jeans." At one point in his life, Elvis even decided (based on a book he had just read) that certain colors had healing powers, especially purple. Therefore, for quite a while, Elvis wore a lot of purple shirts and scarves.

Bartel, Pauline. *Everything Elvis: Your Ultimate Sourcebook to the Memorabilia, Souvenirs, and Collectibles of the King!* **Dallas: Taylor, 1995.   172 pp.   Bibliography.**

Bartel was the author of one of the better books on Elvis' film career. Here, she has outdone herself and about anyone else who has collected Elvis. To begin with, she wrote directly to collectors, gathering information on everything from how to start collecting to adding to an existing collection, regardless of the level. Major sections were included on how to find memorabilia, from statues to books. She even advised on how to get what was desired at an auction, or, on the other hand, how to sell or trade from an existing collection.

She also explained how to judge authenticity, how to get into the network of collectors already in existence, as well as how to display and care for valuable collectibles. The information included addresses of suppliers and fan clubs, ways to insure a collection, and even the return policies of those entrepreneurs who sell Elvis items. The list of sources for acquiring old and new records was one of the lengthiest ever compiled. The list of books on Elvis was one of the most complete ever assembled (in a collectibles guide), especially the more obscure ones.

She made some very aggressive plans for the future, inviting readers to inform her of anything that should be included in future editions. Her expressed goal was to make her book "the definitive reference for Elvis collectors." As collector and author, she wrote that she spends her time "sniffing out and pawing through display cases at collectible shows, bins at movie memorabilia shops, and buy-and-sell ads in collector magazines." She has kept "her eye on the prize," remembering that, where souvenirs and memorabilia are concerned, especially those worth a lot of money, "half the fun is the pursuit."

Buskin, Richard. *Elvis: Memories and Memorabilia.* **London: Salamander, 1995.   96 pp.   Bibliography.**

Templeton, Steve. *Elvis!: An Illustrated Guide to New and Vintage Collectibles.* **London: Quintet, 1996.   Published in the United States by Courage Books/Running Press, Philadelphia.   128 pp.   List of where to buy items, list of films, discography, index.**

Buskin and Templeton both placed their emphasis on photographing and explaining some of the most unique Elvis collectibles. They showed lunch boxes, magazines, belt buckles, and movie posters, among hundreds of other items. An added bonus in the Templeton book was the listing of where souvenirs and memorabilia could be purchased. He also noted that "if you want something more personal," D. J. Fontana would autograph drumsticks (if you were to write to him at the given address).

Templeton is a recognized expert, having published, in a major collector's magazine (during 1997), a lengthy article on the Elvis collectibles market. He first wrote about Elvis memorabilia in a hastily prepared book (done in collaboration with Rosalind Cranor) entitled *The Best of Elvis Collectibles.* He has also been, for quite a while, co-editor of the magazine, *Elvis Collectors.*

In his estimation, the Elvis collectibles market currently exceeds $10 billion. The most valuable items have always been, of course, the rarer items, those issued during Elvis' lifetime. One of the fastest growing areas of collecting have been the Elvis movie items and posters. For example, the poster for his first movie, *Love Me Tender,* recently commanded a price in excess of $500. The section in Templeton's book entitled "The Movies" captured, in full color, not only the major movie posters, but lobby cards, movie stills, press book covers, and even an admission ticket for *G.I. Blues* that came with a "*G.I. Blues* hat."

Buskin's book featured a full chapter on concert memorabilia from the fifties, which, as an added bonus, thoroughly examined the live shows Elvis did during that decade. His chapter on "media madness" explored various printed items, from scrapbooks and songbooks to magazine spreads and bubble gum cards. Scattered throughout the book was an array of ticket stubs, concert posters, and record covers, both albums and singles. One of the ticket stubs was for Elvis' final show, held at the Indianapolis Market Square Arena.

Cotten, Lee. *The Elvis Catalog: Memorabilia, Icons, and Collectibles Celebrating the King of Rock 'n' Roll.* **Authorized by Elvis Presley Enterprises. Garden City, New York: Doubleday, 1987. 255 pp. List of licensed manufacturers.**

With Elvis dead, the closest anyone could get, save a trip to the grave at Graceland, was a piece of memorabilia. Collecting Elvis souvenirs has become a big business. In an attempt to catalog the best items, Cotten compiled his book (though he failed to cross-reference it). As co-author of the definitive work on Elvis bootleg recordings, he has always been an adept chronicler.

He succeeded again, this time presenting useful and intriguing insights into Elvis collectibles. He has seen and evaluated an incredible amount of merchandise, and was thus able to present details as an expert. "The merchandise" consisted of every type of memorabilia and souvenir having to do with Elvis.

The most interesting section of Cotten's book detailed the glut of "official" souvenirs that began within six weeks of Elvis' death. That glut included buttons, key chains, posters and more that all bore the logo, "The King lives on." In addition to the value this book had for collectors, it was a godsend for researchers because of the unique view it took of the Elvis fan phenomenon. Being authorized by Elvis Presley Enterprises gave it a much wider access to "official" souvenirs.

Cranor, Rosalind. *Elvis Collectibles.* **Steve Templeton and Ted Young, contributing editors. Paducah, Kentucky: Collector Books, 1983. New editions 1987, 1994, published by Overmountain, Johnson City, Tennessee. 400 pp.**

In the introduction to the 1994 edition, Cranor wrote that the Elvis Presley souvenir industry was a result of "the first major promotion aimed primarily at the teenager." In three succeedingly more comprehensive editions, beginning in 1983, she examined the market value of a wide variety of Elvis collectibles, not just ones from her collection but from others as well. The materials she presented ranged from novelty items such as pencil sharpeners and watches to marketing props like hanging mobiles and rack dividers.

The amount of material she initially presented in the 1983 edition, unfortunately, was too limited. She wrote that she put that initial edition out primarily to share information with other collectors. At least her approach was to concentrate on pre-1977 material. The dollar values she placed on mid-fifties items such as Elvis dog tags showed an astonishing increase in their worth. The dog tags, for example, were estimated at $290 as of 1994.

In 1987, then again in 1994, Cranor published newer editions of the book. The latter two editions went out courtesy of Overmountain Press of Johnson City, Tennessee. In each edition, the book's printing and layout appeared amateurish (limited to mostly black-and-white photographs) and uninteresting, reflecting the fact that it was published by a small publishing company (the initial edition came from Collector Books of Paducah, Kentucky) with limited resources. Some highly unique items were presented, such as the magic skin Elvis doll, rare because its skin deteriorated unless regularly treated with baby powder. How many could still be available today?

In 1992, Cranor compiled a specialized price guide compendium, entitled *Elvis Collectibles Price Guide Supplement*. She also collaborated in 1992 with Steve Templeton on a 116-page "addition" to the 1987 edition, adding color photos and more items. Overmountain Press published the "addition" under the title *The Best of Elvis Collectibles*. Altogether, the three editions of *Elvis Collectibles*, the 1992 price guide supplement, and the 1992 "best of" book covered a wide range of valuable material.

Doll, Susan. *Best of Elvis*. **Lincolnwood, Illinois: Publications International, 1996. 216 pp. Index.**

Doll, who chronicled Elvis in a number of different ways, presented the "best" of the "things" about Elvis books, recordings, magazines, films, and more. Her book was quite visual, presenting photographs of the covers of the "best" books, magazines, recordings, and so on. Elvis' first two albums topped her "best albums" list. The two best books on Elvis, according to her, were *Mystery Train* and *Dead Elvis*, both written by Greil Marcus.

Mabe, Joni. *Everything Elvis*. **New York: Thunder's Mouth, 1996. 135 pp.**

A huge eighteen-wheeler has been crisscrossing the country to bring fans everywhere the Joni Mabe Elvis collection, known as the "Traveling Panoramic Encyclopedia of Everything Elvis." The book was stuffed full of pictures of her collection that contained locks of Elvis' hair and more than one hundred other items. Most were as innocuous as any other collection except for the little vial containing an Elvis wart (she said she purchased it from a doctor who once treated Elvis) and the picture of the toenail that she claimed to have dug out of one of the carpets at Graceland.

Mabe became a fan and avid collector in 1977, soon after the King's death. The full-color photographs of her collection were amazing. The most useful part of the book was the chronology of all the things that have happened relative to Elvis since his death. In addition to her traveling show, her collecting, and this book, Mabe has also sold limited editions of Elvis prayer mats. Elvis must have become a new religion, at least in her eyes (and in the eyes of the people who bought her product)!

Just like Mabe's unique showables, the wart and the toenail, many people have a unique story they could recall about Elvis, a chance encounter, a photo opportunity, or a memory from a show. Mabe's Elvis toenail was the topic of one person's unique Elvis story. Richard Paul Evans, the author of 1997's best-seller, *The Christmas Box*, told me he was actually bumped from a book signing by that toenail.

Evans was not quite as well known then as he waited inside a small bookstore only to have Joni Mabe and all her notoriety and traveling show roll into town. The store, without hesitation, cancelled his signing and turned the evening over to the woman who could show off Elvis' toenail. Nonetheless, his book went on to become a number one best-seller while hers has gone into the cutout bins. Each author got their fifteen minutes of fame.

Osborne, Jerry, Perry Cos, and Joe Lindsay. *The Official Price Guide to Memorabilia of Elvis Presley and The Beatles.* **New York: Ballantine, 1988. 91 pp.**

Osborne, Jerry. *The Official Price Guide to Elvis Presley Records and Memorabilia.* **New York: House of Collectibles, 1994. 430 pp.**

Umphred, Neal, editor. *Elvis Presley Record Price Guide.* **[n.p.]: O'Sullivan Woodside, 1985.**

Osborne's 1994 book on Elvis recordings and memorabilia has taken its place as the most recent and complete one on Elvis' recordings. It can be obtained through the House of Collectibles in New York. The emphasis was on market values of the most collectible of the Elvis albums, singles, and unique pressings. Promotional items and bootlegs were covered. The valuation part not only gave price ranges but detailed instructions on how to grade the condition of a collectible recording, from "mint" down to "good."

In addition to the recordings, Osborne included a detailed chronology and a section on memorabilia. His directory of buyers and sellers was much more inclusive than one would have expected. Even with all the information presented, the guide has proven difficult to use because of a lack of any kind of indexing or cross-referencing.

Osborne (with Bruce Hamilton) first put together much of this information in 1980 in a book entitled *Presleyana* (which is now well into its fourth "new" edition, according to an ad in *DISCoveries*). The other prior book (done in 1988 on both Elvis and The Beatles), though quite thin, was extremely useful for its extensive detail and price guidelines. It covered major Elvis items as well as ones of equal stature attributed to The Beatles.

Before Osborne put out his definitive catalog in 1994, the most useful reference guide on Elvis recordings was the one compiled in 1985 by collector Neal Umphred. Umphred has not limited himself to Elvis when it comes to catalogs on collectible recordings, he has also done a very useful and complete one on country music. Though the valuations he recommended in 1985 have become outdated, his guide has remained useful because he did more than merely price items. He presented session-by-session and record-by-record detail, with information on covers, label variations, and changes in vinyl color.

Putnam, Stan P. *Memento, Souvenir, Keepsake and Collector's Kit on the Life and Music of Elvis Presley.* **[n.p.]: Research Improvement Center, 1987.**

Putnam, Stan P. *Newfound Facts and Memorabilia on Elvis Presley.* **[n.p.]: Research Improvement Center, 1987.**

In the late eighties, Putnam decided he had compiled some very interesting material covering the memorabilia and collectibles relative to Elvis. Not finding a major publisher, he put them out through something called the "Research Improvement Center," which euphemistically meant they were self-published. Though they presented some unique insights and items, their lack of availability to collectors and fans kept them from becoming useful guides. Not to be daunted, Putnam put out a second volume in which he claimed to have discovered some new facts about Elvis.

Yenne, Bill. *All the King's Things: The Ultimate Elvis Memorabilia Book.* **San Francisco: Bluewood Books, 1993. 31 pp.**

Yenne's book documented the huge personal collection of Elvis collectibles owned and shown by Robin Rosaaen. Her collection has been described as the "largest anywhere outside Memphis, Tennessee." She owned statues, figurines, books, knickknacks, and more, ranging from kitchen displays to garage settings. The Elvis Library portrayed many very rare Elvis books, including one written in Russian.

Overall, the photography done on the items was larger than life and brought out the visual beauty that most collectibles have for their owners. The final section depicted "the ultimate Elvis shrine" which encompassed a lock of Elvis' hair, a rose that had been placed at Elvis' mausoleum (before the body was reburied at Graceland), and a Bible opened to one of his favorite passages, in the twenty-first chapter of the Book of Revelation. Yenne closed his book with the inscription, "Ladies and Gentlemen . . . Elvis has left the building."

The Photograph Collections

How many ways could Elvis be seen? He could be seen through other people's eyes, of course, because he did not let us know how he saw himself through his own eyes. There were other "eyes" that saw Elvis: mechanical, glass ones–camera eyes. They say you can't fool the camera and even for Elvis that was true.

In his younger years, the charisma was so obvious that most of the time his image had a love affair with the camera. When he was captured performing, the sheer electricity and enthusiasm made the pictures almost come to life. But as he aged and grew in the wrong places, the camera showed every blemished fault for all the world to see, especially up close. His pictures never ceased to fascinate and were always in demand. Those from 1956 were the most dynamic.

For years, since birth, someone was snapping pictures of the King. His first twenty years consisted mostly of informal, almost fuzzy, images. Then came 1956, when a photographer literally lived with Elvis. Since then, the photo collections have been invaluable, especially when they went beyond specific publicity opportunities. The best pictures showed every mood swing and feeling he ever had. The camera revealed as much about Elvis as any insider story.

Accordingly, some photographers, because of their concentrated bird's-eye view of Elvis, saw him directly in ways others could not. For example, photographer Ben Mancuso was sent, in 1957, by a movie magazine, to cover Elvis in New York City, where he was to appear on *The Ed Sullivan Show* for the third time. He took pictures in Elvis' hotel room, then they went to the coffee shop, where the conversation did not often flow. On the way back up the elevator,

Mancuso caught Elvis considering his reflection in the elevator mirror, perhaps, as Mancuso concluded, to avoid more conversation. His memory of the session with Elvis centered on being "struck by the fact that in spite of all his fame and all his fans, this was a very lonely guy." Even then, Mancuso saw what others took years to understand.

All the collections of photos in this section focused on Elvis posing as both a public person and persona. Beyond these collections, there were two other, more informal, pictorial sets, the first of which came out in 1978 in honor of Elvis' death, a "family keepsake" collection of fan photographs compiled by editors Angela and Jerome Shapiro (entitled *Candidly Elvis* and published privately by Anje Publishing). Originally offered in more of a magazine-style format, the soft-covered compendium featured some really awful photographs (in terms of quality) that revealed a very accessible Elvis, as devoted fans saw him. The physical differences that could be seen in Elvis in mid-1974 as opposed to 1976 were astounding. He didn't look fat as much as he looked bloated.

The other significant collection was entitled *Elvis Town: Volume I, 1991–1992,* and offered through Graceland Gifts of 3734 Elvis Presley Boulevard, Memphis. The text featured information not only about Elvis but his hometown as well. The snaps around which the text was woven came significantly from the Parker collection.

A beautiful book of stills from *The Ed Sullivan Show* recently appeared. The ones on Elvis revealed yet another side of the photogenic king. The pictures, even the Elvis ones, came from the vaults of CBS, the network that brought Ed's show to the world.

The book, edited by Claudia Falkenberg and Andrew Solt with text by John Leonard, was entitled *A Really Big Show: A Visual History of the Ed Sullivan Show.* The 1956 spread on Elvis (in the rock and roll section) totaled only nine shots but they spoke volumes, showing Elvis talking to a fan, listening to Ed, and spread out on a couch. The highlight pose captured Elvis sporting the biggest, most natural, innocent grin ever.

Cahill, Marie. *Elvis*.   Greenwich, Connecticut: Brompton Books Corporation, 1992.   New edition published in 1994 by World Publications.   64 pp.   Index.

In 1991, Cahill edited, for American Graphic Systems, a book on Elvis Impersonators (see the Elvis Impersonator section). It was one of the better books in that category. For a follow-up, she has compiled this pictorial collection consisting largely of what once appeared to be glossy publicity photos.

There was one very well-shot color picture of Elvis' Tupelo birthplace. Most of the posed photos were available from other sources on superior paper (i.e., glossy). The book must not have done much for Elvis' fans because it soon appeared in cutout bins everywhere, where it has been readily available for under $5. The notes with the pictures were too succinct and uninformative.

Curtin, Jim E. *Unseen Elvis: Candids of the King.* **Boston: Little, Brown, 1992.   207 pp.**

Curtin, Jim, assisted by Renata Ginter. *Elvis and the Stars.* **Wayne, Pennsylvania: Morgin, 1993.   144 pp.   List of stars.**

Curtin was able to obtain many unposed snapshots of Elvis at play, with friends and family, and generally looking quite relaxed. The pictures in *Unseen Elvis* came from hundreds of unknown amateur photographers and many were acquired by accident. Over an approximately thirty-year period, Curtin has collected more than 25,000 Elvis pictures of varying quality, from Brownie camera 1950s shots to professionally posed publicity stills. He captured a side of Elvis that has rarely been shown.

His collection of "Elvis and the stars" photographs portrayed Elvis at ease and often clowning with various celebrities from Dean Jones to numerous leading ladies, the most poignant of which showed him dancing with *Jailhouse Rock* co-star Judy Tyler, who died tragically soon after after the film was shot. Elvis dominated every picture except for the one with Muhammed Ali. He towered over Brenda Lee. Elvis may have been portrayed as grittier and more soulful than Pat Boone, but, surprisingly, in their picture together they looked almost too similar with their tailored white shirts.

In 1998, Curtin announced a "new" book, a 288-page work entitled *Elvis: Unknown Stories Behind the Legend,* that featured 500 intimate stories about Elvis, all said to be "previously unknown." Also awaiting release was a cooperative effort by Curtin and Ginter, *2001: A Fact Odyssey.* It was to be published by a company called Celebrity as was another Curtin book entitled *Christmas with Elvis.*

Hirshberg, Charles, and the Editors of *Life.* **Elvis:** *A Celebration in Pictures.* **Introduction by Charles Hirshberg. New York: Warner, 1995.   128 pp.**

Life Magazine has always been renowned for its spectacular photography, especially its presentation of such work. Charles Hirshberg, along with various editors of the magazine, collaborated to bring together the richest photograph collection on Elvis ever assembled. Bringing together boyhood snapshots, spectacular concert footage, and some very relaxed casual shots, the team captured the definitive pictorial of Elvis' life. Surprisingly, the majority were in black and white.

The best color Elvis shot was a family portrait with Priscilla and a very young Lisa Marie. The most vulnerable depiction appeared on page 80, showing Elvis and his dad, Vernon, crying over the death of wife and mother, Gladys. It was a blunt reminder that whatever anyone may have attributed to Elvis, he was human, with very basic, loving emotions.

Israel, Marvin. *Elvis Presley 1956.* **Photographs by Marvin Israel. Edited and designed by Martin Harrison. New York: Harry N. Abrams, 1998. [unnumbered].**

Kricun, Morrie E., and Virginia M. Kricun. *Elvis: 1956 Reflections.* **Wayne, Pennsylvania: Morgin, 1991. 192 pp. Chronology, discography, filmography, bibliography.**

Leviton, Jay B., and Ger J. Rijff. *Elvis Up Close: Rare, Intimate, Unpublished Photographs of Elvis Presley in 1956.* **Introduction by Kurt Loder. New York: Simon & Schuster, 1987.** Originally entitled *Florida Close-Up*, **published by Ger Rijff, Tutti Frutti Productions, Amsterdam, Holland, 1987. New edition 1988. 135 pp.**

Wertheimer, Alfred, and Gregory Martinelli. *Elvis '56: In the Beginning: An Intimate, Eyewitness Photojournal.* **New York: Macmillan, 1979. 149 pp.**

In 1956, Elvis was being discovered by the mass media, the public, and a number of great photographers. Four books captured the wealth of photographs taken that year. The best appeared in a collection put together by Wertheimer. He was asked by RCA publicist Anne Fulchino to shoot the pictures, though prior to being asked he'd never heard of Elvis. The most dynamic photographs centered around Elvis' first appearances in the spotlight, on such venues as the Steve Allen and Jimmy Dorsey TV shows.

He appeared exuberant and excited over his newfound fame. The crowds he drew clearly enjoyed the young, uninhibited spectacle. Never has a set of photographs so captured the electric energy given off at the beginning of Elvis' performing career. In contrast, Wertheimer added a number of shots showing Elvis at home, where he appeared like a big lovable dazed boy just waiting to be cuddled.

Marvin Israel was never renowned as a photographer, though he did serve as art director for both Atlantic Records and *Harper's*

Bazaar. Nevertheless, he took over 200 photos of Elvis while following his 1956 tour. Because of the unflattering black-and-white nature of the shots, they were considered too stark and uncompromising for Elvis fans, so only two were published at the time. Today, they have become considered as excellent examples of spontaneous, moving photographic work. The pictures in this book were among the last allowed by Elvis' management prior to cutting off informal access to the star.

The Kricun book, like the similarly titled Wertheimer book, presented never-before published shots of Elvis as he began his career. The photos were mostly informally posed snapshots of Elvis reading, telephoning, playing records, and even just "slouching" around, as folks would have said back in the fifties. Overall, they depicted an unguarded and naively happy Elvis. The energy level Elvis had in 1956 was markedly clear in these pictures.

Rijff, who has published more than a dozen Elvis books through his Dutch production company (and who placed some of his Elvis sketches in Roger Taylor's *Elvis in Art* book), collaborated with photographer Leviton to produce a photojournal of immense value because the shots were unique and well cataloged. Leviton originally snapped the pictures (more than 120) as part of a *Collier's* magazine assignment to chronicle the emerging rock star's tour of places Southern. He captured Elvis in hotel rooms, at theaters, with lots of girls, and on stage making music. The book was first self-published by Rijff (in Holland) as *Florida Close-Up*.

Reid, Jim. *Fond Memories of Elvis: 1954-Twenty-Three Years of Photos-1977.* **Memphis, Tennessee: James R. Reid, 1987. New editions 1992, 1994. 52 pp.**

Reid served twenty-eight years as staff photographer for the *Memphis Press-Scimitar.* During that time he had many invited opportunities to photograph Elvis. This thin book encapsulated his best shots. Dedicated to Elvis' mother, Gladys, Reid began with a juxtaposition of Elvis' first house in Tupelo against the Graceland mansion. Later in the book, a full-color aerial view of Graceland stood out. Reid proved to be more than a photographer, including a touching self-penned tribute poem entitled "Sweet Dreams, My Friend." One of his closing photos of an Elvis statue utilized a great quote that said "The sun never sets on a legend."

All phases of Elvis' life and career were featured. There were Army photos and sad snapshots taken when his mother died. Every picture was unposed and informal. Many were quite emotional. Reid completely understood how to use the camera to capture the intimate side of people. He even caught the King during his final concert. His feelings for Elvis came pouring out in a poignant poem superimposed over a beatific Elvis standing above adoring fans.

Stern, Jane and Michael. *Elvis World.* **New York: Harper & Row, 1987.   196 pp.   Literature.**

Too many pictorial collections became huge coffee table extravaganzas hampered by fluff writing and a lack of organization even though they contained some worthwhile pictures. The book by the Sterns, who have been called the "ranking experts on Elvis glitter," was a coffee-table creation yet quite worthwhile because the descriptions were well done and because the authors did a great job of organizing the beautiful photographs from their collection. The first part of their "glitter" book centered on much of the literature that popped up when Elvis first became popular. Featured here were articles with titles like "Why Elvis Is Every Girl's Idol" and "An Elvis Fan Tells All." There were also family snapshots, family recipes, and a lavish four-page Graceland centerfold.

For film enthusiasts, there was a concise section that briefly overviewed each film and listed the songs in each soundtrack. As an added bonus, full-color theater posters were reproduced. For fans, there was a lengthy write-up on the Sterns' encounters with some very unique Elvis devotees. Finally, for the more literate Elvis followers, there was an excellent, though too short critical commentary on the major Elvis books available at the time.

Tunzi, Joseph A., with Sean O'Neal. *Elvis: The Lost Photographs.* **Chicago: JAT Productions, 1990.**

Tunzi compiled, in the nineties, more than half a dozen Elvis books, the majority of which focused year by year on his exploits. Tunzi also compiled a reasonably useful Elvis sessionography as well as a videography. In this book, he presented some poignant "lost" photographs that were uncovered by author and collector Sean O'Neal, who has since become known for two books, an investigation of Elvis Presley Enterprises and a biography of Colonel Parker. The photographs were mostly informal ones, the most incredible of which was a 1953 snapshot of Elvis and a friend posing as "cowboys" at the Memphis Mid-South Fair. Overall, they were a great addition to the thousands and thousands of other pictures taken of the most photographed performer ever.

The Pictorial Books

Most huge oversized hardback books dominated by glossy pictures have come to be known as "coffee-table" books. That means they will be put on some coffee table to display them because they are beautiful and cost a great deal more than the average book. Obviously, given the extent of Elvis fandom, quite a few "coffee-table" books were going to find a niche, and they did.

The gaudiest picture book had no attributed author but did feature an introduction by Glen Campbell, who wrote, in part, that "I have a hard time talking or writing about Elvis without tears welling up." This $90 (retail) work (of art?) boasted that it was sold as a "limited edition" collection with each book "individually numbered" and featuring a "gold-embossed slipcase." It was entitled *Elvis Immortal* and came complete with 190 photos, ninety of which had "never been published before." Was it a great book? It certainly was lavish!

The best of the lot had text and commentary by Dave Marsh. Marsh, who began his career writing for *Rolling Stone,* has authored several books, most notably a biography of Bruce Springsteen. His work on Elvis was worthy of being classified a biography. As far as the rest of the pictorial books, most were at least worthy of display.

The Sean Shaver one was not only beautiful, it was quite in depth on how he went about photographing the King. There were two collections on the bottom end of this genre. That meant their photos were merely of the mediocre, run-of-the-mill variety overlaying a text with no unique information. Basically, they were amassed only to briefly satisfy fan clamoring at some particular point, either the height of Elvis' popularity or his death.

At the bottom-end of the spectrum was a book, published in 1958 by Fan's Star Library with the panoramic title, *The Amazing Elvis Presley.* The source spoke for the contents. The contents, for fans only, suffice it to say, were not amazing. Because of its age, it has become a sought-after collector's item. The going price for a clean, near-mint copy has moved into the $50 range.

Allen, William (text by). *Elvis.* **Godalming, Surrey, England: CLB, 1992. New edition published by Smithmark, New York, 1994. 192 pp. Bibliography, filmography, discography.**

Frew, Timothy. *Elvis: His Life and Music.* **New York: Mallard, 1992. New editions 1994 and 1997. 176 pp. List of television appearances, filmography, fan clubs, million-selling singles and noteworthy recordings, reading list, index.**

Glade, Emory. *Elvis: A Golden Tribute.* Wauwatosa, Wisconsin: Robus Books, 1984. [unnumbered].

Harmer, Jeremy. *Elvis.* White Plains, New York: Longman, 1982.

Matthews, Rupert. *Elvis: The King of Rock 'n' Roll.* New York: Random House/Gramercy Books, 1998. 110 pp. Index.

Allen wrote the text for the huge, glossy book on Elvis, first published in 1992 in England (and re-released in 1997 in a "20th Anniversary Edition"). Actually, William Allen was a pseudonym for W. A. Harbinson, a London-based writer, who had previously (1975) authored *The Illustrated Elvis* (see the Harbinson entry in this part) and later collaborated (in 1994) with Ger Rijff and Kay Wheeler on *Growing Up with the Memphis Flash.* For coffee-table book prose, it was well written, informative, and understandable.

It had some depth, though there was no firsthand information given or primary sources listed. The bibliography contained books only, but the commentary on each was useful and informative. The film listing could be found in any number of other works, as could the listing of recordings. The pictures were, on the whole, more than worthwhile, from many informal early poses to the Million Dollar Quartet. The best unique shots were of Elvis signing autographs and a colorful Graceland scene.

The Frew book (especially in its 1997 Barnes & Noble edition) was almost as big and every bit as glossy as the Allen book. It was just as informative. Content-wise it came across quite similar to Allen's book by being as general in its biographical overview. With four appendices, it was just as comprehensive in its listings.

A version of his Elvis book was included as part of a boxed set that also presented the essential Elvis recordings along with a detailed sessionography. Frew has also compiled an ultrathin Elvis photograph book, which concentrated on photographs from his movies (*Elvis: A Life in Pictures*). This was not the only time Frew did such a book. He compiled a similar work on Lucille Ball.

Using a magazine-layout approach, the Glade book was only about thirty pages long. Like other run-of-the-mill tribute books, it appeared to have been published only to make money while masquerading as an honoring of a dead star. It came out in time for the seventh anniversary of Elvis' death.

Over the years, Harmer's publisher, Longman, has become known for thin, tall, cheaply made books that wound up in cutout bins, which was where copies of this book were quickly placed. The Matthews book came originally from Regency House (England) with all photos courtesy of Todd Slaughter (president of the Elvis Presley Fan Club of Great Britain). In the United States, it was marketed by Gramercy, an imprint of Random House Value Publishing.

Anonymous.   *Elvis: A Tribute to the King of Rock n' Roll: Remembering You.* **London: IPC Magazines, 1977. 62 pp.**

Anonymous.   *The Life and Death of Elvis Presley.* **New York: Harrison House/Manor Books, Inc., 1977. [unnumbered].**

Anonymous.   *Elvis Presley 1935-1977: A Tribute to the King.* **Wednesbury, Staffordshire, England: Bavie Publications, 1977.**

Anonymous.   *Elvis Tear-Out Photo Book.* **London: Oliver Books, 1994. [unnumbered].**

Anonymous. *Elvis Immortal.* **Introduction by Glen Campbell. Tempe, Arizona: Legends Press, 1997. 256 pp.**

The first three "anonymous" books, all published after Elvis died, added nothing to either the Elvis literature or pictorial collections. The first was an output of a British magazine publisher, IPC, and came complete with numerous glossy, previously published stills which emanated mainly from Elvis' movies. The second, an amateurishly written rehash of Elvis' career, did feature some interesting but poorly reproduced color photos. The third anonymous book was actually comprised of a series of five paperback compendiums (each one about thirty-pages long), with the poignant word "goodbye" slapped across the front covers. The set of publications made no pretensions about playing off Elvis' death. Along with a series of portraits, each booklet featured some morbidly sad poetry designed to commemorate "the King" for his fans.

The two anonymous published in the 1990s likewise added nothing to the Elvis literature. The first one, from 1994, was limited to forty-five pages and contained approximately twenty primarily black-and-white pictures, all seen before. The "tear-out" aspect enabled fans to frame their favorite shots. The final anonymous book, published in 1997, did present ninety "new" photos. Did that make it worth its $90 mail-order retail price tag? Though value may rest in the eye of the beholder, the ad for the book left no doubt about what the public was expected to conclude, that one could "swoon over the pouty-lipped, blue-eyed Hollywood star." Actually, the best part of the book was a companion compact disc, in which Elvis shared "candid thoughts about himself, his life, and his love for his fans."

The publisher, Legends Press, claimed that its book was the "ultimate Elvis book." Glen Campbell sold their claim very well in his introduction, telling fans that "this book will help you share in his incomparable legacy. Like me, you can treasure those moments you get to spend to with Elvis." There was even a gold star "guaranty" in case the purchaser was in any way dissatisfied.

Bangs, Lester (text by). *Elvis Presley: The Rebel Years.* **New York: W. W. Norton/Schirmer's Visual Library, 1994.   119 pp. Chronology, discography of singles 1954-1960, filmography 1956-1958, select bibliography.**

There had to have been a basis for all the claims that Elvis was, in the sedate fifties, a rebellious personality who turned American popular culture upside down. The pictures in this book captured that persona to prove its existence once and for all. The late Lester Bangs provided a sparse but insightful text, beginning with his 1987 *Village Voice* essay in which he wrote that when he looked at Elvis, he "went mad with desire, and envy, and worship, and self-projection." He ended with the observation that "nobody you can come up with ever elicited such hysteria among so many."

Bentley, Dawn, text, and Allison Higa, design. *Elvis Remembered: A Three-Dimensional Celebration.* **Kansas City, Missouri: Pop-Up Press, 1997.   [unnumbered].**

Fitzgerald, Jim, and Al Kilgore. *Elvis: The Paperdoll Book.* **New York: St. Martin's, 1982.   [unnumbered].**

King, R. G. *Elvis on Stamps.* **Greenville, Tennessee: K & K Publishing, 1997.**

Fitzgerald once again proved that just when one might think everything possible about Elvis had been done, there was one more approach to be utilized. This one presented (in about thirty pages) Elvis paper dolls (artwork by Kilgore), complete with the kind of outfits the King was known to have worn or would have been expected to use. It was part of a series of serious paper doll books covering everything from Victorian costumes to the British Royal family.

Now, could there have been an Elvis coloring book out there? Yes, was the resounding answer. It was called *Elvis Goes Hollywood* and enabled fans to color in scenes from Elvis' movies. That's not all, folks. There was also a beautiful pictorial book documenting Elvis on stamps, appropriately entitled *Elvis on Stamps*. It was compiled by R. G. King. According to the advertisements trumpeting its release, the book contained "color framable pictures of Elvis on stamps," as well as the "geographical location of each country, denomination & quantity issued." Carrying a $29.95 price tag, it was the first of four proposed volumes.

1997 also brought forth a ten-page pop-up book that focused on the highlights of Elvis' life and career. With text by Dawn Bentley, the book unfolded from the days at Sun Studios to the final days. At a suggested list price of $29.95, the cost came out to about $3.00 per page. At least there was the added bonus of "computer retouching and tinting" that put the King in a much better light pictorially. The book bore a sticker that stated it was an official EPE product.

Celsi, Theresa. *Elvis.* **Kansas City, Missouri: Andrews and McMeel/Ariel Books, 1993. 77 pp. List of No. 1 singles, basic recording library, list of movies and theater productions based on or inspired by Elvis' life, factoids.**

Golick, Jeffrey, editor. *Elvis.* **Adapted from the research and writing of Todd Morgan, with Laura Kath. New York: Abbeville, 1997. 286 pp.**

Hardinge, Melissa. *They Died Too Young: Elvis.* **Avonmouth, England: Parragon Books, 1995. 74 pp.**

Lannamann, Margaret, editor. *Elvis: The Legend.* **Kansas City, Missouri: Andrews McMeel Publishing/Ariel Books, 1998. 127 pp. Facts and figures.**

If nothing else, these four books would count as the smallest (in physical dimensions) Elvis books ever published! Abbeville presented Golick's book as a "Tiny Folio" (measuring four and one-half by four inches), though it did come in a tall volume as well. The Celsi book measured about one-half inch shorter than the Hardinge book, which was, in turn, a quarter of an inch shorter than the one edited by Golick. Lannamann's book, reaching a mere two inches in height, took the prize as the shortest Elvis book to date.

A large part of Golick's book was adapted from original research done and text written by Todd Morgan (with Laura Kath). Morgan was listed in the book credits as "Graceland Director of Creative Services." The limited amount of text was pedestrian at best, and the pictures were mostly movie stills or publicity shots. Any original research was not readily apparent while the chronology of Elvis' life was limited to three and one-quarter pages. The publisher, Abbeville, also marketed a thirty-count set of Elvis postcards.

The size, pictures (nothing new), and generic text found in the Celsi book rendered it suitable for a small coffee table. Its most valuable asset was a short listing of films and theater productions based on Elvis' life. Its biographical parts were basic, devoid of analysis, and "too cute." One statement, that "Colonel Parker made sure that Elvis never disappeared again," stood out as the best example of a lack of analysis and trivialized writing.

Andrews McMeel Publishing of Kansas City published both the Celsi and Lannamann books. They must have wanted to corner the market on the smallest Elvis books. Whereas Celsi's book had something to offer, the Lannamann book did not. Even the facts and figures section offered no new information. The book did make a great display item, however.

The Hardinge book came out as part of a series on popular music stars who died "too young," stars like Marvin Gaye, Buddy Holly, and, of course, Elvis. Published in England, the book did not dwell exclusively on Elvis' death. Rather it purported to tell a simplified, no-frills version of his life, ending by informing readers that Elvis' recordings have sold more than one and one-half billion units.

Doll, Susan, contributing writer. *Elvis: A Tribute to His Life*. **Lincolnwood, Illinois: Publications International, 1989. 256 pp. Listing of films, singles, index.**

Doll, Susan. *Elvis: Rock 'n' Roll Legend*. **Lincolnwood, Illinois: Publications International, 1994. 239 pp.**

Doll, Susan. *Elvis: Portrait of the King.* **Lincolnwood, Illinois: Publications International, 1995. 239 pp.**

The first of the three Susan Doll books had obvious coffee-table pretentiousness and artiness. However, the range of illustrations and thoroughness were unusual for a work of such intent. Content-wise, the book bordered on being a good general history and biography of Elvis and his family, especially when it placed him in context relative to his musical peers. The publicity shots (of those peers) effectively captured how the teen idols of that era were presented to the public.

Not only did the full-color Elvis photos, ranging from studio shots to snapshots, capture his visage, they focused on Graceland and various other tourist attractions. There were even pictures of Elvis' funeral. The second Doll book, *Elvis: Rock 'n' Roll Legend*, did not merit similar favorable comments. To begin with, it included no reference material. Though quite clear and glossy, the photos were intended for fan display only, not for visual analysis.

In 1995, Doll churned out a very disappointing third book. This time the biographical chapters were so hurriedly written as to trivialize the entire tone of the book. While Doll did not denigrate Elvis in any way, she added nothing to the literature. Her final section on Elvis impersonators was at best a thumbnail sketch.

Gibson, Robert, and Sid Shaw. *Elvis: A King Forever.* New York: McGraw-Hill, 1985. Reprinted 1986. New edition 1987. 176 pp.

Giuliano, Geoffrey, Brenda Giuliano, and Deborah Lynn Black. *The Illustrated Elvis Presley.* Edison, New Jersey: Chartwell, 1994. 96 pp.

Nelson, Pete. *King!: When Elvis Rocked the World.* New York: Proteus, 1985. 111 pp. Discography, list of films 1954-1956, chronology 1954–1958.

Parish, James Robert. *The Elvis Presley Scrapbook.* New York: Ballantine, 1975. Revised edition 1977. 218 pp. Discography, filmography.

Reggero, John. *Elvis in Concert.* Introduction by David E. Stanley. New York: Dell, 1979. 120 pp.

Ridge, Millie. *The Elvis Album.* New York: Gallery, 1991.

The books by Gibson and Nelson were poorly written, intended only for fans of oversized productions. The photos were of the souvenir variety and were neither well explained nor presented. Both sets of texts were uninformative and uncritical. The books appeared just for people who already loved Elvis dearly. Of all the photo books, they have become the two most often found in cutout bins. Incidentally, Gibson's coauthor, Sid Shaw, was the individual who fought Elvis Presley Enterprises in court (in England) and won the right (after six long years) to continue to market Elvis artifacts under the name Elvisly Yours.

The chronology in Gibson's book, presented as "The Elvis Diary," did help to keep the pictures in perspective. Coauthor Shaw also previously compiled *Elvis in Quotes*, a sparse set of quotations from the King. He published that work in 1974 through his company Elvisly Yours. It was an approach recently utilized more effectively by Jeff Rovin and Mick Farren.

The book by the Giulianos (and Black) boasted an interesting text, culminating in a quote from Southern novelist, William Price Fox, whose words, "he wasn't like anyone else," neatly summed up

Elvis. Format-wise, it was a typical Chartwell book, consisting mainly of posed studio photos, though some of the informal funeral shots did reveal intense, raw emotions. Geoffrey Giuliano has also written extensively on The Beatles, though some critics viewed his "foursome" books as overkill. In 1996, through Laserlight Digital, he marketed three "audio" books consisting of numerous brief Elvis interviews.

Gallery Books has consistently marketed coffee-table books similar to those from Chartwell. Thus, Ridge's book appeared very close to the Giuliano book in tone and material. The Parish book relied on a scrapbook approach to present Elvis news stories and articles (from before Elvis died). It was similar to a 1982 Richard Peters book that covered newsworthy aspects of Frank Sinatra's life.

Reggero's 1979 book, *Elvis in Concert*, presented some very colorful performance pictures (taken by the author) that were taken from a number of late seventies concerts. As a bonus, one of the Stanley brothers (Elvis' stepbrothers), David, wrote the introduction. Otherwise, the book offered interesting poses of a less than dynamic performer, yet one who was still able to pose and move his audience.

Harbinson, W. A. *The Illustrated Elvis.* New York: Grosset & Dunlap, 1975. New editions 1976, 1977, 1987, 1988. Originally published as *Elvis Presley: An Illustrated Biography*, England, 1975. 160 pp.

Marsh, Dave. *Elvis.* Art direction by Bea Feitler. New York: Thunder's Mouth, 1982. New edition 1992. 245 pp. Discography, filmography, bibliography.

Marsh's pictorially-elaborate opus featured a thorough, albeit brief, biographical overview, well-written and researched. Some valuable perspectives were effectively interwoven with the dozens of wonderful studio and home-quality pictures. The photographs of Elvis on the road were especially revealing, showing an outgoing and charismatic demeanor even in a relaxed mode. An original first edition hardcover copy (the one published by Straight Arrow Publishers) has become quite valuable, worth up to three times the original cover price, depending on condition.

Grosset & Dunlap published the first American edition of Harbinson's book in 1976 (it was originally published in England in 1975 by Michael Joseph) and then, following Elvis' 1977 death, reissued it in abridged form as *Elvis: A Tribute to Elvis, King of Rock*. Postmortem demand pushed the book onto the American best-seller lists. Since 1977, there has been a 1987 edition from Putnam/Perigree and a 1988 one from Treasure Press of London, England.

In his presentation of Elvis' life, Harbinson never went beyond the familiar generalities found in too many Elvis biographies. As far as illustrations, he did include an abundance of movie-related poses but nothing from Elvis' Army years. The back page of the abridged version captured the funeral motorcade as well as Elvis' casket and a grieving Vernon Presley.

Lawrence, Greer. *Elvis: The King of Rock & Roll.* **New York: Smithmark, 1997.   48 pp.**

Taylor, John Alvarez. *Forever Elvis.* **New York: Smithmark, 1991.   New edition 1994.   64 pp.   Index.**

Both the Lawrence and Taylor books came from Smithmark, a publisher known for marketing a multitude of coffee-table books on subjects ranging from art to architecture. Though only forty-eight pages in length, Lawrence's work was lavishly illustrated. The author wrote that it "fulfilled her long-standing ambition to honor the King in prose and picture."

Taylor's book had hardly any writing and only a very common set of photos, albeit some great movie stills. On the valuable side, there was an index (not found in other pictorial books) which enabled the identification of people who posed with Elvis. Most of the pictures came courtesy of American Graphic Systems Archives.

The ending shots in the book were poignant, from the picture of the newspaper proclaiming Elvis' death to the photo of flowers ringing his grave. The pictures inside Graceland, though of poor quality and only in black and white, did give a good overview of the kind of displays to be found inside. All that was disclosed on the author was that he had been a freelance writer for over a decade.

Shaver, Sean, and Hal Noland. *The Life of Elvis Presley.* **Kansas City, Missouri: Timur, 1979.**

Shaver, Sean. *Elvis: Photographing the King.* **Kansas City, Missouri: Timur, 1981.   256 pp.**

Shaver, Sean. *Elvis's Portrait Portfolio.* **Kansas City, Missouri: Timur, 1983.**

Shaver, Sean, Alfred Wertheimer, and Eddie Fadal. *Our Memories of Elvis.* **Kansas City, Missouri: Timur, 1984.**

Shaver, Sean. *Elvis in Focus.* **Kansas City, Missouri: Timur, 1992.**

Shaver got numerous chances to photograph the King, especially in concert. Between 1970 and 1977, he said he "filmed 497 different shows." In *Elvis: Photographing the King* and *Elvis's Portrait Portfolio*, he presented his collection and wrote about how he did what he did. He also discussed his views of Elvis, the kind of impression Elvis made on him, and why he thought Elvis got where he did. Though the books had much to recommend them, they were limited in publication, making them hard to find.

Some of the insights Shaver offered in *Elvis: Photographing the King* were that Elvis was "humble to the point of insanity," he had a photographic memory, and he feared he would be forgotten. Most of Shaver's disclosures came from working closely with Elvis on a daily basis. One conclusion became crystal clear: Shaver did not like most of the people that surrounded Elvis.

He wrote that he saved his best story for last. It concerned a seventeen year old boy who had been collecting Elvis items for years. When he finally got to meet Elvis, the boy showed Elvis his collection. Elvis actually got down on his knees and looked over each item. Why, Elvis wanted to know, did the boy bring his collection here (to Elvis' house where the two met)? The boy simply said he just wanted Elvis to see it. Later, when the boy left he had one of Elvis' diamond rings on his finger.

Shaver parlayed his role as a unique photographer of the King into three other books, also published by Timur. In 1979, to cash in on the King's death, he collaborated with Hal Noland on *The Life of Elvis Presley*. Not to be outdone, in 1984 he compiled (with Alfred Wertheimer and Eddie Fadal, an Elvis army buddy) a tribute to Elvis, entitled, *Our Memories of Elvis*. 1992 saw the appearance of *Elvis in Focus*.

In *Our Memories of Elvis*, the pictures came from both Wertheimer and Shaver and concentrated on the beginning and ending periods of Elvis' career. Some shots were doctored, given an eery touch, such as the one supposedly of Elvis the baby, "only a few months old." Fadal added anecdotal memories of Elvis, from the days when the pair were Army basic training buddies. In all, Shaver's photograph collection has been said to total in excess of eighty thousand unique pictures.

Tobler, John, and Richard Wootton. *Elvis: The Legend and the Music*. New York: Crescent Books, 1983.

Although this book purported to cover Elvis' music, it was a very surface excuse to merely present a large number of beautiful pictures, most of which had been shown before. Tobler has become known for presenting compendiums on rock stars that belong on coffee tables, not in research libraries. The highlights of Elvis' life, though not detailed, did cover the major events. Wootton, on his own, wrote a book about Elvis for a juvenile audience.

The Representations of Elvis in Art

Pictorial and art books fittingly rounded out an amazingly extensive body of published material that has presented a view so complex of one man that truly there could never be any one way of understanding either that man or his place in his world. Betty Harper, an artist who captured Elvis in every period of his life, said that "every time I draw him I see another side . . . almost another person." She added that "there was something incredibly inspiring about him. He pushed right to the limit of his potential."

Elvis was a humanitarian, a homebody, a drug and sex-crazed lunatic obsessed with guns, a religious guru, a night owl, and even the subject of extensive FBI files. He was dominated by his mother, his manager, his friends, his relatives, yet his was one of the most successful show business careers ever. He was a visionary, yet he was delusional. He read some of the most complex spiritual books yet, as poor Southern white trash, he could barely read or write.

How could one person have spawned so many views, been so complex yet so simplistic, and have attained such a legendary status? Harper, the artist, didn't want her audience to merely "see" Elvis, she wanted them to "experience him." Because he was so "incredibly inspiring" to her, she intended her drawings to have so much emotional impact that Elvis, as the subject, would become "secondary."

DePaoli, Geri, editor. *Elvis & Marilyn: Two Times Immortal.* **Foreword by David Halberstam. Commentary by Thomas McEvilley. Poem on Elvis by Bono of U2. New York: Rizzoli International, 1994. 170 pp. Notes, index.**

DePaoli, director of Educart projects, compiled, with assistance from a museum exhibit curator, Wendy McDaris, an extensive compendium of artwork featuring Elvis and Marilyn Monroe. In an editor's statement written with McDaris, he explained that the book "offers the opportunity to witness the transfiguration of Elvis and Marilyn from a cultural state of stardom to an iconic state of spiritual and religious resonance." The Elvis prints ranged from the Andy

Warhol silkscreen, "Elvis I and II," to a Marc Solomon Dennis oil on canvas, "Study of Severed Elvis Head with Salmon."

The Warhol work, "Elvis I and II," had an interesting history. The image came from a movie publicity still of Elvis, depicting him pointing a six-gun toward the camera. The still was one of several taken from the 1960 movie, *Flaming Star.* In 1962 Andy created the work (on canvas), using silkscreen ink (for a silver screen effect) to print the images on both a hand-painted background and a background of aluminum paint.

The "Elvis I and II" work was initially part of a large number (of similar Elvis paintings) Warhol created on a single roll of canvas for a one-man show displayed at the Ferus Gallery in Los Angeles. According to David Bourdon, in his book on Andy Warhol the artist, simply entitled *Warhol*, Irving Blum, in charge of putting on the show, said that "Andy sent me the Elvises in one continuous roll. It was an enormous roll of canvas, roughly six and one-half feet high and about 150 feet long." The paintings were displayed at the gallery, hung, at Warhol's request, "edge-to-edge along the gallery walls." They were complemented by twelve forty-inch-square Warhol portraits of Elizabeth Taylor hung in an adjoining room.

Blum, at first glance, appraised the Elvis (and Liz) paintings as not looking "enough like art," elaborating that "they looked machine-made." After the showing, according to Eric Shanes, in his book, *Warhol: The Masterworks*, Gerald Malanga, Warhol's painting assistant, cut up the paintings on the long roll, turning three of them into "Triple Elvis" in 1962 by overlapping the images. Also created was "Elvis I and II" (the single paintings flanked by two closely adjacent paintings). The "Elvis I and II" work was separately displayed in 1964.

One of the Elvis paintings Warhol created wound up in the possession of Bob Dylan, as payment for Dylan agreeing to possibly act in one of Warhol's movies. Dylan and friends took the painting, tied it to the top of Dylan's car, and drove off. Without telling Warhol, Dylan, who didn't want the painting, traded it to his manager, Albert Grossman, for a small couch Grossman had in his office. Warhol heard about the transaction, noting, in his diaries, that Grossman "has my silver Elvis." Andy was puzzled, writing, "I don't understand that, because I gave it to Dylan, so how would Grossman get it?"

That led Warhol to later quiz Robbie Robertson of The Band. Again in his diaries, Andy wrote that "Robbie said that at some point Dylan traded it to Grossman for a couch! (laughs) He felt he needed a little sofa and he gave him the Elvis for it. It must have been in his drug days. So that was an expensive couch." Supposedly, when Grossman died, the Warhol painting of Elvis was appraised at about $400,000.

Not only did the painting grow in monetary value over the years, but in reputation and meaning as well. Cecile Whiting, in a 1997 book from Cambridge University Press, *A Taste for Pop: Pop Art, Gender and Consumer Culture*, wrote that "in the case of Presley, Warhol's aesthetic contrivances actually end up unsettling the star's display of masculine heterosexuality. Although Presley assumes the movie role of the gun-toting cowboy in *Elvis I* of 1964 with feet spread and gun cocked, the silk-screen undercuts Presley's demonstration of cowboy machismo by coloring his costume a garish red and purple, while smearing his face with orange lipstick and purple eye shadow."

The author saw a basic similarity between the Elvis silkscreen paintings and one done by Warhol of Marlon Brando. In her opinion, "the silk-screens of Brando and Presley depict the stars in memorable moments from their movies when they pose with all of the accoutrements of tough masculinity: motorcycle, gun, black leather jacket, cowboy boots. By extracting these images of Presley and Brando from their narrative context and repeating them in shining metallic colors, however, Warhol's silk-screens have the consequence of revealing the stars' masculine bravado as nothing more than a combination of ostentatious costumes and stiffly staged poses." Both the Brando and Presley silk-screens (and perhaps others done by Warhol) "draw attention to masculine heterosexuality of the stars as public, theatrical performances, which, at least in the case of Presley, do not even promise a secure or stable gender identity."

Editor DePaoli wrote that each work of art in the book was selected because it presented "a new way of seeing, one that challenges the current holdover of a nineteenth-century visual language." That's why a gold bar with the logo "Elvis Lives" was included along with a photographic print by Louis Lussier entitled "Elvis Shadow." Elvis now "belongs to the even smaller and more elite rank of those who are forever known as the inhabitants of empty tombs–again like Jesus."

Along with all the artwork, many insightful essays by writers such as Kate Millett and Lucinda Ebersole were presented. Ebersole raised the issue that "the postmodern myth of Elvis presents us with a god." As a result, "the resurrected Elvis, whether dead or alive, turns up in the most amazing situations." Pulitzer Prize-winning journalist David Halberstam wrote in the foreword that Elvis "was the leader of a larger revolution, the coming of a youth culture."

Of all the books that featured Elvis images, this one captured the widest variety, both pictorial and written. Even the most casual peruser could learn that Elvis' mother walked Elvis to school "until he was fifteen," while viewing artwork that portrayed a "Frog Elvis: The Lounge Act." Artist Carol Robison wrote about Elvis that "I have always been obsessed with Elvis, not for his music but for his inner torment. Perhaps it is through the tears of our icons and idols we gain hope and possible deliverance from our own sorrow."

Harper, Betty. *Suddenly and Gently: Visions of Elvis Through the Art of Betty Harper.* **Foreword by Bill E. Burk. New York: St. Martin's, 1987.   87 pp.**

This book captured the classic black-and-white sketches of Elvis done by Betty Harper. As an artist, she was formally trained at the American Academy in Paris, where she studied Monet and Renoir. Her Elvis artwork went beyond being technically flawless to capturing the various moods and emotions inherent in his facial expressions.

She viewed Elvis as having "had such a wonderful face, so varied. From one angle it's soft, baby-like. From another, it's harder; almost cruel." Actress Joan Crawford likened Harper's work to that of Norman Rockwell. Harper hoped her work enabled the viewer to go beyond "seeing" Elvis to "experiencing" him. Prior to this classic collection, she had a book on "newly discovered drawings of Elvis" published in 1979 by Bantam Books. After *Suddenly and Gently*, she worked on finishing the second in a series of Elvis lithographs distributed by Osborne Fine Art Images.

Taylor, Roger G. *Elvis in Art.* **New York: St. Martin's Press, 1987.   145 pp.   (unnumbered).**

The black-and-white and full-color artwork in Taylor's book presented Elvis in a variety of sequences, poses, settings, and expressions. The outstanding works came from Andy Warhol, Stanislaw Fernandez, and other modernists. Through their eyes, the King took on many radically different personas and auras.

The quotes from others, such as Colonel Parker, James Brown, and Pat Boone, did much to personalize the various ways of perceiving the man and the star. Included were several album cover artworks from RCA/Ariola, specifically the ones for the Sun Collection and the *Return of the Rocker*. The book, though published in 1987, has become a valuable collector's item. Mark Knopfler said in one of the quotes that "Elvis was a beautiful young person." The images Taylor presented captured that observation and more.

Heartbreak Hotel:
WHAT DID ELVIS LEAVE BEHIND?

Elvis was like a battery that had been drained too
many times. His body could no longer hold a charge."

- **Ed Parker**,
Inside Elvis

Elvis is gone. That's the stark fact, whether one believed Elvis died
or disappeared. What did he leave behind? For the fans, he left
countless memories. Otherwise, the years have blurred his legacy.
For some, like the author of the book, *Elvis Presley: King of Kings,*
Elvis had become the messiah, the risen Christ. That book was
available only by telephone order (330-339-9111).

Elvis has yet to become a religion. He likely never will. He has
been turned into a set of impersonators. Former football coach Jerry
Glanville wrote in his memoirs, *Elvis Don't Like Football,* that one
estimate he heard had Elvis impersonators growing to become one out
of every seven people in this country. An impersonator is the
personification of memories.

Elvis left anywhere from nothing to $5 million when he died,
according to various estimates. His image and name have become
worth hundreds of millions of dollars today and his estate grows each
year at a rapid rate. Ex-wife Priscilla turned that venture around.
The bulk of it eventually goes to Lisa Marie Presley, his only legally
recognized daughter. I say that because the claims of women having
his child have literally risen from the woodwork.

Politically, Elvis never got involved during his lifetime, except
for that now legendary trek to see Nixon and obtain a special drug
agent badge. In all likelihood, Elvis' lifestyle and the rumors
surrounding it would have been too much a liability for any politician
needing to appeal across all political and moral persuasions. In
death, though, Elvis did influence at least one election.

According to political analyst Douglas Rushkoff, in his book, *Media Virus*, George Bush might have hurt himself in the 1992 election because he appeared to have spoken "badly about the King." Then-President Bush used a couple of Elvis analogies on Bill Clinton, saying that challenger Clinton had "been spotted in more places than Elvis" and with Clinton, "America will be checking into Heartbreak Hotel." Deepening his rift with "white American Southerners," Mr. Bush further likened Clinton to Elvis, by saying that "the minute he takes a stand on something he starts wiggling." As Rushkoff noted, Bush's comments made him appear like "a reactive, impotent candidate whose only alternative was to attack the virility of his challenger."

As far as the physical aspects of Elvis' legacy, there was, of course, Graceland, his home and mansion. Though the upper floor has been blocked off, Graceland is toured by hundreds of thousands of people every year–more visitors than the White House. One collector/fan even claimed to have found one of Elvis' toenail clippings in the rug. So, perhaps a part of him really does live on, if, of course, toenails have a life of their own. The Elvis persona certainly does.

Eventually, all that any person leaves behind are his or her progeny and his or her estate. Beyond Graceland, Elvis' estate obviously consisted of money, awards, gold and platinum records, a famous name, a marketable image, and lots of material things. His progeny consisted of one person, Lisa Marie Presley. Who is the offspring that Elvis left behind?

She was nine when he died. They had been close, as close as a daughter could be to a superstar, traveling, night-living father divorced from the mother. After his death, she stayed relatively clear of the limelight, surfacing once in a while in the tabloids or in the memoirs of Mike Edwards, her mother's live-in lover, who claimed to have had a lusty crush on her.

Then she surfaced big time. Just prior, there had been reports she had cut some demonstration records and had an agent out shopping the recordings to major labels. Since nothing happened, in spite of the famous name, either the recordings were never made or they were unacceptable to any label, meaning they had to have been awful (if indeed they did exist) because her name alone would have accounted for hundreds of thousands of sales to curious Elvis fans.

The big surfacing came when she married Michael Jackson, the self-proclaimed King of Pop. Michael had been amazingly successful since leaving the Jackson Five to become a superstar in his own right, selling millions of albums, acting as a major force behind the "We Are the World" project, and taking dance videos to new heights. Then

Michael ran into trouble with charges of homosexual relationships with underage children.

The case almost went to trial when Michael supposedly bought off one or maybe two boys and their parents with payments well into the millions. The district attorney who would have prosecuted told his story to *Vanity Fair*. He said at least one boy had a credible story, complete with full identification of various private Jackson parts. Michael's health and career fell into shambles. Liz Taylor rushed to the rescue but even she couldn't save him.

Enter Lisa Marie and her marriage to Michael. The comments surrounding that marriage have ranged from their being two lovebirds to their hardly even speaking to each other, let alone consummating their wedding. The two finally appeared on a major news show to show the world they were indeed two starstruck lovers. Unfortunately, soon after, they were divorced. Michael then impregnated a longtime female acquaintance and soon after the baby was born he supposedly took it over completely. That relationship floundered (though the two did produce a second baby).

Since then, tabloids have had he and the mother together again as well as him going back to Lisa Marie. One even had a "live" Elvis telling Lisa Marie to "divorce Michael." All the public really knew was that Lisa Marie and Priscilla did appear at the August 1997 Elvis week in Memphis. A huge video player showed Lisa singing (overdubbed, of course) with daddy Elvis. Reportedly, not a dry eye was to be seen anywhere.

So, the question remained, what did Elvis leave, in human terms? No one has really tried to answer that, except one Hollywood private investigator, Don Crutchfield. Why should he be believed? Crutchfield related in his book (written with Gene Busnar and published by Dunhill of New York) entitled *Confessions of A Hollywood PI*, that he was hired to "investigate the relationship between Michael Jackson and the Chandler boy," the boy whom Jackson was accused of molesting. By way of his investigation into Michael's troubled world, Crutchfield came into close contact with the equally troubled life of Lisa Marie.

There is no reason to rehash Crutchfield's conclusions on the Jackson side of his detective work. The interesting part was what he observed and pieced together on Elvis' heir. To begin with, he viewed both Michael and Lisa Marie as being "products of sick family backgrounds." Lisa Marie was the daughter of a woman (Priscilla) whose own mother "essentially sold" her to Elvis "at the age of fourteen." Both Lisa and Priscilla became members of the Church of Scientology, or as Crutchfield described them, two of the "most devoted celebrity parishioners." Lisa Marie married another practicing Scientologist, Danny Keogh (some books have spelled it Keough), and together they had two children before divorcing.

So, how did Lisa Marie come to marry Michael in a wedding ceremony which afterward, according to Crutchfield, had the presiding judge (in the Dominican Republic) expressing "shock when bride and groom refused to kiss at the conclusion of the ceremony" and describing Lisa Marie as "one of the unhappiest brides" he'd ever seen? After the ceremony, Crutchfield learned that Lisa Marie (during the time the couple was supposed to have been honeymooning) had really checked into a plastic surgery clinic to "have breast augmentation and liposuction performed on her thighs," procedures that "prevent a patient from having sexual relations for some time." The answer that made "a great deal of sense" to him and which could "explain why Lisa dumped Michael" centered around her involvement in the Church of Scientology.

Crutchfield's perception was that Lisa "did try to recruit Michael" into the church. He felt the perception made sense for two reasons. The first was that Michael could bring "a tremendous influx of cash" into the organization. The second reason centered around the church's "blood feud with the psychiatric community." Crutchfield's view was that the church would have gained quite a "feather in their cap" by taking "an alleged pedophilic homosexual" and converting him "into a normal heterosexual male."

Of all the accounts of the Jackson/Presley nuptials, the one that came out in the February 1998 issue of *Q* magazine became the most precise yet detailed and believable reporting on the the nonevent. The uncredited "eyewitness" article entitled "Michael Jackson's Wedding" quoted the presiding judge, Hugo Alvarez (of the Dominican Republic), as saying he "felt they weren't taking it seriously" and adding that "they were not what I would call a loving couple. There were no cuddles or canoodling but they did hold hands. Jackson kept looking at the floor and seemed embarrassed." During the ceremony, Alvarez disclosed that "Lisa Marie seemed unmoved by the whole event." The judge also "got the feeling Michael was being led." Incidentally, there were two "witnesses" brought along to the ceremony, according to the *Q* article, one of whom had the last name, Keogh (first name Thomas–brother of Danny).

In Crutchfield's final analysis, "the breakup of Michael Jackson and Lisa Marie proved to be the least surprising event in the entire sordid affair." According to his findings, "the couple live mostly apart" and their public displays of physical attraction were "as transparent as a piece of plastic wrap." The only public togetherness came in front of cameras during Diane Sawyer's televised interview with them for ABC-TV. The marriage ended after Michael collapsed trying to film an HBO special. Lisa Marie told him (as quoted by Crutchfield), in the hospital, that "the show was over" and from that point on her lawyers spoke for her as the divorce proceedings went forward.

Away from Jackson, Lisa Marie disappeared from the public spotlight again. Did she come forward just to save Michael and lure him and his money into her church? Has her life become as aimless and isolated as her father's? Was that what her father left behind a manipulative, isolated, confused daughter? Elvis' life began with the accompaniment of a mysterious blue light that must have signified something of a major spiritual nature, according to his father. Yet Elvis never found his purpose in the world, so he chose to isolate himself from it.

To a white Southern country musician, Ira Louvin, Elvis was a "white nigger." To a black artist like Muddy Waters, he was just another "whitey." The rest of the world never really knew who he was. Finally, his life ended in a bathroom, either due to heart failure or brought on by years of drug abuse. To some, he was just another overweight overly indulged reclusive superstar way beyond his prime, while to others, who saw so much more in him, he was gifted, he was electrifying, and he was a near-deity sent to earth to bring joy, harmony, and peace through his music.

If nothing else, Elvis was genuine. It was something that people sensed and it played a large part in drawing them to him. Elvis also had a great natural musical talent on which to build. Before the excesses of stardom (and the demands for writer credits or half the publishing rights) kept the music from being innovative, there were indications that Elvis knew how to be (and wanted to be) a continuing musical trendsetter.

Jimmy Day, one of country music's finest pedal steel players, recently disclosed that Elvis asked to him join his band when he first went out to Hollywood. Day declined but reminisced that "it would have changed rock 'n' roll forever. Rock 'n' roll would have had a steel guitar." Elvis was a strong enough musical force to have pulled it off (rocking with a steel guitar) just as he pulled off his legendary television special in the sixties and later made such a powerful recording of the song "Suspicious Minds."

Elvis had flashes of musical explosiveness throughout his career. Yet even though his most devoted fans acknowledged that "he gave us good songs," that was not necessarily what all of them remembered most about him. Elvis was eulogized as having possessed a "sincere caring about other people" and having been a man who gave the world "a little glimpse of what God is like."

All the hoopla that surrounded the twentieth anniversary of his death (1997) spawned even more idolization and collector mania. Did you know, for example, that the magazine, *Pop Culture Collecting*, named a 1955 poster advertising an Elvis appearance in Texas as the number one collectible rock concert poster? Russell Stover Candies released a twentieth anniversary Elvis memorial tin.

The *Elvis International Forum* magazine, edited by Darwin Lamm, released a *Limited Edition 20th Anniversary Collector's Edition Book* that boasted fifty "breathtaking rare photos," many of which were previously "unpublished." Even more books were printed, though most of them weren't necessarily written to foster deeper understanding. Instead their intent seemed to be to either make more money off the Elvis memory phenomenon or to foster more glorification. Every year, in fact, it seemed like January (Elvis' birth month) and August (Elvis' death month) would spawn new rounds of celebrations, vigils, publications, memorials, and memorabilia marketing.

In a short span of forty-two years, Elvis had come and gone, appearing completely burned out at the end. But did he really die? Those who believed Elvis continued to live by faking his death concluded he did it (or would have done it) because he was through with the trappings of stardom and wanted to get away to a simpler, more spiritual life out of the adoring but demanding public eye. Those who believed he really did die (and didn't get to view the body) based their conclusions on how they saw him live his life, especially the final several years.

One of the best Hollywood columnists, Sheilah Graham, reached her conclusions about what happened to Elvis by observing his activities firsthand over many years. In her 1984 book, *Hollywood Revisited* (published by St. Martin's), she focused on Elvis' health problems, saying that "as the pressures of his life mounted, he began to put on weight. How he hated the blubber on the body that had been slim and handsome when I saw him make his first picture in Hollywood, 'Love Me Tender.' " She watched as he and his Memphis Mafia would have "junk food sent up to the suite." In the end, she decided that the "junk food" along with "the uppers and downers, and all the one-night concert stands, finally caught up with him."

Perhaps the best clue as to what really went on in Elvis' mind (at least early in his career) came from Natalie Wood, who, at eighteen, dated him when he first started making movies. She recalled (as captured by Warren G. Harris in his book, *Natalie & R.J.: Hollywood's Star-Crossed Lovers*) that going out with Elvis was "like having the date that I never had in high school. I thought it was really wild." Not only did she find him to be "so square," he was deeply religious, even then. In her words, according to Harris, "I'd never been around anyone that religious. He felt he had been given this gift, this talent, by God. He didn't take it for granted. He thought it was something he had to protect. He had to be nice to people, otherwise God would take it all away." Maybe Elvis wanted it all taken away in the end.

Syndicated columnist (specializing in the entertainment world) Marilyn Beck was one of a number of writers (in the 1995 book conceptualized by Michael Viner, for Dove Books, entitled *Unfinished Lives: What If . . . ?*) who posed the question, about several celebrities, "what if they had not died?" She speculated on what would have happened if Elvis had not passed away in the Graceland bathroom. Her interesting speculation began with Elvis furtively (and alone) racing (in an old Chevy van) away from Graceland, leaving the body of an imposter behind (laying on the bathroom floor).

From there the story backtracked to Elvis privately viewing the show of an impersonator so much like him that even Elvis thought it uncanny. Elvis invited him to Graceland for a private meeting to discuss the imposter playing some of Elvis' Vegas dates. The imposter turned out to be a "druggie" so Elvis gave him some pills, which caused the look-alike to accidentally overdose and die. In that brief moment Elvis knew that he "found my way out." Did it all sound preposterous? It has been alleged that Elvis really did hire imposters to play some of his shows when he either couldn't or didn't want to.

The rest of the story proceeded from Elvis leaving the dead imposter on the bathroom floor and driving the man's van to "freedom." The "freedom" he found brought him no money, no peace, and no women. So, several months later, he decided to go back. However, no one would believe him, not his dad, not his chief of security (Dick Grob), not even Joe Esposito. So, he became an Elvis "clone," an impersonator, but when he went to do his first show, he couldn't sing anymore. Frustrated, he slit his wrists. However, no one recognized him and his passing went unnoticed, proving, yet again, there never was a way out for Elvis!

Still, die-hard fans needed to believe their idol remained alive because that would negate the tales of overeating and drug use that caused a bloated corpse and an untimely death. Thus, increasing numbers of rumors have surfaced that he went into hiding for reasons ranging from witness protection to physical burnout. The tabloids have profitably fueled such stories and their sensational headlines.

For many people, who have accepted Elvis' physical death, he "still lives" because "there is a need for his effect on culture." Dr. Clarissa Pinkola Estes wrote in her essay, "Elvis Presley: Fama, and the Cultus of the Dying God" (part of the book, *The Soul of Popular Culture*, edited by Mary Lynn Kittelson), that Elvis will remain "alive" as long as "the culture is parched and unresponsive to the body." It is his "energy" and "ecstasy" that will never die.

Otherwise, from the most credible people around Elvis when his dead body was discovered, there has never arisen even the slightest hint that he did not die. From J. D. Sumner to Charlie Hodge, uncompromising statements have been made that Elvis' body was indeed in his coffin. In 1996, the man who ran the funeral home that buried Elvis came forward with his definitive statement.

Kemmons Wilson, the founder of the Holiday Inns chain, was also the co-owner of Forest Hills, which, in his words (from his autobiography), was "the funeral home that handled Presley's arrangements." He unequivocally wrote that "I can guarantee Elvis is dead, because we buried him." That statement should quell any further rumors that Elvis is not permanently resting in his coffin.

To those unequivocal words Wilson added, "I owned half of Forest Hills at the time. M. N. 'Doc' Murray owned the other half. We buried Elvis and put him in a mausoleum at Forest Hills Cemetery. But then it was just misery for us. So many people were trying to get in the mausoleum, trying to sneak over the fence at night. We were so happy when they moved his body out to Graceland that we didn't know what to do." One group of people caught breaking in only wanted to look at the body to see if it was really Elvis. So much for resting in peace.

The Elvis Commentaries

And, Paul Simon's "Graceland" notwithstanding, it is
overwhelmingly sad to visit Graceland and see how
the life and death of the King have been turned
into a slick and sick Elvis Theme Park.

−James F. Harris,
Philosophy at 33 1/3 rpm:
Themes of Classic Rock Music

12

Treat Me Nice:
THE INTRODUCTION TO THE ELVIS
COMMENTARIES

Since August 16, 1977, hundreds of books have appeared,
some seeking honestly to explain a popular phenomenon,
many simply looking to cash in on that phenomenon or, more
often than not, to place the writer at the center of Elvis's life.

–Ernst Jorgensen,
Elvis Presley: A Life in Music:
The Complete Recording Sessions

I was ten years old when my brother sat me down and told me to listen
to this incredible new song, "I'm Left, You're Right, She's Gone." The
singer was Elvis Presley, or as my brother called him, Pelvis Presley.
As for me, I was hooked. So my brother played two more RCA singles
by Elvis, "My Baby Left Me" (explaining, in a very low, reverential
tone, that it was written by Arthur "Big Boy" Crudup, a blues singer
from Mississippi) and "I Want You, I Need You, I Love You."

Both of us always loved stuff we thought no one else knew about,
so when he showed me Elvis' first album, I was close to ecstacy. We
were first in our tiny town to have acquired the recording. He had me
listen to songs like "Tryin' to Get to You" and "I'll Never Let You Go
(Little Darlin')." From there I started reading about Elvis in my
sister's fan magazines and soon learned that my new favorite song,
"I'm Left, You're Right, She's Gone," was based on a 1954 Campbell
soup commercial. Humming the new songs in my head, I wrote down
the words to try to figure out what made Elvis and his songs get to me.
When I discovered I *could* curl my lip like he did and I *could* wear my
hair long (styled with flat top wax), I just as quickly discovered I
could not drive the girls wild the way he did.

That was when I first became engrossed in trying to understand
how (and why) Elvis affected so many people so deeply. I never
became the fan so many people became, instead I became an Elvis
student. My fascination did stop for a while when he became bland
(and oblivious to the changes in the world) by singing songs like "Love
Letters" and "Indescribably Blue." It took Greil Marcus to bring him

back into focus with his great book on American music, *Mystery Train*, of which Elvis was the centerpiece.

After his stunning televised "comeback" special, Elvis went back out on the road. Within the next few years, I heard the overdone excesses of the Aloha concerts and stopped wondering; it didn't matter to me anymore. I assumed people were chasing a memory. Then he died. Elvis worship started and I wrote it off as dead idol worship. I couldn't mourn someone I never knew but since others did, I began wondering anew what the hold was.

The postage stamp controversy arose. Would it be the young, dapper Elvis, or the older, glitzy, Las Vegas Elvis, or the final, speech-slurred, weight-challenged one? They were all some manifestation of Elvis. How could one choose? Personally I wanted to see a collage of all three because together the Elvis personas affected people in this country seemingly like no one before or since, not George Washington, not James Dean, not John Kennedy, not even Michael Jordan. True, we get fascinated, deeply so, by some phenomenons now and again, like O. J. Simpson and his murder trial. When that happens, media outlets become flooded by literature on the subject. Then we tire of the flood and it disappears.

But Elvis hasn't gone away. The literature about him started in 1956 and has continued virtually unabated through this moment. In fact, the books on Elvis are now flowing out faster than they ever have and it seems like there are even more waiting in the wings. I find myself asking over and over again, why, *why* such a fascination with the King? Not being one to leave such a fascinating topic alone, I set out to answer the question.

I wasn't the only one. Author Larry Nager posed a similar question and succinctly tried to answer it in his 1998 book, *Memphis Beat*, published by St. Martin's Press. He observed that "even after the mountain of books about the Elvis phenomenon, the question remains: Why Elvis?" To him, Elvis "was a phenomenon whose impact an entire industry has tried tirelessly to re-create for more than forty years since, always falling short of the mark."

As a possible but superficial answer, Nager wrote that Elvis "may have filled the alienated teen-idol void James Dean left vacant when his Porsche Spider crashed on September 30, 1955, but there was more to it than that." His very general overall conclusion was that "Elvis was simply the right person at the right time." That conclusion left out anything intangible and special Elvis might have had inside which bound record numbers of fans to his persona forever.

In his book, *Revolt Into Style*, renowned British writer and critic George Melly characterized rock and roll as "screw and smash music." In doing so, he analyzed Elvis' impact strictly in terms of sex appeal.

In his estimation, Presley "came on as though confident in his ability to attract women without appealing in any way to their protective instinct. He was the master of the sexual simile, treating his guitar as both phallus and girl, punctuating his lyrics with animal grunts and groans of the male approaching an orgasm. He made it quite clear that he felt he was doing any woman he accepted a favour. He dressed to emphasize both his masculinity and basic narcissism, and rumour had it that into his skin-tight jeans was sewn a lead bar in order to suggest a weapon of heroic proportions."

Melly also noted that Elvis' appeal "in the first place was to young males. He said something which had never been admitted so openly in public, at any rate not for a century and a half: that most young men are promiscuously inclined and that a smaller but significant number of girls have strong sexual appetites on their account." Yet sex couldn't have been the only answer, especially with all the spiritual overtones attached to the Elvis mystique.

Not only did the books on or about Elvis total in the multiple hundreds; by the mid-1990s, the number of photographs available on him in the commercial marketplace ranged in the millions and "new" ones (ones that have never been distributed publicly) kept appearing, even though he's been dead twenty years. In 1997, one of his old girlfriends came out with a treasure trove of never-before-published photos of a young Elvis.

It wasn't until 1998 that former *Life* photographer Bill Ray discovered he had put aside and forgotten about a "stash" of photos he took in 1958. The photos captured a twenty-three-year-old Elvis about to set sail for Germany. As Ray told *People* magazine, when he looked at the "never-published" pictures, untouched for thirty years, he felt "an electricity in the air. Elvis was one of those people who made your heart beat faster when you were around him."

All the books, articles, manuscripts, films, and photographs have effectively made Elvis the most written about and photographed person in the history of the world. How can we not know this man? How can we not recite every fact and close the books? How can we not agree on every fact and story? The answers are surprisingly simple. Elvis has truly become all things, good and bad, to all people.

Anyone could have a view on Elvis and present it. Because he was such an overwhelming public figure, no view could be adequately defended, denied, or even sued over. People don't necessarily want to get to know Elvis. They want Elvis to become what they thought they knew. So, if they thought he was dirty and angry, he became corrupt and crazed. If they held devout views or saw him in a pious light, then Elvis touched their lives with God's love.

As a result, too many supposed facts and stories have become convoluted. For example, authors Peter Harry Brown and Pat H. Broeske reported in their book, *Down At the End of Lonely Street,* that Elvis once used a .22 to blow up a TV set showing Robert Goulet's image, supposedly because Elvis was not a Robert Goulet fan. Their reporting of the incident with no further explanation made it appear that Elvis was either bored, or "wacko," or just prone to acting impulsively for no sane reason.

What the two authors didn't report but what Marty Lacker had previously revealed was that Elvis had a particular vendetta toward Goulet dating back to the time when his then-girlfriend Anita Wood, an aspiring actress and singer, was part of a Goulet tour and Elvis was stuck in Germany. On one of the letters Anita wrote to Elvis, Goulet added a postscript that read, "Hey, Elvis, don't worry, I'm taking pretty good care of Anita!" Lacker said that really "burnt the shit out of" Elvis.

The postscript on the letter "ate at him all those years" and was the real reason why he shot at a television showing the face of Robert Goulet. Though it was a senseless and stupid thing to do, it was not a random act of insanity. There was a time he blasted a TV screen showing a hemorrhoid cream commercial; that might have been a little out-of-control. At least he had a reason to hate Robert Goulet, and not for his singing style.

The concept of Elvis has not only become convoluted, but incredibly complex. Even though Joe Esposito said this and Priscilla said that, very few irrefutable conclusions could be drawn with respect to the "real" Elvis. Instead, it would require multiple views or paradigms (that's why we've been literally flooded with multiple "Elvises") to project a systematic insight into Elvis as a private, thinking, and feeling person. There would be Elvis the actor, musician, star, husband, father, and, if possible, a persona encompassing Elvis the person. That strictly personal picture would generate many subviews, such as Elvis the angel of God, drug-abuser, cancer victim, overeater, isolated, oversexed, and perhaps even the "faker-of-his-own-death."

So, to place an extended focus on the more important and controversial aspects of the Elvis persona, I created a set of Elvis commentaries. Into each of the topics, his phenomenal success, his relationship to the music of black Americans, and the mysterious enigma behind the enigma, Colonel Tom Parker, many here to fore overlooked insights have been incorporated. Most of the insights came from sources outside the specific books written exclusively about Elvis or about others close to him.

13

If I Can Dream:
ELVIS AND HIS PHENOMENAL SUCCESS

> But though Elvis was idolized, and
> fussed over, and treated after
> his death as though he actually
> were a king, he was only a man.
>
> –Carl Perkins,
> *Disciple in Blue Suede Shoes*

One of the major reasons why Elvis outshone every other male rock star was because he turned on the women without turning off the men, affecting the men in such a way that they all wanted to be like him. Marc Eliot, in his book, *Rockonomics: The Money Behind the Music*, saw Elvis as "a mama's boy," whose "peculiar qualities" somehow "translated into a personal appeal that cut across gender, age, economics and class." That appeal, Eliot analyzed, "made real mothers want to smother him and teenage girls want to mother him." Additionally, it "allowed teenage boys to like him, instinctively knowing that Elvis was no threat to take away their girlfriends."

However, the sexual feelings Elvis engendered in both men and women cannot be overlooked. David Sanjek observed, in *Sexing the Groove* (a book edited by Sheila Whitely), that Elvis "crossed all gender boundaries." The women "wanted not simply to fuck Elvis but, instead, to assimilate a portion of his authority and cultural power." Some men even found him more than just attractive. The best expression of that kind of feeling came, as Sanjek pointed out, from a character, Clarence Worly (played by Christian Slater), in the 1993 movie, *True Romance*. The character said, to no one in particular in a little bar, that "I ain't no fag, but Elvis, he was prettier than most women." He continued his soliloquy, adding that "if I had to fuck a guy–had to if my life depended on it–I'd fuck Elvis."

Even his hair added to his allure. Miss Pamela of the GTO's (a Frank Zappa brainchild) told of how she got shivers watching "those old black and white films of Elvis getting shorn for Uncle Sam. When he rubs his hand over the stubs of his former blue-black mane, I get a twinge in my temples." She summarized that "I tried to believe that Elvis was doing his duty as an American, but even at eleven years old, I realized his raunch had been considerably diminished."

Actress Shelley Winters had a view of Elvis that he really liked being conspicuous. In fact, she wrote in her 1989 autobiography, that when Elvis dated Natalie Wood, their idea of "being inconspicuous was wearing all white and driving a huge, convertible white Cadillac. Sometimes I would go to the movies with them. When we entered, I often felt we were the entertainment. They would sit close to each other, down front. I would hide somewhere on the side, but they gave off such an aura of success and happiness and fun that it seemed as if the projectionist had put a spotlight on them. The audience ignored the movie, stood up, and watched Elvis and Natalie. Finally, to get some privacy, Natalie forced him to go to the movies incognito. She taught him that the audience's reaction was very important and must be studied. I believe, after that romance, Elvis never again went into a movie theater unless he'd bought out the whole house."

Shelley used her understanding of Elvis to turn a made-for-television movie about him (starring Kurt Russell) into, in her words, "a very good TV show." In the movie, Shelley played Elvis' mother, Gladys, and was able to "help Kurt Russell play Elvis very authentically-not just to imitate the musical legend but to get at the essence of this young, aspiring, yet sad man." She related that during the time she knew Elvis, "he would call his mother in Memphis at precisely 7:00 p.m. every single night."

During the filming of that 1979 movie, *Elvis*, Winters said she "got Kurt to find the disappointments in his own experience that were perhaps parallel to Elvis's." In fact she talked to Kurt "about Elvis and his sweetness and aspirations for many days." As a result, she believed "he captured the essence of Elvis Presley in that film rather than just imitating him."

When it was all said and done and Elvis was laid to rest, he had accomplished something few performers ever have, he kept himself at the top for three decades, through major societal upheavals and changes. Even after death, in the best American tradition of dead idol worship, Elvis retained his legendary status. Critic John Hellow wrote in a 1998 issue of *The Audiophile Voice* that, in retrospect, the coverage surrounding his death was the kind "usually reserved for the heads of state or royalty." Even today, he noted, not only do the most loyal fans refuse to admit Elvis really died, the growing number of reported sightings have begun to be "tracked on web pages."

Although Elvis himself never felt he was a great musician and all too often his repertoire was criticized as not consisting of great songs, his musical legacy has become too overwhelming to be dismissed. Billy Poore, in his 1998 book, *Rockabilly: A Forty-Year Journey*, wrote that "Elvis was the one who stumbled onto what became the first rockabilly record." He concluded that "if Elvis hadn't walked into that little Memphis studio, do you think we would have ever heard of Buddy Holly, Gene Vincent, Carl Perkins, Eddie Cochran, Jerry Lee Lewis, Roy Orbison, or even The Beatles?"

Of all the popular musicians of the twentieth century, only Frank Sinatra and perhaps The Beatles ever attained and held the stature to which Elvis so naturally gravitated. Statistically, according to Joel Whitburn in his compendium on the *Billboard* album sales charts, *Top Pop Albums 1955–1996*, Elvis had more charted albums (ninety-three) than anyone else. Sinatra, who started recording in 1939 and has four to five times as many albums to his credit, was second with sixty-nine.

Elvis also had the greatest number of gold- and platinum-selling albums (forty-two). Additionally, he had forty-eight top-forty albums (second to Sinatra who had fifty-one) and twenty-five top-ten sets, fourth behind The Rolling Stones and Frank Sinatra, who tied for the most with thirty-three. Elvis' nine number-one albums put him second behind The Beatles and their seventeen top-of-the-chart items. Such sales figures seemed ironic considering that the Jordanaires remembered Elvis saying, "I can't dance. I can't sing. What the hell do they want me for?" They truly wanted him for his music, which was as dominant a factor in his "myth" as his presence and movie star looks.

Who could deny the greatness of his key recordings, such as the early hit, "Don't Be Cruel"? The song was good enough on first listen by the publisher to land its composer, Otis Blackwell, his first staff writing job at Shalimar Music in New York City. Then there was the late sixties powerhouse "Guitar Man," written by country music guitarist Jerry Reed, who played, along with Scotty Moore, some powerful innovative guitar lines on the single. Elvis' final top-ten smashes were equally mesmerizing, "Suspicious Minds" and Dennis Linde's pulsating rocker, "Burning Love."

As far as his successful recording career was concerned, Elvis was one of the few major artists who stayed with one label, even after making it big. That company, RCA, not only reaped huge profits from making and selling Elvis records, their name became almost synonymous with Elvis' name. It would somehow not seem right to see an Elvis recording without the dog or the RCA logo. And to think they got Elvis for the paltry sum of $35,000 (or $45,000, as some people supposedly close to the deal have stated). Jerry Wexler, of Atlantic Records, a company that had wanted to sign Elvis, wrote, in his autobiography, that RCA got Elvis for $45,000. Even that offer had to be "underwritten by Gene Aberbach of publishers Hill and Range," according to Jerry.

Yet when Elvis was still with Sun Records and his contract was up for sale, at least two other companies could have signed him. One of them was, of course, Atlantic. Wexler, one of the original partners of the company (along with Ahmet Ertegun), revealed (in his autobiography) that "we bid up to $30,000" for Elvis' contract. When the bid didn't succeed, "we didn't think much about it and, if truth be known, might have been relieved that the final price was over our heads. If Elvis had accepted our offer, we would've had to scramble even to come up with the thirty grand." Of course, had they had even an "inkling" of Elvis' future as "the Jesus of Rock," he said he might have "found a way to outbid RCA."

Ertegun divulged to *Billboard* magazine that "I tried to sign him up," meaning Elvis, of course. He explained that "Colonel Parker needed $45,000 and we didn't have $45,000. Our biggest purchase of a contract was when we paid $3,000 to get Ray Charles." Authors Dorothy Wade and Justine Picardie (in their book *Music Man: Ahmet Ertegun, Atlantic Records, and the Triumph of Rock 'n' Roll*) quoted Ertegun as saying that the $25,000 bid encompassed "all the money we had then." With more than a little bitter irony, he recalled that "the president of RCA at the time had been extensively quoted in *Variety* damning R&B music as immoral. He soon stopped when RCA signed Elvis Presley."

Dick Jacobs, an A&R executive at both Decca Records and a subsidiary label, Coral, beginning in the fifties, told the story of how Decca was the other major label that had a shot at signing Elvis. According to Jacobs (writing in his book *Who Wrote That Song*), Decca (back in the early fifties) "had an A&R man by the name of Paul Cohen. Paul built Decca's country division into a formidable force in the record industry and signed most of the major artists to the label: Red Foley, Ernest Tubb, Kitty Wells, Loretta Lynn, Webb Pierce, Brenda Lee, Patsy Cline, and many others. Paul had a friend in Memphis, Sam Phillips, who had a label called Sun Records. Sam needed money and offered to his friend, Paul Cohen, the contract to a young singer Phillips had recording for him. The price was $30,000. Cohen brought the deal back to New York, where it was turned down. Management felt that was too much money for a weird looking rock-a-billy singer."

To conclude his story, Jacobs added, "and that's how Decca lost Elvis Presley." It wasn't meant to be. With an attitude like that, Decca probably would not have been able to turn Elvis into the huge record seller he became for RCA. Jacobs saw it as "a lack of vision."

Others saw it as something Phillips had to do. Author and musician Billy Poore, in his history of the Memphis musical scene, explained that "if he hadn't sold Elvis's contract when he did, he'd have gone out of business." Phillips had to have $40,000 with $5,000 going to Elvis for back royalties.

There may have been more than simply financial considerations involved. In the August 1, 1998, issue of *Dateline: Memphis* (a local Memphis entertainment paper), writer Woody Deegan reported that "several sources" had told him that "Oscar (The Baron) Davis, a 'major player' from Boston, came to town with a couple of large bodyguards and met with Sam Phillips in order to 'negotiate' the contract." He concluded that "perhaps Sam really didn't have much of a choice."

Even as successful a businessman as Kemmons Wilson, founder of the Holiday Inn chain, advised Phillips to sell. On the night Sam had to decide to sell Elvis' contract, he called Wilson. Kemmons, in his autobiography, *Half Luck and Half Brains*, wrote that he didn't even hesitate to rhetorically quiz Phillips by saying that although Elvis was a nice young man, "$35,000 for a performer who is not even a professional? I'd sell that contract!"

Eventually Wilson decided his advice was absurd, but only with hindsight. At the time it made a lot more sense, because "Frankie Lane, then a much bigger star than Elvis, had just been sold by Mercury to Columbia Records for only $25,000. In fact, $35,000 was the highest amount ever paid for an entertainer at that time, and RCA considered its acquisition of Elvis a huge gamble."

There was more to the picture, as Wilson recalled. He knew, as Phillips himself has often reminded people, that Phillips "really needed the cash." One reason for that need was his just-completed buyout of his brother Jud's (also spelled Judd) share of the label: he had to obtain cash to cover that transaction. He had also just, according to Wilson, "completed the recording of Carl Perkins' new single, *Blue Suede Shoes*, and believed it could become a big hit."

Wilson, continuing his explanation, said that "the only problem was Sun did not have the resources to get it manufactured and on the market nationally, an expensive proposition for a tiny record label. The money Phillips got for selling Elvis not only enabled him to release *Blue Suede Shoes* and have a huge classic hit with it, it also provided the seed money for him to launch many of the other performers who got their start at Sun." Phillips himself always said he never regretted selling Elvis' contract. Author John Floyd, in his book *Sun Records: An Oral History*, wrote that "Phillips was sure that recent Sun signees Carl Perkins and Johnny Cash would do for him what Elvis did before."

Somewhere along the line Elvis heard about the advice Wilson gave Phillips. He was said to have enjoyed "ribbing Kemmons about his advice." Wilson recalled that Elvis would, every time he saw him, "put his arms around me" and say, "Boss, you made a big mistake, didn't you." Every time it happened, Wilson said he always replied, "I sure did." But did he?

In the scheme of things, Elvis was doubtlessly destined to sign with RCA and become the mega star he became. Another record company executive, Bob Thiele, speculated (in his autobiography) that Steve Sholes, the man who had the "distinction to be the executive who signed Elvis Presley," probably wound up with "eternal job security." Because Elvis stayed with the company for the rest of his career, RCA reaped huge benefits and profits.

The company has yet to stop making mega bucks off the King. In August 1992, RCA Records and the Recording Industry Association of America (RIAA) jointly presented the Elvis Presley Estate with gold, platinum, and multi-platinum sales awards for every Elvis recording that had reached that status. When the presentation was completed, 110 different singles and albums had been duly recognized. In the first six months of 1993 (more than fifteen years after Elvis died), according to a trade press report, Elvis sold 750,000 recorded units (CDs, cassettes, singles). Twenty years after he died, in August 1997, the boxed set of his recordings, fittingly entitled *Platinum: A Life in Music,* jumped onto the *Billboard* album sales charts at number eighty. No such equivalent chart activity on other deceased legendary rockers, R&B artists, or pop stars, Janis Joplin, Buddy Holly, Sam Cooke, John Lennon included, ever occurred, not ten, not fifteen, and definitely not twenty years afterwards.

Michael Omansky, RCA Vice President of Strategic Marketing reached his own conclusion as to why sales of Elvis' RCA recordings have remained so high for so long. He told *Goldmine*'s Gillian G. Gaar that he thought "it's a combination of devotion of the fan base, but I think it's more what he was. He was really one of a kind. He sort of paved the way. He really was great at what he did. And nobody's come along, in spite of the changing time and the multimedia, nobody has come along in his league to knock him off."

Elvis likewise gained undeniably huge benefits from his successful career (profits many others shared in beyond their wildest dreams). Yet he still spent most of his life trying to figure out why God picked him to become who he was. Didn't Lord Tennyson once wax poetic that, "theirs not to reason why, theirs but to do and die"?

If one had to have a reason, Dr. Robert Cole, history professor at Ripon College, offered one of the best. He concluded that "Elvis was the opening beat and boom heard round the world for an era of cultural and social change that has not yet run its course." Yet Elvis died, according to a handwriting expert who analyzed his 1977 will, a "broken, sick and lonely man."

When country legend Merle Haggard wrote a tribute to Elvis (after he died), "From Graceland to the Promised Land," he said that the song "never was for the fans–or even for me. It was for Elvis because, like everybody else, I loved him. Hell, we all loved him to death." To Merle, Elvis "had become an American institution, more than just an entertainer. He was like Casey Jones or Babe Ruth." One final observation by Merle was that "success, with all its promise and glitter, had demanded the ultimate payment from Elvis Presley."

Country singer Ronnie Milsap, who worked with Elvis and also knew him personally, believed that Elvis "wanted nothing more than simply to be normal." Yet he couldn't be. Ronnie said that after he got to know him, "I realized how hard it was to be Elvis. The pressure of this might have been what prompted his alleged drug use, perhaps the entertainment industry's biggest open secret, until it became publicized after his death."

Another great country artist, Willie Nelson, once said he "went to see Elvis one night on the strip and I thought, 'What is going on here?' There was Elvis up there working his ass off, and the crowd was just kind of politely exhausted. They clapped and whistled, but you couldn't feel them giving anything back. I felt like jumping up on top of a table and yelling, 'Hey everybody, that's Elvis Presley up there! You should be jumping up screaming.' "

It was not that Elvis failed to take Vegas by storm. He did! John Giovenco, president of the Hilton's gaming division, once remarked that though people "used to say that Elvis didn't draw a gaming crowd," the hotel management "made more money when he played than with anybody else, because he drew tremendous crowds." In Gary Provost's book, *High Stakes*, Giovenco explained the charts that were kept on how various entertainers "did." With Elvis, Giovenco said he "understood what they meant by 'off the charts.' "

Elvis had such a presence it was impossible to remain neutral about him. It was also next to impossible to follow him, even early in his career. Texas country singer Billy Walker told *Country Weekly* that soon after he met Elvis in 1955, he booked him for his own traveling show. Billy immediately discovered that "after the first night, I realized you didn't follow Elvis Presley. He was the only true phenomenon I've ever been around."

That realization came to almost every singer who ever tried to go on stage after an Elvis performance, from Pat Boone to Hank Snow. Only one performer ever drove a crowd wilder than Elvis did, at least in Johnny Cash's eyes. Cash related, in his 1998 autobiography, that there was one night when Elvis "had to take a backseat to Carl Perkins," even though Elvis "was the headliner."

Not being the star act, Carl went on first and "tore the place up; the fans went absolutely nuts." Finally Elvis went on and though he got a fabulous reception, "he wasn't even all the way through his first song when half the audience started shouting for Carl. It was so bad that he only did one more song before giving up. He left the stage and Carl came back on to thunderous applause." Cash later heard that Elvis vowed to "never work with Carl again."

Perkins went on to have a near-fatal automobile accident on the road and was forced to stop performing for a long time. Elvis went on to bigger and more exciting venues and no one ever came close to touching him again. His impact grew and grew. A would-be country singer, Bob Luman, from Nacogdoches, Texas, told how Elvis influenced him away from becoming anything else but a rock and roll singer.

Writer Paul Hemphill captured Luman's recollections of watching a nineteen-year-old Elvis in Kilgore, Texas. Luman said that Elvis "made chills run up my back. Man, like when your hair starts grabbing at your collar." His most indelible memory was Elvis just standing there with "these two strings dangling, and he hadn't done anything except break the strings yet, and these high school girls were screaming and fainting and running up to the stage, and then he started to move his hips real slow like he had a thing for his guitar."

Johnnie Allan, a longtime Louisiana-based performer, similarly recalled (for interviewers Shane K. Bernard and Charles Adcock) the impact Elvis made on him during one live show. Allan said that Elvis "just stole the show from everybody. I mean, it was just unreal. I was eighteen years old and this is thirty-five years ago–I still remember what he wore that night. That's how much of an impression he made on me. But he just stole, he just blew everybody off of the stage." When asked what Elvis was wearing, Allan unhesitatingly replied, "he had on pink shoes, he had on light green pants with a shirt to match, chartreuse coat, and a tie to match the coat!"

Elvis' friend and associate, Joe Esposito, in his November 1997 column for *Pop Culture Collecting*, conjectured that Elvis' appeal was "unexplainable," that he "simply had an effect on people that they can't describe." However, at least at the beginning of his career, Elvis may have calculatingly enhanced that innate appeal. Country music singer David Houston, who traveled with Elvis during some of his early live appearances, recalled (according to Elvis biographer Albert Goldman) that he "would take the cardboard cylinder out of a roll of toilet paper and put a string on one end of it. Then, he'd tie that string around his waist. The other end, with the cardboard roller, would hang down outside his drawers, so as when he got onstage and reared back with that guitar in his hand, it would look to the girls up front like he had one helluva thing there inside his pants."

There was obviously more to Elvis' magnetism than a mere toilet paper roll! Jim Dickinson, Memphis musician and producer, was there to see the audience impact right from the start. In Floyd's book, *Sun Records: An Oral History*, he was quoted as saying he "never saw anything like Elvis Presley. Just the way he walked on the stage. He didn't even have to sing. And you lose sight of it in terms of contemporary society, but what he was doing was completely revolutionary and liberating. Just shaking his leg—just the simple act of shaking his fucking leg—began the whole sexual revolution and changed the way every man on earth walked, talked, and combed his hair. To this day."

Elvis, who became, in Dickinson's mind, "the most recognizable human being on the face of this earth," has yet to go away, not even in the "cyber-age" of the 1990's. In fact, he resides all over the worldwide Internet. Writer Ben Greenman observed, in a special "net music" article for the August 1998 issue of *Yahoo!: Internet Life*, that Elvis' "minions" have "taken to the Net" and created "sites for their idol that range from comprehensive (members.aol.com/petedixon/elvis) to kitschy (members.aol.com/nudeelvis) to conspiracy-minded (www.robyn.on.net/elvis/essay_whodunnit.html)." In the virtual world of today, he doesn't need a physical body in order to live on.

It has taken an unbelievable multitude of fans to place and keep Elvis at the high levels of popularity he reached during and after his life. Worldwide, the total count of Elvis fan club members stood at more than 300,000 people as of late 1997. That translated to almost 600 different clubs nationally and internationally. When Elvis was alive that number stood at over 1,000. There is even a person who coordinates all those organizations. Her name is Patsy Anderson and she has been working out of Graceland for more than a dozen years.

She told *Country Weekly's* Catharine S. Rambeau that "the clubs carry on where Elvis left off. He gave and gave and gave; he was so generous. One club in Australia raises money to buy kids with defective hearts new machines that allow doctors to check their hearts over the phone. Hospitals are not just around the corner there, so it saves lives. Charity and the music . . . that's what our fan clubs are about." Memphis fan club president Mary Stonebraker told Rambeau that "Elvis was unique. He wasn't at all stuck up, just benevolent and down to earth. He gave to the point of exhaustion and he might still be with us had he not done so."

Elvis' fans have remained more devoted than any group of admirers for any other performer. In the August 16, 1997, issue of *Goldmine*, numerous devotees described their adulation for Elvis and what was behind it (even twenty years after he died). Marvin Madsen of Houston, Texas, wrote that "Elvis started it all. In the last 20 years a lot has been said about Elvis, good and bad, but one thing we can't deny is the great music he left us and maybe that's the way it should be." Debbie Patterson of Lexington, Tennessee, effectively summarized that "there will never be another Elvis. The King will live on in the hearts of millions. I will never forget him. In my eyes he was the best that ever was."

A multitude of awards and honors (Grammys and more, both during his life and posthumously), including his 1998 Country Music Hall of Fame induction, have helped keep him at the forefront of public attention. Country musician and songwriter Merle Kilgore, who toured with Elvis when both performers worked for the Louisiana Hayride, told *Country Weekly* that "Elvis was raised country, he was country and he cut a lot of country songs." In Kilgore's view, he "just blended it all together. Made the dandiest milkshake you ever drank. He poured in a little rhythm and blues, a little C&W and sprinkled it with a lot of action." More than twenty years too late, the country music hierarchy finally recognized what most people already knew.

To Canadian singing star k. d. lang, "Elvis was the 20th-century Jesus Christ," not because of a spiritual equivalency, but because he "basically sacrificed himself to teach young artists like myself what can happen to you in the music industry. His death has taught a lot of people a big lesson about excess, and the heavy-duty responsibility it is to be a public figure. It's very difficult to handle, and I think Elvis must have been devastated by the amount of responsibility."

I Feel So Bad:
ELVIS AND THE MUSIC OF BLACK AMERICANS

Sam Phillips, Elvis Presley, and their coconspirators were outsiders in their own culture; Phillips and Presley had grown up among folks who referred to the music they favored as "vulgar animalistic nigger rock and roll bop.

–Robert Palmer,
Rock & Roll: An Unruly History

Sam Phillips, who recorded Elvis at Sun studios, supposedly felt that, in Elvis, he found a white singer who had a "black" sound. In the racially polarized South that was perfect because white kids wanted to listen to black music but either couldn't or were not allowed to identify with black performers. Elvis became the ideal artist for the times, because not only was he white, he had succeeded in "mixing up black and white musical influences." At least, that was the way producer Jim Rooney expressed it (as quoted by Texas author, songwriter, and artist Nanci Griffith in her book, *Other Voices*).

In the view of black musicologist and former *Billboard* columnist, Nelson George, Elvis' success emanated from his "immersion in black culture, both the blues and gospel." Gospel music historian Anthony Heilbut wrote in his groundbreaking study of the genre, *The Gospel Sound: Good News and Bad Times*, that Elvis, as part of denying "any prejudice against black people," actually claimed he attended East Trigg Baptist Church in Memphis "every Sunday." East Trigg was "not just another black gospel church," according to Heilbut, it featured Queen C. Anderson, a singer "by legend the greatest gospel singer the South has produced."

Years later, Elvis would tell Darlene Love, lead singer for the Blossoms, one of the black gospel-based singing groups he utilized as part of his musical backup, that he "loved gospel music, and most everything he learned about it he got by going to black churches in Tennessee when he was a teenager." Love wrote in her autobiography, *My Name Is Love: The Darlene Love Story*, that Elvis claimed to have been "too afraid to go in, but would just stand outside with his ear pressed to the door, like a kid with his nose against the plate glass of a candy store." She observed that "he didn't need money for the prize on the other side, only a pair of golden ears."

In George's mind, Elvis "did more than listen" (to people like Arthur "Big Boy" Crudup and Big Mama Thornton, two black artists George cited as Presley influences), he was able "to inhale their passion into his soul." In Elvis, George saw "a reverse integration so complete that on stage he adopted the symbolic fornication blacks had unashamedly brought to American entertainment." The result was, as he perceptively wrote in his book, *The Death of Rhythm and Blues*, that "as a young man Presley came closer than any other rock & roll star to capturing the swaggering sexuality projected by so many R&B vocalists."

Elvis also utilized "bits of black culture" to achieve his "stylized look." According to George, "even before he'd made his first record, Elvis was wearing one of black America's favorite products, Royal Crown Pomade hair grease." His famous "rockabilly cut" was "clearly his interpretation of of the black 'process,' where blacks had their hair straightened and curled into curious shapes. Some charge that the process hairstyle was a black attempt to look white. So, in a typical pop music example of cross-cultural collision, there was Elvis adapting black styles from blacks adapting white looks." George pointed out, too, that Elvis also bought and wore the kind of clothes that were "essential to black style in the early 1950s."

How did black artists feel about Elvis? The reactions, over the years, have been noticeably mixed. When Muddy Waters heard one of his early blues riffs in a 1958 Elvis song, he said (according to his biographer, Sandra B. Tooze), "I better watch out. I believe whitey's pickin' up on the things that I'm doin'." The "Queen of the Blues," Dinah Washington, was quoted by her biographer, James Haskins, as observing that "rock 'n' roll" was "based on blues and jazz, but Elvis Presley has done something to it." She concluded, however, that it would not only quickly "die out," but "after a while even the FBI won't be able to find Elvis Presley."

Little Richard, on the other hand, was pleased to note that Elvis had covered four of his songs in one year, 1956. The songs were "Rip It Up," "Ready Teddy," "Long Tall Sally," and "Tutti Frutti." While only two of the four songs were ones Richard co-wrote, all four were big hits for him in 1956. To Richard, Elvis was a musical integrator who opened "that door so I could walk down the road."

Initially for Elvis, there was a close Little Richard connection, which pioneering black vocalist Eartha Kitt clearly heard. Kitt, who recorded for RCA around the time Elvis signed with the label, recalled that Elvis "was singing like a black then, very much in the Little Richard style, but getting the recognition Little Richard never got." Bo Diddley, who recorded for the Chicago-based Chess Records, contended that at first, Elvis "couldn't sing, he couldn't play, an' I couldn't see anythin' that merited the action that he got."

Later on though, Bo came to realize that after Elvis "really got his act together," he became "a magnificent entertainer." Mort Shuman, who wrote or co-wrote (usually with Doc Pomus) between sixteen and twenty songs for Elvis, ensured that Elvis utilized the "Bo Diddley sound" at least once, revealing that "I stole Bo Diddley's riff for 'His Latest Flame,' " a highly infectious song that became a top five hit for Elvis in 1961.

Elvis' fellow Mississippian, blues singer B. B. King, recalled (in his autobiography) that "Elvis was different. He was friendly. I remember Elvis distinctly because he was handsome and quiet and polite to a fault. Spoke with this thick molasses Southern accent and always called me 'sir.' " So, how did King feel about Elvis' music? He wrote in his autobiography that "Elvis didn't steal any music from anyone. He just had his own interpretation of the music he'd grown up on." Most of all, King felt that "Elvis had integrity."

Writing in his autobiography, James Brown partially echoed B. B.'s sentiments. When Elvis was first starting out, Brown thought "he was copying B. B." From there, however, Brown saw Elvis "really get into his own thing." "Elvis was great," he concluded. He knew something that others didn't, that Elvis "found his own style. Elvis was rockabilly; he wasn't rock 'n' roll, he was rockabilly. He was really a hillbilly who learned to play the blues."

In Brown's mind, "Elvis always had soul, or he couldn't have done those records." Two of Elvis' black musical peers (in Memphis), Rufus Thomas and Roy Brown, agreed with [James] Brown's assessment. Thomas said that "Elvis was doing good music, blues and rhythm and blues, because that was his beginning." [Roy] Brown was even more complimentary, saying that "there was something about Elvis that was different from the Fabians and them other guys. Elvis could sing. And he had a heart."

The music of black Americans was always at the heart of Elvis' success, especially in the beginning. A black radio personality and musician from Memphis, Robert "Honeymoon" Garner, remembered that a young Elvis used to drop "into Sunbeam Mitchell's Club with Dewey Phillips" when Honeymoon played there. According to author Louis Cantor, in his book *Wheelin' on Beale*, black disc jockey Nat D. Williams told two reporters that Elvis "had first come to him in the old days, wanting a chance to get on Amateur Night at the Palace Theater on Beale Street." Not only did Nat D. say he "put him on several times," he added, "Elvis Presley on Beale Street when he first started was a favorite man."

However, Memphis radio personality Dewey Phillips revealed that, in the very early going, Elvis "considered himself a country singer." Bill Black, one of two musicians who backed Elvis for Sun Records, told interviewer Billy Poore (as quoted in Poore's book, *Rockabilly: A Forty Year Journey*) that not only did Elvis "only" like "to sing pop-style ballads" when he first joined Sun, "he made fun of the black blues then." But as Black added, Elvis quickly learned it was the black blues that "really made him hit it big-time."

In one of his earliest performances, Elvis sang two country songs and immediately discovered that "nothing" happened. So Phillips told him to try a rhythm and blues song, "Good Rockin' Tonight," by black musician Roy Brown, and "not to sing any hillbilly songs." Once Elvis was well into the song and "started to shake," the place "just blew apart." Elvis made such an impact, as Phillips recalled, that "the people wouldn't let him leave."

It was no coincidence that Elvis' second single for Sun Records was none other than "Good Rockin' Tonight." Elvis had actually learned the song from listening to a version by Wynonie Harris, a black dancer turned singer who was big in the forties and early fifties. Author Nick Tosches wrote in his book, *Unsung Heroes of Rock 'n' Roll*, that "Elvis learned more than songs from Wynonie Harris. The pelvic jab-and-parry, the petulant curlings of his lip, the evangelical wavings of his arms and hands–these were not the spontaneities of Elvis, but a style deftly learned from watching Wynonie Harris perform in Memphis in the early 1950s." An interview Tosches did with Henry Glover, the man who produced Harris, brought out Glover's assertion that "when you saw Elvis, you were seeing a mild version of Wynonie."

Even a white artist, pop singer Johnny Ray, criticized Elvis. In 1956, Ray observed, after watching one of Elvis' shows in Las Vegas, that "it was pretty obvious he was doing it by rote, something that about 300 other black guys had done before him." Yet unlike other white rockers of the fifties, including Jerry Lee Lewis and Ricky Nelson, Elvis actually studied black American performers. He even sat in the audience at the Apollo Theater in New York to observe, in the words of Ralph Cooper, emcee and producer there for four decades, "moves Elvis never saw in his mama's church."

While in New York to appear on Tommy and Jimmy Dorsey's "Stage Show," Elvis "saw how black music affected the world's toughest audience." According to Ted Fox, in his book on the Apollo, Elvis absorbed and emulated "the pounding rhythms, the prancing and dancing, the sexual spectacle of rhythm and blues masters like Bo

Diddley. In fact, watching Bo "charge up the Apollo crowd" had a most profound effect on Elvis.

Yet, as author Stanley Booth found out, even though Elvis may have studied the moves of black performers (like Wynonie Harris), his own moves came naturally to him. Booth wrote in his book, *Rhythm Oil*, that Elvis told his mother, "I just have to jump around when I sing. But it ain't vulgar. It's just the way I feel. I don't feel sexy when I'm singin'. If that was true, I'd be in some kinda institution as some kinda sex maniac." He was a natural man and a shrewd one as well. From then on, not only did he move like a black performer, many of his biggest songs such as "Mystery Train," "That's All Right (Mama)," "All Shook Up," "I Feel So Bad," and numerous others came directly from black artists and songwriters.

In addition to all the songs he recorded by black writers, quite a few of the excellent white songwriters who created hits for Elvis, such as Jerry Leiber and Mike Stoller (composers of Elvis' 1955 chart-topper, "Hound Dog"), had the uncanny knack of writing songs that sounded like they came from the heart of black America. In 1957, Leiber and Stoller were credited with writing one of Elvis' most popular numbers (and the title of his third movie), "Jailhouse Rock." The accuracy of that credit, however, was disputed by Roy Porter, former big band drummer and composer.

Porter claimed the song was written much earlier by a black musician named Shifty Henry. In his 1991 autobiography, *There and Back*, Porter wrote that, when he moved to the Los Angeles area in the mid-forties, Henry, a jazz trumpet player, was one of the first musicians he worked with–they "put a five piece band together and ended up at the Do-Dee Club downtown." According to Porter, Henry went on to become "a respected bass player" as well as "the composer of 'Dark Shadows,' the song that Earl Coleman sang on Charlie Parker's third recording date for Dial Records, and 'Jail House Rock,' which Elvis Presley recorded and made a mint on. But Shifty didn't get a dime from Elvis for that song."

How could Henry have expected to get money from Elvis? The song was credited to Leiber and Stoller. The writing duo said they wrote the song specifically for the movie, *Jailhouse Rock*, in answer to a request for "a big production number in a jail." At least they mentioned the name, Shifty Henry, in the lyrics, in the part about sticking around and getting some kicks. When it came to making a break, Bugs said to Shifty, "Nix, nix."

So, the famous songwriting duo of Leiber and Stoller, who have been honored by a Broadway play highlighting their lives and musical works, was accused of ripping off the work of a black artist. Ironically, Leiber told interviewer Ted Fox he felt Elvis "was not quite authentic" because "he was a white singer." Stoller added that "one of the things we felt was not authentic was a white singer singing the blues."

Ultimately, Leiber (as quoted in an interview with *Goldmine*'s Harvey R. Kubernik) saw Elvis as "the greatest ballad singer since Bing Crosby." However, because his rhythmic styling came through even when he sang ballads and older pop songs (that originated from Tin Pan Alley), at least one classic pop songwriter, Irving Berlin, detested the way Elvis treated at least one of his established songs. Laurence Bergreen wrote in his biography of Berlin that when "he heard Elvis's rendition of 'White Christmas,' he was appalled. He immediately ordered his staff to telephone radio stations around the country to ask them not to play this barbaric rock-and-roll version, which he considered a sacrilege."

Actually Berlin was not objecting so much to Presley's version of his classic song as he was to the original arrangement Elvis used, which, according to Tony Allan and Faye Treadwell, was a duplicate of the one created in 1954 for The Drifters. Allan and Treadwell (manager of the group) stated, in their book *Save the Last Dance for Me: The Musical Legacy of The Drifters, 1953-1993*, that Howard Biggs developed the "complex arrangement" that "featured a shared lead between the bass of Bill Pinckney and the tenor of Clyde McPhatter" enabling the song to be stretched "much further than it had been before." Berlin, by making it clear he did not care for Elvis' version, was in effect expressing contempt for the interpretation of his song as done by one of the premier black American vocal groups, The Drifters.

Gospel music historian Heilbut noted, in his history of the genre, that because Elvis "looked the part of a hillbilly racist, he received some criticism for his musical borrowings." Brian Ward, in his book, *Just My Soul Responding*, presented a much harsher criticism from black musicologist Portia Maultsby. Maultsby concluded that "the cover syndrome, together with the success of white singers like Bill Haley and Elvis Presley," was the "most wide-spread, systematic rape and uncompensated cultural exploitation the entertainment industry has ever seen."

However, New Orleans musician and composer Harold Battiste saw the situation a bit differently at first. To him, "the advent of an Elvis Presley (or even a Pat Boone)" opened doors for black musician and composers by offering them "a white vehicle . . . so that black music began to reach a bigger market." Unfortunately, the "white vehicle" didn't go away. Battiste quickly discovered that "rather than white kids being able to come and accept the real thing, more black kids began to go for the imitators."

Black musician and music authority Preston Love (in his autobiography) pointedly contended that "Elvis Presley became the biggest star in the history of show business and was referred to as the king of rock and roll while many thousands of great Afro-American folksingers and musicians with thousands of times more talent than Presley wallowed in comparative obscurity." Love also wrote that "if the genius of Ray Charles is valid and Aretha Franklin's singing is the wonderful art that I perceive it to be, then Presley's singing and that of the female rock stars are as lacking and horrid as I think they are. I can hardly think of anything less inspiring than Presley's 'Love Me Tender,' for instance."

Swing drummer Panama Francis, who began playing in the big bands of the thirties and forties, was even more critical and specific. He made no bones that "Elvis Presley was nothing but a carbon copy of Otis Blackwell." Blackwell was "the guy that wrote all of Elvis' first big hits" and he "was a black guy." He was one of many blacks in America during the fifties who fell victim to "what they do in America." What that meant, in Panama's words, was that "as soon as a white learns what the black is doing that is popular, they shove the black aside. And they bring the white out front and they give him all the publicity."

Francis played drums "on demos of songs Blackwell wrote," which, when they were completed in New York, were shipped to Elvis in Tennessee. Using, as a reference point, the demo recording Blackwell made of one of the songs he wrote for Elvis, "Don't Be Cruel," Francis noted how Elvis "copied just the way Blackwell sang it on the demo: the emphasis, the phrasing, the feel. Moreover, Blackwell's voice is in the same range. Their timbres are similar." Then Francis concluded that "Elvis sang it in the same style, same exactly like Otis. That's why Otis Blackwell is suing the estate now."

What did Blackwell have to say? In 1976, *Village Voice* contributor Gary Giddins talked with him and came away with some incredible insights. Blackwell told Giddins, "You know, there had to be a deal, share this and that. I said no at first, but they said Elvis is gonna turn the business around, so I said okay." Blackwell remembered that the first song of his Elvis picked up was placed "on the other side of 'Hound Dog.' "

Fortuitously, Blackwell pointed out, "we sounded alike and had the same groove, so I began doing demos for other publishers for Presley-'Teddy Bear,' 'All Shook Up,' 'Easy Question,' 'Don't Drag That String Around.' The cat was hot, that's why his name is on the songs. Why not? That's the way the business is anyway." As he informed Giddins, he realized quickly that the music in the fifties was "in categories and all black artists were classified as blues, so if you wanted to make money with a song like 'Don't Be Cruel,' you had to have a white singer."

Blackwell estimated that, of the records Elvis made of the songs he wrote for him, "90 percent" were "exact copies." He was happy to have had Elvis as his "white singer." In the interview with Giddins, he said he knew, even when Elvis first started, that he would be around for a long time, because Elvis would "try any kind of song that was given him."

Elvis and Blackwell never met, though Blackwell did admire and respect him. So, why didn't they ever meet? Blackwell had a "superstitious fear" that "their working relationship might crumble if Presley did not measure up to his preconceptions." Once, in appreciation, the Colonel asked Blackwell to appear in an Elvis movie, *Girls!, Girls!, Girls!* Otis declined (same fear). By 1976, he was ready to meet Elvis and even tried once, but it was too late.

Giddins talked to others about the Otis/Elvis relationship. One of them was Grelun Landon, who became RCA's Los Angeles manager of press and information after being responsible, during the fifties, for working with Colonel Parker and various song publishers. Landon not only said that "Elvis' musicians had to copy the Blackwell arrangements off the demos because they couldn't read music," he revealed that "Elvis learned how to deliver the songs from Otis."

Another person Giddins talked with was songwriter Doc Pomus, who wrote quite a few songs recorded by Elvis (and a host of other rockers, including The Drifters, Jimmy Clanton, and even Fabian). Pomus acknowledged that Elvis was "an extraordinary talent, the first white singer to get real recognition for the blues, and he could sing anything. He's an original–always Presley–but on certain things–fast tempos–he comes from Otis."

When Giddins asked Pomus about the prevailing notion that Elvis created "head arrangements" on songs he recorded and was, by default, his own producer, Pomus replied that the notion was "absolutely untrue. Elvis did not create those sounds, and I can tell you he managed to get his name on songs he had nothing to do with writing. One thing I can assure you is that his singing was significantly influenced by Otis. If you compare the demos, you will find it incredible how close Presley copied them, especially the sound of Otis's voice."

In Giddins' own analysis, "since their voices and vocal styles were remarkably alike, Blackwell's demos provided Presley with delivery cues that didn't force him appreciably to alter his own impulses, while Blackwell could hear his material performed almost exactly as he imagined it." Blackwell expressed no regrets, to

Giddins or anyone else. He had no ambition, in the early days of rock and roll, to be a performer and he loved the way Elvis interpreted his songs. He said he enjoyed working with Elvis (and other white singers) because he could hear a "part of me coming through."

Speaking on the fact that Elvis' management required him to share songwriting credits and royalties with Elvis, Blackwell told a Philadelphia reporter in 1983 that he realized "songwriters who'd been in the business much longer than I had, and who were much better off financially, were going along with this. Some people would even have paid to have a song done by Elvis, So I figured what the hell. And I can't complain about how I made out."

What about black American audiences: did they "go for" Elvis? Eartha Kitt, who said she was dropped from RCA about the time the company signed Elvis, recalled that black audiences "accepted Elvis thinking he was black, until they saw his photograph on his records." Yet, even when one black audience knew Elvis was white, they still clamored for him, as Memphis disc jockey Nat D. Williams remembered about a 1956 Elvis appearance.

Early in his career, Elvis made an appearance (he did not perform) at the 1956 Goodwill Revue held in Memphis and sponsored by radio station WDIA. The audience was largely black, there for two shows, one strictly gospel and the other dominated by current rhythm and blues music. Deejay Williams asked Elvis to be at the revue and introduced him by saying, "Folks, we have a special treat for you tonight-here is Elvis Presley." At that point, the thousands of people in the audience rushed the stage and began, in the words of one of Elvis' closest friends, George Klein, "grabbing at Elvis."

Williams recalled that "a thousand black, brown and beige teenage girls in that audience blended their alto and soprano voices in one wild crescendo of sound that rent the rafters and took off like scalded cats in the direction of Elvis." Another of WDIA's staff, Robert "Honeymoon" Garner, said that even his kid "loved Elvis. He made me buy him one of those Elvis Presley toy guitars for Christmas." Unfortunately, after Elvis became massively popular and played in the large venues dominated by rich, older fans, "less than one percent of his audiences at concerts were black," according to Klein.

After Elvis became massively popular, a lot more changed for him besides the makeup of his audiences. He continually moved away from his black influences. For example, when he recorded at the black-owned and -operated Stax studios in Memphis in 1974, Bobby Manuel, a Stax session player, recalled that "the vibe didn't work. It was like, 'Who is this guy? So what!' coming in with all this mess and all these clowns around him." Manuel explained that when it came time to record, "they laid out these goofy pop songs. It was just ridiculous."

Yet this was the same Elvis who brought the Reverend Jesse Jackson to tears when he sang "In the Ghetto." While Manuel was reacting to the kind of music Elvis made later in his career, it seemed apparent, at least to one other artist, that Elvis was no longer at the top of his form. In 1975, after recording a song ("If You Talk in Your Sleep") that Elvis had already done, blues guitarist Little Milton observed that "we probably won't sell the kind of records that he sells but we can damn sure do this song better than he did it."

Nonetheless, critic Robert Ward, writing for *Crawdaddy,* concluded that Elvis' "life was a triumph over low birth, lack of education, and a deadening conformist era that broke many a more advantaged man's heart." In an almost book-length article, "Elvis: A Body of Controversy," Professor John Fiske conjectured that the "loose body of Elvis 'loosened' the multiple bodies of his fans until they threatened the body of society." To Fiske, Elvis' body "was not just muscle and movement but a point of intersection for the social axes of age, gender and race."

Don't leave out sex. British music analyst George Melly observed that Elvis' performing persona radiated a "boasting of sexual prowess," which was essentially an old "blues tradition." In fact, in Melly's analysis, "the blues were far more open about it than Presley." Black performer [Darlene] Love observed that once Elvis "got in front of an audience," and "whirled around the stage, got down on his knees and swiveled those hips with a seismic force," it was clear that his concert "was all about hot flashes and goose bumps." [Nelson] George similarly wrote that "Elvis was sexy; not clean-cut, wholesome, white-bread, Hollywood sexy but sexy in the aggressive earthy manner associated by whites with black males." If Elvis acted and looked like a black male, how did he relate to a black female?

Love wrote that when she worked with Elvis on the movie *Change of Habit,* they wound up alone in his trailer during a lunch break. At first, they talked, then all of a sudden, she realized, "I wasn't being looked at. I was being looked over." Whereupon, Elvis told her, "I've never been with a black woman before. I've never even thought about it. But I'm thinking about it now."

Love thought he was "joking," but then saw that "Elvis wasn't laughing." She said she wasn't "really attracted to him, but sometimes it's easy to confuse awe with sex appeal, and besides . . . this was Elvis! Elvis had been married to Priscilla for a little more than a year, but even so, once I thought he was serious, I found myself being drawn into his current. Who would believe I was on the verge of having sex with the King of Rock and Roll?"

Attempting to reply, she found herself stammering a bit, but "just when I thought he was going to make a move, he fell back on his futon and said, 'Hell, what would my people think? My grandma and granddaddy might spin in their graves.' " At that point, Love didn't know what to think. She wondered if he was saying "that black women weren't good enough for him," or that "I wasn't good enough for him." Ironically, it occurred to her that "this was the man who twitched like a black man on stage." She wondered again, "was that all that blacks were good for?"

Then she said she "remembered how Elvis felt about gospel music," that often, his only relief from the pressures of recording "would be a dose of gospel music." To her, then, this became "just another threshold he couldn't cross. If he did, he just wouldn't be able to explain it to all the conflicting voices in his head." So, the moment passed and they "ended up just talking until the lunch break was over."

She did hold on to her memories of Elvis as the performer who "presided over the musical miscegenation of the fifties." In fact, there was one special vision of Elvis she kept, which occurred when he sang, "If I Can Dream," during his comeback special, and "took it to another level altogether." During his performance, she saw a distinct parallel to her daddy, "ready to leap over the pulpit if that's what it took to shake loose the faith from any reluctant parishioner."

Elvis never lost his love for gospel music, especially black gospel. When he made his regular return to the stage in Las Vegas (and via national tours), he wanted to have Love and the Blossoms backing him with their unique gospel-based vocal harmonies. They couldn't afford the drop in pay (they were making $5,000 per week and the Colonel only wanted to pay them $1,500 weekly to back Elvis). So, the group declined but recommended Cissy Houston and the Sweet Inspirations, who immediately accepted, labeling it (as Houston recalled in her autobiography, *How Sweet the Sound*) "a real plum assignment."

Houston's husband John said he used to call him "Elvis Pretzel." He also watched him rehearse and remembered kidding him by asking, "Are you sure you're not part black, Elvis?" Elvis would, in [John] Houston's words, "act kind of 'aw, shucks, John' about it. 'I don't know about that,' he'd say. 'You do look kinda like my uncle. You'll have to ask my daddy.' Used to crack me up."

From gospel to blues and rhythm and blues, Elvis not only felt the inner emotions of the music of black Americans, he understood how to interpret it (as opposed to merely "cover" it as Pat Boone did). He also understood how to deliver the music in tandem with "naturalistic body movement," which was capable, according to black psychologist and lecturer Dr. Alfred B. Pasteur, "of delivering many messages to onlookers." For males, those messages most often encompassed shows of manliness and seductive behavior.

It was Elvis who turned "the black sound and dance" into big business. Pasteur wrote in his groundbreaking work on black expressiveness, *Roots of Soul*, that "the coming of Elvis Presley, who utilized the motions and rhythms made popular long before by black performers like Bo Diddley and a Harlem dancer of the 1920s, Earl Tucker," enabled America "for the first time" to accept "almost completely black vernacular music and dance movements." Significantly, the author noted that Elvis' "initial popularity was among white youth who began to dance in the black vernacular."

From there, "in less than ten years, Elvis Presley sold 100 million records." There was no doubt in Little Richard's mind that Elvis reached that level of commercial success because he "was more acceptable being white back in that period." In a 1990 interview with *Rolling Stone*, Richard disclosed that he believed "if Elvis had been black, he wouldn't have been as big as he was. If I was white, do you know how huge I'd be? If I was white, I'd be able to sit on top of the White House! A lot of things they would do for Elvis and Pat Boone, they wouldn't do for me."

The commercial and social fact was that Elvis, the white performer with the natural movements, successfully turned black music into big business because black musicians were not able to, or more accurately, were kept from doing it. One of Elvis' peer performers who might have succeeded was Chuck Berry, a black singer/songwriter from St. Louis who had successfully fused country music stylings with black rhythm and blues structures and beat.

In 1957, Chuck Berry was as big as Elvis, perhaps bigger because not only did he and Elvis perform the same kind of music, Berry composed it as well. His songs, in the words of John Edwin Mason, professor at the Center for African Studies, the University of Florida, "addressed the preoccupations of white teens in a musical language that was black enough to thrill and familiar enough to be instantly accessible." The music "evoked a primitive, shockingly joyful, and specifically black sexual license." Unfortunately for Chuck, in playing and marketing such music to a white audience, he ignored "the limitations that white America had placed on the actions and aspirations of blacks."

In fact, he became conspicuously rich, in Dr. Mason's words, by "selling rock & roll to white teenagers and young adults, some of whom were women and some of whom he laid." Whereas when Elvis had sexual encounters with young white girls, he was winked at, Chuck was arrested and put on trial, actions by a white hierarchy that Mason saw as "largely exercises in boundary maintenance," especially the boundaries between black men and white women. Chuck's downfall occurred during one of his drives to a 1958 musical gig, when he had a white woman with him in his car. That was 1958, when fan magazines were fraught with pictures of Elvis and young white girls draped all over him.

On the way home from the concert, Berry had pulled off the road due to a flat tire, after which he was observed by a white police officer. Elvis, even if he were accompanied by a young white girl as Chuck was, might have been helped by such an officer and probably would have signed an autograph. In Berry's case, his car was searched (the officer thought it might have been stolen) and when a weapon was found, Chuck was arrested. Though the arrest was based on a concealed weapons charge, the Assistant U. S. Attorney who wound up with the case told Berry that "if he continued to associate with white women in a way that he [the attorney, Frederick Mayer] thought was improper," the concealed weapons charges would be prosecuted (according to the research done by Mason).

It was not uncommon in the 1950s and before for Southern white police officers to "bust" black men traveling with white women. Etta James told a similar story in her 1995 autobiography, *Rage to Survive.* Sometime in the mid-fifties, R&B musician Floyd Dixon was driving, with her in the back seat, through eastern Texas, trying to get to Texarkana. Floyd stopped and asked a white "patrolman" for directions. That was a big mistake.

The white officer looked in the car and saw the light-skinned James in the back seat and, as James remembered the incident, asked Dixon, "Is that a white woman you got back there?" Dixon told him it was not but the officer was not convinced. Finally, Dixon woke up James with the words, "Wake up, Etta, and tell the man you a nigger." It was not until James told the policeman, "Yeah, I'm a black woman," that he relented and let them go on their way.

During the following year, 1959, Berry was found to have consorted in some way with a supposedly underaged girl from Mexico (she said she was fourteen, others thought she was seventeen, though her true age was never established). In contrast to Berry's situation stood both Elvis and Jerry Lee Lewis. Lewis had sex with and subsequently married his thirteen-year-old cousin and Elvis was about to move a teenage Priscilla Beaulieu into his Graceland mansion. Their actions did not upset any authorities, at least not enough to begin legal proceedings, as it did in Chuck's case.

In Chuck's case, the jury of his peers was all white. He was eventually tried for an alleged sexual relationship with the underaged girl, which got him convicted. He was also tried on the old weapons charge, from which he was acquitted. His conviction in the "underaged girl" case was overturned and a new trial was granted because the white judge repeatedly, according to Dr. Mason's findings, made "remarks reflecting upon the defendant's [Berry's] race."

Berry's defense lawyer had charged that the judge "disparaged" Berry solely because he was "a Negro (associating with a woman outside his race)." Significantly, Berry's lawyer's claims were upheld. Just as significantly, Berry was tried again and subsequently found guilty, serving nineteen months of a five-year prison term.

In Mason's analysis, Berry's arrest and subsequent trials and appeals effectively "took him out of the rock & roll scene for over two and a half years. He all but disappeared from concerts and the recording studio at the very height of his fame. His career never truly recovered." Chuck Berry, one of black America's finest performing talents and a creative genius, was prevented from being the one to transform the music of his race into one of the most popular musical formats of all time. Since he couldn't do it, Elvis did.

Mason's research and findings in this case were brought together as a paper presented in 1993 to the Society for Ethnomusicology. At the end of his document, he charged that Chuck Berry "went to jail because he was a black rock & roller, who got too close to white women. The prosecution of Berry was in some measure a defense of racial boundaries." Since, in 1959, "Chuck Berry was demonstrating how permeable those boundaries could be" and since he "represented cultural miscegenation, a miscegenation initiated not so much by rapacious black men, as by willing white teens," he was prosecuted and convicted "largely because of the direct and indirect influence he had on legions of white female fans."

Mason wrote that "Berry was arrested, tried, and convicted at a time when African-Americans seemed bound and determined and likely to upset the racial hierarchy." As one who might well have overcome the limits imposed on blacks, he was effectively eliminated. His elimination may well have been one of the biggest reasons why Elvis succeeded so well with the music of black Americans. Berry could no longer contend for audiences and sales and he could not stand in Elvis' way. The question will always remain: if Chuck Berry had remained unfettered, how big would Elvis have been?

Another question has lingered as well. Given all that Elvis got from black musicians, did he ever give anything back? R&B singer [Etta] James wrote in her autobiography that Elvis "touched" her heart "when my good friend Jackie Wilson was down and out, vegetating in some funky convalescent home. Elvis moved Jackie to a decent hospital–and paid for everything." Wilson, a pioneering black song stylist, suffered a severe heart attack and fell into a coma while performing in 1975, coming out of it with massive brain damage that kept him confined to nursing homes up until his death in 1984.

In 1981, Bill Bentley wrote in the *Los Angeles Weekly* that when the black Memphis-based musician Roy Brown got into tax trouble, he sought help from Elvis, who was in Little Rock attending a party in his honor. The doorman at the party would not let Brown in to see Elvis, so Brown said he "got the doorman to give him a note telling Mr. Presley his yardman is here. When Elvis got it, he came right out, asking me if I needed anything and gave me enough to get straight with the IRS. That's the kind of guy he was."

Elvis' involvement didn't end there. Robert Palmer, author of *Rock & Roll: An Unruly History*, quoted Brown as saying that "when the sickle-cell anemia telethon would come on, for this disease that blacks get mostly, after they raised whatever money they took in that night, Elvis would double it, I don't care if it was a million dollars; Elvis didn't have to do that. The guy was a beautiful human being; he had style, and he had soul."

He also had an opportunity to help Arthur "Big Boy" Crudup, but may have failed to do so, for reasons that have never become clear. In 1954, black blues singer Crudup was dropped by RCA Records because his blues recordings had stopped selling. Even when his records sold he never made much money because, although RCA released his records, his contract was with Lester Melrose. The contract with Melrose did not allow Crudup to own his own copyrights or gain royalties from current and future sales. Melrose paid Crudup a flat fee and took ownership of the copyrights himself. It was a "take it or leave it" contract most black musicians had to sign or never record at all.

In 1954, Elvis cut Crudup's song "That's All Right." It had failed to become a hit when released as a Crudup single first in 1946 and again in 1948. Though Elvis didn't use drums when cutting the song, he did utilize, almost completely, the identical arrangement Crudup created for his 1946 recording. Elvis even told an interviewer in 1956 that "I used to hear Arthur Crudup bang his box the way I do now, and I said that if I ever got to the place where I could feel all that Arthur felt, I'd be a music man like nobody ever saw."

In spite of all that Elvis absorbed from Crudup, only Elvis and Melrose (and later Hill and Range, which bought that song and others from Melrose) profited from Presley's recording. Crudup did not. Though he tried to sue Hill and Range, he had no success; they had legally purchased all rights to the song from Melrose.

Elvis could have stepped in and ensured that Crudup would get some of what should have gone to him. Rumor had it that he did. He was said to have paid for a 1959 Nashville recording session for Crudup, that resulted in quite a few tracks, notably "That's All Right." Most of the recordings done at that Nashville session went out on Fire Records, a Harlem-based company, and later on a 1960s album released by Delmark Records.

According to writers Jim Dawson and Steve Propes (recounted in their book, *What Was the First Rock 'n' Roll Record?*), the owner of Fire, Bobby Robinson, contradicted the rumors. He said it was he who found Crudup and brought him to New York to record. It was also he who paid for the session with no help from Elvis.

Steve Chapple and Reebee Garofalo complemented the Dawson Propes account, writing in their book, *Rock 'n' Roll Is Here to Pay*, that "Crudup was reputed to have received nothing more than an appreciative plaque from Presley and his manager." Perhaps Elvis didn't intervene because Hill and Range was involved. Due to the many known and unknown ties Elvis and the Colonel had with Hill and Range, Elvis may have been precluded from doing anything for Crudup.

Was the relationship between Elvis and the music of black Americans an exploitative one or one in which Elvis took as much as he gave back? Elvis didn't necessarily sing the music of black Americans out of a desire to profit from it, he did it because he liked and appreciated it. In his younger years, he also took considerable heat for his musical preferences because, as Memphis musician/producer Jim Dickinson pointed out, "it was not socially acceptable to play black music and be a white man in the city of Memphis in 1956."

Still, because he was white, his career took off, seemingly overnight. The biggest performing gig Otis Blackwell could get at the start of his career paid him, according to Doc Pomus, "five dollars a night." Late in life, not long before Elvis died, the best venue Otis could find was a tiny club, the Other End (in New York). Though it wasn't Madison Square Garden, the club nearly filled up to see the man "who made Elvis Presley and Jerry Lee Lewis."

Steadfast, Loyal, and True:
ELVIS AND THE COLONEL

I think a monkey could have managed Elvis,
and maybe done a better job.

-Waylon Jennings,
Waylon: An Autobiography

Before Elvis, Colonel Tom Parker managed country music stars Eddy Arnold and Hank Snow. Snow wrote (in his autobiography) about Parker that "my impression of him as a person dwindled day by day." Though refusing to go into detail, Snow did add that "it makes my blood run cold to read the praise that went to Tom Parker-the most egotistical, obnoxious human I have ever had dealings with." Knowing what he did of Parker's background, he said, "I refuse to call him 'Colonel.' "

According to Nashville sideman, Howard White, who once played in Snow's band, some of that acrimony may have resulted from a Christmas present. White recalled, as part of his memoirs, that "Hank really thought a lot of the Colonel. One Christmas Col. Tom gave him a great big RCA television set. Hank was real proud of that TV until he found out that Col. Tom had somehow negotiated that TV through Hank's RCA recording contract and in actuality, Hank was paying for the TV set Col. Tom had given him."

Arnold, on the other hand, claimed he parted amicably from the Colonel. He even wrote (in his autobiography) that "when Tom's your manager, he's all you. He lives and breathes his artist." Once, Arnold asked him, "Tom, why don't you get yourself a hobby-play golf, go boating, or something?" The Colonel looked him in the eye and replied, "You're my hobby."

Parker also managed teen idol Tommy Sands (who married Nancy Sinatra in 1960) in the early fifties. Even after the Colonel took over exclusive management of Elvis, he still reached back and did Sands a favor. In 1957, Elvis was offered the lead part in a television drama, *The Singing Idol*. After the Colonel turned it down, he suggested that Sands be considered. He was and actually got the part, which had him singing a great song, "Teenage Crush." When released as a single, the song became Sands' first and biggest hit ever, peaking at number two on the *Billboard* charts.

In spite of all the Colonel had accomplished by the mid-fifties, with talent like Arnold, Snow, and Sands (and a host of others), he had yet to fulfill one major goal: to find a client with superstar potential, on whose behalf he could devote all his efforts. In the late summer of 1955, he revealed to Arnold Shaw, a New York music industry executive (for Edward B. Marks Music Corporation, one of the city's oldest song publishing companies), that he was planning, "in less than a year," on signing (to a management contract) a young performer then "unknown north of the Mason and Dixon line." According to Parker, "in Georgia and Florida, the girls are tearing off his clothes."

The budding superstar Parker identified was, in Shaw's words, a "tough-looking white youngster." His name, of course, was Elvis Presley. When Elvis began to take off as a regional recording artist and performer in late 1954 and early 1955, one of the first places he showed flashes of his crowd-exciting potential was on the stage of the Louisiana Hayride. Horace Logan, then producing the Hayride shows (he started in 1948 and continued into the late fifties), observed, in early 1955, that what the young Elvis needed was a "real" manager, "somebody" who could "start making the critical decisions that could move the kid's career into high gear." Elvis also knew that, expressing to Logan that he especially wanted "somebody I can trust."

He turned first to fellow musician, Scotty Moore, who in Logan's words "didn't have the contacts or experience." He then tried Bob Neal, a Memphis radio personality, and even asked the very successful Nashville promoter Tillman Franks, as well as Logan himself, to step into the void. It was "a fermenting situation," as Logan described it, and into it "came one of the crudest, most overbearing, most universally detested men in show business. He called himself 'Colonel' Tom Parker–although he was no more a real colonel than I am. And he came with just one purpose in mind: to take total control of Elvis Presley and claim half of every dollar the kid would ever make."

As Logan wrote, "that's exactly what he [Parker] did, too." Along the way, Elvis became one of the most successful show business personalities of all time. How much was due to the Colonel's efforts, expertise, and shenanigans? Often, results speak for themselves. In

Elvis' case, he wound up, in the words of Clive James, a "planetary presence," because "Colonel Parker did think big about maximizing his boy's home market."

Chet Atkins, who wore many hats for Elvis' label, RCA, observed that "there are precious few good personal managers." He concluded that "men like Colonel Parker, who has guided Elvis for so many years, and Dub Allbritton, who managed Brenda Lee until he died, and X. Cosse, who has handled so many stars, are few and far between. Perhaps that is why a lot of the stars don't remain big stars long enough." So, at least in the eyes of one who was there, Colonel Parker was indeed a critical factor in keeping Elvis on top for so long, even years after both passed on.

A view among many who have studied Elvis has been that Colonel Parker almost wrecked Elvis' career in the sixties by signing him up to do formulaic musicals that had no redeeming screen qualities. The Colonel certainly had a hold on Elvis and Elvis almost blindly followed him. According to Marty Lacker, the Colonel would "couch everything in terms of Elvis losing his career." Lacker added that Parker told Elvis, when he started making movies, to "do everything" the Hollywood people wanted him to do or else "they'll ruin your career and you'll go back to being just a poor kid again."

Since Elvis was paying his career expenses on top of giving close to 50 percent of his gross to the Colonel, he may have continually felt an intuitive fear of going broke. During the filming of his fourteenth film, *Kissin' Cousins*, he learned that actor Donald Woods, who played the General in the film, had a moonlighting second career as a real estate broker. According to Woods, Elvis became strangely "fascinated by this and eager to learn the ins and outs of the profession." Woods said Elvis told him he wanted to learn about the part-time profession "just in case I may need it some day."

The Colonel told Elvis and everyone else around that when the two first met, Elvis "had a million dollars worth of talent." He never let Elvis forget that, thanks to him, he "now had a million dollars." Tempest Storm revealed that, as her "torrid" affair with a young Elvis was winding down, she asked him if he believed what the Colonel was telling him, about how easily his career could be ruined. She quoted Elvis as replying, "He's been right on everything so far. He's made me what I am." In a mid-sixties interview printed in the British trade paper, *New Musical Express*, Elvis told George Rooney that "I always place the greatest trust in Colonel Parker. He is the man who has done the most for me and I am convinced that if he says for me to do something, that is the best thing in my interest."

Peter Guralnick, who did more than any writer to pierce the veil surrounding Elvis, wrote that the Colonel "avowed that it was his patriotic duty to keep Elvis in the ninety percent tax bracket." Guralnick added that by the late sixties, "when it was time to let his boy step out," Parker negotiated a "remarkable financial deal for a special to be shown at Christmas time." The Colonel even knew when and how to let Elvis loose so that he could create what Guralnick called the second "flourishing of the art of Elvis Presley." Even "the barriers that the Colonel erected around Elvis" contributed to Elvis remaining at the pinnacle of the American entertainment world.

Above all, Parker was a promoter and a master at creating anticipation. A very young Jimmy Bowen (who would go on to be a recording star and music industry executive) recounted that when he first saw Elvis (in the fifties), Parker would set up Elvis' shows "so that the anticipation would build and build and then explode." How did he do that? According to Bowen, one night the Colonel "had a classical violinist open for Elvis." That dichotomy (the crowd wanted rock and roll and Elvis but for openers they got the exact opposite) created agitation and a heightened yearning for what they came to see–Elvis. Bowen said the crowd not only "threw stuff at the poor guy [the violinist]," they became so aroused emotionally that "when Elvis came on you couldn't hear a word for the next hour."

Danny Dill, who worked for Eddy Arnold when the Colonel managed Arnold, observed that Parker "was a carny. He was raised a carny, and he was still a carny." The greatest thrill Parker got, according to Dill, was conning somebody out of something, anything at all, from a free lunch to free publicity. When Parker got something for nothing from people, Dill quickly realized that "it was not the money. It was just that he conned them out of it."

The Colonel had a huge ego. Arnold's biographer, Michael Streissguth, discovered that when Parker managed Arnold, he promoted his own name right along with Eddy's, thereby guaranteeing that, in the Colonel's words, "anyone in show business, in our field especially, would know that the minute they think of Eddy Arnold, they would think of me as his manager." Another of Parker's clients, Hank Snow, learned firsthand that the Colonel "would never let anyone forget how great he was." He never made a mistake either, or at least, that was the impression he worked hard to give.

One of RCA Records' field representatives, Jack Burgess, remembered that the Colonel's nature was to "always point the finger if somebody else didn't do something. When things went right, he had to take front and center." In other words, Burgess said, "if things weren't going right," Parker would "start reaching out to blame everybody and anybody."

Nonetheless, for every top star (or even promising star) who should have become what Elvis became, there was the ceaseless observation: if only that performer had been managed by a Colonel Parker. The Beatles had Brian Epstein, who discovered, on meeting the Colonel that the two had, according to Epstein's biographer Ray Coleman, a "common tenacity" in launching the careers of their clients. Just as Parker "sold tickets in the dance halls where Elvis appeared," Epstein "took around my own posters and and sold tickets when they [The Beatles] were earning less than twenty pounds a week."

Epstein also learned from his meeting with the Colonel (as reconstructed by Coleman in his book, *The Man Who Made the Beatles*) that "Elvis has required every moment of my time, and I think he would have suffered had I signed anyone else." At their August 1964 meeting, one of the more interesting topics was security. Parker observed to Epstein that "you don't have to protect the Beatles as we protected Elvis because with them there is no jealousy. You don't have to fear the boyfriends as we did, because your artists are characters loved in a different way. Your problem is to protect the small fans from getting hurt in the crush. We have never had them so little."

Who could have used a Colonel Parker? When it seemed like Jerry Lee Lewis might have made it big (and stayed there) in the late fifties, one of the people around him noted that all he needed was a Colonel Parker. Even his cousin, country music veteran Mickey Gilley, said (in an interview with Robert Cain for the book, *Whole Lotta Shakin' Goin' On*) that if Jerry Lee had "used somebody like Parker did with Presley, I think that Jerry Lee would have been as big, or very close to Presley."

Though Lewis once claimed Elvis was "just Colonel Parker's puppet," Elvis seemed happy with his situation, replying to Jerry Lee, "How is it that I'm playing the main room and you're playin' the lounge?" Jud (or Judd) Phillips, older brother of Sam Phillips (founder of Sun Records) and one-time Lewis manager, concluded, according to Myra Lewis, Lewis' ex-wife and co-author (with Murray Silver) of the Lewis biography, *Great Balls of Fire!*, that the Colonel "handled Elvis just right." Why did Jud think so? He observed that Parker "manipulated the personal-appearance fee to top dollar, he's a genius at promotion and has marketed everything from buttons and photos to T-shirts, jewelry, bubble-gum cards, pens, notebooks, dolls—hell, they even got Elvis Presley cologne and lipstick."

Lewis, however, seemed to harbor some long-standing hostility toward the Colonel. When Elvis opened in Las Vegas, he invited Lewis to be one of his guests. After the show, a lengthy raucous party ensued. Finally, according to Linda Gail Lewis, sister of Jerry Lee and author of *The Devil, Me, and Jerry Lee,* the Colonel came in and told Elvis, "It's time for you to go to bed. You've got shows again tomorrow, and you need your rest. Tell these folks good night."

Whereupon, Jerry Lee "got in the Colonel's face" and spouted, "Elvis, I wouldn't let no son of a bitch tell me what the hell I could and couldn't do. What do you think of that, Sergeant Parker?" It didn't matter what Lewis said because the Colonel said, according to Linda Gail, "Elvis, let's go." Elvis then "told everyone good night and left with the Colonel. He was completely under his control."

Elvis concluded early on that he absolutely needed the Colonel, a fact driven home by a simple Milton Berle anecdote. Berle said that when Elvis appeared on his show in 1956, comic and songwriter Solly Violinsky approached Elvis and told him he "had a great number for the kid to record." Solly was having fun, but Elvis was dead serious when he replied, "Most of my material is picked out by my manager, Colonel Parker. I couldn't even look at your song." Violinsky humorously countered, "Okay, kid, you're still going to be big, but it's going to take you longer!"

When Elvis had to reinvent himself as a live performer (after watching his career dwindle down on the heels of so many formulaic movies), he did so without changing managers. Whenever other stars, like Vanna White, for example, have felt the need to redirect their career paths, they have, in Vanna's words, "changed agents." That was not true with Elvis, who stayed with Parker for nearly a quarter of a century, even though, from time to time, there was speculation he tried to break away from the Colonel.

Just before Elvis took off by himself on a jaunt that landed him an audience with then-President Nixon, Priscilla remembered (in her autobiography) hearing him and his dad fighting about the Colonel. Elvis told the elder Presley, "Goddamn, Daddy, call and tell him we're through. Tear up the goddamn contracts and I'll pay him whatever percentages we owe him. To that, "Daddy" Presley replied, "Are you sure you want to do this?" Elvis emphatically retorted, "Goddamn right I am. I hate what I'm doing and I'm goddamned bored." With that, Priscilla watched Elvis stomp "out the front door." He did nothing about Parker, instead he went to the White House.

A few years (approximately late summer 1973) before Elvis died, he and the Colonel had a fight that almost resulted in a complete severing of their relationship. According to Lamar Fike, Elvis and the Colonel got into a screaming match. Marty Lacker said the situation did reach the point where Parker told Elvis he'd call a press conference and announce he was no longer Elvis' manager because of the "weird, stupid things you do." The Colonel also convinced Elvis it would cost $2 million to buy Parker out of his contract. Lacker vividly remembered Elvis saying, "I guess we're going to have to go down and make up with the old bastard."

British writer Colin Macfarlane, Tom Jones' biographer, claimed that Gordon Mills, who managed Jones, revealed that Elvis "asked him if he could take up his management." Mills elaborated that Elvis "was not getting along too well with his manager, Col. Tom Parker." Supposedly, according to Macfarlane, the two men "rarely met and when they did, hardly ever talked, so Elvis began to look for a way out." In the end Mills said he had to turn Elvis down because of, among other factors, "legal and financial complications."

There were other critics and observers would swear that the Colonel and Elvis had a very smooth ongoing relationship. Sheilah Graham wrote that Elvis "was grateful to the Colonel for advising him to make those nine successful films with Hal Wallis." Joe Esposito has maintained that not only was Elvis always very close to the Colonel, so was he, Esposito. In a column for *Pop Culture Collecting*, Esposito wrote that he "enjoyed a great relationship with the colonel, who I consider my very dear friend as well as being a business associate."

No matter how Elvis personally felt about the Colonel, he believed he couldn't last, career-wise, without him. As a result, Elvis would not stand up to him (at least not for long) nor would he disobey him in any major way. When Elvis and Tempest Storm were "lovers" (according to Storm), Elvis admitted, when it seemed like they were too serious, "the colonel pitched a fit." Elvis told her that Parker said, "If you keep hanging around that stripper, those screaming teenagers are going to stop screaming. And when they stop screaming, they'll stop buying your records and then where the hell are you going to be? Back in Memphis driving a goddamn truck." In an aside to Storm, Elvis confided that Parker was "really in a rage."

Storm proceeded to ask Elvis what he thought. His reply was that "if the Colonel said it," Elvis believed it, because "he's been right on everything so far. He's made me what I am." To Storm, Elvis was a "naive country boy" who depended on Colonel Parker as a "surrogate father." She considered the Colonel to be "a dictatorial jackass."

There were times when Elvis pushed back, in his own way. Sammy Davis, Jr. recalled in his memoirs, *Hollywood in a Suitcase*, a time when he and Elvis worked together determinedly to reverse a "decision" made by the Colonel. Davis said the situation occurred after "it was seriously suggested that Elvis Presley and I should play the leads in *The Defiant Ones*, later cast with Sidney Poitier and

Tony Curtis. Both Elvis and I were anxious to do the picture. But Elvis's manager, Colonel Tom Parker, thought it was 'controversial' as a vehicle for his 'boy' and turned it down. We both put up a terrific fight, but by the time everything got settled we had gone on to other things. It was a shame because both of us would have been wonderful in the parts, and we all would have recognized at last Elvis's burning ambition and ability to act his butt off."

One area in which Elvis did not push back hard enough was making a foreign tour, the kind that proved so successful for artists like Bob Dylan and The Rolling Stones. Though he was as popular all over the world as he was in the United States and the people around him felt such a tour would rejuvenate him, the Colonel, according to Lamar Fike, "would always talk him out of it." Speculation ran rampant that Elvis never went overseas because Parker was afraid his own illegal immigrant status might have been discovered. It was also rumored that the Colonel feared Elvis' drug habits might have been discovered by overzealous customs officials.

Fike, a self-described friend, employee, confidant, and partner to Elvis for twenty-three years, was convinced that the "real" reason why Colonel Parker "didn't want to go to Europe" stemmed from the fact that he was "an illegal alien in the United States. He jumped off a boat to get into this country. In fact he jumped off twice. The first time they caught him and sent him back to his native country, the Netherlands. The second time, he stayed and never got caught."

Because of Parker's illegal alien status, Fike concluded that "the Colonel was afraid that if he left the U.S., he'd never be able to get back in, and that's why he prevented Elvis from taking a Europe tour." Fike remembered that whenever the subject of a foreign tour would come up, the Colonel "always had a reason for not going. Security problems. Tax problems. Technical and production details. God knows what else. Elvis would blow up at the Colonel about it, say he was damn well going–but he'd always end up backing down."

It was not as if Elvis needed to tour Europe or any other foreign country, because the crowds he drew stateside, especially early in his career were so large that even his co-performers, who were almost as popular as he was, couldn't get to see him. The Everly Brothers, when they performed with Elvis, remembered trying to visit with him after a show in Nashville, but "because he caused such a riot," all they got was "a quick handshake and kind of a quick look in the eye."

Two English promoters, Bill Benny and Vic Lewis, did get as far as seriously discussing with the Colonel a possible European concert tour (to begin in England in 1961). The Colonel's reaction to the proposed tour was positive yet far too costly. According to Lewis, the

Colonel's terms were that "if we come to England, gentlemen, I want all the cash to go to charity. I want to play at Wembley Stadium and I want the owners to make no rental charges for our use of the venue. All the refreshments are to be given away free to the fans–the Coke, the ice cream, that stuff."

The Colonel wasn't finished as he added the condition that he be given "the use of our own chartered Boeing jet to fly the entourage from Los Angeles to London and back." Finally, the Colonel wanted "your personal guarantee that the Queen of England would be our guest of honour." He viewed the whole prospect as "a royal charity gala at Wembley Stadium. That's the way I want to do it."

Lewis, writing in his autobiography, *Music & Maiden Overs: My Showbusiness Life*, recalled that the meeting closed with "fond farewells." He promised the Colonel he would see what "we could do about his concert proposals." He also said he "knew we had no chance of satisfying his conditions." At least Lewis tried. Given the Colonel's outlandish demands and expectations, it was easy to see why no foreign tour for Elvis was ever scheduled.

Though the Colonel never made it possible for Elvis to tour outside the United States, Parker did consistently deliver in ways that would not have occurred to other managers. When Elvis opened in Vegas at the International Hotel, the Colonel obviously wanted all the attention focused on his client. As big as Elvis was, even then, Parker still ran somewhere around two hundred radio spots touting Elvis' upcoming International appearance.

Because Elvis hadn't played a major live venue in three years, a lot of newspaper people came to town to cover opening night. At the same time, according to syndicated entertainment columnist Earl Wilson, there were competing opening shows, from Las Vegas favorites like Dinah Shore, Jerry Vale, Jane Powell, and Myron Cohen. Many of the newspaper folks planned on catching Elvis' show beginning at 9:00 p.m. and then going to at least one of the midnight shows by another performer. The result would have been, in their next day reviews, coverage being split between Elvis and some other act.

In a stroke of genius, the Colonel announced that Elvis would, after the nine o'clock show, hold a 12:30 a.m. news conference. Wilson recalled that "most of us newsmen were afraid to miss the press conference," because "there had been rumors that Elvis might be making an announcement about his marital situation." So, he said, they all "went and waited for a dramatic announcement." Unbelievably (or perhaps too believably), there wasn't any. Elvis merely came out and said how glad he was "to be there." As Wilson ruefully concluded, "Colonel Parker had effectively kept us from seeing the other competing stars and giving them publicity."

Throughout his career, the Colonel had excelled at focusing all the attention on Elvis whenever appropriate or, in the Colonel's mind, necessary. Country music talk show host and radio personality Ralph Emery recalled that in the mid-fifties, when he worked at a Nashville radio station, he was asked by an RCA promotion man, Ed Hines, to announce that Elvis "would be leaving the RCA studio on Nashville's Seventeenth Avenue South about 2:00 p.m." Supposedly, the call was made at the request of Colonel Parker.

Emery said he made the announcement and "thought little about it," actually feeling sorry for "the kid," because "he was probably going to get his feelings hurt because nobody cared that he was going to be walking outside the RCA studios. It was a weekday and people had better things to do than show up hoping to get a glimpse of a hopeful singer." After all, Emery noted, "Presley had done only one hit at that time for RCA."

There needn't have been any "sorry" feelings for Elvis. Not long after his on-the-air announcement, and with a little additional work by the Colonel, Emery found out that "city authorities subsequently said hello to mayhem." What happened was that "typical of the colonel's promotional savvy, he did not let Presley leave RCA that day until three hours after his scheduled departure. Soon, the streets were hopelessly clogged with fans hoping for a peek at the soon-to-be king. Apparently someone touting Presley just 'happened' to arrange for photographers to come by about the same time Elvis was leaving the studios. The frenetic mob was captured on film and was reproduced by newswires throughout the country."

Stanley Brossette, formerly part of the MGM publicity department, told Alexandra Brouwer and Thomas Lee Wright, for their book, *Working in Hollywood*, that when he joined the studio he never dreamed he would wind up working with none other than Colonel Tom Parker. At the time Brossette started as a "junior publicist," Elvis was "under contract to MGM" and Parker "was his manager." Since, in Brossette's words, "Elvis was one of MGM's most valuable 'properties,' people would do anything to please the Colonel." Unfortunately, the trained publicists at MGM had been taught "exactly the opposite of the way the Colonel was managing Elvis' career." So, Brossette was assigned to work with Elvis and Parker and "learn the Colonel's way."

What exactly was the Colonel's way? Brossette quickly discovered that it did not consist of the traditional Hollywood publicity releases and press coverage. Early on, based on his "carny" experience, the Colonel had come to understand that devoted fans had a deep-seated need to buy products associated with their favorite star or stars, because, as Jib Fowles analyzed in his book, *Starstruck: Celebrity Performers and the American Public,* those products "serve as an emotional link between devotee and idol."

According to Fowles, "beginning in the mid-1950s, Col. Tom Parker arranged to have between fifty and one hundred Elvis products always available for fans – lipstick, phonographs, jeans, fountain pens, and so forth." He never stopped, even after Elvis was dead, prompting Fowles to observe that "in 1986, the two leading expired performers for commercial purposes were Elvis Presley, with approximately 100 different licenses, and Marilyn Monroe, with about half that number of agreements." Today there are "hundreds of items that are now collectible," in the words of Steve Ellingboe (writing for *Warman's Today's Collector*), all of them having an appeal to fans, who "collect with their hearts."

In one of the most perfectly timed moves of Elvis' career, Parker succeeded in getting him on national television just as his first RCA single, "Heartbreak Hotel," was ready to break (though Jackie Gleason supposedly claimed RCA was pushing the flip side, "I Was the One"). *The Ed Sullivan Show* (on Sunday nights) would have been the most logical place to have begun, but Sullivan made it known early on that he "wouldn't have Elvis Presley on my show at any time." There was a similar shying away from Elvis at each of the national networks, so the Colonel turned to an old friend, none other than Jackie Gleason.

According to research done by writer James Bacon (for his biography of Gleason), the Colonel knew Gleason from their days together at "Toots" Shor's New York City saloon. Parker's "dancing turkeys" show had led to his becoming the road manager for a very popular vocalist, Gene Austin (whose big hit was "My Blue Heaven"). Austin introduced Parker to Shor's, where, sometime before 1954, the Colonel met and became friends with Gleason.

In late 1955, when Parker was looking for TV exposure, Gleason had his own *Stage Show* on CBS-TV, starring the Dorsey Brothers, Tommy and Jimmy (instrumentalists and bandleaders during their illustrious careers and Gleason's drinking buddies at "Toots" Shor's). Parker sent Elvis' picture to Gleason, who said he had this reaction (as quoted by Bacon): "Marlon Brando was all the rage then. I sensed that Elvis had the same animal magnetism as Brando. I said that if this kid could make any kind of noise, let's sign him for six weeks for our show."

Gleason went on to add that "I sent someone on my staff to see if we could get a record by this guy. If I remember correctly, we had to send to Sun Records in Memphis for it. It was 'That's All Right.' We had a hell of a time finding it; that's how unknown he was. When I played the record, I saw that his voice matched his looks. We grabbed him fast." Elvis was first booked on the January 28, 1956, telecast of *Stage Show*.

Though Gleason had wanted Elvis for six weeks, that's not what happened. As he explained the situation (to Bacon), "there was a problem." Elvis "was so damn good that first show that Tommy and Jimmy got pissed off. They argued that they were supposed to be the stars, not Elvis. Tommy had been through this same thing with Sinatra. As a result, we only used Elvis a few times, not the six weeks I wanted." Though Elvis didn't get the six weeks, he did get some special exposure. It was on that Gleason show, according to biographer Bacon, that film producer Hal Wallis first saw Elvis perform.

Not content with that level of exposure, the Colonel proceeded to send pictures of Elvis' appearance on Gleason's show to the folks at *The Milton Berle Show*, which resulted in a spring 1956 telecast with Uncle Miltie from the deck of the USS *Hancock* in San Diego. Elvis capitalized on that opportunity, of course, causing once again, in Bacon's words, "a riot with the women." That telecast was watched by more than forty million viewers, a majority of whom were thought to have seen Elvis for the first time.

More appearances followed: *The Steve Allen Show*, another segment of *The Milton Berle Show*, and finally, Sullivan's show (but not until September 9, 1956). Though it was nine months prior that Elvis first went on national television (with Gleason), Bacon (Gleason's biographer) noted that Sullivan "got all the page-one headlines," largely because of "his moralistic stand against Elvis' pelvis movements, which many mothers said were exciting glands in girls too young to know what glands were." Those "page-one headlines" brought out the largest television audience ever, an estimated fifty-three million viewers tuned in to watch Elvis (minus his lower body), a record which stood until The Beatles appeared on Ed's show in 1964.

Colonel Parker always seemed to open up opportunities and get results exactly when they were needed. How did he know to do what he did when he did? How did he come up with some of his most offbeat but successful schemes? The Colonel almost completely kept his thoughts to himself, even up to his death in 1997. At one time, he supposedly started writing an autobiography and even turned down a huge advance, because he wanted to sell advertising inside the book.

Parker told country music personality Ralph Emery that if he didn't finish his autobiography, his second wife Loanne would (he married her after Marie, his wife of forty-two years, died). Until then there could only be a reliance on other people's opinions as far as theorizing what kind of person the Colonel was. He, like Elvis, was most likely a dichotomy. For every negative opinion about the Colonel there usually appeared to have been a positive one.

In her autobiography, Sheila MacRae revealed that at least one very powerful Hollywood personality, Ann Warner, wife of Warner Bros. head, Jack Warner, fostered a loathsome impression of Parker. MacRae quoted [Ann] Warner as saying that "there's a man to avoid. Truly crude. And bigoted. Every third word from his mouth is 'nigger.' " Yet Louise Draper, board member of King's Daughters Day Home, felt compelled to write an unsolicited letter to the *Nashville Tennessean* and disclose that "the continued service this day care renders is due to the fine, caring people like Colonel Parker." Her letter was written following the Colonel's death because she "felt it was time that others knew a different side of this man who seemed to be a controversial figure in the media and public's eye." She closed with the words that "we are indeed grateful for this special man, who always asked that no mention be made of his gifts."

Though the Colonel claimed, "I never talk about myself," he did open up to music industry executive Arnold Shaw, in what became as close to a full personal interview as he ever gave. Shaw, writing in his book, *The Rockin' '50s*, told of being invited out to Colonel Parker's home in Madison, Tennessee (just outside Nashville), in 1955, before his contract with Elvis was executed. The evening began with the two men in Parker's basement where the Colonel showed Shaw a four-page, legal-size, printed document, his standard contract.

He told Shaw that it was "the contract promoters have to sign if they want to book one of my artists." He said he had "prepared that contract myself." After Shaw read and duly showed his "amusement" at the contract's language, the Colonel told Shaw, "I prepared that contract myself, every single clause of it."

With that, Parker launched into one of the longest stories he ever told about himself. He proudly explained to Shaw, "I started in the carny business when I was very young. County fairs, livestock shows, rodeos, circuses, tobacco promotions, Saturday-night dances, carnivals–cleaning, doing odd jobs, selling programs. Finally, I got to where I sold an act to a promoter and I had to sign a contract. Took me all night to read that piece of paper. But I read every word, signed it–and got taken to the cleaners, as you city folk say."

The Colonel had a point, which was that he "raised a ruckus but couldn't do a thing. It was all legal. So I went home, found the clause that did me in, cut it out, and pasted it on a piece of paper. The next time I got a contract, I went lookin' for this son-of-a-bitchin' clause. It wasn't there. But I got taken by another clause. So I pasted that one on a piece of paper. After several years, I had all these stinkers that I was watchin' out fer." To conclude, Parker said that "one day, I put all those smart-assed clauses together–and that's the contract you're holding in yer big-city hands." In sum total, the contract, according to what one lawyer at a booking firm told Shaw, "was a gem."

Whatever other thoughts or wisdom the Colonel may have had in his life were seemingly lost when he passed away at the beginning of 1997 (January 22). In the bombshell of early 1998, the Colonel's widow announced that an "authorized" biography would be forthcoming. She said the book "would be the only authorized biography approved by the estate and will include access to her husband's massive collection of photos, memorabilia and records." Her stated intention was to "detail the true story behind the incredible relationship between the colonel and Elvis." But would it include anything from the truckloads of memorabilia the Elvis estate purchased from the Colonel after the Colonel died?

Would the widow's proposed book also include the kind of story that Link Wray recently told about the pre-Elvis times of Colonel Parker? It seemed that, according to Wray, the Colonel had a vaudeville act called Tom Parker and His Dancing Chickens. The chickens "danced" because Parker put them on a hot plate and they had no choice. Dave Marsh wrote a similar story about the chickens.

Could this have been possible? There was a corroborating source, who said it wasn't chickens, but turkeys. According to Gene Autry, writing in his 1978 autobiography, his longtime sidekick, Pat Buttram, met the Colonel sometime in the mid-thirties, when the Colonel had an act called "Colonel Tom Parker and His Dancing Turkeys." Parker's spiel to the customers was, "they dance, they do the hoochie-coochie; come and see these amazing creatures. Only a quarter."

Buttram disclosed to Autry that the Colonel "had a large table with sawdust on it and underneath was a metal plate. He would arrange about twenty live turkeys on it and then he'd throw on a switch and it would become, literally, a hot plate. At the same time the colonel would turn on the record player and the turkeys would seem to be jumping around in rhythm to the music. The farmers would turn to their wives and say, 'Ma, how does he do it?' And the little kids would go home and beat their pet turkeys, trying to teach them to dance."

That was not the end of the story. Autry went on to relate that Buttram asked the Colonel "just one question: when the tempo picked up, how did he get them to stay in time to the music?" According to Pat, the Colonel said, "That's easy. I got a thermostat in there and when I want them to dance faster I just turn it up a little hotter."

None of this seemed to have shocked or bothered either Autry or Buttram in any way. To end the story, Autry commented that "it didn't surprise me when Tom Parker emerged as the genius behind Elvis. He saw the whole world as a carnival. Late in his career, when Buttram played a character called Mr. Haney on the television series, *Green Acres*, he patterned him after Colonel Parker."

The "dancing chicken legend" didn't end there (with Buttram's story). In the mid-seventies, country star Roy Clark had been tapped to host *The Tonight Show* for a week. One of the first people he called was Colonel Tom Parker. After the two men chatted briefly, the Colonel asked Clark what he wanted. Clark said he began his pitch by telling Parker he was hosting *The Tonight Show*.

Parker immediately cut him off, saying "Elvis don't do those kind of shows. They don't pay anything. If I did the show I'd have to change the name of my book." Whereupon he told an inquisitive Clark that the book was "called, *How Much Does It Cost If It's Free?*" Then he added, in Clark's words, that he would "do the show if they let him set up an Elvis souvenir stand in the lobby."

Clark turned the tables on the Colonel by telling him, "Wait a minute, Colonel, I don't want Elvis on the show. I want you." It was then that the Colonel retorted back, "Aw, kid, I'm harder to get than Elvis! But I do have this dancing chicken act I'll give you!"

Actually, Clark had (by the mid-seventies) known the Colonel off and on for about twenty years, beginning when Clark was a professional music novice working with country music entrepreneur and promoter Connie B. Gay. Clark wrote in his memoirs that the Colonel had come to see Gay to obtain the services of Roy and his band to back Elvis for a gig in the Washington D.C. area. At the same time, Parker also offered to sell Elvis' contract to Gay for "something like eight million dollars." According to Clark, Gay told the Colonel, "I think he's great but I don't think he's got a future."

What happened to the Colonel after Elvis' death? Palm Springs promoter (whom Parker also briefly mentored) Greg McDonald disclosed that Rick Nelson, late in his career, often "went to 'The Colonel' about all sorts of things, even personal matters, and could really talk openly with him." Nelson's biographer, Philip Bashe, added that "The Colonel," who was "deeply fond of Rick, came to function as a casual adviser." Whenever Rick was in Palm Springs, he "dropped in at the Parker home." Years before, Parker had also "casually" advised Rick's father, Ozzie, from time to time. It would appear the Colonel had more to offer than many of his critics would care to admit.

Even today, the question has remained: Was the Colonel good for Elvis, or was he a detriment? To music commentator Dave Marsh, the

Colonel was "in the running for the most overrated person in show business history." On the other hand, Western star Gene Autry saw Parker as a definite plus. In an interview with Jerry Osborne, Autry related that he knew "Colonel Tom Parker very well and don't know of anybody that could have handled Presley's career any better. I knew Tom when he managed Eddy Arnold years ago and consider that he made Elvis bigger than anyone else could have done."

Gene Austin, one of the first entertainers the Colonel represented, had some amazingly positive memories of the man. He was quoted (in his biography, *Gene Austin's Ol' Buddy*) as saying, "I cannot shower enough praises on Tom Parker." When Austin began experiencing harsh financial times, as his career dwindled down, the Colonel didn't desert him. Instead, he obtained credit at a local grocery store and, according to Austin, sold "the tires off the truck to meet the pressing bills." The Colonel explained, "Don't worry, Gene, I have made a deal with a tire company to let us have new tires on credit."

Austin expressed amazement that Parker "could keep manipulating against such difficulties." When his financial situation worsened, Austin remembered that "only Tom's knack of handling people" kept him out of serious trouble. Finally, when Austin had to permanently break off from Parker because he couldn't afford to pay him (or anyone else) anymore, he observed that "Tom" was not only "loyal to the end," he braved some severe weather "to see me off."

Austin's final words on Colonel Parker were: "How I hated to leave that man. My estimation of Tom has been confirmed by his career through the years, with Eddy Arnold, Tommy Sands, and as the guiding light of Elvis Presley." Perhaps that was the definitive conclusion about Elvis and the Colonel.

Andy Warhol immortalizes Elvis on canvas. Reproduced courtesy of ARS. Copyright © 1998 Andy Warhol Foundation for the
Visual Arts/ARS, New York.

The look that created the empire. Reproduced courtesy of MICHAEL OCHS
ARCHIVES/Venice, CA.

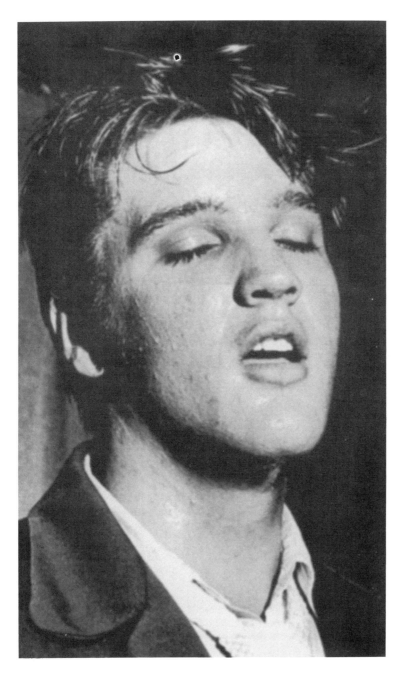

Elvis lost in the moment as he sings to his adoring fans. Reproduced courtesy of MICHAEL OCHS ARCHIVES/Venice, CA.

The King and Nixon shake hands as Elvis receives a "special assistant" badge from the Bureau of Narcotics and Dangerous Drugs. Reproduced courtesy of The Nixon Presidential Materials Staff, National Archives.

The Elvis legend continues as Antigua and Barbuda dedicate stamps to the King's memory.

A fan captures Elvis' likeness in stone.

ADDENDUM I
THE GUIDE TO COLLECTING ELVIS BOOKS

When the publishing world discovered Elvis Presley
in 1956, it found a virtually inexhaustible source of
interest to readers around the world.

–Steve Templeton,
*Elvis!: An Illustrated Guide to
New and Vintage Collectibles*

Given the rising value of Elvis books and the diminishing availability of many earlier works, collecting such books is not that different from collecting any rare or increasing-in-value book. The first challenge is knowing what to look for, what to buy, and how much to pay. The second is finding where to look and who to go to in any and all searches for items.

What to Look for

Beginning right now, every Elvis book is worth something. A *new book* is worth either the suggested list or some discounted price (usually up to 40 percent) at retail. Once a customer has bought a new book, it becomes, automatically, a *used book*, regardless of condition. The closer the owner of a book keeps that book to its new condition, the more value that book will retain over the years.

Being in an almost new condition means the book has had a prior owner (it is "used") but it is in mint or "as-new" state. Anything below that will put the used book into one of several categories: fine, very good, good, fair, or poor. The poor condition means pages are falling out, the jacket is missing, the copy was once a library book, and so forth. Library and book club copies rarely have a marketable value. In general, poor condition books will have value only if there are no other available copies anywhere in better condition.

When buying a new or used book, the best value will be the *first edition*. That notation will usually be printed on the copyright page. It means the copy was part of the first set of that particular book to be printed by the publisher. It was part of the original print run. Most collectors and dealers prefer anything that was done first and books are no exception. They also prefer copies of books that have been signed by the author or subject, especially if the individual doing the signing has attained a high level of fame.

From there every copy of every book is relatively worth less and less. When buying a used book, the older the book the more value it will have. Like all other collectibles, age almost automatically breeds scarcity. For example, a rookie Mickey Mantle baseball card is almost priceless because so few remain available today. A copy of that card manufactured in the past few years is currently worth only about ten cents because of its wide availability.

A signed hardback copy (in mint condition) of Vester Presley's *A Presley Speaks* (which were sold as part of a special edition) would be worth as much as $500 to certain collectors. That same book, in paperback and unsigned, would be virtually worthless. In the case of some of the souvenir books issued on Elvis in the mid-to-late 1950s, age and scarcity have pushed their market value (for mint to fine copies) into the low hundreds (of dollars).

To conclude the advice on what to look for, even when the object or objects are something as specific as a book on Elvis, the collector will find a "road map" to be more than useful. A road map is any kind of guide or bibliography that lists books on the subject (being collected)-in this case Elvis. Fortunately for the collector or researcher, the most complete listing of Elvis books is right here, in this book, *The Printed Elvis*. A final bit of obvious advice is to stay away from paperbacks unless no other copy is available and the book must be acquired in some format.

Paperbacks generally have no resale value and are useful only in trade situations, where one can trade some number of used copies for another number of used copies of other books. Used book dealers will generally not buy paperbacks and serious collectors will not acquire them. They deteriorate too quickly and even one serious reading renders them in poor condition.

How to Find It

In-Print: Almost anything that has been published in the past five years is probably "in-print," meaning that the publisher maintains an active stock of the book. If the book has sold relatively well, most retailers will have a copy for sale. The copy, unless the book is brand-new, will probably not be a first edition. First editions usually disappear within weeks of the initial release of the book to the general public. Many first edition copies never get to the general public. They are often used as gifts or promotions, or are snatched up by collectors just prior to release.

Nonetheless, when collecting Elvis or any other kind of book, the first edition in mint condition is the most valuable and will increase in value faster than any other version. Indeed, there are book dealers who sell only first editions. They will, of course, be the best supplier of any past first editions a collector may wish to acquire. Whenever a book is initially sold, by all means, make sure the first edition copy is the one that you purchase.

If a book is beyond its first edition status yet is still in-print but no longer available at retail, it can be ordered either through a store or directly from the publisher (most have 1-800 numbers). Anything out of print will have to be found through used book sources and dealers. The major sources for used books are used book stores. Most will not carry a used book of any great value or rarity.

Used Bookstores: An average state in the eastern part of the country will have from one hundred to one thousand used bookstores, from the very small, which specialize in popular paperback trading, to the very large boasting thousands of books in every major category. The total number of used bookstores in New York, New Jersey, and Connecticut number in the tens of thousands. Every major state has an antiquarian society of used book dealers.

From any used bookstore one can obtain a copy of the listing of members for that state. Additionally, there are "used book lovers' guides" to used bookstores by region, such as the central states or the southeastern states. The first place to look for any out-of-print books is always one or more of these stores. They will be of great value in building up the basic part of any collection.

The Search Specialist: When the collector decides to acquire more difficult to obtain books, the search progressively becomes more demanding, time-consuming, expensive, and specialized. That is when the specialist should consulted. The specialist is usually a dealer who does not exclusively sell at retail but who spends much or all of his or her business time on retainer for various collectors, looking through hundreds of sources for client requests.

While searching for books for specific clients, specialists will always keep one eye out for exceptional items, especially first editions, and will purchase them on their own, knowing they will be able to sell them somehow and somewhere. The specialists are also the ones given the first opportunity to acquire major collections, something that will rarely be possible for the average collector.

The collector's challenge then, once he or she has perused retail stores, used bookstores, garage sales, thrift stores, and outlet centers is to locate the specific search specialist that will optimally fulfill collection requirements. In both the United States and Great Britain, the Antiquarian Book societies are the best place to begin a search for the best search specialist. For this entire country, the Antiquarian Book Association of America has a headquarters shop in New York City at 50 Rockefeller Plaza.

In the shop, there are some representative samples of rare items available through association members. There is also available, free of charge, a member list of over three hundred of the finest used book dealers. In England, there is the Antiquarian Bookseller's Association located at 154 Buckingham Palace Road, London. That association maintains and makes available a similar list.

Almost any member on either list should be able to serve as a suitable search specialist or point you to a member best able to assist you. You only need to work with one member because that member will network to all the other members to find what has been requested by a specific client. However, if a collector were to go through some of the members and did not achieve satisfaction, there are a number of excellent search specialists outside both associations.

Normally, these specialists advertise regularly in book collecting magazines and in the *New York Times* book section. Peruse those ads and inquire accordingly. In England, there is one further guide that might prove helpful. It is called *A Directory of Dealers in Secondhand & Antiquarian Books in the British Isles*. In the United States, there is also a guide that can prove to be very useful.

It is now entitled *AB Bookman's Weekly* and is available from its headquarters in Clifton, New Jersey (P.O. Box AB). Eight thousand people subscribe to *AB Bookman's*. It is primarily used by searchers to advertise their want lists to other book dealers and search specialists. Along with this general guide are the specialized catalogs issued by specific dealers. Those catalogs are directly available from each dealer. If the collector can find an item in a catalog, the collector will save paying a finder's fee to the dealer. A relatively new online search facility available through the Internet is Interloc, which currently lists two thousand subscribers.

Each year at particular times all across the country there are antiquarian book fairs in which dealers of various sizes and specialties maintain booths to show off their most valuable items. Oftentimes, dealers save their best and rarest acquisitions to show off at one or more of these fairs. For each year, either the national antiquarian society can advise of fair dates or any of the state societies can disclose specific state or local fair information. Go to such a fair and if possible find a dealer with wares similar to your wants. That dealer could wind up being a very valuable search specialist in the future.

In my opinion, to cover the western half of this country, the best search specialist has been M. Taylor Bowie, of Seattle, Washington. Taylor is one of those unusual specialists who operates from a very high-priced used bookstore in downtown Seattle. He has associates to run the store and he uses it mainly to attract collectors and to bring in those occasional rare books that someone may sell.

Most of the time he is on the road, accessible only by telephone or the Internet. The rare books he has found have continually astounded me. He tries to keep the cost down but, like every other specialist, his costs are high and the people from whom he buys know what their items are worth and charge accordingly, knowing that there are few other sources available beyond themselves. He also distributes a regular newsletter on his finds.

In the eastern part of the country, I have turned to Phil and Anne Haisley, of Books, Inc. in Gainesville, Florida. They can be reached at 352-374-4241. They, like Bowie, own a bookstore that staff members run for them while they attend book dealer shows and antiquarian festivals, and search for major private collections to acquire and distribute through their own special channels.

The Haisleys are great to work with because their initial searches are usually fruitful and inexpensive. They specifically advertise for each client's wants in an issue of *AB Bookman's Weekly* and do a lengthier search through Interloc. They also personally call on their vast list of dealer contacts. These are sources they have built up over many years from their earlier days of bookselling in Marion, Indiana, to the present. They always maintain lengthy and up-to-date lists of client wants as they search through book fairs, estate sales, and private collection auctions.

Other major search services (especially for Elvis books) are available through Bluff Park Rare Books of Long Beach, California (310-438-9830) and Art Carduner's Booksearch of Philadelphia, Pennsylvania (215-843-6071). Both firms ask the collector to supply them with book title, author name, publisher name, and date of publication. They will get back to the collector with a price quote and an extensive description of the acquirable copy. If you want a first edition, you must let them know. Each firm will try its best to resolve your search request within a month or less, if possible.

Other Sources: Even though book dealers (new and used) and search specialists are the best avenue for acquiring everything from in-print to rare out-of-print books, there are other means to pursue in building your Elvis book collection. One is attending auctions personally and another is contacting memorabilia collectors. In the case of Elvis books, the collector can have great success by contacting dealers in Elvis memorabilia, because Elvis books are often considered by such dealers to be part of that large body of collectible items that fans demand almost insatiably.

Auction information can be found in local newspaper listings or obtained from auction houses through the mailers they send out well in advance of a major auction. Writing to auction houses will get you on their mailing list and get you a copy of their catalog for upcoming auctions. Perusing catalogs will enable you to decide which auctions to attend and how much to make available in funds for bidding.

Contacting other collectors is often worthwhile. The best way to get in touch is through fan clubs. Calling on members of various fan clubs will open to the collector a vast number of people who are usually doing something very similar, which is looking for anything Elvis. Finding fan clubs is a relatively easy thing to do. In the second part of this book, *The Printed Elvis*, there is a discussion of three authors' books, each of which contains a very useful listing of Elvis fan clubs.

Finally, there are collecting magazines. The elite publication is entitled *Biblio: The Magazine for Collectors of Books, Manuscripts, and Ephemera*. It comes out monthly and boasts of an international editorial advisory board. For a magazine more attuned to popular culture, there is *Pop Culture Collecting: Memories & Memorabilia*. This publication is more in line with Elvis collecting as it features a regular column on Elvis collectibles by Joe Esposito.

Finally, consult the books written by experts on book collecting. Robert Wilson, the proprietor of the Phoenix Book Shop in New York City, has become one of the most renowned. He has also written the definitive book on how to collect books of all kinds. His advice is contained in the book, *Modern Book Collecting*, published in 1980 by Alfred A. Knopf (of New York). Peruse it for all its worth and there probably won't be a book printed that will remain unlocatable.

Two "Collector" Profiles

Most fans collect Elvis memorabilia of some kind, but their collections usually consist of recordings, trinkets, pictures, keepsakes, and special items (special to the particular fan), such as scarves, belt buckles, and even prayer mats. Very few people collect information about the King. Columnist Phil Patton of the *New York Times* discovered one who does, in an extraordinary way. In one of his "Public Eye" columns (August 1998) for the paper, he discussed the phenomenal Graceland Too located in Holly Springs, Mississippi, run by Paul MacLeod and his son, Elvis Aron Presley.

For a mere $5 fee, Patton toured through an antebellum house MacLeod inherited and converted into a shrine to Elvis, complete with "rare records, clothing, one of Elvis's school report cards," all part of a massive collection of memorabilia worth, according to MacLeod, in excess of $10 million. Patton quoted the elder MacLeod as saying that his house, dedicated as it is to memorializing the King, "has made their lives complete." Surprisingly, the house, over a hundred years old (built circa 1840), sits in a quiet, unassuming small town neighborhood about an hour's drive south of Memphis, where, in Patton's words, "it's not surrounded by the used-car dealerships and fast-food joints of Elvis Presley Boulevard."

What made the MacLeod enterprise stand out above all the other shrines constructed by fans all over the world were what Patton called "the media logs" put together by the MacLeods. These logs have documented "millions of references from the obvious to the miniscule," all having information capable of disclosing, for example, "that on 6:30 p.m., Dec. 23, 1995, a poster of Elvis appeared in the back of the set of the TV show, *Entertainment Tonight*." In addition to the logs were dozens (actually trunkloads) of VCR tapes and hundreds of books the MacLeods have used to document "all references to Elvis" ever been made in the media, to their knowledge.

This would include, as Patton discovered, "every time a deejay plays a record," as well as every time Elvis "shows up in a movie." Father and son MacLeod have made it their lives' work to literally "take turns monitoring the media for all references to Elvis." Their "museum" is literally the place to go for anyone who needs or wants to know how Elvis has been used by or has appeared in almost every form of popular communications networks and mediums.

Are the MacLeods "nuts," as some could be tempted to label them? They did, after all, purchase as much of the Graceland carpet (rubber backing and all) as they could when the mansion was remodeled, though that might someday prove to be high-yield investment. They simply have turned their home into, in Patton's eyes, "a larger, more obsessive version of any number of shrines to athletes or rock stars in teen-agers' rooms." In some ways, he mused, it was like "a grandiose enlargement of the sports fan's den, with his Dallas Cowboys satellite television package and ESPN." Patton admitted that it reminded him of his "own media-monitoring decor, my stacks of magazines, tapes and notebooks."

The MacLeods have collected informational "references" so they can track Elvis' appearances. Other fan/collectors have acquired books, magazines, and pieces of written ephemera (like concert programs and newspaper articles) so they can not only possess those items but learn from them as well. One such collector is Charlotte Campana, a transplanted Floridian by way of a Chicago suburb.

The "forty-plus"-year-old Charlotte is on the verge of realizing her dream of devoting an entire room, in her recently purchased home, to Elvis and her collection of Elvis books, records, and ephemera. Short of that goal, she has files of clippings, cases of books (well over a hundred), photo books, magazines, concert programs, and much more. She also has a huge and ever-growing set of scrapbooks that contain almost every article, newspaper column, or published picture relevant to Elvis, especially his death.

Charlotte has been a single mother on and off throughout her life. She spends her limited resources on a few pleasures, namely, cigarettes, the occasional going out to an unplanned party, a foray to a movie, or a friendly dinner. What she has left, whenever she has it, has consistently been spent on something pertaining to Elvis. In addition to her files and scrapbooks documenting Elvis' career, she has managed to purchase hundreds of albums and singles, but no compact discs: They lack the "warmth and intimacy" of vinyl.

I recently had the opportunity to interview Charlotte and I asked her both why and how she had become so devoted to collecting Elvis. It was a great interviewer question, one that doesn't allow a subject to merely answer yes or no, and smile, knowing he or she just got off the hook. No, it wasn't that kind of question, I thought to myself.

Still, I was not prepared for her answer. That's because it wasn't an answer; she just smiled at me, as if to say, "You big dummy, don't you know?" I recovered by asking what she specifically collected. This time she answered and said, "Everything written on him except for all that stuff about drugs. I don't keep anything that ever said he did drugs. Elvis never did drugs."

Now I was on to something. I pursued the question with a statement about how the people close to Elvis revealed that he did drugs for all kinds of reasons. She listened politely and waited until I finished dispensing my evidence, then she said, just as pointedly, that Elvis did not do drugs. I learned my next lesson, Elvis was clean. He wasn't completely wholesome, no, nobody would admit being that deluded. Elvis fooled around, he had many women (no men, of course!); indeed, that was part of his mystique, that he seemed accessible to any woman who really wanted him.

So much for Charlotte's feelings about Elvis. I was ready to discover more about her collecting and her collection. We cut right to the heart. She had become an Elvis collector and fan at the age of seven (somewhere in the fifties). Her multilayered fascination quickly progressed into a desire to know everything about her hot young idol.

From her seventh year right up through today, she has acquired records, books, and magazines while clipping newspapers from all over the United States. She also attended concerts and personally took photos at shows from Las Vegas all the way to Jacksonville. Mostly, she joined fan clubs and lived because Elvis brought her a joy like no one else did, except her now seven-year-old child. Whenever that baby sings or does something cute and entertaining, she remarks how much the child resembles Elvis.

As our interview progressed, she described her memorabilia and souvenirs in terms of hundreds of concert programs, ticket stubs, and even brought out her two favorite picture sleeves, the ones from the 45 singles, "Blue Christmas" and "Way Down." Then she showed me her scrapbooks, her magazines, which contained everything from features on Elvis to entire editions devoted to him, and her files, bursting with newspaper clippings of concert and record reviews, items about Elvis that someone deemed newsworthy, and every conceivable written word on every move Elvis ever made.

As Charlotte opened the scrapbooks and began describing the contents, her personality transformed into a young girl doting on the love of her life, the one who would always be her "doll." She especially glowed over the pictures she took in Jacksonville with a last-minute borrowed camera. Sure enough, there was Elvis as he pirouetted in his white studded jumpsuit through numbers she could still recall. From the blazing color pictures she took me to her very first news item. It was on the "king of rock and roll" and featured a smiling 1957 Elvis sitting next to a hound dog.

The items placed on any given page were not in any particular chronological order. Instead, they flowed one after the other based on their importance to Charlotte. After all, *she* was the collector. Right after the 1957 piece was a news column that noted how in 1955, in Cleveland, Presley opened for Boone. Pat closed by saying, "It was the first and last time I followed him."

1955 gave way to 1968 and the cover of a newspaper television section featuring Elvis' upcoming TV special. Then there was a picture of Elvis kissing his mother in 1958. A tabloid article "exposing" the bizarre behavior of a fat, aging Elvis filled the succeeding page. Finally, the first scrapbook unfolded into a ninety-nine-point list of little known Elvis facts. The little known points ranged from the name of Elvis' favorite horse to the revelation that Elvis regularly held Bible readings for his fans in his home.

On and on the clippings and the scrapbooks unfolded until we arrived at Charlotte's "proudest" article. The headline summed up the article and her feelings at once, that "Presley Did Not Die of a Drug Overdose." That article gave way to Dr. Nichopoulos' press release stating Elvis suffered from low-grade diabetes. TV evangelist Rex Humbard disclosed that in December 1976 he had prayed with Elvis and Elvis had confided in Humbard that he would soon die.

Above and beyond the scrapbooks, Charlotte's files were massive. They contained much more recent material, such as all the details about the Elvis stamp controversy, alongside a 1980 *People* magazine purporting to explain "how" Elvis died. Right behind that wonderful piece was "the last photo of Elvis alive," featured on a tabloid page as snapped by a fan standing outside Graceland.

In all, Charlotte has enough resources to write a very interesting book on Elvis. In fact, she and every other Elvis fan/collector like her should go public. From their stories and collections (and favorite concert photos) could come the next memorable Elvis book. It would be about all the great Elvis collections worldwide. The book would present the "perceived" Elvis, the Elvis who exists collectively in the minds of all the Charlottes of the world, those people who want simply to remember Elvis, not make a buck off him.

At the conclusion of our interview, Charlotte continued talking about Elvis. Of the many thoughts she expressed about him, one in particular caught my attention. She said that, to her, the most memorable Elvis feature was his "sexy eyes." Thurl Ravenscroft, of the Mellow Men, related a similar sentiment in a book by Joseph Tunzi (*Photographs and Memories*). What Ravenscroft remembered most about Elvis "was his eyes," because "when he looked at you, he was looking way beyond you." Charlotte also perused my manuscript (an early version of *The Printed Elvis*). I noticed that she passed over any of the books she knew had discussed or exposed Elvis' purported drug problems. Truly Elvis was whatever someone wanted to see, not whatever he really might have been.

ADDENDUM II:
THE CHRONOLOGICAL LISTING OF ELVIS BOOKS

Elvis has been the subject of several hundred
publications. Books and magazines have analyzed
every conceivable shred of fact and fiction about the
man, his professional as well as his personal life.

-Jerry Osborne,
Official Price Guide to Elvis Presley
Records and Memorabilia

The 1950s: The first two Elvis books came out in 1956, strictly for
teenage fans. By 1957, just one important book was published, a
compendium of fan-oriented insights written by Richard Gehman and
edited by Mary Callaghan. With Elvis in Germany, only an
anonymously compiled fan-oriented book came out in 1958. Finally in
1959, an original Elvis book hit the market, focusing on his film
career. Two foreign books came out, from Germany and England.
British fan club president Albert Hand (now deceased) self-published
(for the English market only), in 1959, his first two very short fan-
oriented "booklets."

 The 1960s: In 1960, two books looked at Elvis' service career soon
after it ended. By 1961, though Elvis was back from the Army, only
superfan Hand's "handbook" came off the presses. 1962 saw the
release of two books, both from England. By 1964, Elvis books had
literally stopped. The Beatles hit that year and interest waned up
through 1970, with only the English fans Albert Hand, Roy Barlow,
and David Cardwell keeping up via their 1963 encyclopedia. The
first look at Sun Records was published in 1969.

 The 1970s: It wasn't until the year Elvis died that more than ten
new books (in one year) devoted to him appeared on the market.
Before that, the first major 1970s Elvis book came out in 1971 in the
form of Favius Friedman's publication for juvenile readers. The Jerry
Hopkins biographical classic also came out in 1971. Two years passed
before another significant Elvis book hit the market, Tomlinson's 1973
work from Great Britain. Other seventies books, such as one by Mae

Boren Axton and another by Greil Marcus, discussed Elvis but were not exclusively devoted to him.

In 1975, Paul Lichter came out with the first major film compendium. May Mann, though she had considerable access to Elvis, wrote little more than gossip column material. The Zmijewsky brothers released an Elvis film critique in 1976 that stood for years as the definitive work in that area. Ron Barry came out with the first discography while Kathleen Bowman brought out a children's book.

It really took Elvis' 1977 death to kick off a major surge in the writing and publishing of Elvis books. The very controversial scandal sheet from the West boys, which appeared just before Elvis' death, topped off the year. During the year after Elvis died, more books by fans appeared along with two family member memoirs from Elvis' Uncle Vester Presley and Cousin Harold Loyd.

Elvis had only been gone two years when the stepfamily books began with mother Dee's mean-spirited memoirs, written with her three sons. Robert Mathew-Walker did the first serious study of Elvis' music. Otherwise, there was a whole spate of books from people who had somehow been around Elvis: his nurse, a backing musician, fans, a member of the Memphis Mafia (Marty Lacker), a photographer who had followed Elvis closely for a while.

The 1980s: The eighties began slowly with Harley Hatcher's highly implausible book about Elvis' secret time in the Army. Speculations that Elvis didn't die already dominated the tabloids as did possible spiritual visitations from the King. Jess Stearn released his book on Elvis' spirituality while the Gregory's put out their book that covered every known aspect on Elvis' death.

In 1981, Albert Goldman released his infamous "debunking" of the Elvis myth while Hopkins completed the successor to his classic Elvis biography, this time covering the "final years." Steven Chanzes raised the first book-length specter of Elvis faking his death. Marge Crumbaker and Gabe Tucker marketed the first book that examined Colonel Parker.

The highlight of the 1982 book crop was Dave Marsh's coffee-table book along with an Elvis paper-doll book. The Lee Cotten and Howard DeWitt bootleg discography covering 1970 through 1983 came out in 1983. Ken Brixley and Twyla Dixon (with photographs by William Eggelston) also took a trip to Graceland in 1983 while fellow soldier Rex Mansfield wrote about Private Elvis. The total number of books dropped off from the previous year.

In 1985, the year Elvis would have turned fifty, Memphis newspaperman Bill Burk did a thirty-year overview of all things Elvis. The anniversary sparked the marketing of many more books than the previous year. Patsy Hammontree's bio-biblio-discography came out as did Elaine Dundy's mother/son study.

Another Stanley stepbrother (David) book again attacked Elvis in 1986. Then one by stepbrother Rick came out that was almost sycophantic in tone. The total number of books on Elvis decreased in 1986 with none even close to being standouts, though the Pearlman book "for beginners" took an unfamiliar, lighthearted approach.

To commemorate Elvis being gone ten years in 1987, more than twenty useful books saw release that year. Rosalind Cranor illuminated her readers on Elvis collecting, while Lucy DeBarbin claimed to have been Elvis' secret lover and mother of his child. Elvis in art was a big item with Betty Harper's book of drawings and Roger Taylor's book of artwork featuring Elvis. Elvis' backup singer and sometime lover, Kathy Westmoreland, speculated on Elvis having cancer when he died, thereby needing to take massive amounts of medicine. Rounding out 1987 was a discography of Elvis novelty and tribute records.

By 1988, Gail Brewer-Giorgio claimed Elvis faked his death while Dirk Vellenga exposed the Colonel as an illegal alien. Memphis Mafia man Charlie Hodge got his memoirs out and Priscilla's ex-boyfriend told how he lusted after Elvis' daughter, Lisa. Yet another Stanley brother book (by Billy) came out in 1989 along with Larry Geller's diaries of his times with Elvis. Geller had so much success that he marketed a two-volume cassette "reading" of the diaries. In all, more than ten Elvis books appeared that year.

The 1990s: The 1990s became a time for analytical works about Elvis, even though the decade opened with a quickie about Lisa Marie, another "Elvis Is Alive" rip-off, and one more cousin book. On the bright side for 1990, some beautiful photographs from Elvis' first movie surfaced, thanks to the Michael Ochs Archives and Steve Pond. Bill Burk wrote about Elvis in high school.

Albert Goldman's Elvis suicide theories topped off more than twenty 1991 books partially or wholly about Elvis. Marie Cahill walked through the world of Elvis impersonation while Greil Marcus viewed Elvis as a dead icon. Charles Thompson and his co-author revealed the truest possible view of the cause of Elvis' death and Colin Escott completed the definitive history of Sun Records.

1992 marked fifteen years since Elvis died. More Memphis Mafia stories (by Alan Fortas and judge-to-be Sam Thompson) came out alongside a push to elect a dead Elvis president of the country. Over thirty books discussed everything from Elvis religious cults, to Elvis collectibles, to Elvis the soldier. Jim Curtin brought out a set of photos from his collection of over 25,000 and Rick Stanley revealed even more extensive memories of Elvis.

Of the more than twenty Elvis books released in 1993, Chet Flippo stood out with a massive, epic-proportion work on Graceland. John Parker got into some of the FBI files while Howard DeWitt detailed Elvis' work at Sun Records. Ernst Jorgenson got his massive Elvis sessionography published in the United States.

In 1994, another secret Elvis girlfriend surfaced and Peter Guralnick completed a definitive study of the early Elvis, the first installment of a two-part work (the second part would appear in late 1998). Nixon aide Egil Krogh detailed the day the King met the president. The idea of Elvis as religious leader got a roasting from A. J. Jacobs while David Stanley really exposed Elvis with an encyclopedia. Joe Esposito finally told his "whole" story. Jerry Osborne's best collectibles book also became available.

By early 1995, Elvis would have turned sixty and almost twenty books came out, either completely or partially about Elvis. Three Memphis Mafia members told their stories together. The highlight of the 1996 book crop was a study of Graceland by Karal Ann Marling. An investigation of Elvis, Inc. (or Elvis Presley Enterprises) was compiled by someone who had felt its litigious tentacles, Sean O'Neal. Elvis also got a psychological examination and a university professor discussed the postmortem Elvis phenomenon.

By 1997, Elvis had been gone for twenty years. The year in books started fast with the papers from the first Elvis conference and a book that may turn out to be the best single-volume Presley biography, written by Brown and Broeske. Scotty Moore wrote his autobiography and ex-girlfriend June Juanico published her memoirs. Priscilla finally rated a full-length, though largely unflattering, biography.

Over the years, some books were published by small presses and some were self-published, so the noting of information such as date of publication, city, and so forth was not always made available. Were any of these books important? Not really, although the photographs presented in *Elvis Town* were quite unique.

The 1950s

Anonymous. *Elvis Presley: His Complete Life Story in Words and Illustrated with More Than One Hundred Pictures.*
Anonymous. *The Amazing Elvis Presley.*
Aros, Andrew A. *Elvis: His Films and Recordings.*
Gehman, Richard. Edited by Mary Callaghan. *Elvis Presley: Hero or Heel?*
DeVecchi, Peter. *The Sounding Story.*
Editors of *TV Radio Mirror Magazine. Elvis Presley.*
Hand, Albert. *A Century of Elvis.*
Hand, Albert. *The Elvis They Dig.*
Holmes, Robert. *The Three Loves of Elvis Presley: The True Story of the Presley Legend.*

The 1960s

Anonymous. *Elvis Presley: El Re Del Rock.*
Barlow, Roy, David T. Cardwell, and Albert Hand. *The Elvis Elcyclopedia.*
Buckle, Philip. *All Elvis: An Unofficial Biography of the "King of Discs."*
Gregory, James, editor. *The Elvis Presley Story.*
Hamblett, Charles. *Elvis the Swingin' Kid.*
Hand, Albert. *The Elvis Pocket Handbook.*
Hand, Albert. *Meet Elvis.*
Leigh, Spencer. *Elvis Nation.*
Levy, Alan. *Operation Elvis.*
Primus, Claire. *Elvis: "The King" Returns.*
Taterova, Milada, and Jiri Novak. *Elvis Presley.*
Vernon, Paul. *The Sun Legend.*

1970–1974

Axton, Mae Boren. *Country Singers: As I Know 'Em.*
Fraga, Gaspar. *Elvis Presley.*
Friedman, Favius. *Meet Elvis Presley.*
Goldman, Albert. *Freakshow.*
Hopkins, Jerry. *Elvis: A Biography.*
Jahn, Mike. *Rock: From Elvis Presley to the Rolling Stones.*
Langbroek, Hans. *Hillbilly Cat.*
O'Grady, John, and Nolan Davis. *O'Grady: The Life and Times of Hollywood's No. 1 Private Eye.*
Pleasants, Henry. *The Great American Popular Singer.*
Saville, Tim, compiler. *International Elvis Presley Appreciation Society Handbook.*
Shaw, Arnold. *The Rockin' 50s.*
Sumner, J. D., and Bob Terrell. *Gospel Music Is My Life.*
Taylor, Paula. *Elvis Presley.*
Tomlinson, Roger. *Elvis Presley.*

1975–1976

Barry, Ron. *All American Elvis: The Elvis Presley American Discography.*
Bowman. Kathleen. *On Stage: Elvis Presley.*
Cohn, Nik. *King Death.*
Ellison, Harlan. *Spider Kiss.*
Gripe, Maria. *Elvis and His Friends.*
Harbinson, W. A. *The Illustrated Elvis.*
Jones, Peter. *Elvis.*
Lichter, Paul. *Elvis in Hollywood.*
Mann, May. *The Private Elvis.*
Marcus, Greil. *Mystery Train: Images of America in Rock 'n' Roll Music.*
Parish, James Robert. *Solid Gold Memories: The Elvis Presley Scrapbook.*
Rijff, Ger. *Elvis Presley: Echoes of the Past.*
Tatham, Dick. *Elvis: The Rock Greats.*
Zmijewsky, Steven and Boris. *Elvis: The Films and Career of Elvis Presley.*

1977

Anonymous. *Elvis: A Tribute to the King of Rock n' Roll.*
Anonymous. *Elvis Presley Poster Book.*
Anonymous. *Elvis Presley 1935–1977: A Tribute to the King.*
Anonymous. *The Life and Death of Elvis Presley.*
Bagh, Peter von. *Elvis! Amerikkalaise Laulajan Elama Ja Kuolema.*
Benson, Bernard. *The Minstrel.*
Berglind, Sten. *Elvis: Fran Vasteras till Memphis.*

Bowser, James W., editor. *Starring Elvis: Elvis Presley's Greatest Movies.*
Farren, Mick, and Pearce Marchbank. *Elvis: In His Own Words.*
Grove, Martin A. *The King Is Dead: Elvis Presley.*
Hanna, David. *Elvis: Lonely Star at the Top.*
James, Antony. *Presley: Entertainer of the Century.*
Mann, Richard. *Elvis.*
Marchbank, Pearce, editor. *Elvis Aaron Presley 1935–1977: The Memorial Album.*
Osborne, Jerry, and Randall Jones. *The Complete Elvis.*
Page, Betty. *I Got Ya, Elvis, I Got Ya.*
Slaughter, Todd. *Elvis Presley.*
Stanley, Billy. *Elvis: The Last Tour.*
Tatham, Dick. *Elvis: Tribute to the King of Rock.*
Tello, Antonio, and Gonzalo Otero Pizarro. *Elvis, Elvis, Elvis: La Rebelion Domestica.*
Trevena, Nigel. *Elvis: Man and Myth.*
Verwerft, Gust. *Elvis, de Koning die Niet Sterven Kon.*
West, Red, Sonny West, and Dave Hebler, as told to Steve Dunleavy. *Elvis: What Happened?*
Yancey, Becky, with Cliff Linedecker. *My Life With Elvis: The Fond Memories of a Fan Who Became Elvis' Private Secretary.*

1978

Adler, Bill. *Bill Adler's Love Letters to Elvis.*
Anonymous. *Elvis Lives.*
Anonymous. *The Official FBI File on Elvis A. Presley.*
Canada, Lena. *To Elvis With Love.*
Cortez, Diego, editor, Duncan Smith, and Rudolf Paulini. *Private Elvis.*
Corvino, Nick. *Elvis: The Army Years: 1958–1960.*
Grust, Lothar, F. W., and Jeremias Pommer. *Elvis Presley Superstar.*
Hansen, Mogens. *Elvis: Er Ikke Dod.*
Hill, Wanda June. *We Remember, Elvis.*
Lohmeyer, Henno. *Elvis Presley Report: Eine Dokumentation der Lugen und Legenden, Thesen und Theorien.*
Loyd, Harold, with George Baugh. *The Graceland Gates.*
Nash, Bruce M. *The Elvis Presley Quiz Book.*
Palmer, Robert. *Baby, That Was Rock & Roll: The Legendary Leiber & Stoller.*
Parker, Ed [Edmund K.]. *Inside Elvis.*
Perkins, Carl, with Ron Rendleman. *Disciple in Blue Suede Shoes.*
Presley, Vester, as told to Deda Bonura. *A Presley Speaks.*
Rosenbaum, Helen. *The Elvis Presley Trivia Quiz Book.*
Shapiro, Angela and Jerome, editors. *Candidly Elvis.*
Staten, Vince. *The Real Elvis: Good Old Boy.*
Wallraf, Rainer, and Heinz Plehn. *Elvis Presley: An Illustrated Biography.*
Wiegert, Sue. *For the Good Times.*

1979

Alico, Stella H. *Elvis Presley–The Beatles.*
Boone, Pat. *Together: 25 Years with the Boone Family.*
Busnar, Gene. *It's Rock 'n' Roll: A Musical History of the Fabulous Fifties.*
Cocke, Marian J. *I Called Him Babe: Elvis Presley's Nurse Remembers.*
Gripe, Maria. *Elvis and His Secret.*
Grob, Richard H. *The Elvis Conspiracy?*
Guralnick, Peter. *Lost Highway: Journeys & Arrivals of American Musicians.*
Harms, Valerie. *Tryin' to Get to You: The Story of Elvis Presley.*
Harper, Betty. *Newly Discovered Drawings of Elvis Presley.*
Hatcher, Holly. Edited by Terry Sherf. *Elvis Is That You?*

Hill, Ed, as told to Don Hill. *Where Is Elvis?*
Kelly, Joe. *All the King's Men.*
Kling, Bernard, and Heinz Plehn. *Elvis Presley.*
Lacker, Marty, Patsy Lacker, and Leslie S. Smith. *Elvis: Portrait of a Friend.*
Long, Reverend Marvin R. *God's Works Through Elvis.*
Matthew-Walker, Robert. *Elvis Presley: A Study in Music.*
Panta, Ilona. *Elvis Presley: King of Kings: Who was the Real Elvis?*
Presley, Dee, Billy, Rick, and David Stanley, as told to Martin Torgoff. *Elvis: We Love You Tender.*
Reggero, John. *Elvis in Concert.*
Shaver, Sean, with Hal Noland. *The Life of Elvis Presley.*
Tharpe, Jac L., editor. *Elvis: Images and Fancies.*
Thornton, Mary Ann. *Even Elvis.*
Wertheimer, Alfred, and Gregory Martinelli. *Elvis '56: In the Beginning.*
West, Joan Buchanan. *Elvis–His Life and Times in Poetry & Lines.*

1980

Anonymous. *Elvis: The Other Side: World Spirit Messages from Edie (Spirit Guide).*
Gregory, Neal and Janice. *When Elvis Died.*
Hatcher, Harley. *Elvis Disguised: The "John Crow" Recording.*
Hegner, Mary. *Do You Remember Elvis?*
Lichter, Paul. *Elvis: The Boy Who Dared to Rock.*
Loyd, Harold, with Lisa DeAngel. *Elvis and His Fans.*
Osborne, Jerry, with Bruce Hamilton. *Presleyana.*
Pearl, Minnie, with Joan Dew. *Minnie Pearl: An Autobiography.*
Presley, Vester, and Nancy Rooks. *The Presley Family Cookbook.*
Stearn, Jess. *Elvis: His Spiritual Journey.*
Wallis, Hal, with Charles Higham. *Starmaker: The Autobiography of Hal Wallis.*

1981

Anonymous. *Elvis: The Man & His Music.*
Chanzes, Steven C. *Elvis . . . 1935–?: Where Are You?*
Clark, Alan. *Elvis Presley Memories.*
Collins, Lawrence. *The Elvis Presley Encyclopedia.*
Crumbaker, Marge, and Gabe Tucker. *Up and Down with Elvis Presley.*
Goldman, Albert. *Elvis.*
Greenfield, Mane. *Elvis: Legend of Love.*
Hawkins, Martin, and Colin Escott. *Elvis: The Illustrated Discography.*
Hopkins, Jerry. *Elvis: The Final Years.*
Mordden, Ethan. *The Hollywood Musical.*
Shaver, Sean. *Elvis: Photographing the King.*
Thompson, Patricia, and Connie Gerber. *Walking in His Footsteps.*
Tucker, Gabe, and Elmer Williams. *Pictures of Elvis Presley.*
Whisler, John A. *Elvis Presley: Reference Guide and Discography.*
Worth, Fred L., and Steve D. Tamerius. *All About Elvis.*

1982

Cabaj, Janice M. Schrantz. *The Elvis Image.*
Carr, Roy, and Mick Farren. *Elvis Presley: The Illustrated Record.*
Clark, Alan. *The Elvis Presley Photo Album.*
Covey, Maureen, Todd Slaughter, and Michael Wells. *Elvis for the Record.*
Fitzgerald, Jim, and Al Kilgore. *Elvis: The Paperdoll Book.*
Gates, Graham, and John Tobler. *The A–Z of Elvis.*
Harmer, Jeremy. *Elvis.*

Lewis, Myra, with Murray Silver. *Great Balls of Fire!: The True Story of Jerry Lee Lewis.*
Mann, May. *Elvis: Why Won't They Leave You Alone?*
Marsh, Dave. *Elvis.*
Pasteur, Alfred B., Ph.D., and Ivory L. Toldson, Ed.D. *Roots of Soul: The Psychology of Black Expressiveness.*
Torgoff, Martin, editor. *The Complete Elvis.*
Wootton, Richard. *Elvis!*

1983

Brixley, Ken, and Twyla Dixon. *Elvis at Graceland.*
Cotten, Lee, and Howard A. DeWitt. *Jailhouse Rock: The Bootleg Records of Elvis Presley 1970–1983.*
Fontana, D. J. *D. J. Fontana Remembers Elvis.*
Mansfield, Rex, and Elizabeth Mansfield. *Elvis the Soldier.*
Pierson, Jean. *Elvis: The Living Legend.*
Shaver, Sean. *Elvis's Portrait Portfolio.*
Tobler, John, and Richard Wootton. *Elvis: The Legend and the Music.*

1984

Glade, Emory. *Elvis: A Golden Tribute.*
Grizzard, Lewis. *Elvis Is Dead and I Don't Feel So Good Myself.*
Jenkins, Mary, as told to Beth Pease. *Elvis: The Way I Knew Him.*
Olmetti, Bob, and Sue McCasland. *Elvis Now–Ours Forever.*
Pabst, Ralph M., as given to. *Gene Austin's Ol' Buddy.*
Panter, Gary. *Invasion of the Elvis Zombies.*
Rooks, Nancy, and Mae Gutter. *The Maid, the Man, and the Fans: Elvis Is the Man.*
Sauers, Wendy, compiler. *Elvis Presley: A Complete Reference.*
Shaver, Sean, Alfred Wertheimer, and Eddie Fadal. *Our Memories of Elvis.*

1985

Anonymous. *The Wonder of You Elvis Fans Cookbook, Volumes 1 and 2.*
Anonymous. *The Elvis Story.*
Bleasdale, Alan. *Are You Lonesome Tonight?*
Burk, Bill E. *Elvis: A 30 Year Chronicle.*
Cogan, Arlene, and Charles Goodman. *Elvis: This One's For You.*
Cotten, Lee. *All Shook Up: Elvis Day-by-Day.*
Dundy, Elaine. *Elvis and Gladys.*
Gibson, Robert, and Sid Shaw. *Elvis: A King Forever.*
Giddins, Gary. *Riding on a Blue Note: Jazz & American Pop.*
Hammontree, Patsy Guy. *Elvis Presley: A Bio-Bibliography.*
Henderson, William McCranor. *Stark Raving Elvis.*
Hill, Wanda June. *Elvis Face to Face.*
Latham, Caroline. *Priscilla and Elvis: The Priscilla Presley Story: An Unauthorized Biography.*
Lichter, Paul. *Elvis Memories.*
Lichter, Paul. *Elvis: A Portrait in Music.*
Matthew, Neal. *Elvis: A Golden Tribute.*
Nelson, Pete. *King!: When Elvis Rocked the World.*
Peters, Richard. *Elvis: The Golden Anniversary Tribute.*
Presley, Priscilla Beaulieu, with Sandra Harmon. *Elvis and Me.*
Roy, Samuel. *Elvis: Prophet of Power.*
Taylor, Paul. *Popular Music Since 1955: A Critical Guide to the Literature.*
Umphred, Neal, editor. *Elvis Presley Record Price Guide.*

1986

Booth, Stanley. *Elvis Presley's Graceland*.
Bourgeau, Art. *The Elvis Murders*.
Leigh, Vanora. *Elvis Presley*.
Love, Robert. *Elvis Presley*.
Pearlman, Jill. *Elvis for Beginners*.
Rijff, Ger. *Faces and Stages: An Elvis Presley Time-Frame*.
Stanley, David, with David Wimbish. *Life with Elvis*.
Stanley, Rick, with Michael K. Haynes. *The Touch of Two Kings*.

1987

Banney, Howard. *Return to Sender: The First Complete Discography of Elvis Tribute and Novelty Records, 1956-1986*.
Burk, Bill E. *Elvis Through My Eyes*.
Cash, June Carter. *From the Heart*.
Charlesworth, Chris. *Elvis Presley*.
Cotten, Lee. *The Elvis Catalog: Memorabilia, Icons, and Collectibles Celebrating the King of Rock 'n' Roll*.
Cranor, Rosalind. *Elvis Collectibles*.
De Barbin, Lucy, and Dary Matera. *Are You Lonesome Tonight?: The Untold Story of Elvis Presley's One True Love and the Child He Never Knew*.
Haining, Peter, editor. *Elvis in Private*.
Hallum, Boen. *Elvis the King*.
Harper, Betty. *Suddenly and Gently: Visions of Elvis Through the Art of Betty Harper*.
Leviton, Jay B., and Ger J. Rijff. *Elvis Up Close: Rare, Intimate, Unpublished Photographs of Elvis Presley in 1956*.
Lewis, Vic, with Tony Barrow. *Music & Maiden Overs: My Showbusiness Life*.
Lichter, Paul. *Elvis: Behind Closed Doors*.
Loyd, Harold. *Elvis Presley's Graceland Gates*.
Moody, Raymond A., Jr., M.D. *Elvis After Life: Unusual Psychic Experiences Surrounding the Death of a Superstar*.
Nicholson, Monte W. *The Presley Arrangement*.
Nixon, Anne E. *Elvis: Ten Years After*.
Pritchett, Nash. *One Flower While I Live: Elvis As I Remember Him*.
Putnam, Stan P. *Newfound Facts and Memorabilia on Elvis Presley*.
Putnam, Stan P. *Memento, Souvenir, Keepsake and Collector's Kit on the Life and Music of Elvis Presley*.
Reid, Jim. *Fond Memories of Elvis: 1954-Twenty-Three Years of Photos-1977*.
Shaw, Sid. *Elvis in Quotes*.
Smith, Bill. *Memphis Mystery*.
Stanley, Bill. *Living in the Shadow of the King*.
Stern, Jane and Michael. *Elvis World*.
Storm, Tempest, with Bill Boyd. *Tempest Storm: The Lady Is a Vamp*.
Taylor, Roger G. *Elvis in Art*.
Townson, John, Gordon Minto, and George Richardson. *Elvis UK: The Ultimate Guide to Elvis Presley's British Record Releases, 1956-86*.
Van Doren, Mamie, with Art Aveilhe. *Playing the Field: My Story*.
Westmoreland, Kathy, with William G. Quinn. *Elvis and Kathy*.
Wiegert, Sue. *Elvis: Precious Memories*.
Winegardner, Mark. *Elvis Presley Boulevard: From Sea to Shining Sea, Almost*.

1988

Black, Jim. *Elvis on the Road to Stardom*.
Brewer-Giorgio, Gayle. *The Most Incredible Elvis Presley Story Ever Told*.
Edwards, Michael. *Priscilla, Elvis and Me: In the Shadow of the King*.
Hodge, Charlie, with Charles Goodman. *Me 'n Elvis*.

Kirkland, K. D. *Elvis.*
McNutt, Randy. *We Wanna Boogie: An Illustrated History of the American Rockabilly Movement.*
Osborne, Jerry P. *Elvis: Like Any Other Soldier.*
Osborne, Jerry, Perry Cos, and Joe Lindsay. *The Official Price Guide to Memorabilia of Elvis Presley and the Beatles.*
Rijff, Ger. *Memphis Lonesome.*
Tunzi, Joseph A. *The First Elvis Video Price and Reference Guide.*
Vellenga, Dirk, with Mick Farren. *Elvis and the Colonel.*
Worth, Fred L., and Steve D. Tamerius. *Elvis: His Life from A to Z.*

1989

Carson, Lucas. *Elvis Presley.*
Doll, Susan, contributing writer. *Elvis: A Tribute to His Life.*
Editors of *Consumer Guide. Elvis: The Younger Years.*
Fox, Sharon R., editor. *Elvis, His Real Life in the 60s: My Personal Scrapbook.*
Geller, Larry, and Joel Spector with Patricia Romanowski. *"If I Can Dream": Elvis' Own Story.*
Jenkins, Mary, and Beth Pease. *Memories Beyond Graceland Gates.*
Lichter, Paul. *Elvis: All My Best.*
McLafferty, Gerry. *Elvis Presley in Hollywood: Celluloid Sell-Out.*
Newton, Wayne, with Dick Maurice. *Once Before I Go.*
Schuster, Hal. *The Magic Lives on: The Films of Elvis Presley.*
Stanley, Billy, with George Erikson. *Elvis, My Brother: An Intimate Family Memoir of Life with the King.*
Wiegert, Sue. *Elvis: Precious Memories, Vol. 2.*
Winter, Shelley. *Shelley II: The Middle of My Century.*

1990

Adler, David, and Ernest Andrews. *Elvis, My Dad: The Unauthorized Biography of Lisa Marie Presley.*
Brewer-Giorgio, Gail. *The Elvis Files: Was His Death Faked?*
Brouwer, Alexandra, and Thomas Lee Wright. *Working in Hollywood.*
Burk, Bill E. *Early Elvis: The Humes Years.*
Burk, Bill E. *Elvis: Rare Images of a Legend.*
Childress, Mark. *Tender.*
Danielson, Sarah Parker. *Elvis: Man or Myth.*
Doll, Susan. *The Films of Elvis Presley.*
Doll, Susan. *Elvis: The Early Years: Portrait of a Young Rebel.*
Esposito, Joe. *Elvis: A Legendary Performance.*
Glanville, Jerry, and J. David Miller. *Elvis Don't Like Football: The Life and Raucous Times of the NFL's Most Outspoken Coach.*
Greenwood, Earl, and Kathleen Tracy. *The Boy Who Would Be King: An Intimate Portrait of Elvis Presley by His Cousin.*
Latham, Caroline, and Jeanne Sakol. *"E" Is for Elvis: An A-to-Z Illustrated Guide to the King of Rock and Roll.*
Pond, Steve. *Elvis in Hollywood: Photographs from the Making of Love Me Tender.*
Tunzi, Joseph A. *Elvis: Encore Performance.*
Tunzi, Joseph A. *Elvis Highway 51 South Memphis Tennessee.*
Tunzi, Joseph A., with Sean O'Neal. *Elvis: The Lost Photographs.*

1991

Barth, Jack. *Roadside Elvis.*
Booth, Stanley. *Rhythm Oil: A Journey Through the Music of the American South.*
Brown, Christopher. *On Tour with Elvis.*

Cahill, Marie, editor. *I Am Elvis: A Guide to Elvis Impersonators.*
Choron, Sandra, and Bob Oskam. *Elvis!: The Last Word: The 328 Best (and Worst) Things Anyone Ever Said About "The King."*
Editors of *Consumer Guide. Films of Elvis Presley.*
Escott, Colin, with Martin Hawkins. *Good Rockin' Tonight: Sun Records and the Birth of Rock 'n' Roll.*
Goldman, Albert. *Elvis: The Last 24 Hours.*
Greenwood, Earl, and Kathleen Tracy. *Elvis: Top Secret: The Untold Story of Elvis Presley's Secret FBI Files.*
Kricun, Morrie E., and Virginia M. Kricun. *Elvis: 1956 Reflections.*
Marcus, Greil. *Dead Elvis: A Chronicle of a Cultural Obsession.*
Moore, W. Kent, and David L. Scott. *The Elvis Quiz Book.*
Parish, James Robert, and Michael R. Pitts. *Hollywood Songsters: A Biographical Dictionary.*
Pollard, Mark, editor. *Elvis Is Everywhere.*
Porter, Roy, with David Keller. *There and Back.*
Ridge, Millie. *The Elvis Album.*
Rijff, Ger, DeNight, Bill, and Sharon Fox. *The Elvis Album.*
Rijff, Ger, with Jan Van Gestel. *Elvis: The Cool King.*
Rijff, Ger, with Jan Van Gestel. *Elvis: Fire in the Sun.*
Rubel, David. *Elvis Presley: The Rise of Rock and Roll.*
Sumner, J. D., with Bob Terrell. *Elvis: His Love for Gospel Music and J. D. Sumner.*
Taylor, John Alvarez. *Forever Elvis.*
Thompson, Charles C., II, and James P. Cole. *The Death of Elvis: What Really Happened.*
Tunzi, Joseph. *Elvis '69: The Return.*
Wombacher, Marty. *Elvis Is a Wormfeast.*

1992

Adair, Joseph. *The Immortal Elvis Presley, 1935–1977.*
Allen, William (text by). *Elvis.*
Brown, Hal A. *In Search of Elvis: A Fact-Filled Seek and Find Adventure.*
Butler, Brenda Arlene, editor. *Are You Hungry Tonight?: Elvis' Favorite Recipes.*
Cantor, Louis. *Wheelin' on Beale.*
Charters, Samuel. *Elvis Presley Calls His Mother After the Ed Sullivan Show.*
Clark, Alan. *Legends of Sun Records: Number One.*
Clark, Alan. *Legends of Sun Records: Number Two.*
Committee to Elect the King, the. *Elvis for President.*
Cranor, Rosalind, and Steve Templeton. *The Best of Elvis Collectibles.*
Curtin, Jim E. *Unseen Elvis: Candids of the King from the Collection of Jim Curtin.*
Flinn, Mary C. *Elvis in Oz: New Stories and Poems from the Hollins Creative Writing Program.*
Fortas, Alan. *Elvis: From Memphis to Hollywood: Memories From My Twelve Years with Elvis Presley.*
Fowles, Jib. *Starstruck: Celebrity Performers and the American Public.*
Frew, Timothy. *Elvis.*
Gelfand, Craig, and Lynn Blocker-Krantz. *In Search of the King.*
Gilmore, Brian. *Elvis Presley Is Alive and Well and Living in Harlem.*
Harrison, Ted. *Elvis People: The Cult of the King.*
Hazen, Cindy, and Mike Freeman. *The Best of Elvis: Recollections of a Great Humanitarian.*
Holladay, John. *Where's Elvis?*
Jones, Ira, as told to Bill E. Burk. *Soldier Boy Elvis.*
Kalpakian, Laura. *Graced Land.*
Lichter, Paul. *Elvis: Rebel Heart.*

McKeon, Elizabeth, Ralph Gevirtz, and Julie Bandy. *Fit For a King: The Elvis Presley Cookbook.*
Peters, Richard. *Elvis: The Music Lives On.*
Pritikin, Karin. *The King & I: A Little Gallery of Elvis Impersonators.*
Quain, Kevin, editor. *The Elvis Reader: Texts and Sources on the King of Rock 'n' Roll.*
Rijff, Ger. *Long Lonely Highway: A 1950's Elvis Scrapbook.*
Rovin, Jeff. *The World According to Elvis: Quotes from the King.*
Shankman, Sarah. *The King Is Dead.*
Shaver, Sean. *Elvis in Focus.*
Stanley, Rick, with Paul Harold. *Caught in a Trap: Elvis Presley's Tragic Lifelong Search for Love.*
Svedberg, Lennart, and Roger Ersson. *Aren Med Elvis.*
Thompson, Sam. *Elvis on Tour: The Last Year.*
Tunzi, Joseph A. *Elvis '73: Hawaiian Spirit.*
Van Oudtshoorn, Nic. *The Elvis Spotters Guide: The King Lives!*
Weisman, Ben. *Elvis Presley: "The Hollywood Years."*

1993

Adler, David. *The Life and Cuisine of Elvis Presley.*
Brown, Christopher. *Elvis in Concert.*
Burk, Bill E. *Elvis Memories: Press Between the Pages.*
Celsi, Theresa. *Elvis.*
Curtin, Jim, and Renata Ginter. *Elvis and the Stars.*
DeMarco, Gordon. *Elvis in Aspic.*
DeWitt, Howard A. *Elvis: The Sun Years: The Story of Elvis Presley in the Fifties.*
Eicher, Peter. *The Elvis Sightings.*
Flippo, Chet. *Graceland: The Living Legacy of Elvis Presley.*
Friedman, Kinky. *Elvis, Jesus & Coca-Cola.*
Holzer, Hans. *Elvis Speaks from the Beyond and Other Celebrity Ghost Stories.*
Jorgensen, Ernst, Erik Rasmussen, and Johnny Mikkelson. *Reconsider Baby: The Definitive Elvis Sessionography, 1954–1977.*
Kath, Laura, and Todd Morgan. *Elvis Presley's Graceland: The Official Guidebook.*
Krohn, Katherine. *Elvis Presley: The King.*
Maliay, Jack D. *Elvis: The Messiah?*
Marino, Jan. *The Day Elvis Came to Town.*
Mungo, Ray. *Palm Springs Babylon.*
Parker, John. *Elvis: The Secret Files.*
Rijff, Ger. *The Voice of Rock and Roll.*
Schroer, Andreas. *Private Presley: The Missing Years–Elvis in Germany.*
Sloan, Kay, and Constance Pierce, editors. *Elvis Rising: Stories on the King.*
Tanner, Isabelle. *Elvis: A Guide to My Soul.*
Tunzi, Joseph A. *Elvis Sessions: The Recorded Music of Elvis Aron Presley, 1953–1977.*
Tunzi, Joseph A. *Elvis: Encore Performance Two: In the Garden.*
West, Joe. *Elvis: His Most Intimate Secrets.*
Womack, Jack. *Elvissey: A Novel of Elvis Past and Elvis Future.*
Yenne, Bill. *All the King's Things: The Ultimate Elvis Memorabilia Book.*

1994

Ann-Margret, with Todd Gold. *My Story.*
Anonymous. *Elvis Tear-Out Photo Book.*
Bangs, Lester (text by). *Elvis Presley: The Rebel Years.*
Bartel, Pauline. *Reel Elvis!: The Ultimate Trivia Guide to the King's Movies.*

Bova, Joyce, and William C. Nowels. *Don't Ask Forever: My Love Affair with Elvis: A Washington Woman's Secret Years with Elvis Presley.*

Burk, Bill E. *Early Elvis: The Tupelo Years.*

Clayson, Alan, and Spencer Leigh, editors. *Aspects of Elvis: Tryin' to Get to You.*

Clayton, Rose, and Richard M. Heard, editors. *Elvis Up Close: In the Words of Those Who Knew Him Best.*

Cohen, Daniel. *The Ghost of Elvis and Other Celebrity Spirits.*

DePaoli, Geri, editor. *Elvis & Marilyn: Two Times Immortal.*

DeWit, Simon. *King of Vegas.*

Doll, Susan. *Elvis: Rock 'n' Roll Legend.*

Esposito, Joe, and Elena Oumano. *Good Rockin' Tonight: Twenty Years on the Road and on Tour with Elvis.*

Farren, Mick. *The Hitchhiker's Guide to Elvis.*

Gentry, Tony. *Elvis Presley.*

Giuliano, Geoffrey, Brenda Giuliano, and Deborah Lynn Black. *The Illustrated Elvis Presley.*

Goodin, Vera-Jane. *Elvis & Bobbie: Memories of Linda Jackson.*

Green, Margo H., Dorothy Nelson, and Darlene M. Levenger. *Graceland.*

Guralnick, Peter. *Last Train to Memphis: The Rise of Elvis Presley.*

Hannaford, Jim, and Ger Rijff. *Inside Jailhouse Rock.*

Higgins, Patrick, editor. *Before Elvis There Was Nothing.*

Hutchins, Chris, and Peter Thomson. *Elvis Meets the Beatles: The Untold Story of Their Untold Lives.*

Jacobs, A. J. *The Two Kings: Jesus, Elvis.*

Krogh, Egil "Bud." *The Day Elvis Met Nixon.*

Ludwig, Louie. *The Gospel of Elvis: The Testament and Apocrypha of the Greater Themes of "The King."*

McKeon, Elizabeth. *Elvis in Hollywood: Recipes Fit for a King: A Cookbook and a Memory Book.*

Osborne, Jerry. *Official Guide to Elvis Presley Records and Memorabilia.*

Peabody, Richard, and Lucinda Ebersole, editors. *Mondo Elvis: A Collection of Stories and Poems About Elvis.*

Petersen, Brian. *The Atomic Powered Singer.*

Pierce, Patricia Jobe. *The Ultimate Elvis: Elvis Presley Day by Day.*

Rijff, Ger, with Gordon Minto. *60 Million TV Viewers Can't Be Wrong.*

Rijff, Ger, W. A. Harbinson, and Kay Wheeler. *Growing Up with the Memphis Flash.*

Roberts, Dave. *Elvis Presley.*

Robertson, John. *The Complete Guide to the Music of Elvis Presley.*

Sammon, Paul M. *The King Is Dead: Tales of Elvis Postmortem.*

Smith, Gene. *Elvis's Man Friday.*

Snow, Hank, with Jack Ownbey and Bob Burris. *The Hank Snow Story.*

Stanley, David E., with Frank Coffey. *The Elvis Encyclopedia: The Complete and Definitive Reference Book on the King of Rock & Roll.*

Tunzi, Joseph A. *Elvis '70: Bringing Him Back.*

Tunzi, Joseph A. *Elvis Standing Room Only.*

Urquhart, Sharon Colette. *Placing Elvis: A Tour Guide to the Kingdom.*

1995

Bartel, Pauline. *Everything Elvis: Your Ultimate Sourcebook to the Memorabilia, Souvenirs, and Collectibles of the King!*

Burk, Heinrich. *Elvis in Der Wetterau: Der "King" in Deutschland 1958–1960.*

Buskin, Richard. *Elvis: Memories and Memorabilia.*

Cotten, Lee. *Did Elvis Sing in Your Hometown?*

Davis, Arthur. *Elvis Presley: Quote Unquote.*

DeWit, Simon. *Auld Lang Syne: Elvis' Legendary New Year's Eve Show in Pittsburgh, Pa., 1976.*

Doll, Susan. *Elvis: Portrait of the King*.
Duff, Gerald. *That's All Right, Mama: The Unauthorized Life of Elvis's Twin*.
Hardinge, Melissa. *They Died Too Young: Elvis*.
Hirshberg, Charles, and the Editors of *Life. Elvis: A Celebration in Pictures*.
Lewis, Jerry Lee, and Charles White. *Killer!: The Baddest Rock Memoir Ever*.
Nash, Alanna, with Billy Smith, Marty Lacker, and Lamar Fike. *Elvis Aaron Presley: Revelations from the Memphis Mafia*.
Nash, Bruce, Allan Zullo, and John McGran. *Amazing But True Elvis Facts*.
Palmer, Robert. *Rock and Roll: An Unruly History*.
Prince, James D. *The Day Elvis Presley Came to Town*.
Rose, Frank. *The Agency: William Morris and the Hidden History of Show Business*.
Strausbaugh, John. *E: Reflections on the Birth of the Elvis Faith*.
Taylor, William J., Jr. *Elvis in the Army: The King of Rock 'n' Roll as Seen by an Officer Who Served With Him*.
Viner, Michael (conceptualized by). *Unfinished Lives: What if . . . ?*
Wilson, Charles Reagan. *Judgment & Grace in Dixie: Southern Faiths from Faulkner to Elvis*.

1996

Burk, Bill E. *Elvis in Canada*.
Daily, Robert. *Elvis Presley: The King of Rock 'n' Roll*.
Dickerson, James. *Goin' Back to Memphis: A Century of Blues, Rock 'n' Roll, and Glorious Soul*.
Doll, Susan. *Best of Elvis*.
Dowling, Paul. *Elvis: The Ultimate Album Cover Book*.
Eversz, Robert M. *Shooting Elvis*.
Gordon, Robert. *The King on the Road: Elvis Live on Tour: 1954 to 1977*.
Gray, Michael, and Roger Osborne. *The Elvis Atlas: A Journey Through Elvis Presley's America*.
Kath, Laura, with Todd Morgan. *Elvis Presley's Graceland: The Official Guidebook (Updated and Expanded Second Edition)*.
Kluge, P. F. *Biggest Elvis*.
Mabe, Joni. *Everything Elvis*.
Marling, Karal Ann. *Graceland: Going Home with Elvis*.
O'Neal, Sean. *Elvis Inc.: The Fall and Rise of the Presley Empire*.
Perkins, Carl, and David McGee. *Go, Cat, Go: The Life and Times of Carl Perkins, The King of Rockabilly*.
Rodman, Gilbert B. *Elvis After Elvis: The Posthumous Career of a Living Legend*.
Shamayyim, Maia C. M. *Magii from the Blue Star–The Spiritual Drama and Mystic Heritage of Elvis Aaron Presley*.
Stanley, David, with Mark Bego. *Raised on Rock*.
Templeton, Steve. *Elvis!: An Illustrated Guide to New and Vintage Collectibles*.
Tunzi, Joseph A. *Elvis '74: Enter the Dragon*.
Whitmer, Peter, Ph.D. *The Inner Elvis: A Psychological Biography of Elvis Aaron Presley*.
Wilson, Kemmons. *Half Luck and Half Brains*.
Wright, Daniel. *Dear Elvis: Graffiti from Graceland*.

1997–1999

Anonymous. *Elvis Immortal*.
Anonymous. *Elvis: 30 Postcards*.
Bentley, Dawn, and Allison Higa. *Elvis Remembered: A Three-Dimensional Celebration*.
Braun, Eric. *The Elvis Film Encyclopedia: An Impartial Guide to the Films of Elvis*.

Brown, Peter Harry, and Pat H. Broeske. *Down at the End of Lonely Street: The Life and Death of Elvis Presley.*
Burk, Bill E. *Early Elvis: The Sun Years.*
Cajiiao, Trevor. *Talking Elvis.*
Chadwick, Vernon, editor. *In Search of Elvis: Music, Race, Art, Religion.*
Coffey, Frank. *The Complete Idiot's Guide to Elvis: The King Lives on!*
Columbus, Maria. *Elvis in Print.*
Cotten, Lee. *Did Elvis Sing in Your Hometown, Too?*
Crutchfield, Don, with Gene Busnar. *Confessions of a Hollywood P. I.*
Curtin, Jim. *Elvis: Unknown Stories Behind the Legend.*
Dickerson, James. *Colonel Tom Parker: The Carny Who Managed the King.*
Doss, Erika. *Elvis Culture: Fans, Faith, and Image.*
Early, Donna Presley, Edie Hand, and Lynn Edge. *Elvis: Precious Memories.*
Erwin, Sara. *Over the Fence: A Neighbor's Memories of Elvis.*
Esposito, Joe, with Darwin Lamm. *Elvis Intimate & Rare: Memories & Photos from the Personal Collection of Joe Esposito.*
Finstad, Suzanne. *Child Bride: The Untold Story of Priscilla Beaulieu Presley.*
Floyd, John. *Sun Records: An Oral History.*
Golick, Jeffrey, editor. *Elvis.*
Guralnick, Peter. *Careless Love: The Unmaking of Elvis Presley.*
Guttmacher, Peter. *Elvis! Elvis! Elvis!: The King and His Movies.*
Hazen, Cindy, and Mike Freeman. *Memphis Elvis-Style Rock Music Anthology.*
Henderson, William McCranor. *I, Elvis: Confessions of a Counterfeit King.*
Israel, Marvin. Edited and designed by Martin Harrison. *Elvis Presley 1956.*
Jorgensen, Ernst. *Elvis Presley: A Life in Music: The Complete Recording Sessions.*
Juanico, June. *Elvis: In the Twilight of Memory.*
Keenan, Frances (aka "Baby Jane"). *Elvis, You're Unforgettable.*
King, R. G. *Elvis on Stamps.*
Klein, Dan, and Hans Teensma. *Where's Elvis?: Documented Sightings Prove That He Lives.*
Krebs, Gary M. *Rock and Roll Reader's Guide.*
Lamm, Darwin, editor. *Limited Edition 20th Anniversary Collector's Edition Book.*
Lannamann, Margaret, editor. *Elvis: The Legend.*
Lawrence, Greer. *Elvis: The King of Rock & Roll.*
Lewis, Donna, with Craig A. Slanker. *"Hurry Home, Elvis!": Donna Lewis' Diaries, Vol. 1 (1962-1966), Vol. 2 (1967-1968), Vol. 3 (1968 - 1977).*
Lewis, Linda Gail, with Les Pendleton. *The Devil, Me, and Jerry Lee.*
Logan, Horace, with Bill Sloan. *Elvis, Hank, and Me: Making Musical History on the Louisiana Hayride.*
Matthews, Rupert. *Elvis: The King of Rock 'n' Roll.*
Maughon, Dr. Robert. *Elvis Is Alive.*
McKeon, Elizabeth, and Linda Everett. *The Quotable King: Hopes, Aspirations, and Memories.*
McLemore, P. K., editor. *Letters to Elvis: Real Fan Letters Written by His Faithful Fans.*
Moore, Scotty, as told to James Dickerson. *That's All Right, Elvis: The Untold Story of Elvis's First Guitarist and Manager, Scotty Moore.*
Nager, Larry. *Memphis Beat: The Lives and Times of America's Musical Crossroads.*
O'Neal, Sean. *My Boy Elvis: The Colonel Tom Parker Story.*
Poore, Billy. *"Rockabilly": A Forty-Year Journey.*
Rijff, Ger, Trevor Cajiao, and Michael Ochs. *Shock, Rattle & Roll.*
Rijff, Ger, with Linda Jones and Peter Hann. *Steamrolling Over Texas.*
Roy, Samuel, and Tom Aspell. *The Essential Elvis: The Life and Legacy of the King as Revealed Through Personal History and 112 of His Most Significant Songs.*
Rubinkowski, Leslie. *Impersonating Elvis.*

Skar, Stein Erik. *Elvis: The Concert Years, 1969-1977.*
Streissguth, Michael. *Eddy Arnold: Pioneer of the Nashville Sound.*
Tunzi, Joseph. *Elvis '68: Tiger Man.*
Tunzi, Joseph A. *Photographs and Memories.*
Ward, Brian. *Just My Soul Responding.*
Wolf-Cohen, Elizabeth. *The I Love Elvis Cookbook: More Than 50 Hit Recipes.*
Woog, Adam. *The Importance of Elvis Presley.*
Wray, Matt, and Annalee Newitz, editors. *White Trash: Race and Class in America.*
Yenne, Bill. *The Field Guide to Elvis Shrines.*
Zimmerman, Peter Coats. *Tennessee Music: Its People and Places.*

Unknown Dates of Publication

Anonymous (published in Japan). *Guts: Elvis.*
Anonymous. *Elvis Town: Volume I, 1991–1992.*
Beeny, Bill. *DNA Proves That Elvis Is Alive.*
Fox, Sharon. *Elvis: He Touched My Life.*
Friesner, Esther M., and Martin H. Greenberg, editors. *Alien Pregnant by Elvis.*
Goodge. *We're So Grateful That You Did It Your Way.*
Grandlund/Holm. *Elvis–As We Remember Him.*
Hamilton, Bruce. *Love of Elvis.*
Hannaford, Jim. *Elvis: Golden Ride on the Mystery Train* (volumes 1–3).
Loper, Karen. *The Elvis Clippings.*
McEnroe, Colin. *Lose Weight with Great Sex with Celebrities (the Elvis Way).*
Streszlewski, Leszek C. *Elvis.*
Watkins, Darlene. *Elvis: We Still Love You Tender.*
Yeovil, Jack. *Comeback Tour.*
Zeller, Alexander. *The King Lives On.*
Zemke, Ken. *Elvis on Tour.*

ADDENDUM III:
THE NOTES ON SOURCES

Elvis, he wasn't doing nothing but what the colored
people had been doing for the last hundred years.
But people . . . people went wild over him.

-Robert Henry,
Beale Black & Blue

Beyond the primary purpose of this book which was to present and critique all the books on Elvis (that had some measure of worth), a secondary purpose arose. That was to present pertinent statements, quotations, and viewpoints on or about him made by others and included in publications that were not necessarily devoted to Elvis. This secondary purpose was intended to give a much deeper and broader basis upon which to further understand either the man or the various reviews, critiques, and analyses presented herein.

As a result, many, but not all, of the critiqued books served as sources for quotes and information about Elvis. To fulfill the requirement of disclosing the origins of quotations, statements, reviews, critical viewpoints, and historical information that became integral to the analysis, it has become appropriate to state that, unless otherwise noted, the source for any quoted material used in this book came from one of the entries discussed in the main body of the book or in one of the commentaries. Following below, I have also listed other source material that was essential. If I have erred in my listing of sources and credits, I will make every effort to correct such mistakes and print the results in future editions.

The Introduction

The Lester Bangs comments were made in: Lester Bangs (text by), *Elvis Presley: The Rebel Years*, p. 14.

The Chadwick observation came from: Vernon Chadwick, editor, *In Search of Elvis: Music, Race, Art, Religion*, p. xvi.

The Columbus comment came from the introduction to: Gail Brewer-Giorgio, *The Elvis Files: Was His Death Faked?*, p. xi.

Dahlin wrote in: "Unique Appeal of Elvis Presley's Music Now Carries Over to Books About Him," *Publisher's Weekly*, September 5, 1977, p. 34.

Booth expressed his view in: Stanley Booth, *Rhythm Oil: A Journey Through the Music of the American South*, p. 132.

Chapter 1

The Cassata interview came from: Mary Anne Cassata, "Precious Memories of Elvis," *A Tribute to Elvis*, 1997, p. 52.

Sumner's conclusion came from: J. D. Sumner with Bob Terrell, *Elvis: His Love for Gospel Music and J. D. Sumner*, p. 94.

Parsons' writing was quoted in: Myra Lewis with Murray Silver, *Great Balls of Fire!: The True Story of Jerry Lee Lewis*, p. 191.

Elvis' comment was quoted in: Myra Lewis with Murray Silver, *Great Balls of Fire!: The True Story of Jerry Lee Lewis*, p. 191.

Myra Lewis' comment came in: Myra Lewis with Murray Silver, *Great Balls of Fire!: The True Story of Jerry Lee Lewis*, p. 191.

Chapter 2

Graham's comments came from: Sheilah Graham, *Hollywood Revisited: A Fiftieth Anniversary Celebration*, p. 249.

Alden's comments were recorded in: "Love Him Tender," *People*, August 18, 1997, p. 86.

Ward's disclosure appeared in: Peter Knobler and Greg Mitchell, editors, *Very Seventies: A Cultural History of the 1970s, from the Pages of Crawdaddy*, p. 132.

Sumner's disclosure came from: J. D. Sumner with Bob Terrell, *Elvis: His Love for Gospel Music and J. D. Sumner*, p. 95.

Darin was quoted in: Boze Hadleigh, *Hollywood Babble On: Stars Gossip About Other Stars*, p. 169.

The pool man's comment came from: Ray Mungo, *Palm Springs Babylon*, p. 135.

Schutte's recollections were recorded in: "Love Him Tender," *People*, August 18, 1997, p. 83.

Egan's and Paget's comments came from: "The Women Who Adored Him . . . and Those Who Broke His Heart," *Elvis Presley: A Photoplay Tribute*, p. 77.

Wood's comments came from: John Parker, *Five for Hollywood: Their Friendship, Their Fame, Their Tragedies*, p. 140.

Stevens' statement was recorded in: "Love Him Tender," *People*, August 18, 1997, p. 88.

Lewis' comment came from: Jerry Lee Lewis and Charles White, *Killer!: The Baddest Rock Memoir Ever*, p. 178.

Esposito's comments were made in: "Esposito on Elvis: Elvis Week Amazed Everyone," *Pop Culture Collecting*, November 1997, p. 36.

Chapter 3

John's comment was recorded in: Philip Norman, *Elton John: The Definitive Biography*, p. 327.

Little Richard's recollection was presented in: Charles White, *The Life and Times of Little Richard: The Quasar of Rock*, p. 140.

Hutton's comment about Grant came from: Boze Hadleigh, *Hollywood Babble On: Stars Gossip About Other Stars*, p. 192.

Lennon was quoted in: Boze Hadleigh, *Hollywood Babble On: Stars Gossip About Other Stars*, p. 26.

Cole's comments were made in: Richard Cole, *Stairway to Heaven: Led Zeppelin Uncensored*, p. 279.

Shamayyim statement came from: Maia C. M. Shamayyim, "Elvis and His Angelic Connection," *Angel Times*, p. 21.

Shepherd's comments were found in: "Love Him Tender," *People*, August 18, 1997, p. 88.

Chapter 4

Fontana's comments were recorded in: Steve Otfinoski, *The Golden Age of Rock Instrumentals*, p. 146.

Thompson's appraisal was in: "Country Notes," *Country Weekly*, October 21, 1997, p. 5.

Parton's recollections came in: Paul Kingsbury, "Once More With Feeling: A Conversation with Dolly Parton," The *Journal of Country Music*, p. 36.

Lewis was quoted in: Richard Peters, *Elvis: The Music Lives on: The Recording Sessions, 1954-1976*, p. 83.

Burton's comments were from: Richard Peters, *Elvis: The Music Lives on: The Recording Sessions, 1954-1976*, p. 83.

Brown was quoted in: Jody Farr, *Moguls and Madmen: The Pursuit of Power in Popular Music*, pp. 217-219.

Twitty's comments were in: Wilbur Cross and Michael Kosser, *The Conway Twitty Story*, p. 56.

Chapter 5

Capote's remarks were captured in: Boze Hadleigh, *Hollywood Babble On: Stars Gossip About Other Stars*, p. 12.

Duke and Amar were both quoted in: Stephanie Mansfield, *The Richest Girl in the World: The Extravagant Life and Fast Times of Doris Duke*, p. 326, p. 426,

Billups comments were written in: Andrea Billups, "The King & Cookin'," *The Gainesville Sun*, July 16, 1998, p. 1D.

Pittman's remarks were quoted in: Ellis Amburn, *Dark Star: The Roy Orbison Story*, p. 175.

Chapter 6

Beeny's remarks were from: "Elvis Lives, and Bill Beeny's Museum Has the Proof," *People*, July 13, 1998, p. 56.

Graves wrote his remarks in: Tom Graves, "Natural Born Elvis," *The Oxford American*, Issue 16, p. 84.

The observation by the Everly Brothers came in: Phyllis Karpp, *Ike's Boys: The Story of the Everly Brothers*, p. 80.

Esposito's insights appeared in: "Esposito on Elvis: Elvis and Religion," *Pop Culture Collecting*, March, 1998, p. 44.

Chapter 7

Denson's comments came from a personal interview with the author, August, 1998.

Presley's remark was quoted in: Jane and Michael Stern, *Elvis World*, p. 198.

Burk's comment was captured in: Jane and Michael Stern, *Elvis World*, p. 198.

Chapter 8

The blurbs about the Rijff book appeared in: "Elvis Book Recalls King's '56 Visit to Berle Show," *Pop Culture Collecting*, March 1998, p. 9

Chapter 9

The Hodge and Grob comments about *The Minstrel* came from: Fred L. Worth and Steve D. Tamerius, *Elvis: His Life from A to Z*, p. 313.

The comments by Carol Henderson (wife of author and professor William McCranor Henderson) came from her article, "Married to the King," *The Oxford American*, Issue Number 27 & 28 (Third Annual Double Issue on Southern Music), Summer 1999, p. 86.

Chapter 10

Esposito's views were related in: "Esposito on Elvis: Elvis' Personal Wardrobe," *Pop Culture Collecting*, July 1997, p. 20.

Evans' remarks came from a personal interview with the author, December, 1997.

Chapter 11

Day's recollections were captured in: Dennis Scoville and Lisa Sorg, "King for a Day," *No Depression*, November-December 1997, p. 76.

The analysis by Estes appeared in: Dr. Clarissa Pinkola Estes, "Elvis Presley: Fama, and the Cultus of the Dying God," *The Soul of Popular Culture*, edited by Mary Lynn Kittelson, p. 50.

Wilson's comments were from: Kemmons Wilson with Robert Kerr, *Half Luck and Half Brains: The Kemmons Wilson Holiday Inn Story*, p. 129.

Chapter 12

Marty Lacker made the Goulet comment in: Alanna Nash with Billy Smith, Marty Lacker, and Lamar Fike, *Elvis Aaron Presley: Revelations from the Memphis Mafia*, p. 145.

Chapter 13

Miss Pamela's observation was printed in: Ben Watson, *Frank Zappa: The Negative Dialectics of Poodle Play*, p. 251.

Nelson's comments came from: Sandra Choron & Bob Oskam, *Elvis!: The Last Word*, p. 69.

Luman's comments were in: Paul Hemphill, *The Nashville Sound: Bright Lights and Country Music*, p. 273.

Allan's recollections were taken from: Shane K. Bernard, *Swamp Pop: Cajun and Creole Rhythm and Blues*, p. 153.

Lang made her comments to Denise Donlon in: Victoria Starr, *k. d. Lang: All You Get Is Me*, pp. 75-76.

Chapter 14

Little Richard's recollection about the four Elvis cover versions was presented in: Charles White, *The Life and Times of Little Richard: The Quasar of Rock*, p. 77.

Little Richard's statement about Elvis was from: David Dalton, "Little Richard," *The Rolling Stone Interviews*, p. 371.

Kitt's comment about Elvis' style was from: Eartha Kitt, *Confessions of a Sex Kitten*, p. 122.

Diddley's appraisal of Elvis came from: George R. White, *Bo Diddley: Living Legend*, p. 78

Shuman's quote came from: Mort Shuman, "Writing for Elvis," *Aspects of Elvis: Tryin' to Get to You*, edited by Alan Clayson and Spencer Leigh, p. 145.

Thomas' statement came from: Robert Palmer, *Rock & Roll: An Unruly History*, p. 27.

[Roy] Brown's opinion was in: Robert Palmer, *Rock & Roll: An Unruly History*, p. 28.

Ray's comment came from: Jonny Whiteside, *Cry: The Johnnie Ray Story*, p. 206.

The Leiber and Stoller comment came from: Robert Palmer, *Baby, That Was Rock & Roll: The Legendary Leiber & Stoller*, p. 24.

Panama Francis was quoted in: Chip Deffaa, *Swing Legacy*, p. 194.

Kitt's comment was from: Eartha Kitt, *Confessions of a Sex Kitten*, p. 123.

Manuel's recollection was quoted in: Rob Bowman, *Soulsville U.S.A.: The Story of Stax Records*, p. 304.

Little Milton's observation came from: Rob Bowman, *Soulsville U.S.A.: The Story of Stax Records*, p. 305.

Chapter 15

The observation by Atkins came from: Chet Atkins with Bill Neely, *Country Gentleman*, p. 208.

Bowen made his comment in: Jody Farr, *Moguls and Madmen: The Pursuit of Power in Popular Music*, p. 191.

Berle's story came from: Milton Berle, *B.S. I Love You: Sixty Funny Years with the Famous and the Infamous*, p. 268.

Vanna White's comment came from: Jib Fowles, *Starstruck: Celebrity Performers and the American Public*, p. 86.

Esposito's comment about his relationship with Colonel Parker came from: "Esposito on Elvis: Elvis to Hit the Big Screen Again," *Pop Culture Collecting*, February 1998, p. 37.

The comment by the Everly Brothers came from: Consuelo Dodge, *The Everly Brothers: Ladies Love Outlaws*, p. 48.

Wilson's recollections were captured in: Earl Wilson, *The Show Business Nobody Knows*, p. 25.

Emery's account was in: Ralph Emery with Tom Carter, *Memories: The Autobiography of Ralph Emery*, pp. 73-74.

Emery's comments on Colonel Parker's autobiography came from: Ralph Emery with Patsi Bale Cox, *The View from Nashville*, p. 281.

Draper's letter was reprinted in: Ralph Emery with Patsi Bale Cox, *The View from Nashville*, pp. 282-283.

INDEX OF AUTHOR NAMES

The new 1960 Elvis Presley was no longer a
word-mangler–and gone were the hiccups.
Why, this man could develop into a fine tenor.

–Ian Whitcomb,
Rock Odyssey: A Musician's
Chronicle of the Sixties

INDEX OF SONGS, FILMS, AND ALBUMS

When he first broke, critics said Elvis Presley
sang hillbilly in r & b time.

-Steve Chapple & Reebee Garofalo,
*Rock 'n' Roll Is Here to Pay: The
History and Politics of the Music Industry*

INDEX OF BOOKS, MAGAZINES, AND PUBLICATIONS

I thought Elvis Presley was the greatest ballad
singer since Bing Crosby.

–Jerry Leiber,
In the Groove

GENERAL INDEX

I get so tired of being Elvis–
I don't know what to do.

–Elvis to D. J. Fontana,
The Big Beat

Jim Hannaford Productions, 155
John, Elton, 32
Johnson, Robert, 73
Jones, Dean, 187
Jones, Tom, 17, 32, 38, 67, 80, 149, 249
Joplin, Janis, 222
Jordan, Michael, 214
Jordanaires, The, 34-35, 37, 43, 55, 77, 219
"Jungle Room, The," 89

Kalamazoo (Michigan), 94
Karen (cerebral palsy patient), 51
Kennedy, John F., 19, 93, 178, 214
Kennedy, Robert, 178
Keogh (or Keough), Danny (Lisa Marie Presley's first husband), 138, 208; and daughter Danielle (Elvis' granddaughter), 138
Keogh (or Keough), Thomas (Danny's brother), 208
Kilgore, Merle, 226
King's Daughters Day Home, 255
King, Martin Luther, Jr., xii
KKK, 172
Klein, George, 29, 235
Knopfler, Mark, 204
KWKH (radio station), 158

Lanchester, Elsa, 60
Lang, k. d., 226
Las Vegas (Nevada), xi, 23, 31, 32-34, 35, 36, 43, 71, 79, 85, 106, 107, 130, 132, 139, 144, 214, 223, 230, 237, 247, 251, 267
Laserlight Digital, 198
Lauderdale Courts, 90, 116-17
Leap Frog Productions, 69
Led Zeppelin, 43, 156
Lee, Brenda, 42, 187, 220, 245
Legend Books, 101
Leiber, Jerry, and Mike Stoller, 146, 231
Lerner (publisher), 135
Lewis, Bunny, 66
Lewis, Jerry, 10
Liberace, 31-32
Libertyland roller coaster, 90
Library of Congress, xii
Linde, Dennis, 219
"Lisa Marie" (airplane), 89, 91
Little Egypt, 59

Little El (impersonator), 106
Little Milton, 139, 236
Little Richard (real name Richard Penniman), 32, 38, 228-29, 238
Little, Brown (publisher), 128
"Lizard Tongue" (fan), 141
Locke, Dixie, 19
Longman (publisher), 192
Lord, Jack, 153
Louisiana Hayride, 36, 71, 143, 158, 226, 244
Louvin, Ira (Louvin Brothers), 209
LSD, 122
Luman, Bob, 224
Lussier, Louis, 203

MacLeod, Paul, 265-66
MacLeod, Elvis Aron Presley, 265-66
Madison Square Garden, 132, 242
Madsen, Marvin (Houston, Texas), 226
Mafia, the, 97
Majors, Lee, 153
Mancuso, Ben, 185-86
Manilow, Barry, 163
Mantle, Mickey (baseball card of), 260
Manuel, Bobby, 235
Marcos, 141
Marley, Bob, 131
Martin (Dean), and (Jerry) Lewis, 63
Martin, Janis, 162
Martindale, Wink, 125
Mayer, Frederick, 239
MCA Records, 66
McDonald, Greg, 257
McPhatter, Clyde, 232
Meditation Garden, 90
Mellow Men, 268
Melrose, Lester, 241-42
Memphian Theater, 90
Memphis Mafia, the, xv, 8, 13-14, 16, 20, 29, 60, 74, 79, 83, 124, 126, 170, 178, 210, 270-72
Memphis Mid-South Fair, 190
Memphis State University, 89
Memphis YMCA, 86
Mercer, Johnny, 66, 149
Mercury Records, 221
Merman, Ethel, 69
MGM Studios, 252
Michael Joseph (publisher), 198

About the Author

STEVEN OPDYKE runs a performing arts consulting service and music publishing company. He received his Master of Arts degree from the University of Florida and has written music articles and discographies and a book on Willie Nelson.